WILDWOOD DANCING

WILDWOOD DANCING

DANCING

Juliet Marillier

WITHDRAWN

Alfred A. Knopf

New York

THIS IS A BORZOI BOOK PUBLISHED BY ALFRED A. KNOPF

Published in the United States by Alfred A. Knopf, an imprint of Random House Children's Books, a division of Random House, Inc., New York.

KNOPF, BORZOI BOOKS, and the colophon are registered trademarks of Random House, Inc.

www.randomhouse.com/teens

Educators and librarians, for a variety of teaching tools, visit us at
www.randomhouse.com/teachers

Library of Congress Cataloging-in-Publication Data
Marillier, Juliet.
Wildwood dancing / Juliet Marillier. — 1st ed.
p. cm.
SUMMARY: Five sisters who live with their merchant father in Transylvania use a hidden portal in their home to cross over into a magical world, the Wildwood.
ISBN: 978-0-375-83364-9 (trade) — ISBN: 978-0-375-93364-6 (lib. bdg.)
[1. Supernatural—Fiction.   2. Magic—Fiction.   3. Sisters—Fiction.]   I. Title.
PZ7.M33856Wil 2007
[Fic]—dc22
2006016075

Printed in the United States of America

January 2007

10 9 8 7 6 5 4 3 2

First Edition

To my granddaughter Claire

Many people assisted in the preparation of this book. Mircea Gastaldo took me to parts of Transylvania I never could have reached on my own, and shared his wealth of knowledge and his love of Romanian culture and landscape. My son Godric was a stalwart minder and assistant on that trip. Elly, Bronya, Ben, and Rain read the manuscript in various forms and provided invaluable feedback and creative input. Fiona Leonard, Tom Edwards, and Satima Flavell helped with brainstorming and critiquing as the book progressed, and kept me sane during some difficult times. My thanks to Michelle Frey, whose perceptive editorial input helped shape the book into its final form, and to Brianne Tunnicliffe, Anna McFarlane, and Stefanie Bierwerth, who worked on the Australian and UK editions. Last but not least, heartfelt thanks to my agent, Russell Galen, for his ongoing support and enthusiasm, and to Danny Baror for his efficient work on foreign rights.

Wildwood Dancing will take you to another time and indeed another world. For proper pronunciation of names and for details about select Romanian terms, please turn to the back of the book.

Chapter One

I've heard it said that girls can't keep secrets. That's wrong: we'd proved it. We'd kept ours for years and years, ever since we came to live at Piscul Dracului and stumbled on the way into the Other Kingdom. Nobody knew about it—not Father, not our housekeeper, Florica, or her husband, Petru, not Uncle Nicolae or Aunt Bogdana or their son, Cezar. We found the portal when Tati was seven and I was six, and we'd been going out and coming in nearly every month since then: nine whole years of Full Moons. We had plenty of ways to cover our absences, including a bolt on our bedchamber door and the excuse that my sister Paula sometimes walked in her sleep.

I suppose the secret was not completely ours; Gogu knew. But even if frogs could talk, Gogu would never have told. Ever since I'd found him long ago, crouched all by himself in the forest, dazed and hurt, I had known I could trust him more than anyone else in the world.

It was the day of Full Moon. In the bedchamber our gowns

and shoes were laid out ready; combs, bags, and hair ornaments were set beside them. Nothing would be touched now, until the household was safely in bed. Fortunately, it was rare for Florica to come up to our room, because it was at the top of a flight of stairs, and stairs made her knees hurt. I did wonder how much Florica knew or guessed. She must have noticed how quiet we always were on the night of Full Moon, and how exhausted we were when we stumbled down to breakfast the next morning. But if she knew, Florica didn't say a thing.

During the day we kept up our normal activities, trying not to arouse suspicion. Paula helped Florica cook fish *ciorbă*, while Iulia went out to lend a hand to Petru, who was storing away sacks of grain to last us over the winter. Iulia did not enjoy the hard work of the farm, but at least, she said, it made the time go more quickly. Tati was teaching Stela to read: I had seen the two of them ensconced in a warm corner of the kitchen, making letters in a tray of wet sand.

I sat in the workroom with Father, reconciling a set of orders with a record of payments. I was good with figures and helped him regularly with such tasks. The merchant business in which he was a partner with his cousin, whom we called Uncle Nicolae, kept the two of them much occupied. Gogu sat on the desk, keeping himself to himself, though once or twice I caught his silent voice—the one only I could hear.

You're upset, Jena.

"Mmm," I murmured, not wanting to get into a real conversation with him while both Father and his secretary, Gabriel, were in the room. My family didn't truly believe that I sometimes knew what Gogu was thinking. Even my sisters, who had long ago accepted that this was no ordinary frog, thought that I was deluding myself—putting my own words into the frog's mouth, perhaps. I knew that was wrong. I'd had Gogu since I was a small girl, and the things he told me definitely didn't come from my own head.

Don't be sad. Tonight is Full Moon.

"I can't help it, Gogu. I'm worried. Now hush, or Father will hear me."

Father was trying to write a letter. He kept coughing, and in between bouts he struggled to catch his breath. Tomorrow he would be leaving on a journey to the port of Constanţa, in the milder climate of the Black Sea coast. His doctor had told him, sternly, that if he tried to get through another winter at Piscul Dracului in his present ill health, he would be dead before the first buds opened on the oaks. We five sisters would be looking after the place on our own, right through the winter. Of course, Uncle Nicolae would help with the business, and Florica and Petru with the house and farm. It was not so much the extra responsibility that troubled me. Father was away often enough on business and we had coped before, though not for so long. What chilled me was the thought that when we said goodbye in the morning, it might be forever.

At supper we were all quiet. I was thinking about what Father had confided to Tati and me earlier. Up till then, none of us had mentioned the possibility that Father might die of this illness, for to say that aloud would be to put the unthinkable into words. But Father had wanted his eldest daughters to be prepared for whatever might happen. Should he die before any of us girls married and bore a son, he'd explained, both Piscul

Dracului and Father's share of the business would go to Uncle Nicolae, as the closest male relative. We were not to worry. If the worst should occur, Uncle Nicolae would see we were provided for.

Uncle Nicolae's family home was called Vârful cu Negură: Storm Heights. His house was quite grand, set on a hillside and surrounded by birch and pine forest. He ran a prosperous farm and a timber business, as well as the trading ventures that had made him wealthy. When we were little, we had lived in the merchant town of Braşov, and Vârful cu Negură had been a place we visited as a special treat. It was hard to say what I had loved best about it: the dark forest, the forbidden lake, or the excitement of playing with our big cousins, who were both boys.

But there was no doubt at all what Father had loved. Next door to Vârful cu Negură was Piscul Dracului, Devil's Peak. Father had first seen the empty, crumbling castle, set on a high spur of rock, when he was only a boy. Our father was an unusual kind of person, and as soon as he clapped eyes on Piscul Dracului he wanted to live there. There'd been nobody to inherit the ruin and the tract of wildwood that went with it; perhaps the many strange tales attached to the place had frightened people away. The owner had died long ago. Florica and Petru had been custodians of the place for years, looking after the empty chambers and eking out a living from the small farm, for they were hardworking, thrifty folk.

Father had waited a long time to achieve his dream. He had worked hard, married, and fathered daughters, bought and sold, scrimped and saved. When he'd set enough silver aside from his merchant ventures, trading in silk carpets and bear skins, spices and fine porcelain, he'd quietly paid a large sum to an influential *voivode*, gone into partnership with Uncle Nicolae, and moved our family into Piscul Dracului.

I think Mother would have preferred to stay in Braşov, for she feared the tales folk told about the old castle. It looked as if it had grown up out of the forest, with an assortment of bits and pieces sprouting from every corner: tiny turrets, long covered walkways, squat round towers, arches, and flagpoles. The eccentric nobleman who had built it had probably been someone just like Father. People seldom ventured into the forest around Piscul Dracului. There was a lake deep within the wildwood, a place unofficially known as the Deadwash, though its real name was prettier: Tăul Ielelor, Lake of the Nymphs. Every family had a dark story about the Deadwash. We got ours soon after we moved into the castle. When I was five years old, my cousin Costi—Uncle Nicolae's eldest son—drowned in Tăul Ielelor. I was there when it happened. The things folk said about the lake were true.

Before Father became so ill, Tati and I had scarcely given a thought to such weighty matters as what might happen to Piscul Dracului, with no son to inherit our father's property. My elder sister was a dreamer, and I had a different kind of future in mind for myself: one in which I would work alongside my father, traveling and trading and seeing the world. Marriage and children were secondary in my scheme of things. Now—with Father's cough ringing in our ears, and his white face regarding us across the supper table—they had become a frightening reality. I remembered Aunt Bogdana saying that sixteen was the ideal age for a young woman to wed. Tati was already in her seventeenth year; I was only one year younger.

Father went off to bed as soon as the meal was over; he'd hardly touched his food. The others disappeared to our bedchamber, but I waited for Florica to bank up the fire in the big stove and for Petru to bolt the front door, and for the two of them to retire to their sleeping quarters. Then it was safe, and I ran up the stairs to our chamber, my worries set aside for now, my heart beating fast with an anticipation that was part joy, part fear. At last it was time.

The long room we sisters shared had four round windows of colored glass: soft violet, blood-red, midnight-blue, beech-green. Beyond them the full moon was sailing up into the night sky. I put Gogu on a shelf to watch as I took off my working dress and put on my dancing gown, a green one that my frog was particularly fond of. Paula was calmly lighting our small lanterns, to be ready for the journey.

With five girls, even the biggest bedchamber can get crowded. As Tati fastened the hooks on my gown, I watched Iulia twirling in front of the mirror. She was thirteen now, and developing the kind of curvaceous figure our mother had had. Her gown was of cobalt silk and she had swept her dark curls up into a circlet of ribbon butterflies. We had become clever, over the years, in our use of the leftovers from Father's shipments. He was good at what he did, but buying Piscul Dracu-lui had eaten up a lot of his funds and, even in partnership with his wealthy cousin, he was still making up for lost ground. I saw the books every day—he had been unable to conceal from

me that finances remained very tight. We sisters had to impro-
vise. We made one new dancing gown anytime a cargo contained a little more of a certain fabric than the buyer had
requested. I wore Tati's hand-me-downs; Paula wore mine.
Iulia, with her fuller figure, did rather better, because she
could not fit into either Tati's clothes or mine. All the same, she
complained; she would have liked a whole wardrobe of finery.
Tati was clever with her needle, and adjusted old things of
Mother's to fit her. Mother was gone. We had lost her when our
youngest sister was born. Stela was only five—easy to dress.

Paula had finished lighting the lamps. Now she crouched to
bank up the fire in our little stove and ensure its door was safely
shut. One year Iulia's junior, Paula was our scholar. While I
was good at figures, she shone in all branches of learning. Our
village priest, Father Sandu, came up to Piscul Dracului once a
month to provide Paula with private tutoring—I shared in the
mathematical part of these lessons—and went home with a bottle of Petru's finest ţuică in his coat pocket. Most folk believed
education of that kind was wasted on girls. But Father had
never cared what people thought. *Follow your heart* was one of his
favorite sayings.

"What is it, Jena?" Paula had noticed me staring at her. The
heat from the stove had flushed her cheeks pink. Her dark eyes
were fixed on me with an assessing look. Tonight she was
wearing dove-gray, with her spectacles on a chain around her
neck, and her brown curls disciplined into a neat plait.

"You look pretty tonight," I said. "So do you, Stela." Stela,
our baby, was rosy-cheeked and small, like a little bird, maybe

a robin. Her hair, the same ebony as Tati's, was wispy and soft, and tonight it was tied back with rose-pink ribbons to match the gown Tati had made for her. She was standing by the oak chest, jiggling up and down in excitement.

"What about your hair, Jena?" asked Tati, doing up my last hook. "It's all over the place."

"Never mind," I told her, knowing nobody would be looking at me while she was anywhere near. My elder sister's gown was a simple one of violet-blue that matched her eyes. Her hair rippled down her back like black silk. Tati didn't need jewelry or ribbons or any sort of finery. She was as lovely as a perfect wildflower. It always seemed to me a generous fairy must have presided over her christening, for Tati was blessed with the kind of beauty that draws folk's eyes and opens their minds to dreams.

I didn't make a big effort with my appearance. When people commented on our family of sisters, Tati was always the beautiful one. If they noticed me at all, they called me sensible or practical. I had bushy hair, brown like Paula's, which refused to do what I wanted it to, and eyes of a color somewhere between mud and leaf. My figure was a lot more straight-up-and-down than Iulia's, even though I was two years her elder. The one special thing about my green gown was the pocket I had sewn into it for Gogu, since he needed a safe retreat if he got tired or upset. Tonight the only ornament I carried was the frog himself, sitting on my shoulder. *You look lovely, Jena. Like a forest pool on a summer's day.*

Tati darted across to make sure our door was bolted. Then,

by the shifting light of the lanterns, we moved to the most shadowy corner of the chamber: the place where we had once sat playing games by candlelight and made the most astonishing discovery of our lives.

We dragged out the heavy oak chest from against the wall and set our lanterns on it so their light was cast into the little alcove where the chest had been, an indentation that wasn't even big enough to store a folded blanket in.

"Come on," Iulia urged. "My feet are itching for a dance."

The first time we had done this, in our earliest days at Pis-cul Dracului—when I was only six, and Stela was not yet born—Tati and I had been amusing the younger ones by making shadow creatures on the wall: rabbits, dogs, bats. At the mo-ment when all our hands had been raised at once to throw a par-ticular image on the stones, we had found our forest's hidden world. Whether it had been chance or a gift, we had never been sure.

It made no difference that we had done this over and over. The sense of thrilling strangeness had never gone away. Every Full Moon, our bodies tingled with the magic of it. The lamp shone on the blank wall. One by one, we stretched out our hands, and the lantern light threw the silhouettes onto the stones. One by one, we spoke our names in a breathless whisper:

"*Tatiana.*"

"*Jenica.*"

"*Iulia.*"

"*Paula.*"

"*Stela.*"

Between the shadows of our outstretched fingers, a five-pointed star appeared. The portal opened. Instead of a shallow alcove, there was a little archway and a flight of stone steps snaking down, down into the depths of the castle. It was dark, shadow-dark. . . . The first time it ever happened, back when there were only four of us, we had clutched one another's hands tightly and crept down, trembling with excitement and terror. For the others the fear had dissipated over the years; I could see no trace of misgiving in any of them now, only shining eyes and eager faces.

I was different. The magic drew me despite myself; I passed through the portal because it seemed to me I must. There were eldritch forces all around, and the only thing sure was that the powers of the wildwood were unpredictable. It was curious: from the first I had felt that without me, my sisters would not be safe in the Other Kingdom.

Lanterns in hand, we made our way down the winding stairway, holding up our long skirts as our shadows danced beside us on the ancient stone walls. It was so deep, it was like going to the bottom of a well. Gogu rode on my shoulder down the twists and turns of the stair, until we came to the long, arched passage at the bottom.

"Hurry up!" urged Iulia, who was at the front of the line.

Our slippers whispered on the stone floor as we glided along under the carved extravagance of the roof. Here, there were enough gargoyles and dragons and strange beasts to decorate the grandest building in all Transylvania. They clung to the corners and crept around the pillars and dripped from the arches, watching us with bright, unwavering eyes. Subterranean mosses crawled over their heads and shoulders, softening their angular forms with little capes of green and gray and brown. The first time we saw this Gallery of Beasts, Tati had whispered, "They're not real, are they?" and I had whispered back, "Just nod your head to them, and keep on walking." I had sensed, even then, that respect and courtesy could go a long way to keeping a person safe in a place such as this.

As we passed now, I felt something jump onto my shoulder—the one not occupied by Gogu—and cling there, its needle claws pricking my skin through the soft fabric of the green gown. It was doing its best to look like a frog, rolling up its long tail and bulging its eyes, while casting surreptitious glances at Gogu.

The frog tensed. *Interloper.*

The little creature poked out a forked tongue, hissing.

"Lights out!" ordered Iulia, and we each covered our lanterns in turn. As our eyes adjusted to the sudden darkness, a pale expanse came into view ahead of us: the mist-wreathed waters of a broad lake, illuminated by the moon. Through the vaporous cloud we could see the bobbing torches of those who were waiting to escort us on the last part of our journey.

"Ooo-oo!" Iulia called in a falling cadence. "Ooo-oo!"

The little boats came, one by one, out of the tendrils of mist—high-prowed and graceful, each shaped in the form of a creature: swan, wyvern, phoenix, wood duck, and salamander. In each stood a figure, propelling the craft by means of a slender pole: push and lift, push and lift. The response to Iulia's call came in five voices, each different, each as uncanny as the others. Our guides were what they were; the only human creatures in this midnight realm were ourselves.

The boats pulled in to the shore. The boatmen stepped out to help us board. The next part, my frog didn't like. He began to quiver in fright, a rapid trembling that went right through his body. I was used to this; he did it every time. I held him against my breast and, as I climbed into the boat, I murmured, "It's all right, Gogu, I've got you. We'll be there soon."

Tăul Ielelor: the Deadwash. This was the place where Costi had drowned. Our mother had warned us about it, over and over: we should never go there, for to do so was to risk harm at the hands of the vengeful fairy folk who had robbed us of our cousin. And yet, since the very first time the portal had opened for us, the realm that lay beyond had shown us warmth and kindness, open arms, and welcoming smiles. I was still cautious; I did not have it in me to trust unconditionally. All the same, it was impossible to believe that the person who had drowned our cousin was one of those greeting us on our nocturnal journeys.

The folk of the Other Kingdom had their own name for this expanse of shining water—at Full Moon, they called it the Bright Between. The lake waters spanned the distance between their world and ours. Once we set foot in their boats, we were caught in the magic of their realm.

Time and distance were not what they seemed in the Other Kingdom. It was a long walk from Piscul Dracului to the Deadwash in our world—an expedition. Gogu and I had made that forbidden trip often, for the lake drew us despite ourselves. At Full Moon, the walk to Tăul Ielelor was far shorter. At Full Moon, everything was different, everything was upside down and back to front. Doors opened that were closed on other days, and those whom the human world feared became friends. The Bright Between was a gateway: not a threat, but a promise.

It was all too easy to lose track of time in the Other Kingdom—to forget where you were and where you had come from. This might be the familiar forest, the same one in which Petru farmed our smallholding, and Uncle Nicolae harvested pines to sell for timber, and Cousin Cezar went out hunting in autumn. It was the same and not the same. When we crossed the Bright Between, we entered a realm that existed at the same time and place as ours, with the same trees and hillsides and rocks. But it was not open to humankind, except for those lucky few who found a portal and its key. And the folk who lived there lived by their own laws, laws not at all like those of the human world. Any aged man or woman with stories to tell knew that. There were tales about men who'd gone through a portal and spent a night among the forest folk, and when they'd come back again, a hundred years had passed, and their wives and children were dead and buried. There were stories about people who had visited the fairy revels and been driven right out of their minds. When they returned to the human world, all they did was wander around the forest in a daze, until they perished from cold or hunger or thirst. There were still more accounts of folk who had gone into the forest and simply disappeared.

So, although we believed such misfortunes would never befall *us*—for we were constantly assured by the folk of the Other Kingdom that they loved and welcomed us—we had made a set of rules to keep us safe. If anything went wrong, the others were to come to Tati or me immediately: they were to do as we told them, without question. There was no eating or drinking while we were in the Other Kingdom, except sips from the water bottle one of us always brought from home. There was no leaving the glade where the dancing took place, however tempted we might be to wander off down beguiling pathways into the moonlit forest. We must keep an eye on one another, keep one another safe. And when Tati or I said it was time to go home, everyone must go without argument. Those rules had protected us through nine years of Full Moons. They had become second nature.

The boats swept across the Bright Between. As we passed a certain point, the air filled with a sweet, whispering music. Swarms of small bright creatures that were not quite birds or insects or fairy folk swooped and rose, hovered and dived around us, making a living banner to salute our arrival. Underwater beings swam beside our craft, creatures with large, luminous eyes, long hands, fronded tails, and glowing green-blue skin. Many dwelled in or on Tăul Ielelor: ragged swimmers resembling weedy plants, their gaze turned always up, up to the surface; the beguiling pale figures of the *Iele*, from whom the lake got its name, reaching out graceful white arms from bank or islet or overhanging willow. Should an unwary man from our world be passing, they would seek to entice him from his path forever. As we neared the opposite shore, an assortment of tiny folk rowed out from the miniature islands to join us, in a bobbing flotilla of boats made from nutshells and dried leaves and the discarded carapaces of beetles. We reached the far shore, and my escort—who was three feet high and almost as wide, with a scarlet beard down to his boot tops—handed me out. He made a low bow.

"Thank you," I said as the gargoyle made a flying leap from my shoulder, then scampered off into the undergrowth.

"Delighted to be of service, Mistress Jenica. I'll expect you to return the favor, mind."

"You shall have the first dance, of course, Master Anatolie," I told him.

The dwarf grinned, revealing a set of jeweled studs in his front teeth. "I'll match you step for step, young lady. You'll find me a more satisfactory partner than that slippery green friend of yours. He's shaking like a jelly—wouldn't know a jig if it jumped up and bit him."

Gogu stopped shivering instantly. I could feel bunched-up irritation in every part of him.

"You've upset him," I said. "Frogs have feelings, too, you know."

The dwarf bowed again. "No offense," he said, his eyes on Gogu. "It should be an interesting night. We've got visitors. Night People from the forests of the east."

A bolt of horror shot through me and I stopped walking. Ahead of us, my sisters and their assorted escorts were disappearing along the broad, leaf-carpeted track that led away under tall trees, following the sweet call of a flute. The branches were festooned with colored lights shaped like birds and beetles and flowers. "Night People?" I echoed, and heard the tremor in my voice. Fragments of dark stories crept into my mind: tales of blood and violence, of evil deeds and terrible retribution.

"Nothing to worry about," said Anatolie offhand.

"Yes, it is!" I protested. "Florica, who works for us, says they come at night and bite people in their beds. She says the only thing they drink is human blood." My sisters were too far ahead to be called back.

"This would be the same Florica who said all dwarves were liars and thieves?" Anatolie asked, feet planted apart and hands on hips. His cloak was ankle length and lined with what appeared to be bear skin.

"Well, yes," I said.

"The same Florica who told you not to go too close to the Deadwash or you'd be scooped up in the magic fishing net of Drăguţa, the witch of the wood?"

"Yes, but . . . but Night People, everyone says—" I stopped myself. Anatolie was right. If I had never met one, it was unfair to judge on the basis of stories.

"You and your sisters are quite safe here," the dwarf said as we started walking again. "Hasn't the forest queen herself allowed you to visit her revels these nine years of Full Moons? Believe me, if her protection did not stretch out over the five of you, you would not be here now."

"I don't like the sound of that at all," I said, wondering whether he meant we would have met the same fate as the foolish folk in the stories: dead, mad, or vanished.

"The Night People will not touch you while Ileana is queen of the wildwood," Anatolie said. "You have my word."

"Thank you," I said, but I was full of doubt. I could not remember hearing a single good thing about the Night People, and I had no wish to meet even one of them. They'd never been to Dancing Glade before; at least, not when we were there. I thought about garlic, and silver crosses, and everything else folk used to keep such dangerous forces at bay. I hadn't brought a thing to protect myself or my sisters.

When we reached the glade, the festivities were in full swing. A circle of autumn-clad trees sheltered the grassy sward, their branches hung with still more lanterns. These cast a warm light over the brightly clad revelers, whose gowns and masks, robes and jewels filled the open space with a swirling mass of color. Above them, creatures performed aerial dances of their own, some borne on delicate, diaphanous wings, some on leathery, creaking membranes. Some of the guests were tall enough to bump their heads on the lanterns; some were so tiny, one had to take care not to step on them. I saw my gargoyle perched on the branch of a holly bush, waving its paws in time with the music and beaming beatifically.

The musicians sat on a raised platform at the far end, under the biggest oak. The instruments were the same as the ones in the village band—flute, drum, goat-pipes, fiddle—and yet they were not quite the same. Each possessed a strangeness that set it apart. What ordinary drum cries out poetry when beaten? What flute plays three tunes at once, each blending perfectly with the others? As for the goat-pipes, they had something of the voice of the creature whose skin had provided their air bag, plaintive and piercing. The fiddle soared like a lark.

The sound of this band was intoxicating to the ears, the kind of felicitous blend a village musician aspires to and may achieve once in a lifetime. It made feet move faster, pulses race, faces flush. It set hearts thumping and coaxed smiles from the most somber mouths. It was a music we would keep on hearing in our dreams, days after Full Moon was over and we were gone from the Other Kingdom.

Iulia was already out there, dark hair flying, her face wreathed in smiles. Tati danced more sedately, her hand in that of tall Grigori, an imposing figure with long, twisted dark hair. It was said he was a kinsman of Drǎguţa, the witch of the wood.

Paula was not dancing, but had gone straight to her usual group of friends, a clutch of witches, astronomers, and sooth-sayers clad in long, raggedy robes and swathing, vaporous cloaks. All wore hats—I saw tall pointed structures decorated with stars, and scholarly felt caps, and here and there a myste-rious shadowy hood. They were gathered around a table under the trees, deep in debate as always, their arguments fueled by a continuous supply of ţuicǎ. Paula was seated among them, wav-ing her hands about as she expounded some theory.

Stela was with the smallest folk, down near the musicians. There was a double ring of them, weaving in and out and around about in a dance of their own. Some had wings, some horns, some feathers, and some shining, jewel-bright scales. They were chattering like a mob of little birds as they pranced to and fro, and still managing to get every step perfect. We'd all started here; as we grew older, we had been welcomed by different folk, collected by different ferrymen, and permitted to mix more widely. Dancing Glade had its own set of rules.

"Hello, Jena!" my little sister called, waving wildly. Then she plunged back into the circle.

The pattern of the night was always the same. The revels

would begin with chain dances, circle dances, devised so every-one could join in, the big and small, the clumsy and dainty, side by side. We sisters had been part of this since the first time we came across to the Other Kingdom, when kindly folk of all shapes used to take our small hands and guide us through the steps. We needed no guidance now, for we were skilled in all the dances. The first was always done with our boatmen by our sides—it was their privilege to lead us onto the sward. At some point in the evening the queen of the forest would hold formal court; this was the opportunity for newcomers to be greeted, petitions made, questions asked. Later on, the music would change, and with it the mood of the crowd. That was the time for couples to dance slow measures in each other's arms, float-ing in their own small worlds. By then my youngest sisters would be getting tired, and we would all sit under the trees and watch until it was time for the last dance—a grand gather-ing of the entire crowd, in celebration of Full Moon. Then we would pass across the Bright Between once more, and go home to another month of hard work and dreaming.

The music was making my feet move even before I trod on the sward. I took the dwarf's hand and we threw ourselves into a jig. The drumbeat made my heart race; the goat-pipes seemed to speak to something deep inside me, saying, *Faster, faster! You're alive!* Anatolie gripped my hand tightly as we ran and jumped, as we turned, and swayed, and pointed our toes. Gogu had re-treated to the pocket, where he was safe from falling and being trampled by the multitude of stamping, hopping, kicking feet. When the dance was over, I fished him out and set him on my shoulder once more.

"All right?" I whispered.

If you could call being shaken about like a feather duster "all right,"
I suppose so.

I was looking around the glade as my heartbeat slowly returned to normal. "Where are the Night People?" I asked Anatolie.

"They will come. Wait until the moon moves higher; wait until you see her between the branches of the tallest oaks. Then you'll catch a glimpse of them, around the edges."

"Don't they dance?"

Anatolie grinned. "I'll bet you a silver piece to a lump of coal that you can't get one of them to step up and partner you," he said. "They stick to their own kind, those black-cloaked streaks of melancholy. They don't come to enjoy themselves, but to observe—to take stock."

Out of long habit, because I was the sensible sister, I checked on the others, one by one, to make sure they were safe. Over at the far side of the sward I saw Stela, now playing a chasing game with her bevy of small companions. Those that could fly had a distinct advantage. Iulia was with a circle of young forest men and women. When I had first seen such folk, I had thought of them as fairies—though they were far taller and more elegant than the tiny figures of my childhood imagination— with their garments constructed of leaves and cobwebs, vines, bark, and feathers, and their features unsettlingly not quite human. There was no sign of Paula, but she would still be at the scholars' table.

There was a ripple of movement. A fanfare rang out and the crowd parted before an imposing figure clad in a gown that seemed fashioned of iridescent gossamer. It was Ileana, the hostess of these celebrations and queen of the forest people, sweeping across Dancing Glade. Folk said every bird of the wildwood had given one feather to make up her crown, which rose from her head in an exuberant crest. Her golden-haired consort, Marin, was a step behind her. This grand entrance was a feature of every Full Moon's revels. Walking behind the queen and her partner tonight was a group of folk I had never seen before.

"That's them," Anatolie hissed. "Sour-faced individuals, aren't they?"

I did not think the Night People were sour-faced, just rather sad-looking. They were extremely pale, their skin almost waxen in appearance, their eyes deep set, dark, and intense. All were clad in jet-black. The pair who led them was especially striking. The woman's lips were narrow and bright crimson in color, whether by nature or artifice I could not tell. Her fingernails had been dyed to match. Both she and the man had bony, aristocratic features: well-defined cheeks and jaws; jutting, arrogant noses; and dark, winged brows. They made a handsome couple—he in billowing shirt, tight trousers, and high boots, she in a formfitting gown whose plunging neckline left little to the imagination.

I spotted Tati, standing in the crowd close by Ileana, her dark hair shining under the colored lights of the glade. The forest queen beckoned; my sister stepped forward and dropped into a low, graceful curtsy. A moment later Tati was being introduced to the new arrivals. I felt a sudden chill. If Ileana singled out anyone for this kind of attention, it was not the little human girls from Piscul Dracului but the most formidable of her own folk, such as the tall Grigori or the most powerful of the sooth-sayers. I saw the black-booted stranger lift Tati's hand and kiss it in a cool gesture of greeting. Then the Night People seemed to drift away into the shadows under the trees.

Ileana and Marin were not the real power in the Other Kingdom. They presided over the revels and sorted out minor disputes between the forest folk. They made sure the daily life of the wildwood went on in its usual pattern. The folk of the Other Kingdom were often less than forthcoming when ques-tioned about their realm and its rules, but Paula had picked up a great deal at the scholars' table. We knew that the one who was the heart of it all—the one who held the ancient secrets and wove the powerful magic—was Drăguţa, the witch of the wood. Drăguţa had been in the forest since before the castle of Piscul Dracului sprang to life in the imagination of the eccentric *voivode* who built it. She had dwelt in the depths of the woods since these great oaks were mere sprouting acorns. Drăguţa did not come to Full Moon dancing. She stayed in her lair, some-where out in the wildest and least accessible part of the woods. If folk needed to ask her something, they had to go and find her, for she wouldn't come to them.

Once, I had questioned whether Drăguţa really existed at all. Only once. A chorus of horrified gasps and hisses had greeted my doubt—"*Don't say that!*" "*Shh!*"—as if the witch were everywhere, watching and listening. Drăguţa was real, all right, and folk's fear of her was real fear. In our world, Florica spoke her name in a trembling whisper, and Petru crossed himself every time he heard it. For every boy or girl from our valley who had perished in the forest or drowned in the lake, there was a story about Drăguţa and her minions, about hands coming up out of the water to drag the hapless under. For every crucifix the villagers had erected on the outskirts of the Piscul Dracului forest to keep evil spirits at bay, there was a tale about someone who had ventured too far and walked into the witch's net. Perhaps it was not surprising that our castle had stood empty for so long.

The forest queen had finished introducing folk to her black-clad guests. Calling for the music to start up again, she moved out onto the sward with her hand in Marin's. I danced with Grigori, whose alarming appearance tended to mask the fact that he was a model of courtesy. I danced with a forest man who had ivy twists for hair, and another clad all in cobwebs. The music wove its way into my blood and made my feet agile and my limbs supple. My head was full of colors and lights: I smiled at nothing in particular and felt that I was beautiful. Only when the earlier dances came to an end and folk stood about the edges of the sward while the band had a rest did I remember that Father was leaving in the morning. Once my mind escaped the lure of the dancing, once my body stopped bending and turning and swaying to the music's enchantment, I found that I was thinking only of the long winter ahead, and how we would cope without him.

Something of my worry must have shown on my face. Grigori came over to ask what was troubling me. Anatolie offered the opinion that I must be unwell. Gogu showed his own awareness of my unease, snuggling up to my neck, under my hair. *It's all right, Jena. I'm here.* It helped that he was close, for I felt suddenly cold and, surrounded as I was by folk making merry, curiously alone.

While we waited for the band to commence the slower, more beguiling music that signaled the start of the couple dances, platters of delicacies appeared: tiny, gaudily hued cakes; creatures fashioned of spun sugar; strange vegetables carved into castles and trees and giants; and mounds of gleaming fruits that in the real world would not appear until next summer. Flasks of țuică and elderberry wine made the rounds. Little glittering goblets were borne on trays that floated conveniently at waist height.

There was no need to keep watch over my sisters. Tati and I had drummed our rules into the younger ones time after time over the years, and they abided by them without question, even when the music had them in its thrall. The rules helped us remember who we were and where we belonged. Dancing Glade was our sanctuary, our joy, our bright adventure. But we did not belong in the Other Kingdom. We were here as guests, through luck, not entitlement. Besides, as Tati had once pointed out, if you had a party every day, parties would soon become a lot less exciting. We were mortal girls, and every one of us would want a mortal life. For most of us that would mean a husband and children.

I frowned, remembering what Father had told us. To be pushed into marrying early in order to provide an heir for Piscul Dracului would be horrible. It would mean not being able to choose properly. It could mean spending the rest of your life with someone you hated. Our father had married for love; he had made his choice with no regard for what folk expected. I did not think we would have that luxury, not until one of us had produced the required son. I shivered as I gazed out over Dancing Glade. We had been lucky so far. We had had the best of both worlds. I hoped it wasn't time for our luck to change.

The music struck up again, and the folk of the Other Kingdom began, languidly, to form couples and move out onto the sward. Gogu nudged me with his cold nose and I felt my skin prickle.

Look. Over there, under the oaks.

I looked over to the spot where the Night People had retreated into the shade of the trees some time before. I did not see the dashing, black-booted man or his crimson-lipped partner. But there was somebody else there. His eyes were as dark and deep as theirs. His face was as pale—though this was an ashen pallor, white rather than waxy—but the somber lips were more generous in shape. He was young, perhaps our cousin Cezar's age. He wore a black coat—high-collared, long-sleeved, and buttoned in front, sweeping down to his ankles. What struck me was his intense stillness. He hardly seemed to blink, he barely seemed to breathe, and yet the eyes were intent, keenly focused as he stared out into the moving throng. I followed his gaze, and there was Tati, moving across the sward to join the dancers.

Now that my sister had turned sixteen, it seemed that Ileana had granted her permission to participate in these far more grown-up dances. Tati was hand in hand with a big, blunt-faced figure: the troll, Sten. Her cheeks were flushed with delicate rose. Her hair, stirred by the dancing, spilled over her shoulders like a dark silken cloak. Her gown was modest in design, yet under the lights of Dancing Glade, its plain cut emphasized her perfect figure. Many eyes were on her.

But these eyes were different. The person in the black coat was looking at my sister as if he were starving. He didn't need to move a muscle for me to read the hunger on his face, and it chilled me.

As I watched my sister dancing—first with Sten, then with Grigori, then with a young man clad in what looked like butterfly wings—my unease grew stronger. I made a decision. We would need to be up soon after dawn to see Father off. We must bid him farewell with looks of cheerful confidence on our faces. That would be impossible if we were exhausted from a night with no sleep.

"Gogu," I murmured, "we're going home early."

He shifted on my shoulder, bunching up his body. *I'm ready to go. Don't worry, Jena. We'll look after things, you and I.*

I gathered up my sisters and we made our formal farewells to Ileana and Marin, thanking them for their hospitality. I cast an eye around, seeking the Night People, but could see none of them, only a group of solemn-looking owls, perched on a branch of the nearest oak.

Ileana said, "Our guests were impressed. Human girls are not bold enough to visit such revels in their part of the world. They asked for your names and commented on your beauty." Her gaze wandered over all five of us as she spoke, which was unusually polite of her. Almost certainly the compliment referred to Tati, or possibly Iulia. Stela was too young to be called a beauty. As for Paula and me—whichever fairies had offered blessings over our cradles, they had clearly valued brains before looks. We were, in a word, ordinary.

We made our way back to the boats, accompanied by a bevy of folk jostling to hold our lanterns for us. But only the designated boatmen took us across the water, through the mist, back to our own world. In my hands Gogu trembled with terror, and I soothed him with gentle fingers. As my feet touched the home shore, I felt the surge of relief that always filled me at this point. *We're back again. I've kept them all safe.*

Then it was along the Gallery of Beasts—the gargoyle's scuttering feet could be heard behind us until he reached his own archway—and up the long, long, winding staircase to the portal.

No shadow play here, just a simple laying of hands on the stone wall. I was last. As my fingers touched the rough surface, the portal swung open, admitting us to the warmth of our bedchamber.

The younger ones were asleep the moment they laid their heads on the pillow. Tati gathered up the gowns they had shed and laid them over the oak chest, while I helped Iulia take the pins out of her hair. By the time I had scrambled wearily into my night robe, she was no more than a gently breathing form under her mounded quilt.

"Jena?" Tati's voice was quiet as she sat up in bed, brushing out her dark locks.

"Mmm?" I was filling Gogu's water bowl from the jug, making sure he would be comfortable for what remained of the night. He sat, watching solemnly—a shadowy green form on the little table next to the bed that Tati and I shared.

"Did you see that strange young man?" my sister asked. "The one in the black coat?"

"Mmm-hm. I thought you hadn't noticed."

"I wonder who he was," Tati mused, yawning.

Once the water dish was ordered to Gogu's liking, I got into bed. The warmth of the goose-feather quilt was bliss over my tired legs. In the quiet of the chamber I could hear little splashing sounds.

"One of *them*," I said, my eyelids drooping with tiredness. "Night People. You know what people say about them. They're dangerous—evil. Dead and alive at the same time, somehow. They can only come out after dark, and they need human blood to survive. I hope Ileana doesn't let them stay. Did you speak to one of them? I saw Ileana introducing you. What were they like?"

"Cold," Tati said. "Terribly cold."

There was a silence, and I thought she had fallen asleep. Then her voice came, a whisper in the shadowy chamber. "I thought the young man looked sad. Sad and . . . interesting."

"If you asked Florica," I said, "she'd tell you that the only thing Night People find 'interesting' is sinking their teeth into your neck."

But my sister was asleep. As the light brightened and birds began a chirping chorus outside, I lay awake, thinking about the winter to come and whether I had been foolish to assure Father that we could cope. After a while, Gogu hopped out of his bath and came to nestle on the pillow by my face, making a big wet patch on the linen. *I'm here. Your friend is here.* I was still awake when the sun pierced the horizon, somewhere beyond the forest, and down in the kitchen Florica began clattering pots and pans in preparation for breakfast.

Chapter Two

We stood in the courtyard. Two horses were saddled and bridled—ready for the ride down to Braşov, where Father would transfer to a cart. Gabriel was traveling with him and would stay by his side through the winter, to watch over him. With our man of all work, Dorin, away at his sister's wedding celebrations in Ţara Românească and not due back for some time, Piscul Dracului would be a house of women, save for the stalwart Petru.

Uncle Nicolae and his son, Cezar, had come down from Vârful cu Negură to see Father off. Both wore sheepskin caps, heavy wool-lined gloves, and long fur-trimmed cloaks over their working clothes. Uncle Nicolae was smiling, his bearded face radiating genial confidence. Maybe he was putting it on for Father's benefit, but I found it reassuring. Uncle Nicolae had always been kind to us girls, ready with jokes and compliments, his pockets housing small treats that could be produced anytime one of us was upset or overtaken by shyness. Now that Tati and I were young ladies, he addressed us by our full names, with affectionate courtesy.

"Tatiana, Jenica, you know our home is always open to you and your sisters. Please come to me or Bogdana, or to Cezar, if anything at all is troubling you. We want to help in any way we can."

"I'll be overseeing your part of the business, Uncle Teodor," said Cezar to our father, who had gone suddenly quiet now that his departure was imminent. At eighteen, Cezar was as tall as his father and a great deal broader, with a short, well-kept dark beard and forceful eyebrows. Our cousin was not a particularly easy person to like, and growing from a boy into a man did not seem to have improved him. I had tried to be a friend to him, thinking I owed him that. When we were little, he had saved my life.

"Of course, I will supervise Cezar's work closely," put in Uncle Nicolae, seeing Father's expression of doubt. "This will be good experience for him."

"I'll be looking after the accounts," I reminded them. "I don't need any help with that, it's all in order. In fact, I can handle everything at this end."

"It's a lot of work for a girl—" Cezar began.

"I wish to speak with each of my daughters on her own for a moment," Father said quietly. "You first, Jena. Nicolae?"

Uncle Nicolae gave a nod and drew Cezar aside. My sisters were standing on the steps before the main entry to the castle, with Florica and Petru behind them. Though the girls looked half-asleep, I could see that every one of them was struggling not to cry. A chill wind blew down from the forest: a messenger of winter. Under the tall pines, all was quiet.

"Now, Jena," Father said, out of the others' hearing, "I suppose in a way Cezar is right—this is a great deal of responsibility, and you are only fifteen. Are you quite sure you understand what I explained to you about the funds, and about dealing with that shipment from Salem bin Afazi when it comes? I've left sufficient silver for your domestic expenses until well into spring, but if anything untoward should happen—"

"Please don't worry about us, Father," I said, putting my hand on his arm. Within his layers of winter clothing, he looked pale and wretched. "I've remembered about keeping business money separate from household, and I know the record-keeping part of things backward. The girls will help with the shipment and Ivan can bring some men up from the village if we need any heavy lifting." Ivan, grandson of Florica and Petru, had his own smallholding not far away. "We'll be fine."

"Tati doesn't have the same head for business that you do, Jena. Let her be a mother to the younger ones—she's always done that job well, ever since I lost Bianca. And so have you, of course. You are good daughters." We knew that Father would never marry again; his love for Mother was in his voice every time he spoke her name.

"Thank you, Father." Curse it, I wasn't going to cry. I was going to be strong, to set an example.

"Perhaps you'd be wise to curtail your trips into the forest over the winter." Father's tone was mild. He was not the kind of man who forbade things. The most he did was offer gentle suggestions. "I know you and that frog love your adventures, but now you are a little older, you should perhaps observe other folk's rules awhile, at least until I'm home again. In this community my method of bringing up my daughters is considered eccentric. They already believe I allow you too much responsibility. Best not give them any more fuel for comment while I'm gone; I'd hate for you to be hurt by foolish tongues. Your aunt Bogdana is a sound source of advice on matters of propriety."

"I'll try, Father." He knew, and I knew, that I was no more capable of staying out of the forest than I was of holding back my opinions when I thought I was right.

You can't mean that. What about our picnics? What about pondweed pancakes?

"Shh," I whispered to the frog, and then it was time to say goodbye. I managed to kiss Father on both cheeks without letting my tears spill. Then I stepped back to allow each of my sisters her moment of farewell. I stroked Gogu's cool, damp skin with a finger as I lifted him from my shoulder to slip him into my pocket. Out of the corner of my eye, I could see Cezar watching me. "It's nearly winter," I murmured. "Too cold for picnics."

After we'd watched Father and Gabriel ride away, I think all five of us wanted to go back to bed and catch up on lost sleep—or just sit quietly, considering how life could change overnight, and how hard it could be to deal with. But Uncle Nicolae and Cezar had made the effort to ride through the forest to bid Father farewell, so we had to invite them in for refreshments. We used the kitchen, which was big, warm, and welcoming, if informal. The floor was tiled in red and the walls were bright with woolen hangings of our housekeeper's own weaving, showing patterns of stripes and trees and little flowers in rows. The fire in the stove was glowing, for Florica had already made two batches of pastries this morning. I loved this room, with its savory scents and its vivid colors. Piscul Dracului was a huge, drafty labyrinth of crooked stairs and oddly shaped chambers, perilous parapets and echoing galleries. I loved that, too—its strangeness, its surprises—but Florica's kitchen was the true heart of the place. As a child I had felt safe here. While Florica had never quite been a mother to us, she had done a good job over the years as confidante and friend. Generously built, with gray hair worn in a neat bun, our housekeeper treated us with a mixture of the respect due from servant to young mistresses and the benign discipline of a mother cat bringing up a brood of unruly kittens.

Our guests sat down at the big table, whose wood was gleaming white from Florica's daily scrubbing. Petru had escaped, muttering something about sheep. Like many of the valley men, he never had much to say in company.

"Shall I take the last batch of pastries out of the oven, Florica?" asked Tati, stifling a yawn. At Florica's nod, she lifted the tray out of the blue-tiled stove, her hands protected by a thick padded cloth, her cheeks flushed from the heat. She was wearing her dark hair in braids pinned up on top of her head, and even in her working gown and apron she looked lovely. The pastries smelled nutty and wholesome. Gogu stuck his nose out of the pocket again, sniffing.

"You look well prepared for winter, Florica," commented

Uncle Nicolae. There were strings of garlic in their dozens hanging from the rafters, along with bunches of herbs and garlands of little onions; the Night People would not be visiting Piscul Dracului this season if Florica could help it. "We've a good supply of cheeses and salted meats set aside this year. You girls must let us know if you run short of supplies for the table." Both houses had storage caves in which such foodstuffs could be kept for months in cold weather: it was one advantage of living in the mountains, where winter gripped long and hard.

"Thank you, Uncle," Tati said. "Would you care for a pastry? Cezar?"

"Jena," said Florica, "that frog's eating my best plum preserve."

Gogu had escaped the pocket and was approaching the nearest jam dish in very small hops, as if he thought this would go unnoticed. I picked him up as unobtrusively as I could and stuffed him back in the pocket.

"You still have the frog," commented Cezar, frowning.

I could see he was about to launch into one of his speeches about how unsuitable a frog was as a young lady's pet: an argument I had no answer for, because I could not explain exactly what Gogu was, only that *pet* was a woefully inadequate description for my dearest friend and advisor. It seemed a good time to change the subject.

"Where's Paula?" I asked. The others were all here. Stela had retreated to the warm nook by the stove and looked more asleep than awake.

"Writing," Tati said. "She has some work to do for Father Sandu. She went straight back upstairs as soon as Father left. Iulia, will you go and fetch her, please?"

Our coffee glasses were of Venetian make, and very fine; I had seen both Uncle Nicolae and Cezar looking them over with the appreciation of born merchants. They were a set of eight, each glass a different color, with holders of silver wirework wrought in an exquisite pattern of stems and butterflies. As for the coffee itself, it was Turkish. The Turks were overlords of Transylvania, and not everyone viewed them kindly, for their presence among us had been attended by conflict, though the princes they set up to rule us were no better or worse than others in the past. Father had said Turkish culture was full of refinements, and that the Turks made excellent trading partners, as long as one knew the right way to talk to them. We had seen the lovely items he brought back after he bartered with their merchants: silk carpets from Persia, which seemed alive with intricate patterns of scrolls and flowers; musical instruments of flawless finish; and cunning boxes with hinged lids and hidden compartments, decorated with brass inlay. We did not take coffee very often—Father was of the opinion that one could have too much of a good thing. It had seemed to all of us that this morning's farewell more than justified a treat.

Gogu wasn't really supposed to have coffee; it made him jumpy. All the same, Iulia had put a little green saucer by my glass. I began to pour the thick, dark brew from the coffeepot into the glasses, hoping I was not so tired I would spill it on someone's lap. Tears pricked behind my eyes. I'd have given up a lifetime of treats to have Father back here now, well and happy, sitting at the table telling a story of some faraway, exotic place he'd visited and the intriguing folk he'd encountered there. I'd have given up coffee and pastries in a flash to see his smile.

As soon as the others returned and sat down, Cezar began an inquisition. "I understand you've been busy writing, Paula." His tone was bland. "Letters?"

"I've been preparing for a lesson." Paula delighted in talking about her studies. "It's about historical invasions of the Transylvanian plateau."

"Go on," said Cezar.

While my cousin's attention was on Paula, I poured some of my coffee into the saucer.

"You know the name Transylvania means *the land beyond the forest* in Latin," Paula told Cezar, sipping her coffee. She always seemed able to drink it piping hot. "The wildwood has played a major part in saving the folk of this area over the centuries, did you know that? Down in the lower regions, the settlements were overcome and ransacked by one conquering force after another. Up here on the plateau, folk just vanished into the woods when they heard the invaders coming. The marauding armies simply couldn't find them."

"Interesting," said Cezar with an edge in his voice. I tried to warn Paula with my eyes, but she was addressing herself earnestly to our cousin.

"Folk are afraid of the wildwood, of course," Paula went on. "There are so many strange stories about it. But it seems to me the forest shelters and protects people. Ow! Jena, you kicked me!"

I caught her eye and she fell silent. It was a long time since Costi's death. All the same, this topic was not a good one to raise with Cezar, nor with his father. For all that, Uncle Nicolae seemed quite unperturbed; he was starting on a second pastry.

"This land's seen cruel times," said Florica. "My grand-mother had tales that would turn your hair white."

"*Shelters and protects.*" Cezar's hands clenched themselves into fists on the table, and the bright chamber seemed suddenly full of shadows. "Hardly! Ensorcells and destroys, more likely. You can't have forgotten what happened to Costin, Paula." His use of his brother's full name indicated how upset he was. "Jena herself nearly drowned that day. This valley has a hundred other tales that echo our own—a hundred other children lost, a hundred other travelers wandered into the forest around Piscul Dracului, never to be seen again. The very names of creatures that dwell in the wildwood put a shiver down a man's spine: lycanthropes, goblins, witches, and Night People."

Gogu had drained the saucer and now crouched by it, trem-bling. *I don't trust him, Jena. He makes me edgy.*

"That's just the coffee," I muttered.

"What was that?" Cezar gave me a sharp look.

"Nothing."

"To call the wildwood a sanctuary is almost . . . sacrile-gious," Cezar continued. "Everyone knows the forests in these parts are places of extreme peril, full of otherworldly pres-ences. Florica would agree with me, I'm certain."

"Folk do say it's unsafe, Master Cezar," said Florica. "On the other hand, maybe it's more a matter of how you look at things. Of getting back what you give. It's always seemed to me that if you offer respect, you get respect in return, even when you're dealing with those beings you mentioned."

"There's a certain wisdom in that," said Uncle Nicolae. "And it sounds as if Paula knows her history."

"I must disagree with you, Father." Cezar's jaw was set, his eyes cold. It was a look familiar to me, one I did not like at all. Once he was in this mood, there was no cajoling him out of it. "Where did your sister learn these theories, Tatiana?"

Tati blinked at him in surprise, a piece of pastry halfway to her lips.

"I can speak for myself," Paula said, her tone level, although her arms were folded belligerently across her chest. "Father Sandu and I have discussed this at some length. As he is a priest of the Orthodox faith, you can hardly claim his lessons to be contrary to the teachings of the Church. It's true about people taking refuge in the forest. There are documents—"

"If you girls will excuse me," said Uncle Nicolae with a smile, rising to his feet, "I'll just go out and have a word with Petru before we leave. Cezar, don't be long. We've work to attend to at home."

If he'd hoped to calm an approaching storm, he was unsuccessful. As soon as he had left the kitchen, Cezar started again. "This should be brought to an end right now," he said, looking as grave as a judge. "Before any more damage is done."

"What do you mean?" Tati stared at him.

"This teaching, these visits by the priest. History, philosophy, Greek . . . Most men get by well enough without that kind of knowledge, and a woman can have no hope of understanding it. It's putting dangerous ideas in Paula's head. In my opinion, Uncle Teodor showed a lamentable lack of judgment in ever allowing it."

There was a silence. Paula went very red in the face, and the rest of us stared at Cezar, appalled. Tati recovered first.

"Father entrusted the welfare of our younger sisters to Jena and me, Cezar," she said calmly. "This is hardly a time to begin questioning his judgment—he's only just ridden out of the courtyard. And I might point out that you're not so very much older than I am. It's not for you to pronounce on such matters."

"Besides," I put in, "there is a purpose to Paula's education, and to mine. Since we have no brothers, Father's going to need us to help with the business as we get older. Paula's languages will be an asset. History helps people avoid making the same mistakes over and over. Geography allows a merchant to find new markets before anyone else does."

"I see." Cezar's tone was chilly. "So your father sees no ill in Paula's view that witches and lycanthropes and bloodsucking Night People are friendly creatures who want only to help us? How would you feel if little Stela here went out into that benevolent forest one day and was torn to pieces by some monstrous beast? What if she fell foul of Drăguţa, the witch of the wood? What price knowledge then?"

I pictured my smallest sister in her pink gown, dancing under the trees of Ileana's Glade with her happy group of assorted friends, her rosy face wreathed in smiles. I thought about the Night People. Cezar was both right and wrong. A person couldn't understand the Other Kingdom if he'd never been there—if he'd never experienced how beautiful it was, how magical and precious. Yes, it was dangerous as well, but dealing with that was a matter of putting Florica's wisdom into practice: to give respect and get respect in return, and at the same time to be always watchful. Our cousin was not alone

among the folk of the valley in his attitudes. There were those who believed the Other Kingdom to be a devilish place, full of presences out to destroy humankind. The margin of the wild-wood was hedged about with crucifixes; the trees on its rim were thick with protective amulets.

"Cezar," I said, working hard to keep my voice calm, "if you think you must challenge Father's opinion on this matter, please do us the courtesy of waiting until he returns from Constanţa, then speak to him personally." I made myself smile at him, ignoring the anger in his eyes. He gave a stiff nod. Then he took my hand and raised it to his lips, startling me so much I sat frozen and let him do it. Iulia exploded into a fit of nervous giggles.

Gogu made a wild leap, aiming for my shoulder and over-shooting by at least an arm's length. He landed heavily on an oak side table, skidded, and thumped into the wall. In an instant I was on my feet and had him cradled between my hands. I could feel his heart pounding like a miniature drum. His body was possessed by a quivering sense of outrage. There didn't seem to be anything damaged, save his pride.

"There's something extremely odd about that creature," said Cezar, eyeing Gogu suspiciously. "It just serves to underline my argument. A place in which a child can find an oddity like that frog is not a safe place to wander about. It is not the benign realm of your theory, Paula. Ideally, the forest around both Vâr-ful cu Negură and Piscul Dracului should be felled entirely."

Perhaps he did not hear our indrawn breath of pure horror, for he went boldly on.

"That would keep those presences I mentioned away from our doorsteps, as well as opening up additional land for grazing. The shepherds don't like coming up here, not even onto the pasture areas, and with good reason. The whole of the eastern hillside is wasted as a result. A complete clearance, that's what I'd like to see. As for the frog, you should get rid of it, Jena. You're a young woman now. If you must have a little companion, and I know ladies are fond of such things, a cat or a terrier would be far more suitable. I would be happy to make inquiries for you. That creature is . . . peculiar."

I could think of nothing to say. I was used to his attitude to Gogu, which had grown stronger as I had become older. As for the forest and its dwellers, there was a reason why Cezar feared them, a reason that made perfect sense to anyone who had not had the privilege of entering the Other Kingdom.

"Aunt Bogdana likes pastries, doesn't she?" I said brightly. "Florica, could you pack up some of these for Cezar to take home? I'll see him out."

On the way to find Uncle Nicolae, Cezar paused in the hallway, arms folded, his face half in shadow. "Jena?"

"Mmm?"

"You're angry, aren't you?"

"No, Cezar. I may disagree with your ideas, but that doesn't mean I'm angry. It's hard to be angry with someone who once saved your life. When you talk about Costi, I can still see it."

His features tightened, his dark eyes turning bleak. "Me

too, Jena. I wish it would fade, but it doesn't. Ten whole years. Every night I dream of it. It won't go away."

"It was an accident," I said, the pale waters of the Dead-wash filling my mind, with the remembered terror of floating away from the shore—farther and farther away—as a thrilling game turned into a dark reality. "Nobody's fault. It was terrible, yes. But you need to look forward now."

"When I've destroyed every one of those creatures out there, when I've broken their world and stamped on the pieces, then I'll look forward," Cezar said. His words set cold fingers around my heart.

"Even if you did all that, it wouldn't bring Costi back." We were going over old ground here. And the more we did so, the less ready he was to change his mind. Ten years was a long time. Wasn't time supposed to ease grief? It seemed to me that Cezar had grown sadder and angrier with every year that passed. "Hating people doesn't mend anything."

"I must go," he said abruptly. "Goodbye, Jena."

"Farewell, Cezar. I'll see you at church, perhaps."

Tăul Ielelor had always been forbidden. Children love forbidden places, especially when they lie deep in a mysterious dark forest, where all kinds of wonderful games can be played, games that last from dawn to dusk and spring to life again next morning. At Full Moon, the lake formed the border where everything began to smell richer and to look brighter, where every sound became honey for the ears. Crossing the Bright Between made our senses come alive in a way we had never known in the human world. But it could not be Full Moon every night. In between, Gogu and I still loved the forest and we still visited the lake, though we stayed a safe distance away from the water.

I hadn't forgotten the frog's crestfallen comment about picnics. I decided that instead of catching up on sleep, I would spend the rest of the day on one last expedition before the weather got too cold. In the eyes of the world, maybe I was too old for such adventures, but Gogu and I needed our favorite ritual, and I was feeling sad enough about Father without having my frog upset as well. Besides, does anyone ever get too old for picnics?

It was a long walk in the cold. When we reached our chosen spot—up the hill from the Deadwash, in a sheltered hollow by a stream—I unpacked the bag I had brought. Then I made a little campfire and cooked two pancakes: a tiny one for him, a bigger one for me. I'd had no appetite for Florica's pastries, but I was hungry now. I draped a garnish of pondweed on top of my creations and called Gogu, keeping my voice low. It was not unknown for certain of the bolder folk of the Other Kingdom to venture out into the human world; they had their own portals. Dwarves might be out and about at any time, and so might Drăguţa, the witch of the wood (if the rumors about her were true). She could be watching me even now. Cezar was sure it was she who had reached from the water and dragged Costi under on that terrible day when I was five years old. If she could do that, she was capable of anything. And if there was any chance that Drăguţa might be close by, I'd be foolish not to be on my guard.

"Come on, Gogu! The pancakes are getting cold!"

Gogu was rummaging about in the leaf mold. Autumn was here, and a thick layer of decaying material lay over all the paths, full of scurrying insects and the eccentric miniature castles of tiny fungi sprouting from the rich soil. He spotted a juicy bug, glanced at me, then shot out his tongue and scooped it up. We had developed a fine understanding for such moments. I pretended I wasn't looking, and he pretended he didn't know I was. A moment later he was by my side, investigating my cookery.

There was no doubt in my mind that Gogu was an Other Kingdom dweller, wandered into our world by chance. His behavior was quite unfroglike, his enthusiasm for human food being only a small part of it. I'd tried to put him back a few times when I was younger, even though I'd desperately wanted to keep him. For three successive Full Moons I'd suggested to him that he stay in Dancing Glade, but when I'd headed for home, there he'd been, on my shoulder as usual. Once I'd tried leaving him in the forest to find his own way back to the Other Kingdom. Only once. I'd walked away while he was dabbling in the stream, tears pouring down my cheeks. After a little he'd come hopping after me. I'd heard his silent voice, its tone full of reproach. *You left me behind, Jena.* I knew I could never do that to him again.

"Today feels odd, Gogu," I said as we began to eat. "As if a whole new part of our lives is beginning. I don't know what it is. It feels bigger than Father going away and us having to do things on our own. Even Cezar was different. He's never spoken out in front of Uncle Nicolae like that, as if he knew better than his own father and ours. And he looked so angry. He's always angry these days. I'm starting to wonder if, one day, he might actually go through with his threats. Could he really damage the Other Kingdom? Would hatred give an ordinary man enough power for that?"

Don't waste your time thinking about him. Eat your pancake.

"That's where it happened, you know. Just over there, near that little island with the birches growing on it. That's where Costi drowned." Picnic forgotten, I gazed down the stream to the shore of the Deadwash—living it again, the awful day neither Cezar nor I had been able to forget, not in ten whole years.

Three children were running through the woods. In front was Costi, his parents' favorite, at ten years old already a leader, arrogant, impetuous, today set free from lessons for a whole month, and determined to wring every last bit of enjoyment out of it. His face was ablaze with excitement as he led his small expedition to the forbidden place where the special game was to be played. Cezar, a stolid eight-year-old, followed in his brother's wake, trying to keep up, adoration in his solemn eyes. And running along behind—chest heaving, heart bursting with the thrill of being permitted to share this secret expedition with the big boys—there was I, five-year-old Jena, in danger of tripping over my own feet as I traversed the forest paths at top speed.

The game was called King of the Lake. The boys talked about it a lot, but this was the first time I'd been allowed to play. Tati and I had been staying at Vârful cu Negură while Father was away on a buying trip. Today, Aunt was helping Tati to make a doll.

"We need a princess." Costi had said this earlier, back at the house. "Or a queen."

"We never had one before." Cezar had sounded doubtful.

"I can be a princess." I'd spoken up with all the confidence I could muster, which wasn't much. In my eyes, Costi had god-like status: I hardly dared open my mouth in his presence. Cezar was intent on impressing his big brother and had little time for me. But the dazzling opportunity that was within my grasp had made me bold. "Or a queen."

"You need special clothes," Cezar had said dismissively. "Costi's got a ring. I've got a cloak. You can't play without special clothes."

"I've got a crown." I had made it the day before, after I heard the boys planning their expedition—just in case. It had taken me all day: laboring with glue and pins, wire and beads, and scraps of braid from Aunt Bogdana's sewing box. It was the most beautiful crown in the world, all sparkles and silver.

"A crown's quite good," Cezar had conceded.

Costi had gazed down at me. He was very tall; it was all too easy to remember that I was only half his age. "Think you can keep up, Your Majesty?" he'd asked me, his mouth twitching at the corners. He'd looked as if he was trying not to smile.

"Of course," I'd said, summoning a tone of bold assurance and lifting my chin. It had mostly been pretense, but it had worked.

"All right, then." Costi's permission had been given casually. Trembling with excitement, I'd fetched the crown and a little patchwork blanket from my bed that would make a colorful cape for a monarch. And I'd followed my big cousins out into the woods.

Costi was wearing his family ring, a big silver one he'd been given at his christening as the eldest son and future master of Vârful cu Negură. I knew he was only allowed to wear it on special occasions. In between, it was supposed to be locked away. Cezar had a cloak of silky fabric in purple, very grand, with fur around the edges. I wished I could have a turn with it. Clad in our finery, we reached the shore of Tăul Ielelor, where willows bowed over the water like mournful, long-haired dryads. Why did the lake gleam so, when the sunlight barely penetrated the canopy of dark firs and tall pines? The surface was dotted with little islands. There was one that had its own soft wildflower carpet—pink, yellow, purple, blue—and on its highest point a miniature birch forest, each tree a little taller than my five-year-old self. Just by looking, I could feel the magic of it. Farther from the shore, mist clung close over the water. I imagined I could see shapes in it: dragons, fairies, monsters. My heart was thumping, and not just from the effort of keeping up with the boys.

Costi and Cezar had been here many times before, and their game had well-established rules. It started with contests of various kinds, in which I had little chance of prevailing. I did my best. Running, climbing, swinging from a rope tied to a tree. Making a fire. They had a secret hoard of useful things there, hidden in a box tied up with rope. I peered into it, expecting marvels—but it held only a flint and a sharp knife, a folded blanket, and a ball of string. And they had a raft. They had made it themselves last summer and kept it tied up to a willow, half concealed under a clump of ferns at the base. I was deeply impressed that they would dare go out on the Deadwash—even at five, I had heard the stories.

"Last race," declared Costi, who had already won most of the challenges, being leaner and quicker than his brother, as well as more confident. "Jena, you run as fast as you can, over to that big oak there. We'll count up to ten, then we'll come after you. Whichever one of us catches you wins. Ready? One, two, three—go!"

Not having time to think about how unfair this was, I ran. I did my best, one hand holding my crown in place, the other clutching my makeshift cape. The ground was uneven, pitted with stones and broken by crevices. I ran and ran: the oak seemed to get farther away the harder I tried. Costi was laughing as he came after me, his feet swift and purposeful. Cezar had been left behind. The waters of Tăul Ielelor flashed by, a bright blur. The dark woods seemed to close in.

All at once I was terrified. I could hear Costi's breathing, and it was like the panting of some monster about to seize me and rend me limb from limb. The faster I tried to run, the slower my legs seemed to go, as if I were wading through porridge. Tears blinded my eyes. I tripped and fell, striking my cheek on a knobbly tree root—and Costi was there, grabbing me by the arms and shouting triumphantly, "I got her! I won! I get first pick!"

Cezar came up, breathing hard. "Jena's crying," he observed.

"Oh," said Costi, and let go abruptly. "Are you all right, Jena?" He had the grace to look a little contrite.

"Here," said Cezar, producing a handkerchief from his pocket.

I sat up and blew my nose. "First pick of what?" I asked them.

"What you get to be, in the game," explained Costi. "King of the Lake, King of the Land, or King of something else. We've never had three before. What do you want to be, Jena?"

"Queen of the Fairies," I sniffed.

"All right. Here's what we do next—"

"It's not so easy."

The three of us froze in shock. We'd had no idea anyone else was there. But as the voice spoke, we saw an old woman, clad all in black, stooped over in the woods nearby. She was gathering yellow mushrooms into a little basket. Maybe she'd been there all the time; she blended into the dark hues of the undergrowth as if she were just another thing that grew there.

"What do you mean?" asked Costi.

"It's only a game," said Cezar.

"Nothing is *only* a game." The old woman hobbled toward us, the basket of mushrooms over her arm. "Whatever you play, you must play it properly. There are rules—rules it seems you don't know."

"What rules?" asked Costi, frowning.

"Ah," said the crone, crouching down beside us. She produced a square of cloth from the basket, which she proceeded to lay out flat on the sandy lakeshore. As if drawn by a powerful charm, the three of us crouched, too, waiting. "You can't claim the title of King without giving something in return. King of the Lake, King of the Land, Queen of the Fairies—such titles are not idly bestowed, nor easily won with foolish demonstrations of strength or speed." She glanced at Costi. I saw his eyes narrow. "You must pay for them."

"Pay?" asked Cezar. "What with? You mean silver?"

There was a little silence. Then the old woman said, "You must pay with what is most precious to you in all the world. The thing you love best. Put that on the cloth. Give it up willingly, and the title will be yours to take and to keep. If it were I, I would give these mushrooms, for they will keep starvation from my door for one more day, and what is more precious than life? What will you give?"

We were all impressed. The boys' faces looked very serious. Costi slipped the chain holding his silver ring over his head and laid it on the cloth. "There," he said. "I want to be King of the Lake."

"Are you sure?" the old woman asked him, and the look she gave him was searching.

"I wouldn't have offered it if I wasn't sure," Costi said.

I was only five. Yet I knew I must be brave and give up my treasure. I took off my beautiful crown, which I'd made with such labor and such love. "I want to be Queen of the Fairies, please," I whispered, setting it down beside the ring.

The old woman favored me with a gap-toothed smile. "Are you sure, little girl?" she said with quiet intensity.

Her voice frightened me even more than her beady eyes. Costi had shown no fear; I felt I had to match him. "Yes," I said.

The old woman's gaze moved to Cezar. "King of the Land," she said thoughtfully. "That's the only one left."

Cezar was pale. He looked as if he was about to faint, and

he was staring at his brother. He didn't seem to be able to think what to offer. I was about to suggest that he give up his cloak when the crone said, "Are you sure?"

Something changed in Cezar's face, and a chill went up my spine. It was as if darkness itself was looking out through those eight-year-old eyes. I dropped my gaze; I could not look at him. I heard him say, "I'm sure," in a voice that sounded like someone else's. Then the crone spoke again.

"It's done," she said. "Play your game. Don't forget, next time: nothing comes without a price." She picked up her basket, turned her back on us, and shuffled away into the woods.

Costi was on his feet, solemnity forgotten. "I'm King of the Lake!" he shouted. Seizing my hand, he ran down to the water, pulling me behind him. "Come on, Jena! I'll give you first turn on the raft. I'll ferry you over to the magic island. The Queen of the Fairies needs her own special realm where she can hold court."

He was so quick. My heart pounding, I let him guide me onto the precarious craft, constructed of willow poles tied with twists of flax and lengths of fraying rope. It rocked in the water as he stood knee-deep beside it, unfastening the line that moored it to the willow. I teetered and sat down abruptly, swallowing tears of fright. My big cousin had allowed me to play his grown-up game. I wasn't going to give him the chance to call me a crybaby. Besides, I'd paid for this with my best thing in the world. It must be all right. And I really did want to be on that island, the dear little one with the flowers. If I looked closely enough, I might find real fairies there, tiny ones, hiding inside the blooms. I was a queen now; I must be brave.

"Ready?" asked Costi. Then, without waiting for an answer, he pushed the raft away from the shore. The pole for guiding it lay across the weathered boards by my feet. Probably he had planned to jump on with me, but somehow, the raft went out too quickly. As I grabbed for the pole, it rolled across the boards and into the waters of the Deadwash. Costi was left standing in the shallows, staring after me.

The raft floated out. Eddies and swirls appeared on the surface around it, carrying the pole farther and farther away. I passed the little island with the flowers. I passed another island thick with thornbushes, and a third all mossy rocks. The figures of my cousins got smaller and smaller. I thought I could see dark figures on the islands, hands reaching out to grab me. The mist seemed to swirl closer, as if to draw me into the mysterious realm beyond. I began to cry. The raft moved on, and I began to scream.

"Hold on, Jena!" Costi shouted. "I'm coming to get you!" He stripped off his shirt and waded into the lake. He was a strong swimmer. On the shore behind him, Cezar stood in shadow. His face was a white blob, his figure no taller than my little finger. He was utterly still. My screams subsided to hysterical sobs, then to sniffs, as Costi came closer. Around him, I saw the lake waters swirling and bubbling. The raft began to move in circles, making me dizzy, carrying me away from his grasp. There was nothing to hold on to. I felt another scream welling up in me, and sank my teeth into my lip. Then Costi was there, his hands clutching the edge of the raft, his face even whiter than Cezar's. His dark hair was streaming water and his teeth were chattering.

I was too scared to speak. The raft began to drift back slowly toward the shore, Costi's strong legs kicking us forward. We moved past the rocky island and the thorny one. Costi was struggling to hold on, fighting the current. His eyes had a fierce look in them, like someone in a fight. His fingers were slipping. I put my hands over my face, listening to him gasping for breath. I felt the raft spin around, then tilt up; I heard splashing. Then someone grabbed my arm, pulling me, and I struck out wildly.

"Stop it, Jena, it's me. You're safe now." The voice was Cezar's. As I opened my eyes, the raft beached itself, and my cousin's hands dragged me onto dry land. My head was spinning. My nose was running. My heart was beating madly.

I fled. I pelted past Cezar, past the cloth where we had laid our offerings, past the clothing Costi had shed, and into the shelter of the bushes, where I crouched down with my colored blanket over my head and surrendered to hiccuping sobs of fright and relief.

Maybe I wasn't there long—to a five-year-old, a few minutes can seem an age. I heard Cezar calling my name, but I ignored him. This was the boys' fault. They had made me play the game, they had made me come to the lake, and now it was all spoiled. And I hadn't gotten to be Queen of the Fairies, even though I'd given away my lovely crown. Now my cousins would tease me for being afraid and for crying, and they'd never ask me to play with them again.

"Jena! Come out! Jena, please!"

Something in Cezar's voice made me get up and walk back

to the shore. The square of cloth still lay on the sand, but the silver ring and my little crown were gone. I couldn't see the raft. I couldn't see Costi.

"Where were you?" Cezar seized me by the arms, hard— I thought he was going to shake me. "Where did you go? Did you see what happened?"

"Ow, let go!" I protested. "See what? What do you mean? Where's Costi?" Then I noticed that, although he was three whole years older than me, my cousin was crying.

Cezar sat me down on the sand and told me what had happened. His nose was running because of the tears, and his eyes were swelling up and going all red. I gave him back his handkerchief. He told me that as the raft was passing the fairy island, Costi had lost his grip. As Cezar had stripped off his own shirt and boots, ready to go to his brother's aid, hands had reached up from under the water, pulling at Costi's arms and rocking the raft as if to capsize it. Cezar had swum out to rescue me, grabbing the raft just in time. He'd propelled it, and me, safely to shore. Then he'd gone back in for his brother. But when he returned to the fairy island, the water was calm and clear. And Costi was gone.

"He's dead." He said it as if he couldn't believe it, even though he'd seen it with his own eyes. "Costi's dead. The witch took him. Drăguţa, the witch of the wood. She pulled him under and drowned him."

I was too little to find words. Perhaps I did not yet quite understand what death was.

"We have to go home." Cezar's eyes were odd, shocked and

staring. He looked more angry than sad. "We have to tell them. You're going to have to help me, Jena."

I nodded, misery starting to settle over me like a dark blanket. Costi was gone. Costi, who was so alive—the most alive person I knew. Costi, whom everybody loved. Watching the light sparkle on the lake water, I thought I could hear someone laughing.

"Come on, quick," Cezar said. "We should get our story straight. We'd better practice on the way."

I remembered that part even now: walking along the forest paths, my small hand in his not much bigger one, and the way he talked me carefully through what had happened—hoping to calm me down, I suppose. Even after ten years, I could still see the expression on Cezar's face as he gave his account to his father. It was a heavy load for a boy just eight years old. I helped all I could, telling the same version of events as Cezar. What had happened was all jumbled up in my head, so it was good that he had explained it to me so clearly. He did not mention the game, nor did I. We confessed that we had been at the forbidden lake, playing with a raft. We told them about the tricky currents and the hands in the water. Uncle Nicolae and Aunt Bogdana were so distraught at the loss of their beloved firstborn, their shining star, that after a certain point in the story they ceased to listen.

My mother came to take me and my sister home to Piscul Dracului. After that, I did not see Cezar so often. He had become the eldest son. He worked hard at it: learning the business; accompanying Uncle Nicolae to village meetings; getting to know the running of the farm. He finished his education, going away to Braşov for several years and returning unrecognizable: a young man. I became shy of him—so tall, so big, so alarmingly solemn. So full of ideas and theories that clashed utterly with mine. All the same, I owed Cezar my life, and I had never forgotten that.

"The problem is," I said now to Gogu, who was sitting on a leaf, practicing being invisible, "that Cezar is so difficult to be a friend to. If I could get closer to him, maybe I could persuade him to give up his talk of vengeance. But he thinks girls are an inferior breed, not suited to anything except cooking and cleaning. This winter I plan to prove him wrong on that count, at least. I'll look after Father's affairs so well that neither he nor Uncle Nicolae will need to do a thing."

What's that old saying: Pride comes before a fall?

"Don't say that, Gogu! I thought you, at least, had faith in me."

I do, Jena. Complete faith. Be careful, that's all. Everything's changing. You said as much yourself. Change can be frightening.

"That's why I'm glad I've got you," I said. "You keep me sane, Gogu. You stop me from making stupid mistakes. Cezar had better not make any more suggestions about terriers. I simply couldn't do without you."

Nor I without you, Jena. We are a pair, you and I. It's getting cold. . . . Winter's close. Can I ride home on your shoulder?

Chapter Three

Dearest Father, I wrote, *we have been very busy since you went away. I will dispatch the consignment for Sibiu as soon as Uncle Nicolae can spare some men to load it onto the carts for us.* I'd have preferred to arrange this myself, but the men who usually came up from the village were all occupied with shoring up the banks of the Grimwater, which recent rains had swollen to a frothing brown torrent. A river in spate was as dangerous as Drăguţa the witch at her most malevolent—it could consume a whole village in one gulp.

The river is up, but the bridge is still passable, so the consignment should get through before the winter, I wrote. *I am expecting the goods you ordered from Salem bin Afazi soon. I will make sure they are safely in storage before the weather gets any worse.*

I sighed and rested my head on my hand, the neat black script blurring on the page before me. It was almost Full Moon again, a whole month since Father's departure. The others were excited, making their preparations, counting the days, then the hours, until it was time to cross over into the Other Kingdom. All I could feel was a profound weariness. This wasn't the first time Father had gone away, of course. But it was the first time both Gabriel and Dorin were absent at the same time as he was, and it would be for much longer than the usual buying trip. It had even been difficult to secure the services of the ever-reliable Ivan, since his own smallholding was threatened by the rising river.

There was too much to attend to—too much to think about. I longed for a whole day on my own with Gogu and absolutely nothing to do. It was hard not to let this show in my letter. I must not worry Father; if he believed we were coping well, that would surely help him recover more quickly. Foolishly, I had hoped to hear from him by now, but no message had come. I had expected the impossible. Constanţa was far away—letters took many weeks to travel such a distance, even supposing there was someone to bring them.

Paula and Stela are helping Florica around the house, I added, *and Iulia has been doing her best.* These days, Iulia's best was falling a little short of what it might be, but I didn't tell Father that. Now that the nights were growing longer and colder, it was a trial getting her out of bed in the mornings. She hated outside jobs like filling the wood baskets and raking out the chicken coop and feeding the pigs.

"Why can't one of you do it?" she would whine, her nose red with cold, the rest of her face icy-pale under her rabbit-fur hat.

And I would tell her what Father would, if he were home: "We all do our share."

We are in good health, I wrote. *Florica and Petru ask to be remembered to you. Father, I hope very much that your own health is improving in the warmer air of the seacoast. If you are well enough to write, it would be wonderful to hear from you. We send our fondest love. We all miss you, even Gogu. Your affectionate daughter, Jena.*

I sealed the letter, put away the quill, and replaced the stopper on the ink pot. Delivery must wait until Uncle Nicolae had a man traveling in the right direction. I hoped that would be soon.

The day before Full Moon, a cart came with Father's goods from the east. Somewhat grudgingly, the two men who had driven the cart up to Piscul Dracului unloaded the bundles and boxes. They carried them into our storeroom, then dropped them unceremoniously on the stone floor. Paula and I had weighed out the correct payment in silver pieces some time ago and stored it in a box with a very good lock. The men tried to argue with me over the amount, but I flourished a document with both Father's and Salem bin Afazi's signatures on it. After a while they took the silver and left, their tempers much improved by the appearance of a smiling Tati with a bottle of țuică and a cloth full of spice cakes for the road.

The rest of the day was spent checking the consignment in full and making sure everything was safely stored until it was time for each item to be sold. Fabrics had to be kept dry and protected from dust and moths; spices had to be tightly sealed and out of the light. Carpets were best unrolled and layered with padded cloth.

The chamber we used for storage was huge. We imagined it had once housed grand entertainments in the early days of

Piscul Dracului. But the polished marble of the floor had been badly damaged long ago, and the slender, vine-wreathed columns rising gracefully to the painted ceiling bore their share of cracks and chips. Practical shelving had been erected where once elegant lords and ladies might have sat on benches, listening to fine music.

All five of us unpacked the boxes and crates. Hard work as this job was, we loved it. It was like the best kind of treasure hunt. Salem bin Afazi's consignments were always full of exotic surprises.

Stela found a box full of tiny glass phials and flasks filled with a variety of sweet perfumes: spicy, floral, musky, pungent. She began to set them out in a row by color, handling each with careful fingers.

Paula had discovered books destined for the monastery near Sibiu: a most precious cargo. Now she sat cross-legged on the marble, spectacles perched on the tip of her nose, engrossed in an old text bound in dark leather.

The rest of us were working together, for there were rolled-up carpets in this consignment, and each had to be checked in its turn and set away. They were long and heavy. By the time we reached the last of them, our backs were aching.

Stela had packed away the bottles and put the box on a shelf. Now she was investigating a basket of curious toys—wooden bees, and dragonflies, and bats, that whirred and buzzed and flapped their wings when they were pushed along. Gogu was by her side, enthralled. His eyes bulged with fascinated apprehension. "They're not real, Gogu," I heard my sister say. "Not really real."

"Oh, look at this!"

Iulia had begun emptying a crate of fabrics. Tati had unwrapped the protective covering of the first bundle to check for imperfections and water damage.

"Oh, it's so lovely, like cobweb!" Tati lifted a length of the silk cloth between her hands. It was not-quite-white—the color of a pale spring flower with the smallest hint of sunshine to soften its stark purity. The cloth was exceptionally fine and clung to Tati's fingers. The whole surface was closely embroidered with a pattern of butterflies done in the same subtle color as the background, so they showed best when light shone through the sheer fabric. Here and there an eye or wing or antenna was accented by tiny pearls, by miniature crystals, by odd glass beads with swirling patterns in them.

"Just wait," I said. "As soon as the wife of one *voivode* appears in this, the others will be knocking down our door, wanting something just the same, only better."

"Oh, Jena." Tati was holding the silk up against her cheek; it was plain to me that she had fallen in love. "This is so . . ."

"There is quite a lot of it," Iulia remarked, eyes thoughtful. "And it's been ages since Tati had a new gown."

"If we all worked on it, we could get it finished for tomorrow night," Paula said without taking her eyes off her book.

"Oh, yes!" declared Stela, clapping her hands and making Gogu jump.

"What?" asked Tati, who had been standing there in a daze.

"How many yards do you need?" I asked her. "Iulia, pass me the shears."

"Oh, we shouldn't—" Tati protested, but her eyes were alight.

"Iulia's right, there's plenty of it," I said. "Father won't mind, and I've already signed for the cargo. We won't be taking much. You're not exactly a big girl. You'll need an underdress with this, it's almost transparent."

"I have an old silk shift we can use," Tati said, coming back to herself. "Are you sure, Jena? Four yards, I think. It's a lot of sewing in one day. We have to unpack the rest of this first."

"A project will be good for us," I said, wielding the shears. This would make a nice change from staring at columns of figures and worrying. "Let's hope we have no unexpected visitors before tomorrow night."

Tati went off with Paula and Stela to make a start while Iulia and I got the rest of the cargo unpacked, labeled, and stored. By the time we'd finished, Tati had cut most of the pieces and Paula was busy altering the silk shift. The sun set early and fine work was difficult by lamplight. When we went down to eat supper, our minds were elsewhere, and both Florica and Petru gave us funny looks.

"We're worn out," Iulia said, helping herself to a second bowl of ciorbă. "That must be some kind of record, unpacking a whole shipment in one day. Tomorrow I'm going to do absolutely nothing."

"Not if I have anything to say about it," I snapped, picking up her cue. It was essential to cover our tracks by acting as we usually would; we always made sure that Petru and Florica got no inkling that the days leading up to Full Moon were different from any others. This time, with the need for a full day's intensive sewing, we required additional cover. In Florica's mind, there would be no reason for us to spend so long on such a frivolous creation. When would Tati need a dancing dress? With Father away, the most exciting outing we could expect was a trip to Uncle Nicolae's to take coffee with Aunt Bogdana.

"We have mending for you to do," Tati said calmly. "I'm planning to go right through Paula's and Stela's things, letting down hems, repairing broken fastenings, adding a few trimmings. . . ." As Iulia began a protest, she added, "It's only fair. Paula and Stela always get clothes last, so they should at least be able to wear them without needing to worry about holes. There are probably one or two more garments of yours that Paula could be wearing, Iulia—you're really shooting up this year."

"I'll help," Stela piped up, understanding what this was about.

"So will I," said Paula. "I wouldn't mind that skirt of Iulia's with the braid around the hem. I've noticed she can't do up the waistband anymore."

"Are you calling me fat?" Iulia's eyes flashed outrage and Paula flinched.

"A man likes a woman with a bit of flesh on her," Florica said, a little smugly. Her own form was ample. "He doesn't want an armful of skin and bones. You're growing into beauties, all of you, in your different ways."

Iulia had pushed her bowl away with the soup half eaten.

"You're not fat," I told her. "You have the same kind of figure as Mother had—and Father thought she was the loveliest woman in all Transylvania. He told me so."

"Early to bed tonight," Tati said briskly. "You all need a good night's sleep so you can work hard for me tomorrow. Florica, I think we'll do the mending in our room. We can sit around the little stove and keep our fingers warm, and we won't get in your way."

"If you're sure," Florica said. All of us knew she would be happy to have her kitchen to herself for once. Since Father's departure, we had taken all our meals there. The formal dining room with its silk carpet and gleaming oak table seemed cold and unwelcoming without him.

Petru was not at supper. When questioned, Florica said tersely that he had gone to bed early. "He's tired, Mistress Jena. We're none of us getting younger. He says the fences around the eastern side of the woods won't last the winter—they'll need mending, or wolves will be at the sheep. It's a big job."

I said nothing. This was the kind of work for which Dorin would have hired extra help, the help I did not seem to be able to secure. Petru had been looking gray and exhausted even at breakfast time. He was so much a part of the fabric of Piscul Dracului, I had forgotten he was an old man. Guilt gnawed at me.

Tati made the younger ones go to bed straight after supper. Without a good sleep tonight, we'd be blundering through Full Moon, dancing with our eyelids half shut. She and I stayed up a little later, working on the shaping of the new gown.

"Jena?"

"Mmm?"

"I wonder if that young man will be there again tomorrow night."

"You mean the one in the black coat?" I had almost forgotten him; I'd been too busy even to think about the Other Kingdom. "Who knows? I don't know why you're interested. All he did was stand around looking mournful and showing how long he could stare at you without blinking."

"Maybe he's shy."

"Shy people don't go out of their way to look different. Besides, he was with the Night People. I wish they'd go back where they came from. I don't like the stories I've heard about them. They disturb me."

"Oh well," said Tati dismissively, "it doesn't really matter. What do you think about the sleeves, Jena? Narrow at the wrist, or cut in a bell shape?"

Tati sewed the last stitches in the hem at about the same time the following night, surrounded by the rest of us in our dancing finery. It was piercing cold outside. I had felt winter's bite earlier, when I had taken a break from sewing to perform some essential tasks. Petru was out on the farm, and Florica could not do everything. By the time I had replenished the wood baskets, taken a steaming mash out to the huddled chickens, and ascertained that the storeroom was staying dry, my teeth were chattering and my ears ached with cold. Tonight we wore fur hats, heavy lined cloaks, and outdoor boots. We carried our dancing slippers. In our bedchamber the chill wind was slipping in through every crack and chink it could find. Shivering, Tati stood close by the stove to take off her day dress and put on the new gown.

"Come on!" urged Iulia.

I gave my elder sister's hair a quick brushing. The gown floated around her like a cloud of mist; her eyes were bright. I helped her put on her thick woolen cloak, blue-dyed, and pull up the fur-lined hood. In the pocket of my green gown, I had tucked Gogu into an old glove made of sheepskin. He did rather spoil the line of my skirt, but I couldn't have him catching cold.

A freezing draft swirled and eddied up the spiral staircase; it tangled and teased its way along the Gallery of Beasts, seeking out victims. The gargoyles had retreated into whatever niches and cavities they could find between the stones. I spotted a group of them clustered together like bats, up in a corner. Nobody wanted to come out tonight.

On the shores of the lake, we stamped our feet and rubbed our gloved hands together, our breath turning to vapor as we watched the line of small lights draw closer. A thin layer of ice crusted the lake's surface. We could hear its shifting music as the boats broke through. By next Full Moon, the water would be hard frozen.

"Hurry, hurry, hurry," muttered Stela. "I'm turning into an icicle."

One, two, three, four boats nudged in to shore. One by one, my sisters stepped in: Stela with a blue-bearded dwarf, Paula with a gap-toothed wizard, Iulia with tall Grigori. As

Sten stepped from the fourth boat and reached out his hand to help me in, I cast my eyes about, confused. Tati was still standing beside me on the shore, waiting. Gogu began to tremble. I could feel it even through the thick sheepskin.

"What about my sister?"

Sten mumbled something. I got Gogu out, glove and all, and held him close to my chest under my cloak.

"What did you say?"

"Late," said Sten. "He's running late. Step in, young lady. And the young master there. That's it." Without further ado, the troll shoved his pole hard into the mud and we shot off across the water in a tinkle of swirling ice, leaving Tati all alone on the shore. I was opening my mouth to protest when I saw the last boat coming. As the craft emerged through the layers of mist, I saw the pale length of the willow pole first, and the white hands holding it—then the black-coated form and ashen, solemn features of that young man, the one who had spent the night of last Full Moon standing unnaturally still with his eyes on my sister. I only got a glimpse, because Sten seemed to think he was in a race and must win; he dug the pole deep and we surged forward, making an icy wave.

"Perhaps we might wait for the others?" I suggested shakily as we stepped out on the opposite shore—so far ahead of the rest that even Stela's boat had not yet emerged from the mist. Then I whispered, "It's all right, Gogu, we're there now."

My boatman bowed low. For a troll, he had exceptionally good manners.

"That young man," I said, "the one poling the last boat . . . do you know who he is?"

"Night People," Sten grunted. "Rubbish. Should go back where they came from, if you ask me. Heard nothing but bad about them."

"If he's rubbish, how is it he was chosen to be my sister's boatman?"

"Ileana tolerates them. Our visitors. He probably went to her. About our dance—can I have that one where we toss our partners up in the air? I was a champion back home." Sten had traveled far to settle in this forest. His home was to the north-west, in a land he had told me was even more icy than ours—though that was hard to believe. "I made a bet with Grigori."

"What bet?" I asked suspiciously, all the time watching as my sisters came into view, one by one.

"Who can throw who highest. I'll win, of course."

"All right." I grinned; I never could resist a good bet. Then my grin faded. All my sisters were now arriving—all but Tati. "He's so slow," I murmured. "And he's strange. He never says a word. He never even opens his mouth."

"Uh-huh," the troll said. "That'd be the teeth."

"What?"

"The teeth. You know, Night People teeth. He doesn't want you to see them. In particular, he doesn't want *her* to see them."

This terrified me. Surely the Night People could have only one reason for showing interest in human girls, and it was noth-ing to do with dancing or making polite conversation. I drew breath to call out for Tati. But at that moment, the last boat came into view. The pale young man guided it without ever taking his eyes off his passenger, who was sitting very still in her hooded cloak. They glided to shore. He stepped out and offered her his hand. Tati disembarked with her usual grace and spoke what must have been a polite thank-you. There seemed nothing untoward about it at all. Teeth or no teeth, perhaps I was just being silly to feel such misgivings. This was Tati, after all: my big sister. At sixteen, surely she knew how to look after herself.

"Come on, then," I said briskly. "If we're going to win this bet, maybe we should get in some practice."

It was a good night. The magic of the Other Kingdom made my weariness fall away. I was enveloped by the sound of the music, the tantalizing smells of the sweetmeats, and the glorious whirl of color under the ancient oaks. In the human world autumn was well advanced, but here in Dancing Glade we could shed our hats and cloaks, take off our boots and put on our party slippers, for the air was balmy and on the lush grass flowers bloomed.

There was a particular tree whose inhabitants looked after items of apparel until it was time to go home. It was full of odd, small folk with snub noses and long arms, who simply reached out, donned cloak or hood or boots, and settled in the branches to wait. Some items were fought over—Iulia's rabbit-skin hat seemed to be a favorite. I wondered how well it would survive the tug-of-war that was taking place, high off the ground, to an accompaniment of screeching and spitting.

Sten won his wager. By the end of the dance I was dizzy and bruised but happy that his pride was undented. Being from foreign parts, he did seem to feel he must prove himself before the others. I had spared Gogu this adventure and left him in Paula's care—while he loved to leap, he most certainly didn't appreciate being thrown about. After that, I danced with Grigori, and Iulia with Sten. Then came a jig and my usual partner for such light-footed capering, the red-bearded Anatolie.

"Your sister's boatman hasn't claimed his dance," the dwarf said with a wink as we twirled arm in arm.

"Really?" That was a surprise. "Perhaps he doesn't dance. It doesn't seem like the kind of thing Night People would enjoy." I let go his arm to jig three paces right, jump, and clap.

"The others are dancing. Look," said Anatolie, executing his own jump with flair and clapping his hands over his head.

So they were. A black-booted man, his features like a tragic carving in pale stone, circled with a black-gowned woman, her scarlet lips unsmiling, her raven head held like a queen's. A jig? Not for them—they moved to some silent, dark music that was all their own. Around them the rest of the Night People moved in concert, pallid and haughty. The jostling, jumping throng of other folk kept their distance. Across the sward, the stately Ileana partnered her consort, Marin. *They* were not above a jig, though they performed it with the air of nobles playing at peasants—drolly indulgent.

"Each to his own, eh?" chuckled Anatolie, seizing both my hands for a prance down the sward. "Nobody does it as well as we, Mistress Jenica! Kings and queens, lords and ladies—what do we care about them?"

"Shh!" I hissed as the music came to a close. "Ileana might hear you. Offend the queen of the forest, and even a dwarf could find himself in very nasty trouble. Now why don't you go and dance with Iulia? I need a rest."

I found a little space to one side of the sward and stood there awhile, watching. I counted my sisters: Iulia, dancing, and Stela sitting on the grass with her friends, making chains of flowers. Paula deep in debate with the scholars, while Gogu, on their table, sniffed at the flask of plum brandy. Paula said something to him and he hopped back to her. Tati . . .

Not dancing. I had not seen her out on the sward all evening, and she loved to dance. What about the beautiful new gown over which we'd all slaved until our fingers ached? Surely she must want to be out there showing it off—it would look magical under the colored lights of Dancing Glade. I glanced about. Where was she? And where was the young man in the black coat? My heart skipped a beat. Our rules were sacrosanct; we never broke them. *No going into the forest on your own. No leaving the glade until home time.*

I started to panic, something I never did. My pulse raced and my palms grew sweaty. Night People . . . bloodsuckers. I made myself look systematically across the crowded glade—up, down, this way, that way. . . . Those others were there, with their waxen skin and dead eyes, but not the somber youth. My younger sisters were all accounted for, but there was no sign of Tati. A terrible doubt crept into my mind. The exquisite fabric, the frenzy of sewing . . . Surely Tati hadn't planned this all along? Wishing to be beautiful not to dazzle the throng of revelers, but just for *him*? If it was true, it would be the first time my sister had ever kept something secret from me.

I began a search, starting with Paula's table. "Have you seen Tati?"

"No," said Paula. "Here, take Gogu—he keeps trying to drink the ţuică. She'll be here somewhere, don't worry."

"I'm not," I lied, and elbowed my way through the crowd to Stela's group and their daisy chains. I squatted down beside her. "Stela, have you seen Tati?"

"No. Not that one, Ildephonsus, the stem is too narrow. Let me show you—"

Ildephonsus, a creature with a snuffling pink snout and gauzy wings, leaned close as Stela demonstrated the best way to add a daisy to the chain, which was now immensely long and wound many times around the circle of busy artisans. I left them to their work.

Iulia danced past me, the tired face and ill temper of recent days entirely gone. She was all smiles, her blue eyes sparkling. I still couldn't see Tati. "Where is she, Gogu?" I muttered.

"Jena?" My sister's voice came from just behind me and I jumped as if I'd been struck.

"Tati! Where were you?" I bit back more words: I was worried about you, I thought you'd gone off. . . . "You still have your cloak on," I said, surprised. "Why aren't you dancing?"

"Maybe later." It seemed to me that her smile was evasive. "I saw you looking for me. I'm fine, Jena. Just go on and enjoy the party."

It was then that I saw, over her shoulder and at some distance—but clearly waiting for her—the young man in the black coat. His features bore their usual forlorn look, like that of a loyal dog unfairly reprimanded. The dark eyes belied that expression: I saw a message there that scared me. Gogu shifted on my shoulder. *He's trouble.* I swallowed and found my voice. "Are you going to introduce me to your new friend?" I croaked.

"Oh. You mean Sorrow? I don't think he's quite ready for that, Jena."

"Who?" I couldn't have heard her correctly.

"Sorrow." She glanced at Black Coat, her lovely features softening in a way that set a chill premonition in my heart.

"I bet that's not his real name," I snapped, anxiety making me cruel. "His parents probably called him something plain and serviceable, like Ivan. Ah, well, pretentious coat, pretentious name."

Tati stared at me. She looked as if she might burst into tears or slap me. We never argued.

Now you've done it.

"Shut up, Gogu," I muttered, furious with myself. "Tell him you can't talk to him," I hissed to my sister under my breath. "He's one of *them.* Don't you understand how dangerous that is?" Then I turned on my heel and plunged back into the crowd.

I didn't dance much after that. I watched the two of them as they went back into the shadows under the trees—she in her night-blue cloak, he in his long black coat—not touching, not even so much as fingertips, but standing close, so close each might have felt the whisper of the other's breath on half-closed lids or parted lips. They were talking. At least, Tati was talking, and Sorrow was doing a lot of listening and putting in a word or two, here and there, though he was certainly not given to opening his mouth very far.

I watched them as the night drew toward dawn and the

jigs and reels and high-stepping dances of the earlier hours gave way to slower tunes, music for lovers. Iulia sat on the bank, watching, her eyes full of dreams. Stela was stretched out with her head on Ildephonsus's stomach, half-asleep. A couple of hedge sprites were making nests in her hair. At Paula's table, the arguments raged on; did scholars never grow weary?

Tati took off her cloak. Sorrow folded it and laid it among the roots of an oak, his eyes never leaving her. A shaft of moonlight illuminated my sister in her delicate gown—her hair tumbling down her back as dark and shiny as a crow's wing, the curves of her body revealed through the sheer, floating silk. She reached out a hand; Sorrow took it in his as if it were something precious. There was no longer a shred of doubt in my mind that Tati had worn the butterfly gown for him. It was a gift—a gift for his eyes only.

They danced. All by themselves, beyond the farthest fringe of the crowd, they circled and swayed, met and parted, turned and passed. Even when the steps of their dance drew them apart, their heads turned to look, and look, and look, as if they would drown in each other's eyes.

"What is she thinking of, Gogu?" I whispered. "She must have gone mad!"

I'm cold. Gogu gave an exaggerated shiver. *Can we go home now?*

Why didn't it surprise me that Tati was the last sister to come down to the boats? I saw where Sorrow had beached their craft at some distance along the shore, half concealed by reeds. I stood with Sten as my other sisters stepped into their boats and headed off across the lake with their escorts. The mist wreathed the water thickly in this predawn hour: in the swirling white I could see strange shapes—wyvern, dragon, manticore. Gogu's trembling felt about to dislodge him from my shoulder. I tucked him into the glove and into the pocket. "It's all right, Gogu."

Dawn, I thought. Since last Full Moon, I had asked Paula a lot of questions about Night People. She'd told me they lost their powers with the rising sun. If I could get Tati out of here safely, she'd come back to herself. Once home, I would be able to make her see sense. Just as long as she could drag herself away in time.

"Ready?" Sten had one big foot in the boat, one on the shore, and a hand extended to help me aboard.

"I'm waiting for my sister."

"She's there." The troll jerked his head. It was true. In the moment I had turned away, Tati and Sorrow had emerged from the trees, a discreet distance apart: he with her cloak over his arm, she a vision in the sheer embroidered gown. Once she set foot on the home shore, she would be freezing.

"Good," I said grimly. "Let's go."

Sten was in fine form. We crossed the Bright Between in a trice, leaving a pathway of roiling water and splintered ice behind us. Next in was Iulia with Grigori, followed by Paula and then Stela. The air on this side was so chill I could feel my face going numb. Deep in the pocket, Gogu was immobile.

We waited, huddled into our cloaks and hats and mittens, trying to escape the cold.

"Hurry up, Tati," muttered Paula. "It's hardly a morning for a leisurely boating expedition."

We waited longer. Sten picked his teeth. The dwarf

tapped his foot, sighing loudly. Grigori put his arms around Iulia to keep her warm.

"He'd want to make haste," said the dwarf. "The sun will soon be up."

The boat's high prow broke the mist then, coming slowly. It touched the shore a little way from us. Tati alighted, still without cloak, hood, or boots. Sorrow got out after her. She turned her back to him; he unfolded her blue cloak and placed it around her shoulders. He did not touch my sister an instant longer than was necessary, and yet there was something in the way his hands lingered above her shoulders, as if he would embrace her if he dared, that was as tender as any caress might be.

Tati turned to thank him. He bowed his head, then took her hood and boots from the boat and gave them to her. We waited while she put them on, balancing with one hand on Sorrow's shoulder to take off her dancing slippers. He stood immobile, pale face set, eyes bleak. The name he had chosen was apt enough; I had never seen anyone with so many different ways of looking sad.

"Goodbye," I heard Tati say, but Sorrow said nothing at all. His eyes spoke for him.

"Come on, Tati," mumbled Iulia through chattering teeth. "It'll be time to get up before we even go to bed."

Above us, beyond the swirling mist that blanketed the water, the sky was beginning to lighten. The other boatmen were climbing aboard their craft. None wished to be on this shore at sunrise.

Tati reached up a hand. She brushed Sorrow's cheek with her fingers, as lightly as the touch of a butterfly on a flower. He closed his eyes, and the ashen pallor of his cheeks warmed with the faintest of blushes. An instant later Tati was by my side and, to the tinkling music of ice fragments shifting in the water and the solitary hoot of an owl, five little boats slipped away through the mist to the Other Kingdom.

We're safe, I told myself as always. But it seemed to me that although we had crossed the margin to our own world and were on our way home once more, this was no longer true.

Chapter Four

Vârful cu Negură was full of lovely things. The house had floors of marble and of fine polished wood, broad passageways, and sweeping staircases, and it was tended by a host of well-trained servants. Aunt Bogdana's coffee cups were of fine porcelain, and she served tiny, exquisitely decorated cakes. For a woman who values beauty, a merchant makes a good husband.

It was the day of the autumn stag hunt, and Paula and I were keeping our aunt company. We were expecting to drink a lot of coffee before the day was over. Aunt Bogdana's maidservant Daniela moved quietly in and out of the sewing room to replenish the refreshments. Uncle Nicolae and Cezar had ridden out early, armed with crossbows and accompanied by a troop of men from the district, dogs at heel. We had been invited to ride with them, as several women were accompanying their husbands and it was considered quite respectable for us to go along. Iulia was the only one of us who had accepted. She loved to ride, and the lack of a horse of her own had long been a sore point.

Hunting did not appeal to me. The forest king, Marin, with his golden hair and noble bearing, had often reminded me of a stag in his prime. I sensed there was not much difference between other hunt quarry such as wolf, boar, or wildcat and certain of the stranger denizens of the Other Kingdom. Besides, it wasn't fair to leave Paula to entertain Aunt Bogdana on her own. Stela had a cold, and Tati had been all too willing to stay home and tend to her.

"I'm sorry Tatiana could not be here today. I wanted to have a word with her," Aunt Bogdana said, sipping her coffee. "But I do applaud her responsibility in watching over little Stela. Of course, at sixteen Tati should be married and thinking about children of her own. It's time you older girls were introduced to a wider circle of eligible young men. Don't look at me like that, Jenica. Your father's a man—he doesn't understand that suitors won't simply come knocking on the door. One does need to *act*. In your own case, some attention to grooming and deportment would not go astray. Teodor will be wanting to see you settled securely. Especially now, with his health so frail." She set the tiny cup down. "You must look to your future, girls."

I saw the expression on Paula's face and spoke swiftly. "Father's physician told him he'd likely make a full recovery," I said. It was only a slight embroidery of the truth. "He just needs rest and warm air."

Aunt Bogdana was not easily diverted. "A party," she said, eyeing me sharply. "That's what Teodor should have done, given a grand party for you, with music and dancing—an opportunity for you to mingle with the young men of the district. As it is, you never go out. Nobody ever sees you. I wonder if Nicolae would agree to hold some kind of entertainment here? He does love his music."

There was a wistful look on my aunt's face. She wore her hair covered by a demure lace cap, and her gown, though of the finest fabric, was plain in design and dark in color. I thought I could remember a time, before Costi's death, when she had dressed in bright silks and worn feathers in her hair. There was a picture of him on a shelf near her chair, right next to an icon of Saint Anne. The little painting had been done on Costi's tenth birthday. I could not look at it without feeling the terror of being on the raft and drifting away, away, into the mist. Looking into Costi's painted eyes, I saw Cezar's frightened tears and heard his voice stumbling through the story. . . .

"We do go out, Aunt Bogdana," Paula said as she darned the worn heel of a stocking. We had brought a basket of mending with us, anticipating a long day. "What about church in the village? We meet everyone there. Father's taken us to all the guild houses in Braşov. We do see people."

"There's seeing and *seeing*," Aunt Bogdana said weightily. "Conducting business in merchants' counting-houses is hardly the same as dressing up and letting folk look at you. A young man needs to view a girl at her best. A young woman clad for dancing is like a dewy flower—she catches and holds the eye."

I met Paula's glance and looked hastily away. Gogu poked his head out of my pocket. *If you were a flower, you'd be pondweed.*

"We won't be having any parties until Father is back home," I said. "But thank you for the suggestion, Aunt."

Aunt Bogdana glanced at me. "Jenica," she said, "for a girl of fifteen, you are somewhat bold in your responses." Her tone was kindly; I knew she meant well. "Your father . . ." She sighed. "He's a lovely man, but he will insist on going his own way, and that does you no favors, my dear. Suitors won't care in the least whether you can add up figures and tell silk from sarcenet or jade from amber. It all boils down to manners and deportment, dress and carriage. And the need to keep your conversation appropriate. The frog is an issue. He may be a nice little creature, but he does tend to leave damp patches on your clothing."

"Yes, Aunt." There was no point in arguing. Aunt Bogdana was the valley authority on what was proper. "Cezar has already mentioned it."

"Ah, Cezar . . ." With another sigh, Aunt set down her cup. Her eyes were on Costi's picture. Daniela got up and bore the tray away. "Life can be very cruel, my dears, cruel and arbitrary," Aunt went on. "I think sometimes it is particularly hard for women, as we cannot so easily divert ourselves with business affairs."

"Some women do," muttered Paula to her stocking.

"What was that, Paula?" Aunt Bogdana had sharp hearing.

"It's true, Aunt," I said, drawn into debate despite my best intentions. "Marriage and children need not be the only future open to us. Father speaks of women in Venice and other foreign parts who wield great influence in merchant ventures—women who manage business enterprises in their own right. I'm already helping Father quite a bit, learning as much as I can—"

"Say no more, Jena. That is not a path you can seriously contemplate. Such women are not . . . respectable. At your age you cannot fully understand what I allude to. Only a certain kind of female seeks to enter the masculine realm of commerce, or indeed"—she glanced at Paula—"that of scholarship. Our strengths lie in the domestic sphere. A truly wise woman is the one who knows her place. You need suitable husbands. They won't just chance along. You must make an effort. Being a man, your father simply doesn't understand. That he has never provided dancing lessons for you illustrates that. There is no point in appearing at a party if all you can do is step on your suitors' toes. Don't smirk, Paula. This is not a joking matter."

"No, Aunt," we chorused.

"Of course," Aunt Bogdana went on, "if your poor dear father does recover his health, this will become less of an issue for you, Jena."

"Oh?" My attention was caught.

"My dear, we all accept that Tatiana will marry first. For all Teodor's neglect of the upbringing suitable to young ladies, your elder sister has great natural charm, and her manners are at least acceptable. She will do well enough for herself, given the right introductions. As the second sister and somewhat less . . . As the second sister, it would be entirely appropriate for you to remain at home and look after your father. Teodor will never take another wife; he was devoted to Bianca. He'll need a companion in his old age. That is one advantage of producing so many girls."

I could feel Gogu's outrage in every corner of his small form, even through the woolen fabric of my gown.

"I expect that one of us will stay at Piscul Dracului, married or unmarried," I said, struggling to stay courteous. "We love the house, we love the forest, and we love Father. Of course we wouldn't leave him all alone." It was interesting that our aunt never raised one obvious possibility: that one of us should wed Cezar. Not that any of us would want to. My sisters disliked him and I—I was not sure I wanted to marry anyone at all. Not without love. And whatever I felt toward my cousin, it was not the kind of passion I had heard about in tales, the feeling that swept you off your feet and into a different world. It was foolish to expect that, of course. In choosing a husband, practical considerations almost always came before the inclinations of the heart. This was something Aunt Bogdana had explained many times before.

A certain expression had entered my aunt's blue eyes, one I knew from experience meant she was planning something. "I'll have a word with Nicolae on the party question," she said. "It's not yet too late in the season, if we move quickly. It is a long time since Vârful cu Negură has seen a night of celebration."

"There's no need, Aunt Bogdana." My heart sank at the thought of yet another complication in my busy existence.

"Believe me, Jena, there's every need. What if the worst should occur? Nicolae is hardly in a position to support the five of you indefinitely. Of course, we must hope poor Teodor recovers from this terrible malady and that he returns to us by springtime. But, as good daughters, you are duty bound to prepare yourselves—"

Behind Aunt Bogdana, the door of the chamber opened a

crack. I glanced up, surprised that Daniela had been so quick. Instead my eyes met Iulia's, and I turned cold. She was standing just beyond the doorway, motioning frantically for me to come out. We had not expected the hunt back before dusk. My sister's face was pinched and strange, her eyes dark with shock. She stayed out of view of both Paula and our aunt.

"Excuse me a moment," I said, putting down my handiwork and going casually to the door.

The moment I stepped out, Iulia clutched violently at my arms. She was babbling something about the snow and an arrow. "The blood," she kept saying. "So much blood."

I drew her along the hallway, out of Aunt Bogdana's earshot. "Take a deep breath, Iulia, and tell me slowly." I was starting to hear noises from outside now, horses' hooves, men calling out, doors slamming, running steps on gravel. "That's it, good girl. Now tell me. What's happened?" My heart had begun to race.

"The man couldn't see—the light was funny in the woods, like dusk, almost. . . . It was the deer he was supposed to hit, but the crossbow bolt—it went straight into his chest, Jena! The blood, I've never seen so much blood. . . ." Iulia was stammering and shaking.

"Who?" I gripped her shoulders, my heart pounding. "Who's been hurt, Iulia?"

"Uncle Nicolae," she whispered. "Oh, Jena—Uncle Nicolae's dead."

A moment later the burly figure of Cezar appeared in the hallway, still in his outdoor woolens and his hunting boots, the front of his tunic soaking wet. And red; all red. I felt sick. Uncle Nicolae—kindly, smiling Uncle Nicolae—who only this morning had hugged us in welcome and made jokes as the hunt rode off.

"I must talk to Mother." Cezar's voice was cold and tight.

"Paula's in with her," I said, struggling to be calm. "You can't walk in like that—you must change your clothing, at least."

My cousin looked down at his blood-drenched garb. It was as if he hardly understood what he was seeing. "I must tell Mother," he said blankly.

"Cezar," I said, blinking back tears. "Wait, while someone finds you a clean shirt."

"Oh." Cezar seemed to shake himself, to force himself into the here and now. "A shirt . . ."

"I'll ask someone to fetch one." Iulia was making an effort to help, even as she wept.

"Tell them to hurry," I said. Noises from the hall suggested they were bringing Uncle Nicolae in. Someone was crying.

"I'll stay, if you want," I offered. My hand was still on my cousin's arm. He felt as tightly wound as a clock spring.

"No," Cezar said, frowning at me as if he'd only just noticed I was there. "No, you must take your sisters home." Then, after a pause during which he stared at the wall: "Thank you, Jena."

We stood there in silence until a servant came with the shirt, which Cezar put on. The servant bore away the tunic. There was a trail of red droplets on the stone floor. I wondered if our uncle had bled to death in his son's arms. The awfulness of it made it difficult to say anything. If this had been someone else, I would have put my arms around him and held him—but Cezar was not the sort of man folk embraced. I hugged Iulia instead, and she clung to me.

"Go now," Cezar said, squaring his shoulders. Watching him, I saw a frightened eight-year-old about to give his parents the news that their elder son would not be coming home. "There's nothing you can do here."

He opened the door of Aunt Bogdana's sewing room. A moment later Paula came scurrying out, workbasket over her arm, an expression of surprise on her face. The door closed. I gathered my sisters and led them away, muttering the terrible news to Paula as we went. Somewhere deep inside I was willing my aunt not to make a sound until we were out of the house. I put a hand in my pocket, feeling for Gogu. He was all scrunched up tight in the bottom corner, as closed in on himself as Cezar had been.

Uncle Nicolae was lying on a board. They had brought him into the hall and laid him across two benches. There was a blanket over his still form with a creeping bloodstain on it. His dog stood nearby, tail down, shivering. There were men everywhere—grooms, villagers, friends of Cezar's who had come for the hunt—standing about, grim-faced and quiet. I just wanted to go. I wanted to be home, to be with Tati and Stela, to be able to lie on my bed and cry. I made myself stop beside Uncle Nicolae. Part of me was still refusing to believe we had lost him. *He can't be dead, he can't. It must be a bad dream. . . .*

I touched his ashen cheek with my finger. It was cold; cold

as frost. This was no dream, but the worst sort of reality. I muttered a prayer; my sisters echoed the words. We had reached *Amen* when Aunt Bogdana's scream tore through the house.

My stomach churned. A wave of dizziness passed through me. *You're fifteen—nearly grown-up,* my inner voice reminded me. I took my sisters' hands in mine. "Come on, then," I said. "We're going home."

Dear Father, I wrote, by now Cezar's messenger will have brought you the terrible news of Uncle Nicolae's death. They held a pomană *seven days later. Florica and Petru came with us, as well as Ivan and his family. There were lots of Uncle Nicolae's friends, and folk from all over the valley, including Judge Rinaldo and, of course, Father Sandu, who spoke very well. The winter has already begun to pinch, and many people are in need of warm clothing and other supplies. All of Uncle Nicolae's things were given away. Aunt Bogdana wanted you to have his best embroidered waistcoat and his special writing materials; I have put them away for you. We have not seen Aunt since then, but Cezar has been at church. He told me his mother is prostrate with grief and wants no visitors.*

I paused, quill between my fingers. It was cold in Father's workroom. Outside, snow lay everywhere: piled up in drifts around Piscul Dracului, frosting the trees with white, blanketing the many odd angles and planes of our roof. Icicles made delicate fringes around the eaves, and the ponds were frozen solid. It was almost Full Moon again—two months since Father had gone away—and we still hadn't received a single message from him.

"I don't even know if he got my first letter, Gogu," I said

out loud. "It's hard to keep reassuring the others that he's getting better when they know there hasn't been any news."

Gogu made no response. He'd not been himself since the terrible day of the hunting accident. Often his thoughts were a complete mystery to me.

"Come on, Gogu," I said in exasperation, "say something."

He turned his liquid eyes on me. *Why not tell your father the truth?*

"What am I supposed to tell him? That I can't get any of the local men to come and work for us this winter? That the fences still aren't fixed and we've started losing stock? I can't worry Father with those things."

Winters were always harsh in the mountains. All the same, Dorin could usually get men from the valley to come up and help us with our heavy work, for a reasonable payment. This year, when the men of the district were not busy keeping their cottages clear of snowdrifts, their hearths supplied with dry wood, and the river away from their doorsteps, they all seemed to be at Vârful cu Negură, working for Cezar. Ivan had come up to give Petru a hand whenever he could, but the immediate work of the farm meant the bigger job of mending the fences had been put off too long. It must be completed before we suffered any more losses.

"I'm worried, Gogu," I told my friend as I dipped the quill in the ink once more. "I thought I'd be able to manage better than this. I know Florica and Petru are working too hard, and it's my job to get help for them, but I don't seem to be able to do it. And I really don't want to ask Cezar. He'll just see it as an opportunity to remind me that girls shouldn't trouble their pretty little heads with such weighty matters."

Don't bother yourself with him. Gogu had found an ink drop on the table and was dabbing it experimentally with a webbed foot.

"Stop it! You're just making more mess for me to clean up, and I'm tired!" My tone was much too sharp for such a minor misdemeanor. I saw the frog flinch, and made myself take a deep breath. "I'm sorry," I told him, reaching a finger to stroke the back of his neck. "I'm upset. It's not just the farm, it's Tati as well. She should be helping me, but she's off in a dream half the time. I know she's thinking about *him*—about Sorrow. It's as if the moment she clapped eyes on him, she forgot every rule there is."

On this topic, Gogu had nothing to contribute. I picked up the quill again.

We would love to know how you are keeping, Father, I wrote. *Could you give Cezar's messenger a brief note? I am not sure if you received my earlier letter; I sent it some time ago. Please be assured that we are all in excellent health and are coping well, though the weather is extremely cold. We've had word that the consignment for Sibiu was delivered safely and unloaded at the warehouse. Your agent there will arrange for the items to be dispatched to their pur-chasers, and he will hold the payments in his strongbox until your return. I have not spoken to Cezar yet about Salem bin Afazi's goods. As I said, we have hardly seen him since the* pomană. Of this I was quite glad. I could not forget the image of our aunt bent over in her grief like an old woman, her hands lingering on each item of Uncle Nicolae's clothing before she passed it to a ragged man, a skinny boy. I could still see Cezar's stony face, which had seemed more furious than sorrowful.

As for Iulia, the shock of our uncle's violent death had at

first left her withdrawn and tearful. Then, just as suddenly, she had become more willful and demanding than ever before, complaining about everything from the cold weather to the endless diet of *mămăligă* to the fact that Tati wasn't doing her share of the work. To my surprise I realized that on this last count, Iulia's dissatisfaction was justified. I kept finding my elder sister gazing out of windows, or staring into space, or taking fifty times longer to perform a simple task than she should. Challenged over this, she gave vague answers: "I don't know what you mean, Jena." "Oh, was I meant to be cutting up vegetables?" I tried to ask her about Sorrow. I tried to explain that things were difficult, that I needed her help. She did not seem to hear me. She was drifting in a little world of her own, her lips curved in a secret smile, her eyes seeing something that was invisible to me.

I signed and sealed Father's letter, wondering whether it was fair to ask Petru to take it over to Vârful cu Negură. I didn't want to go myself. I would never be able to walk in there again without seeing Uncle Nicolae's blood, without hearing Aunt Bogdana's scream.

Someone's coming. Gogu made a leap in the general direction of my pocket. I managed to catch him and scoop him in as the door to the workroom opened and Paula appeared, looking apologetic. "Cezar's here," she said, and a moment later he was marching into the room, where he sat himself down opposite me at the small square table on which my writing materials were laid out. He was neatly dressed, all in black, and around his neck he wore an ornament that had belonged to Uncle Nicolae: a gold chain with a medallion in the shape of a hunting horn.

"Oh," I said. Then: "Cezar, I wasn't expecting you. Paula,

will you fetch Tati, please?" Whether my cousin was here for business or for family matters, I knew I did not want to deal with him alone, not now that his father's death had changed things so much. Besides, to do so would be considered unseemly under the rules of polite conduct that were so important to our aunt.

Paula fled. Cezar was looking at the sealed document on the table before me. I seized on a topic of conversation. "I was just writing to Father. I'm hoping you may have someone who can deliver it to Constanţa for me."

"Of course, Jena." He took it and slipped it inside his jacket. "You realize that it may not be possible for a while. The roads are unreliable at the best of times. And it looks like a bad winter—"

"Yes, I know."

There was an awkward silence. I willed Tati to hurry up.

"How are you, Cezar?" I made myself ask. "How is Aunt Bogdana coping?"

His jaw tightened. His eyes took on a distant expression. "My mother is as you might expect. Women lack the resilience to deal with such losses and move forward."

Such a statement could not be allowed to go unchallenged. "I can't agree with you," I said, twirling the quill pen in my fingers. "I've always believed women to have great strength of endurance. In times of war, for instance, it is they who bear the loss of their men and the disruption to their lives. It is they who keep their communities together. But I do understand how sad and shocked Aunt Bogdana must be."

Cezar stared at me. I had no idea what he was thinking. "You, I should imagine, would be different from Mother in such circumstances," he conceded.

If that's meant to be a compliment, we'd prefer an insult. Gogu circled inside the pocket, his mood indignant.

"Have you had any word from Father since we last saw you? Anything at all from Constanţa?" I tried for an unconcerned, businesslike tone, though his last comment had struck me as quite odd.

"I'm afraid not, Jena. You must not distress yourself." His hand crept out and laid itself over mine on the table.

I snatched my fingers away; something about his gesture felt entirely wrong. "I'm not distressed, Cezar," I snapped. "I realize not much gets through in winter." I made myself take a deep breath.

Cezar gave a small, knowing smile. That irritated me even more than his ill-advised gesture of comfort. I reminded myself that he had lost his father only a month ago, that he must still be grieving. If his behavior seemed a little out of place, that was probably why.

"It's kind of you to pay us a visit," I said, trying to act as Aunt Bogdana might expect under the circumstances. "I'm hop-ing your mother may be able to receive visitors in return—"

A tap at the door—Paula again. "I can't find Tati any-where," she said. "And there's a man at the door, his clothes are all ragged, and he says he has no work, no food, and no money, and his wife and children are starving. Florica said to ask you if we can give him something."

"Some food, of course," I said, getting up and going to the shelf where our store of silver and copper coin for household expenses was kept in a locked box. There had been a steady stream of travelers to the door of Piscul Dracului since the start of winter, and it did not seem right to send them off without a coin or two in their pockets. The pinched features and tattered garb of these wayfarers worried me. For every man we saw, there would likely be a woman and a gaggle of children out in the woods, trying to survive on what they could get from one landowner's door to the next. I wondered how many died between one grand house and another. The fields were thick with snow.

"You are overgenerous," Cezar commented, eyeing the iron-bound box as I placed it on the table and turned the key. "A package of food, a kind word—even that is more than many of these folk deserve. They are wanderers because they don't know the meaning of hard work, because they have squandered their opportunities. You shouldn't waste your money— What is it, Jena? What's wrong?"

I was gaping into the box. Last time I had opened it, to make a small payment to Ivan, it had been three-quarters full, copper well balanced with silver. Now the contents barely covered the bottom, and there were only five silver pieces left. Almost overnight, our winter funds had disappeared.

"Jena?"

I suppose I had gone pale. I sat down slowly, gripping the table for support, my mind desperately seeking explanations. A mistake, some kind of mistake . . . Someone had moved the money. . . . Someone had put the household coins in the business coffer in error. . . . No, I had checked the business funds myself only this morning.

"Jena, what is it?" Cezar leaned closer, frowning.

"Nothing," I said, shutting the box with a snap. "Paula, go and tell Florica to give the man food, and to let him warm himself by the stove before he moves on." My hands were shaking— I clasped them together in my lap as she left. How could this have happened? The only people who knew where the key was kept were Father, my sisters, and me. We all knew this money must be conserved carefully to last all winter and perhaps beyond. How could I pay anyone to come and help Petru? How could I make a family offering at church? How could I go on slipping Ivan a little extra, so that he would see our wares safely transported to Sibiu and beyond? He had come to rely on that, with his family ever expanding and his farm too small to sustain all of them.

"Are you missing some funds? You must tell me," Cezar said. "Your father expected me to look after you and Piscul Dracului. It's my right to know."

Abruptly, I lost my temper. "It is *not* your right!" I retorted, fists clenched on the too-light box. "This place doesn't belong to you, and nor do we! My father is still alive and he's going to get better. Go home, Cezar. I don't need your help. I'm coping perfectly well. I just need to . . . I just have to—" Then I disgraced myself by starting to cry, because it had come to me that I would have to question every one of my sisters about the missing coins, and that each one would then believe I thought her capable of stealing. I sprang to my feet, turning my back on Cezar, every part of me willing him to go away. Instead, I heard the sound of my cousin opening the coffer, then his whistling intake of breath.

"This is all you have left?" The coins clinked as he lifted them and dropped them back into the box. "This will barely last you a month, Jena, and that's only if nothing untoward occurs. You'd best let me handle your domestic expenses from now on. It's clear you have no idea how to manage them."

"That's not true!" I dashed away the tears and turned to face him. "I haven't mismanaged them. I do possess some intelligence, whatever you may think. The money's disappeared in the last few days, and I don't know who's taken it. I had plenty. I was being careful."

"Here." He handed me a silk handkerchief; he was the kind of man who always seemed to have one ready. "Who looks after the key, Jena?"

"Never mind that," I said, blowing my nose. "It was safe. At least, I thought so. I'll deal with this, Cezar. I'll manage somehow."

He gave me a direct look. "You'd best start by curbing your generosity to vagrants," he said. "I want to help you. Let us not argue over this. Let me take care of this box, and the one you use for the business. We can't have that going mysteriously missing, can we? I seem to recall that Uncle keeps it in here—"

I watched, frozen, as my cousin opened what I had believed to be a secret cupboard and helped himself to the much weightier strongbox that held Father's trading funds. Of course he would know where it was—I hadn't been thinking. He had visited many times with Uncle Nicolae.

"There's no need for you to do that," I said, my voice trembling with rage and mortification. "I can cope perfectly well. It's just a temporary setback."

"Trust me, Jena," Cezar said. "I have your best interests at heart. I will ensure you have a little for your expenses, week by week, and if anything untoward occurs, you may come to me for whatever additional funds you require. That way I will be in a position to approve each item of expenditure as it arises. It's only common sense. You are a sensible girl, most of the time."

Arrogant swine.

"This isn't fair!" I snapped, realizing with horror that from Cezar's point of view, his action was perfectly logical. "You can't just take over our funds and expect to decide what we can and can't spend money on. I'm a grown woman, I can deal with this!"

"Let me help you, Jena," Cezar said mildly. "We're friends, aren't we? I want to look after you." He slipped the ring holding both keys into his pocket, then took up one box under each arm. I could see in his eyes that no argument I could muster was going to make any difference to him. He was a big man, tall and strong; there was no point in trying to take the coffers away from him.

"If we're friends," I said, recognizing that I was frightened, "then you'll stop bullying me and let me handle my own affairs. Yes, there's a problem, but—"

"Hush, Jena." He sounded as if he were calming an overexcited dog. "I'm only too happy to be able to spare you this duty. You'll be provided for, I won't neglect that. Trust me."

If a man has to say trust me, Gogu conveyed, *it's a sure sign you cannot. Trust him, that is. Trust is a thing you know without words.*

"I don't think you understand," I said, bitterly regretting that I had lost my temper; no doubt Cezar saw that as yet another indication of my unreliability. "Trust goes two ways. I know I owe you a debt from long ago, but that doesn't mean I'm happy to hand over a responsibility that should be mine. I'm not stupid. You know me, and you should know that."

Cezar had the grace to look a little uncomfortable. "I do trust you, Jena. Of all you girls . . . But you *are* a woman, and inexperienced in such matters. Your father did ask us to assist you. I'm only doing what Uncle Teodor would want for you."

"He wouldn't want you to be the one who decided every last small purchase." My heart sank at the impossibility of it. "What if I need to pay workers day by day? I can't make them wait while I run over to Vârful cu Negură in the snow."

"Send me a message when you need men. I'll arrange to have them here, and I'll take responsibility for paying them. Jena, this will save you a great deal of trouble. Trust me."

There he goes again.

"Let's find out what Tati thinks," I said in desperation. If she were at her charming best and exerted her natural authority as the eldest sister, maybe Tati could persuade Cezar that he was being ridiculous. "Come down to the kitchen. I expect we can manage some black currant tea." I was going to have to break the news to my sisters that we were much lower on basic supplies than they realized. Florica had prepared as well as she could, but there would now be even less in the way of luxuries this winter than we were accustomed to at Piscul Dracului. There was no way I would purchase anything that hinted at extravagance if I had to grovel to Cezar for every copper coin. If

Tati couldn't convince him to change his mind, it was going to be a steady diet of *mămăligă*.

Tati wasn't there. The girls said she'd gone for a walk—an odd thing to do with the snow lying knee-deep on the paths and the sky so dark that noon felt like dusk. I sent Iulia out to look for her while Cezar made awkward conversation with my other sisters. The ball of compressed resentment that was Gogu, deep in my pocket, perfectly reflected my own mood.

After some time, Iulia returned with a message: Tati would be back soon. We waited. The conversation dwindled and died. The tea went cold. It became clear that Tati had either forgotten or had never intended to join us.

"I must be off," Cezar announced, rising to his feet. "Thank you for your hospitality. Jena, I will return soon; I can see you do need my guidance, however reluctant you may be to accept it. Perhaps next time I can speak with Tatiana as well. As the eldest, she should be taking her share of the responsibilities. Goodbye, girls."

"Goodbye, Cezar," they chorused politely. Something in his manner, or mine, had banished the usual giggles and whispers.

I saw our visitor out. In my pocket, Gogu was thinking in a grumble. *Interfering busybody. Supercilious know-it-all. How dare he?*

"Farewell, Jena." Cezar gave a little bow, the two locked coffers under his arms. The sky was lowering; the snowdrifts wore gray shadows.

"Goodbye," I said. "This isn't finished, Cezar. I'm not handing over everything just like that. Once I let Father know—" I faltered to a halt. Who provided my sole means of conveying letters over the difficult tracks all the way to the

Black Sea? Without Cezar's messengers, I had no way to let Father know anything at all.

Gogu shifted uneasily. *He'll say it again, just wait.*

"Trust me, Jena," said Cezar. As I watched, speechless, my cousin turned and strode away from Piscul Dracului, carrying my independence in his brawny arms.

Chapter Five

It was not until after dark, with our sisters asleep in their beds and the waxing moon sending a cool glow through the four colored windows, that I had the opportunity to speak with Tati alone. She had not returned to the house until nearly suppertime. After the meal, she had busied herself washing Stela's hair and brushing it dry before the stove while Paula told a story she'd had from Father Sandu, about a girl who turned into a tree rather than submit to a young man who was pursuing her.

I was more frightened than angry now. My stomach was churning with it, and I couldn't enjoy the story. I'd had plenty of time to think about my confrontation with Cezar, and I could see something in it that truly scared me. He was master of his own estate now; only Father, in frail health, stood between our cousin and Piscul Dracului. If Father died, everything would belong to Cezar, and our future would be in his hands. Cezar, who did not believe women deserved lives of their own—Cezar, who had threatened to pursue and destroy the folk of the Other Kingdom. This afternoon, our cousin had begun to stake his claim.

Tati seemed quite calm, if somewhat remote. Her air of self-possession made me even more cross. I tried to shut out the wise voice of my little green advisor: *Calm down, Jena. This is not Tati's fault.* It was all very well for Gogu to say that. He wasn't the one who had to keep the place going over the winter with no money. It wouldn't be he who had to run to Cezar and beg whenever he needed the slightest thing.

"Jena, I can hear you grinding your teeth from here," Tati said, tucking the blankets more snugly over the slumbering forms of Stela and Paula. Then she turned to face me. "I can almost feel how angry you are. What's wrong?"

"Where were you?" I burst out, though I kept my voice down, not wanting to wake the others. "I needed you this afternoon!"

"I'm sorry, Jena." Tati came over to sit on our bed and reached for her hairbrush. "I was out walking, and I lost track of time. It wouldn't have made any difference anyway. The only one of us Cezar ever takes notice of is you."

"He didn't today," I told her grimly. "I'm worried, Tati. Worried about Cezar, and worried about you. I thought he would help us properly, the way Uncle Nicolae would have done, letting us manage our own affairs and go to him when we had a problem. Cezar's idea of helping is to take over completely. He thinks we're incapable."

"That's nonsense," Tati said. "We all know how good you are at these things, Jena. About the missing money—there were folk at the door a day or two ago, and I did give them some coins."

"How many?" I asked her with a sinking heart.

The brush stilled. "I didn't count, Jena. They looked so pale and tired, and there were little children. Father did teach us to be compassionate. But there was plenty left in the box. I think Iulia had to deal with travelers yesterday—she may have given more. Anyway, can't you just top up the domestic funds from the business coffer?"

I could think of nothing to say. It was possible to see how it might have happened: the drained faces at the door, the small acts of generosity that added up to far more than a wise dispensing of charity. I could see how my sisters might all have believed that the answer was as simple as Tati's suggestion. I had not shared Father's financial system with any of them except Paula. They'd never been interested. Mixing the funds was something we never did—if we had planned correctly, it should never be necessary. Anyway, it was too late now. And it looked as if, in a way, what had happened was my fault.

"Jena?" My sister's voice was soft in the shadows of the candlelit chamber. "Are you cross with me?"

Gogu jumped into his bowl. There was a miniature tidal wave, then he settled, neck-deep.

"I was," I said. "With Father gone, I need to be able to rely on you. I didn't think Cezar would try to take over. He shocked me today. It's not just the money. You've heard the kind of thing he says about felling the forest and destroying the folk of the Other Kingdom. I'm beginning to wonder if he might actually go through with that."

Tati stared at me, horrified. "But it's just talk, isn't it? How could he do it? He doesn't know about the portal, so he couldn't reach them even if he wanted to. It's just . . . bluster. Nobody's as powerful as that."

"I don't know. I think if he cut down the forest in our world, it would be destroyed in the Other Kingdom as well. The way I understand it, from what folk say, the two realms exist side by side. They have the same pathways, the same ponds and streams, the same trees. If you do harm or good in one, it has an effect in the other. I think our world and the Other Kingdom are linked—balanced, somehow—and they depend on each other. That means Cezar could wreak havoc there without even needing a portal. I always thought he'd grow out of his anger over Costi."

"He probably will, Jena, especially now he's master of his own estate and has so much more to occupy him. Anyway, couldn't Ileana stop him?"

I slipped my gown off over my head and reached for my night robe. "I don't know. When Cezar talks about it, his eyes fill up with hate. He seemed different today, so sure of himself that he didn't really listen to me. He scared me."

Tati did not reply.

"Tati," I said, "there's something else we have to talk about."

"What, Jena?" Her voice was suddenly cool. It was as if she had taken a deliberate step away.

"Sorrow. The Night People. I saw the two of you dancing; I saw the way you were looking at each other. You need to be careful—careful you don't forget the rules." I pulled the covers up to my chin; the chamber was freezing.

"I haven't forgotten them, Jena. I just . . ." Tati's voice faded away as she lay down beside me.

I struggled for a way to say what I had to without hurting her. "I know that Ileana said you could join the grown-up dancing. That worries me, too. You may not have seen the way some of your partners were looking at you. I started to think that maybe we shouldn't be going there anymore. It began to feel different. As if danger was coming closer and closer. You and Sorrow . . . That's something that can't be, Tati. Even if he wasn't with the Night People, it would still be impossible. I can't believe I'm having to tell you that. It's in this world that we must find husbands, bear children, make our own households—the world of Aunt Bogdana's parties and polite conversation over the coffee cups. The world of feeding the pigs and needing to be careful with money. Not the world of Dancing Glade."

There was a silence; then came Tati's voice, not much more than a whisper: "Sometimes you're so sensible, you make me angry."

"Someone has to be," I said, swallowing my annoyance. "I'm just trying to keep you safe. To look after things while Father's away."

"I don't really want to talk about this."

"We have to, Tati. Things are hard enough already without you drifting off into your own world and losing touch with common sense."

"If we decided everything on common sense," Tati said, "we wouldn't go to the Other Kingdom at all. We wouldn't take such pains to keep the secret month after month and year after year. We'd just lead the kind of lives Aunt Bogdana thinks are appropriate for young ladies. I can't believe that's what you'd want, Jena. You're the most independent of all of us."

She was right, of course. That didn't make me feel much better.

"We won't be able to keep visiting the Other Kingdom forever," I said. "The portal only opens if all of us make a shadow with our hands. It's possible that as soon as one of us marries and goes away, the magic won't work anymore. Perhaps it was never intended to last after we grew up."

"It worked with only four of us before Stela was born," Tati pointed out.

"All the same," I said, "it didn't work those times one of us was ill or off on a trip with Father. We do need to start getting used to the idea that this may not be forever. We need to make sure we don't form serious attachments, because not going will be hard enough even without that."

Tati said nothing.

"Promise me you won't spend the whole night with Sorrow next time," I said. "Promise me you won't get . . . involved. You know it's against our rules. You're setting a bad example for the others."

Gogu jumped out of the bowl, shook himself like a dog, and made a damp track across my arm and chest to his favorite spot on the pillow, beside my neck. He was cold; I pulled the blanket over him.

"I won't make any promises I can't keep," Tati said, rolling over, her back to me.

"All right," I said grimly, "maybe I need to spell it out for you. Sorrow came to Ileana's court with the Night People. He looks like them. He acts like them. I have no reason at all to think he's not one of them. You know the stories just as well as I do. What about that time there was an attack in the mountains north of Brașov, and everyone was scared our valley would be next? There wasn't a single household that didn't have a sharpened scythe, or an ax, or a pitchfork ready by the door. Folk were too scared even to go outside. You've heard the stories about Night People. They feed on human blood. Without it, they waste away. Once they bite you, if you don't perish, you become one of them yourself: one of the living dead. It doesn't matter how courtly Sorrow's manners are or how much he likes you, Tati. The fact is, even if he has the best intentions, sooner or later he'll be the death of you. You must stop this before it gets too serious."

In my mind was an image of the two of them lost in their solemn dance, a shaft of moonlight capturing them and setting them apart—a vision of wonder and magic. What was between them seemed to have come from nowhere. It had been serious since the moment they set eyes on each other. Was there some spell in play—had the young man in the black coat bewitched my sister?

"You don't understand," Tati said. "I can't turn my back on him now. He's never had a friend before. He's terribly alone."

"I thought he came to Ileana's glade with the Night People." I couldn't summon the least twinge of sympathy.

"He's with them, but not *with* them," Tati said. "It's something he can't talk about, not fully. I think that tall one, their leader, has some kind of hold over him. If Sorrow stays among the Night People, it's not through choice."

"He told you that?"

"More or less, Jena." Tati hesitated. "Where they come from, it's not like Ileana's kingdom. The rules are different. He's desperate to get away, but something's holding him there. Something he can't tell me about. He needs me."

"He's probably just saying that to get your sympathy." This was all wrong: it was like being in a cart hurtling downhill with the reins slipping out of my hands. "How do you know it's not all lies?"

Jena. Gogu wriggled closer. *Shh. Shh.*

"You sound so hard, Jena." Tati's voice was very quiet.

"Someone has to be. Someone has to look after things."

"That's always been you. Sensible Jena. You know, I sometimes envied you that. Being known simply as *the pretty one* can be a little galling, as if I have no other good qualities at all."

I said nothing, but lay back on the pillow, my hand around Gogu for reassurance. The truth was, it was exhausting being the sensible one. I had a simple solution to the Sorrow problem. All I needed to do was refuse to help open the portal. While part of me could not imagine giving up our Full Moon visits— the music, the magic—another part of me, growing steadily stronger, said the time was rapidly approaching when we must do so or see the two worlds touch in a way that spelled disaster. But I had to go once more, at least. I needed to warn Ileana and Marin about Cezar. I needed to tell them that, now he had authority over Vârful cu Negură, the ancient forest might begin to fall on the first day of spring.

"I know it's against the rules, Jena." Tati's voice was a whisper. "I know what I'm supposed to do. But I don't think I can. This is like a tide pulling me along. It's too strong to swim against."

I had wondered whether Tati would wear the butterfly gown again, but she put on her old dancing dress, the violet-blue one. She spent some time plaiting her hair and pinning it up on top of her head, with Iulia's assistance. Around her neck was a fine silver chain that had belonged to our mother. Even clad in such a severe style, Tati could not look less than beautiful, though there was a pallor in her cheeks and an intensity in her eyes that had not been there a month ago.

We were not exactly jubilant as we made our preparations. Iulia and I had argued earlier in the day about the lack of ingredients for such items as fruit pies and sweetmeats. I had perhaps been a little sharp with her when I told her I would not be asking Cezar for the means to acquire such inessential trifles. Now she was sulking. Paula was unusually subdued. On the appointed day for our lesson Father Sandu had not come, and although I had suggested that the inclement weather was the cause, none of us quite believed it. Stela had picked up the general sense of disquiet and complained that her head hurt.

Gogu sat on the little table, watching as I slipped on my green gown and brushed my hair. *Green as grass, green as pondweed, green as home.*

"Do you want to go in the pocket?"

I will ride on your shoulder until the crossing. Don't be sad, Jena.

My frog was perceptive, as ever. I was such a mess of

churned-up feelings that I couldn't tell which was the strongest. I was certainly sad: sad that we had lost the ability to prepare for our special night in a spirit of simple excitement. I felt guilty, too. In a way, Iulia's discontent was my fault, for not keeping a closer eye on the funds and for failing to stand up to Cezar. I had to face the unpalatable fact that I wasn't coping as well as I should be. Above all, I was afraid: afraid for Tati and for the future.

"Hurry up, Jena." Iulia looked me up and down, her eyes critical. "Can't you do something with your hair?"

I had washed my hair earlier and, on drying, it had decided to go bushy. I could not force it into any form of confinement. "No," I said crossly, and headed for the portal. Tati was crouched there already, eyes like stars. I could feel Gogu nestling into the wild cloud of my hair.

Soft. Cozy. Nice.

The Deadwash was a sheet of black ice.

"*Ooo-oo!*" It was Tati who called them this time. I saw the vapor of her breath in the freezing air.

Not even the indomitable Sten could force a boat through this rock-hard barrier. In winter's chill, our escorts came in sledges, each with its particular sound, so we heard them before their lights appeared in the misty distance. The wyvern was fringed with sprays of silver chimes. The wood duck had a cowbell, and the phoenix a row of tiny red birds that kept up a twittering chorus. Iulia, Paula, and Stela were duly greeted and borne away. Tati and I waited on the shore. This time, two of the sledges were late.

"So, are you expecting him again?" I asked her, rubbing my

hands together. I could feel them going numb, even in their sheepskin gloves.

Tati said nothing. Despite the piercing cold, she stood still as a statue, gaze fixed out over the sheet of ice—as if by only looking she could make Sorrow appear.

"What if he's gone home already? Maybe you shouldn't get your hopes up."

"He will come." Tati spoke with complete certainty. A moment later, two sledges emerged from the mist, one accompanied by a tinny fanfare, for a team of straggle-haired gnomes rode the front of the salamander, reed trumpets braying. Like all the other sledges, this one traveled of its own volition, without need for deer or wolves or unicorns to pull it. The driver was tall Grigori. Beside it came another sledge, in the form of a swan, moving in a pool of silence, and at the sight of the occupant, my sister sucked in her breath.

"He's hurt!" she exclaimed.

Sorrow had certainly been in some kind of trouble. He had a black eye and one side of his face was a mass of bruises and grazes. Perhaps he'd been in an accident, but he looked a lot like Cezar's friends did when they'd had too much țuică and gotten into a brawl. Sorrow held himself straight, his dark eyes fixed with unsettling intensity on Tati.

I didn't suggest that Tati travel with Grigori, though I was tempted. I could talk to Sorrow—I could tell him to keep away from my sister. Almost as soon as I thought of this idea, I dismissed it. Those eyes told me he wouldn't listen any more than Tati had. If there was a solution, I'd have to find it elsewhere.

"What happened to *him*?" I asked Grigori as we traversed

the frozen lake and the gnome band entertained us with a selection of old favorites.

"Sorrow? Some of us fellows took exception when he announced that he'd be escorting your sister again. Instead of backing off politely, he challenged us. Put up a good fight, too. I don't think anyone will be standing in his way next time. That's if there is a next time: that tall one, the leader of the Night People, seems to keep him on a pretty tight rein."

An unsettling thought occurred to me. "What if he bit you? I'd have thought that would put anyone off fighting one of the Night People."

"A Night Person's bite can't harm one of us," Grigori said, glancing across at the swan sledge. "All the same, Ileana's watching him. She saw your concern last time and she shares it. Alliances between our kind and your kind do happen, of course, but they're fraught with difficulty."

"I need to speak with Ileana tonight. Maybe I could ask her to send the Night People away."

Grigori ran a hand through his long black hair. "You can try, Jena. I don't think she will. Ileana doesn't direct the course of affairs; that's not our way. She believes in letting folk make their own errors. If that results in disaster, so be it."

"There's a bigger disaster looming than Sorrow and Tati," I said grimly, "and it's my cousin's doing. Will you ask the queen if I can talk to her later?"

"Of course." Grigori swept a bow as we pulled in to the bank. "Remember as you do so that the real power in the Other Kingdom is not Ileana and Marin. In times of deepest trouble, only Drăguţa can help."

"That's what everyone tells me," I said, stepping out to a frenetic fanfare from the reed trumpets and grasping Grigori's arm as my boots slipped on the ice. Gogu was shuddering with cold and distress. I had never really understood why he insisted on coming with us when the lake caused him such terror. "Nobody's ever been able to tell me just where Drăguţa's to be found. Not even you, and I've heard the two of you are kin."

Grigori grinned, showing a phalanx of shining white teeth. "If you truly need her, you'll find her," he said. "That's all you have to remember. Now, about our dance. Sten and I have another bet. . . ."

I persuaded the gnomes to bring their trumpets up to Dancing Glade, for I knew Stela would love them. They marched ahead of us in formation, red-cheeked faces beaming with pride, instruments over their shoulders.

Jena?

The frog had come back to himself. I fished him out and set him on my shoulder.

"Good evening to you, young master." Grigori's deep voice was courteous.

"He would say good evening if he could," I said. "He appreciates your excellent manners. There are many who wouldn't give a frog the time of day."

"In this realm, we understand that to make such a judgment is dangerous," Grigori said. "A friend is a friend, whatever form he may take."

I lost sight of Sorrow and Tati almost immediately. I danced with Grigori and with Sten and with Anatolie. I danced with the young forest men, all of whom had long, complicated names that sounded like stars or rare plants or precious stones. The forest women danced as lightly as gossamer in the wind. Each was as lovely as an exotic bloom, as beguiling as a sparkling gem. As with their men, there was a certain sameness in their features, a certain coolness in their eyes—their beauty lacked the flaws that give individuals character. Myself, I much preferred the less decorative inhabitants of the forest: Anatolie, with his dry humor; honest, craggy Sten; Grigori, whose imposing frame housed the kindest of natures.

"Will you dance?" The voice was deep and dark, like indigo velvet. A chill went down my spine.

"If you wish." I held on to my manners, despite my alarm. Information. An opportunity for information. I took the extended hand of the black-booted, waxen-faced man who was leader of the Night People, and stepped into the dance.

His hand was ice-cold; the grip was strong. Close up, I looked into a pair of lustrous sloe-black eyes, fringed by heavy lashes a young woman would give much to possess for herself. The lips were thin, the nose a haughty beak. He was tall— taller than Cezar. Even with my hair sticking out in all directions, I came up only to his chest.

"Your name is Jenica," the velvety voice said as we began a stately progress across the sward, hand in hand. "A human girl. Interesting."

I struggled for an appropriate response. The one Gogu suggested could not be used: *Do you mean as a source of food? Or are you just making polite conversation?* "Er, yes, that's right. What is your name?"

I had already made up my own names for the leaders of the

Night People, along the same lines as Sorrow. I had dubbed this dashing, dark-cloaked creature Arrogance, and the crimson-lipped siren Allure.

"You may call me Tadeusz," he said, clearly surprised that I had dared ask something so personal. "My sister is Anastasia. You dance well, Jenica." He twirled me under his arm.

"Thank you. We've been coming here since we were little girls; we get plenty of practice."

"You prefer this realm to your own?"

Something in his tone set alarm bells ringing. "No," I told him firmly. "I love it here, but I belong there. Tell me, do you plan to stay long at Ileana's court?"

"Why would you ask this?" We executed a gallop, both hands joined, and turned at the bottom of the line.

I was unable to answer. To come right out with my concerns about Sorrow and Tati to *him* didn't seem right. "Is Sorrow your son? Your brother?" I asked, feeling the clammy sensation of his hand in mine and wondering how my sister could possibly summon warm feelings for people who felt like dead fish.

Tadeusz threw back his head and laughed. People stared. So did I, fascinated and horrified. He didn't exactly have fangs. There was no doubt, however, that the elongated canine teeth were perfectly designed for inflicting a neat and effective puncture wound.

"I have neither son nor brother, Jenica," the dark-cloaked man said, suddenly somber. "We live long, and each of us walks alone."

I felt obliged to correct him. "You said Al—Anastasia was your sister," I pointed out. "So you are not quite alone."

"Sister, lover, daughter, stranger—which of these would trouble you least?" He was flippant now.

"I like the truth, even when it does trouble me," I said.

"Then ask what you want to ask."

"Very well. I want to know when Sorrow is going home. When he's leaving."

"And why would you be interested in such a thing? It is your sister who has attached herself to the young man; you, I think, cannot see past the frog."

What's that to you? If Gogu had had hair, he'd have been positively bristling.

"I ask because of her—Tatiana. She seems to be losing sense of what is possible. I am afraid for her."

"Really?" The dark brows went up. He was mocking me now. "You can't live everyone's lives for them. Maybe it's time to let go; to live your own. You are young and not unattractive. You dance well. You have a spark that's sorely lacking in most human women. Why not abandon the rules with which you hedge in yourself and your sisters, and seek enjoyment, adventure, fulfillment? I would take some pleasure in teaching you. . . ." He ran a chilly finger down my neck and across the part of my chest exposed by the green gown, a gesture of shocking intimacy.

Gogu made an ill-calculated leap, sliding down Tadeusz's immaculate black shirt to land on the grass in an undignified heap. The dark eyes looked down impassively. One boot rose from the ground, wooden heel poised.

I swooped on my frog, snatching him from harm's way. "I'm

sorry," I lied. "I'm afraid Gogu's left a trail on your shirt. I'll take him away now."

"Thank you for the dance, Jenica." The music was drawing to a close. Tadeusz executed an elegant bow. It was not quite a mockery.

"Thank you," I muttered, and lost myself in the crowd.

Shortly after that, Grigori came for me. He led me to the spot where Ileana and Marin sat on thrones of willow wood woven with ivy, resting from their exertions. Word of my request seemed to have gotten about. This would not be a private audience. Anatolie and three other dwarves were there, and Sten, and a good many others.

I swept a low curtsy, cleared my throat, and set it all out for them: Father's illness, his departure, the unanswered letters. Uncle Nicolae's terrible accident. The fact that I believed Cezar might really plan to drive the fairy folk out of the forest. They listened in silence. When I was finished, Ileana said calmly, "But we know all this. We watch you. We are everywhere."

"We must do something," I said. "Don't you understand? This could mean that in time the whole forest will be destroyed. Dancing Glade could be gone. You'd have nowhere to live."

"Your cousin does not own Tăul Ielelor," Marin said gravely. "He does not control Piscul Dracului. You will keep it safe."

"I'm trying," I said through gritted teeth. "But Cezar's doing his best to take the responsibility out of my hands. Nobody sees anything wrong with that. To the men of my world, his actions must seem quite reasonable. They wouldn't expect a family of girls to look after an estate over a whole winter. And as for what Cezar intends to do to the forest, you must know that people fear you—that they blame you for many deaths and disappearances." I caught the sardonic eye of Tadeusz, who had appeared on the edge of the crowd, and looked quickly away. "Now that Uncle Nicolae's gone, there's nobody who can help us. And if Father dies . . ."

"What if he dies?" Ileana's tone was cool.

"If he dies before a male grandchild is born, Cezar inherits Piscul Dracului outright. Then there really will be no forest left."

"Mmm-hm. Why has your cousin made himself into an enemy? Why does he wish to destroy us all?"

"He believes your people drowned his brother, Costin. He was lost in the Deadwash long ago. Cezar swore vengeance on all the folk of the forest. I never thought he would go through with it. I believed in time he would forget his anger, or that I could make him change his mind. I think I was wrong."

"Maybe not," Ileana said, her pale blue eyes meeting mine with a penetrating look. "Your cousin listens to you. Inasmuch as he can care about anyone, he cares about you. Maybe you could drive a bargain, Jena."

I did not like this turn of the conversation at all. "Your Majesty, I have come to you for help. I don't think I can bargain with Cezar. I don't think I have anything I'm prepared to give him. But if Father doesn't come back, if he doesn't get better, I need some way to stop my cousin from carrying out his threat."

All of them just looked at me. I had expected fear, anger, a shared purpose. I had hoped for solutions. This blank acceptance seemed almost like indifference. "This is your whole future!" I burst out, against my better judgment. "Don't you *care?*"

There was a little silence. Gogu twitched. *Uh-oh.*

"What would you have us do?" Ileana seemed eerily calm. "Wage war on this cousin, frighten him from his home? Set fire to his crops, strike his animals dead? Take such a course of action, and we would spark the kind of retribution that comes on the keen edge of a scythe, the piercing tines of a pitchfork. It is not our way. Your Cezar makes his own path. Whether it leads to good or ill, only time will tell."

"So you would just sit back and watch as your kingdom is destroyed?"

"We will not interfere. This will flow as it must; it is not for us to stem the tide. Have you considered that the solution may be no farther away than your fingertips?"

"I don't know what you mean." I could not keep hurt and annoyance from my voice. "I can't even get workers to come up and mend the fences for me—how am I meant to solve a problem as big as this? Cezar's a landholder now. He's got power."

"You must solve your own puzzle," Ileana said. She rose to her feet and picked up a fold of her gold-embroidered gown, ready for another round of dancing. "You can do it. Music! Come, strike up a reel!"

In a trice they were gone, heading onto the sward for more revelry. I was stunned. Not only had the forest queen made no offer of assistance, she'd treated my pressing problems—and her own—as almost inconsequential.

"She does care," Grigori said. He was the only one who had

stayed behind. "It's our way to let things take their course, that's all. What was that you were saying about fences? Sten and I could attend to your heavy work. You should have asked us."

Sudden tears pricked my eyes. "Thank you," I said, "but it's best if you don't. When you come across to our world, especially if you stay awhile, you put yourselves at huge risk. I won't have you doing that for us. Cezar's enough of a threat to you—we mustn't make it worse by giving other folk the chance to see you on the farm. But I value your offer. Now I'd better go and find Tati."

"If I may." A tall, dark form appeared by my side. It seemed that one other had lingered after Ileana's audience. The pallid Tadeusz reached to cup my elbow without a by-your-leave. His eyes met Grigori's and, to my surprise, Drǎguţa's kinsman backed away.

"You have troubles," Tadeusz murmured, drawing my arm through his and starting to walk along the sward so I had no choice but to go with him. "I could help you. This cousin is nothing." He snapped his fingers in illustration. "He can be stopped from interfering in your affairs. That would be an easy matter, Jenica. It would give me pleasure to be of assistance to you. He could simply be . . . removed." I felt long, bony fingers close around mine; he lifted my hand to his lips. The chill touch of his mouth gave my skin goose bumps. In my pocket Gogu was cringing and silent. "Of course, I would require something in return. Nothing comes without a price."

I felt sick. "Thank you, but I will find some other solution to my problems," I said, my heart pounding. "I'm sure I can work something out."

He looked down at me, his dark eyes assessing. "Really?" he asked me, and lifted a hand to toy with my hair, twisting a brown curl around his finger.

"Really. Now I must go—"

"You should not be afraid, Jenica. My kind are not entirely what you believe of us. The tales your villagers tell give one picture of the truth, a picture distorted by superstitious fear. But there are many truths in the Other Kingdom. It is a matter of perception. The eyes of each viewer see a different reality. You would not judge so quickly, would you?"

I swallowed. His voice was a subtle instrument, soft and beguiling. The sound of it seemed to resonate deep within me. "I don't trust easily," I said. "I don't like violent solutions to problems. And I prefer to know exactly what I'm getting into."

"Ah. But you come to the Other Kingdom every Full Moon, trusting that you will be safe, that your friends will be here to welcome you, that your night will be spent in innocent enjoyment."

I stared up at him, wanting to be anywhere but here, yet held by his voice. Despite myself, I was intrigued by what he said. "I'm careful," I told him. "I look out for my sisters. Anyway, it always has been like that. We've always been safe here."

Tadeusz smiled, and I tried not to look at his teeth. "So young and so ignorant," he said. "Yet maybe not so young. You watch your sisters, yes—one in particular you watched two

Full Moons ago, as she danced with one partner and then another. You made her go home before the dancing was over. Why was that, I wonder? And again, at last Full Moon—was there perhaps a touch of jealousy in you, Jenica? A desire to be a little older, and to feel a man's arms around your own waist in intimate embrace?"

I felt myself flush scarlet. "I'm not listening to this," I said. "I must go now—"

"Go," he said airily, but his hand still held mine. "Go—and remain in ignorance, if that is your preference."

"Ignorance of what?" Perhaps he had something to tell me about Sorrow, something that would help me persuade Tati to let him go.

"All these years you've limited yourselves to one visit a month—to one way of entering the Other Kingdom. There is another way. At Dark of the Moon, there is another portal. With my help it can be opened to you. It will unveil a world of knowledge to you, Jena. At Dark of the Moon, you may look into Drăguţa's mirror. If you wish to discover the true nature of your sister's lover, you will do so there. If you can summon the courage for it, you may see your own future and that of those you love." His thumb moved against my palm.

"What do you mean?" I croaked, not liking the way his words made me feel, as if I had glimpsed something I wanted badly and knew I should not have. "That if we passed through this portal of yours, we wouldn't be in Dancing Glade, but somewhere else? In your own realm? I was told you come from the forests of the east."

"There are many paths in the Other Kingdom." He lifted his brows, and his mouth formed a derisive grimace. "I'll wager you are not brave enough to try this one."

I knew I should turn my back and walk away. "What if I did want to?" I whispered. "Where is this portal? How can I find it?"

Tadeusz's teeth gleamed in the moonlight. "There is a price," he said. "Do not forget that."

"What price?"

"A price no greater than you can afford, Jena. I will ensure that."

"You mean you won't tell me what it is? That is asking me to take a foolish risk. I am no fool."

"Ah, well. I am unsurprised that you lack the courage for this."

I swallowed. "If I—if I did decide to try it," I said, hating myself for asking, "how would I get over? Where would I go?"

"If you would cross over, call to me and I will take you there." His voice wrapped about me like a soft cloak.

"Call to you? How?"

"Ah. That is a simple matter. You need only want me, Jena, and I will come to you. I am not bound by man's fences nor fettered by his puny charms of protection. No need of doors or keys, of spells or incantations. I will hear your call in the pulsing of the blood, in the urgent hammering of the heart." He stroked my cheek with the back of his hand; it sent a shiver through me.

"I've heard about your kind," I whispered. "What reason would I possibly have to trust you?"

Gogu had been getting increasingly agitated. Now he startled me by leaping from my pocket and hopping rapidly away to disappear into a clump of long grass. I realized to my alarm that we had walked some distance from the sward of Dancing Glade—much farther than our rules allowed. Under the dark oaks where we stood, all was shadowy and still. The colored lights were a dim glow, the magical music a dim buzzing.

"Oh!" I exclaimed. "My frog! I must catch him—" I wrenched myself away and strode back toward the glade, led by a series of rustling noises in the undergrowth that seemed to mark Gogu's progress.

Tadeusz's voice followed me, soft and deep. "Do not leap to judge me on the basis of old wives' tales. Live your life that way, and you are no better than an ignorant peasant, raised on the dirt of the fields. If you require proof of my good intentions, I will give it, Jena."

I did not look back. My heart was racing and my brow was damp with cold sweat. What had I been thinking? Gogu moved faster and faster. I ran, and there was a curious sound of derision in my ears: not the full-throated laughter of Tadeusz, but the cackling of an old woman.

I was shocked to find, when I reached the glade again, that the dancing was nearing its end—folk were leaping about in a grand finale. In keeping with the strange quirks of time in the Other Kingdom, my conversation with Tadeusz had swallowed up half the night. Gogu was nowhere to be found; a search of the bushes by the path revealed nothing. I retraced my steps to Ileana's throne. I looked under and over and all around. I eyed the confusion of skipping, jumping, stamping feet on the sward, some bare, some shod. Tadeusz had returned to stand with his fellow Night People; disconcertingly, his gaze was still on me. I gathered up Stela and Paula. Neither had seen the frog.

"But Tati's up there," Paula said helpfully. "They've just been sitting there all night."

Tati and Sorrow had found a little hollow near the edge of the sward, under a stand of leafless birches. Tati's blue cloak was spread out on the grass, and she sat on it with her back against a pale trunk. Sorrow lay with his head in her lap. She was stroking his hair; he was holding her other hand. They didn't seem to be talking.

"Go and tell her it's time to leave," I told my sisters. "I have to find Gogu." He'd been trying to warn me; I knew it. He'd heard how I was being lulled and charmed by that insidious voice and had hopped off to lead me back to safety. Now I was safe, and he had vanished.

I went right around the sward, asking everyone I passed: "Have you seen my frog?" Nobody had. I asked the creatures in the cloak-tree, and they chittered a negative as they dropped my things down to me, the winter boots narrowly missing my head. By the time I got back to my starting point I was crying, and my sisters and their escorts were all waiting for me.

"It's nearly dawn," Grigori said. "We must go."

"I can't go! I can't leave Gogu!"

"He'll be all right, Jena," Stela said through a yawn. "He should be safe here until next time."

"I'm not going! I can't! I can't leave him behind!" I heard the shrill tone of my own voice, like a frightened child's. Losing Gogu would be like losing a part of myself—like being ripped apart.

"We must go now," said Anatolie gently.

"Come, Jena," said Grigori. "You must leave your friend behind."

"He probably belongs here anyway," Iulia pointed out. "Maybe it's time to let him go."

I slapped her. She stared at me a moment, eyes wide with shock, a red mark on her cheek. Then she turned her back and put her hands over her face; I could see her shoulders quivering. Misery descended on me. I was going to have to leave him. If I didn't go with them, my sisters couldn't get home. Besides, I could hardly vanish from my own world for a whole month, even supposing I could get by without eating or drinking anything. That was impossible.

As I followed the others down to the lake, I pictured Gogu as I had first found him: alone in the forest, weak, hurt, frightened. He had been with me for more than nine years. He was used to living in the castle, and eating with us, and sleeping on my pillow. He had no idea at all how to look after himself in the wildwood, even supposing he wasn't injured, or worse. He'd get cold; he'd get hungry; he'd be terribly lonely. What if he wandered off and I never saw him again?

Iulia was crying. Paula and Stela were pale and silent. Tati walked hand in hand with Sorrow. They were holding on so tightly that their knuckles were white.

We reached the shore. One by one, my sisters got into their sledges and glided off over the ice. The sky had begun to brighten. Dawn came late in this dark season; we had had a generous night of dancing. My heart was a lump of cold misery in my chest. I pictured the empty sward, after the revelers had departed—and my dearest friend lying there, heedlessly crushed in a desperate effort to find me.

"Jena." Tati stood right next to me, with Sorrow just behind her. "I don't want to go."

A chill ran through me. "What? You have to go—we all do."

"I really don't want to go, Jena. I don't know how I can manage a whole month over there. . . ." Her voice drifted into nothing. She turned and put her face against Sorrow's chest and his hand came up to the back of her neck.

"I could stay and look for Gogu," Tati said, her voice muffled by the black coat.

"You can't," I said, sniffing back more tears. Suddenly I was angry: angry with myself, that my stupidity in listening to Tadeusz had allowed this to happen, and angry that Tati would use my distress to try to win time for herself. "Remember, we can't open the portal without you. You have to come, and I have to leave Gogu here. As for *you*"—I glared at Sorrow and saw his hand tighten against my sister's neck—"you should think twice about what you're doing. You don't belong here, and I wish you would go away."

I turned my back and climbed into the salamander sledge, my eyes blinded by tears. The gnomes struck up a dirge. I was scarcely aware of crossing the Deadwash, or of bidding Grigori a hasty farewell before the sledges sped back, racing the dawn's first rays. My mind was full of Gogu: abandoned, bereft, shivering with cold and fright—or, worse still, lying dead somewhere—

because I had allowed myself to lose sight of common sense. I'd never felt so miserable or so guilty in my life.

Tati stood on the shore with Sorrow. He was leaving his departure until perilously late.

"You'd better go," she said, apparently trying to be strong. An instant later she flung herself into his arms. He held her, his head bowed against her shoulder, his lips on the white neck exposed by her upswept hair. Then he detached himself, backing toward the sledge with his hand still in hers. They held on as he got in; they held on while the swan sledge began easing away from the bank, with Tati balanced precariously on the ice and Sorrow leaning out at a perilous angle. Then, all at once, the sledge sped off into the morning mist and the clasping hands were torn from each other.

We made our way through the Gallery of Beasts, whose occupants were no more than vague bundles up in the corners. We climbed the long, long, winding stair.

"Hurry up, Jena!" called Paula. "Hurry up, Tati!"

I was last, walking behind Tati. I did not trust her to bring up the rear and not decide to bolt back down and go crashing away across the ice in search of her pale-faced sweetheart. Up, up, and up . . . I felt each step as a blow to the heart. At last we reached the portal. We stretched out our hands toward the stone wall—but I snatched mine away, without touching it. I had heard something. . . . I strained to catch it again. For a moment all was silence. Then it came once more, a little, weary thud from down the stairs. *Plop . . . plop . . .*

"Something's coming up," Stela whispered, turning as white as linen.

Plop . . . plop . . . It was getting slower.

"Gogu?" My voice was reed-thin and quavering, an old woman's. A moment later he came into sight, three steps down. He was shaking with exhaustion, a rime of frost over his whole body. A big heaving sob burst out of me. I gathered him up and held him to my breast. He was so cold; his skin felt all hard and crackly, as if his damp body had begun to freeze solid. His eyes were half closed.

You left me. You left me b-b-behind.

"Put out your hand, Jena!" snapped Iulia. "It must be nearly sunrise—quick! We might get trapped in between worlds!"

I hardly heard her. A flood of tears was running down my cheeks. I hugged my frog close, trying to warm him against my body.

"Come on, Jena." Tati had moved up next to me. Her eyes met mine, and some kind of forgiveness passed between us. We each set a hand against the wall. Our sisters placed their fingers beside ours. The portal opened and we went home to Piscul Dracului.

No water bowl this morning. I lay in bed with Gogu on my chest. I had rolled him in a woolen scarf after warming it on the little stove. Monumental shivers still passed through him. Beside us, Tati lay on her back, staring up at the ceiling.

"I'm sorry," I whispered. "I'm so, so sorry. I know you were trying to rescue me. I promise I'll never leave you again."

Gogu made no response, but the shivering began to die down and his eyes took on a brighter look.

"Anyway," I whispered, "how did you get across the

Deadwash? You're too scared to go anywhere near it by yourself. Did someone bring you?"

D-D-D- . . .

"Never mind," I said. "You're safe and we're together again. I don't want to think about anything else right now." I couldn't stop crying. Maybe I was making up for all the times I had stayed calm and sorted out other people's problems. How could I have been so foolish? I had let Tadeusz lull me into forgetting what was right. I'd made it all too easy for him. I must never, ever do that again. His words were still in my mind: the startling revelation that Dark of the Moon allowed a passage to the Other Kingdom; the news of another portal; the tantalizing reference to a way of looking into the future. . . . What if I could see Cezar's future, and somehow use that knowledge to stop him from going through with his threats? What if I could see what would become of Tati and Sorrow? And what would I see for myself, or for Father? I tried to stop thinking about it, but the images filled my mind—images of what might be revealed to me if I only had the courage to look.

After a while I felt Gogu wriggle out of the scarf and hop up to the pillow. He snuggled close to my cheek. *Don't be sad, Jena. I'm here.*

Chapter Six

A heavy blanket of snow lay over the hillside, making the paths treacherous. The forest had a special beauty in winter: frozen waterfalls like delicate shawls; foliage shrouded in a glittering, rimy coating; blue-white snowdrifts revealing, here and there, a rich litter of darkened leaves in a thousand damp colors of brown and gray. The forlorn, peeping cry of a bird . . . neat imprints in the white, the tracks of a hungry wolf or wildcat. The bears would be sleeping, curled deep in their hollows. My breath made a big cloud as we went, Gogu's a smaller one.

I'd found it hard to sleep and had headed out early for a walk. I hoped that exercise would clear my mind, which felt as if a dense fog had descended over it. It was all very well for me to lecture Tati about becoming involved with Sorrow. What I had done was almost worse: I had let one of the Night People lead me off the path and whisper his dangerous lies in my ears—and I had felt, just for a moment, the delicious, forbidden sensation of considering what he had offered. In the cold light of the winter morning, I could not believe I had allowed it to happen.

I walked all the way down to the village. Behind the carved gates of each smallholding, cows lowed and chickens squawked. Here and there, a woman swathed in shawls and scarves could be seen on the muddy pathway, carrying a bucket or a bundle. A long cart loaded with logs passed by, pulled by a pair of heavy horses. Red tassels dangled from their bridles, a charm against evil spirits. The logs would be from Cezar's plantation, and destined for Braşov. I stopped by Judge Rinaldo's house to offer his wife our regards. She invited me in for a glass of rosehip tea and expressed the hope that Aunt Bogdana would be ready for visitors soon. I did not tell her that even we had been told to stay away.

The village church stood on a little hill, its pointed wooden roof reaching toward heaven. I wavered outside, tempted to seek out Father Sandu, but not sure exactly what I wanted of him. I could not speak of Night People. I could have asked him to pray for Father's recovery, but in the end I walked past, for it was early and I did not wish to disturb the priest without good reason. The shutters of his little house were closed fast. I headed back past Ivan's place and his wife gave me a small pot of honey. I suspected that she could ill spare it, but it was impolite to refuse such a gift. Iulia would be happy, I thought—Tati or I could use this to bake something sweet. Maybe Florica had some nuts hidden away.

Gogu and I made our way back into the castle courtyard

under a light falling of snowflakes. I was planning what I needed to say to my sisters. I'd start with an apology to Iulia for hitting her. What she had said to me last night, about letting Gogu go, had made perfect sense. She could not know the mixture of grief and guilt that had made me strike out at her. I would tell them how sorry I was that I hadn't specified we were not supposed to mix up the funds. I would explain truthfully that we had been quite short on both foodstuffs and silver even before Cezar had walked off with our two coffers, and that I had no intention of begging from him. Then they could give me their ideas on how we might get through the winter. I began to feel a little better. Admitting I was wrong did not come easily to me; I preferred not to make errors in the first place. But today, with the echo of Tadeusz's soft voice in my ears and his touch fresh on my skin, I knew I must make peace with my sisters and allow them to help me.

Horses.

"What?"

Horses. Visitors.

Gogu was right. Tied up before our front door were my cousin's black gelding and two other mounts.

"A pox on Cezar!" I lengthened my stride, putting a hand up to balance the frog. "He's the last person I want to see this morning."

The morning after Full Moon wasn't the best time for us to receive visitors. We tended to be tired and cross after too little sleep. In the kitchen Florica was brewing fruit tea and Iulia was slicing a loaf of bread while Paula put out dishes of plum preserve. Stela was setting out glasses and plates—she looked so weary, she could drop something at any moment.

Cezar was talking to Tati, who was pale and drawn and did not seem to be paying much attention. My cousin's two friends sat at the table. Cezar had met Daniel and Răzvan during the years of his formal education in Braşov. They were landholders' sons, the kind of young men deemed suitable to be future husbands for girls like us. I thought Daniel supercilious and Răzvan rather slow. Both were of solid build, like Cezar, and their interests ran along similar lines: hunting, drinking, and discussing their own exploits loudly and at length. The kitchen was full of their presence; I felt as if we had to shrink to make room for them.

Stay calm, Jena.

"Cezar." As I walked in, the eyes of the three young men traveled from the frog on my shoulder down to my wet boots and the sodden hem of my gown. "Another surprise visit?" I saw something on the table next to Tati's tea glass, and my heart lurched. Instantly, Cezar was forgiven. "A letter! A letter from Father?"

My cousin had risen to his feet as I came in. Now he stepped forward and took both my hands in his. I resisted the urge to snatch them away. "It is from Constanţa," he said. "But this is not Uncle Teodor's writing. Paula tells me it is that of his secretary."

"We waited for you, Jena." Paula was solemn. In her eyes I read the unspoken message: if it was bad news, it would be best if we all heard it together.

"Father often gets Gabriel to address his letters," I said,

picking up the folded parchment and reaching for the bread knife. I willed my fingers not to shake. "Thank you for bringing this, Cezar."

"I'm at your disposal, as you know. This came with a representative of my agent in Constanţa. The man had not seen your father, only a messenger, who left this with him. I have no further news for you."

"Excuse me." I couldn't ask him and his friends to leave the room, although I dearly wanted to be able to read Father's letter in private, with just my sisters around me. I went over to the stove, my back to everyone, and slit the seal.

I saw immediately that the message, too, was in Gabriel's writing. My heart plummeted with disappointment. I scanned the letter quickly. If it was the worst news, I needed a moment to collect myself before I told them. I cleared my throat, swallowing tears.

" 'My greetings to you, young ladies, on your father's behalf,' " I read aloud. " 'Teodor is still too unwell to write. The cough has deepened and is causing his physician grave concern. Rest assured that everything that can be done will be done.

" 'Your father is not able to send any instructions for the conduct of his affairs while so severely debilitated. I am aware that you have Salem bin Afazi's consignment in storage. . . .' "
As I spoke, my eyes were scanning the next section of the letter, in which Gabriel suggested that I ask Cezar to deal with the selling of Father's precious goods. I decided I would not read this part aloud. " 'A decision was made not to give your father the news of his beloved cousin's tragic and untimely death as yet. His physician believed that such a blow could well prove

fatal. I would ask that if you write to your father, you take care to shield him from this news.

" 'I will dispatch this by Cezar's agent and hope it reaches you safely. Of course, I will remain by your father's side through this difficult time. As instructed, I have sent word to Dorin that he should not return to Piscul Dracului until he hears from me again, since, in your father's absence, there will be little employment for him there. Your obedient servant, Gabriel.' "

There was a silence after I had finished. Looking from one sister to another, I saw the same look on all their faces. It perfectly reflected what was in my own heart: the cold realization that our worst fears were coming true. *Grave concern. Severely debilitated. Could well prove fatal.* Those phrases seemed to add up to only one thing: we'd probably never see our father again.

After a little, Florica carried the teakettle over to the table and set it down with a rattle. "Praise God, your dear father is still with us," she said, raising a hand to wipe her eyes. "Master Cezar, will you take tea?"

"I'll pour it," I said, wanting a job to help me stay calm. "Răzvan? Daniel? I'm afraid we have only bread to offer you."

"Ah, how could I forget?" Cezar got up and fetched a capacious basket that had been set by the door. "I'm sorry there isn't better news to celebrate, but Florica is right—we should be glad Uncle Teodor is still clinging to life. I brought you some supplies, a few little delicacies. I had a feeling you might be running short. Here." He set the basket on the table and unfolded the cloth that lay over its contents. A delicious smell arose. "Our own store cupboard is amply stocked," Cezar said. "My steward attends to it diligently. We can certainly spare this. Nuts, honey, a little wine for you older girls, some preserved fruits . . . And I had our kitchen people make some spice cakes. We could sample those with the tea. You look as if you need a treat."

I wonder what he wants.

Gogu's suspicions mirrored my own. I was uncomfortable with Cezar in the role of benefactor. His good deeds were seldom performed without some expectation of gain for himself.

"Oh, Cezar, how lovely!" Iulia's cheeks were flushed with pleasure. I noticed Răzvan staring at her in what appeared to be admiration. When she leaned forward to examine the basket's contents, he was taking in the view down the front of her day dress. I frowned at my sister, but she did not seem to notice.

It was clear that Tati wasn't going to say anything. Daniel was seated opposite her. She sipped her tea and stared through him.

"Thank you, Cezar," I made myself say. "I'm sure I speak for all of us when I tell you how welcome these small luxuries are." I noticed that he was wearing his father's gold chain again, the one with the miniature hunting horn—perhaps he wore it all the time now.

"Jena?" The little voice was Stela's.

"What is it, Stela?"

"Is Father dying? Is that what it means, *severely debil— debili—*"

"*Debilitated* just means tired and weak." Paula spoke firmly. "Father needs more rest, that's all. He'll be home in spring-time."

We sat awhile over our feast. Cezar did most of the talking. I had several questions in my mind, questions I could not ask. It seemed to me impossible that Gabriel would have opened my private letters; my father's secretary was the soul of propriety. Yet, if he had not, how could he have shielded Father from learning of Uncle Nicolae's death? Evidently Gabriel himself had been given the sad news. Had Cezar had a hand in censoring my correspondence? Gabriel had said, *if you write to your father*—*if*, not *when*. Was it possible that my letters had never reached Father in Constanţa? And who had decided that we didn't need Dorin back? An able-bodied young man to help Petru would be worth his weight in gold right now.

I waited for an opportunity to ask Cezar about this, but he was holding forth on the perils of the wildwood, one of his pet subjects, and I couldn't get a word in edgewise. Nobody was arguing—today, none of us sisters had the energy or the heart to challenge him. After a while my attention drifted, my thoughts going over the events of last night: the look in Tadeusz's eyes, the honey in his voice, the things he had told me. I could not think why I was the one he had singled out, nor what he hoped to gain by it. In the ancient tales of Transylvania, Night People were not known for doing people favors.

"You'd do well to let me deal with the lower reaches of the Piscul Dracului forest as well, Jena," my cousin was saying. "Since I'll be hiring men to fell the trees around my own house, they may as well be put to work on Uncle Teodor's land straight afterward. We could have the immediate area fully cleared by the end of spring. And the timber would fetch you a tidy profit."

"What?" I must have sounded stupid. I had only just realized what he was talking about.

"My project, Jena." Cezar's tone held exaggerated patience. "Rendering my property, and Uncle Teodor's, safe from the malign presences that haunt these woods."

Your cousin wants a hand in everything. He wants control.

"You can't do that, Cezar. Folk may be afraid of the beings that dwell in the wildwood, but I doubt very much that the people of the valley would support what you suggest." I glanced at Florica; she had gone extremely pale. "Felling the trees over a wide area would only anger those presences. It could bring down retaliation on everyone in our community." Then, seeing the way Cezar was looking at me: "At least, that's what most folk will believe. As Florica said once, if you give respect, you get respect back. If you offend, you get . . . retribution. Nobody will be prepared to work for you on this. Anyway, you can't do anything here at Piscul Dracului without Father's permission."

Cezar's mouth went thin, his eyes turned cold. "It offends me to hear such sentiments issuing from your lips, Jena. I will do you the favor of putting it down to your innocence."

He means ignorance.

"Since you speak of offense and of retribution," my cousin went on, "I must point out to you that there could hardly be a greater offense than robbing a boy of a beloved brother. I've waited years to dispense due punishment for that. The trees are only the first step. As for workers, a man whose family is starving cannot afford to refuse employment on the basis of superstitious fear. Besides, it's easy enough to bring in labor from farther afield: men who don't know the peculiarities of this particular forest."

The atmosphere in the kitchen had turned decidedly chilly. Nobody else was saying a thing, though I could see that Paula was bursting to speak. I gave her a warning glance. We were all tired and upset; this was the time not for challenges, but for wise silence. Cezar's friends had the grace to look a little embarrassed as they applied themselves to the food.

"Enough of this," Cezar said abruptly. "Jena, I want to look over the accounts while I'm here. I trust that your sisters can keep my friends entertained?"

"Of course," said Iulia, who had seated herself between Răzvan and Daniel. Now that she had had her treat, she was in the best of tempers and making the most of her position—smiling shyly, batting her eyelashes, and plying the young men with cakes. I did not like this new behavior at all; I preferred her childish bursts of giggling. Even Cezar was stealing glimpses at her.

"Well," I said, rising to my feet, "let's get on with it. I don't imagine Daniel and Răzvan will be wanting to stay too long. Florica, perhaps you could make more tea for our guests? Paula, please come with Cezar and me. Bring a book."

"Oh, by the way," Cezar said as the three of us made our way up the narrow stairs to Father's workroom, "I noticed on the ride here that you've had all the fencing repaired up by the top pastures. I imagine you'll be needing some funds to pay your workers. Who helped Petru with the job? It's been expertly done— Jena? Is something wrong?"

"Oh—oh, no, nothing." My head was in a whirl, my stomach churned. The fencing all done between last night and this morning? It was not possible. Petru had been working in the barn when I left on my walk. He had still been there when I returned. Besides, even with two or three men, the fencing job would have taken several days. Grigori? No, I had asked him not to risk his safety, and I knew he would not act against my wishes. My heart sank. Tadeusz. It was the only explanation. But I had never asked for his help. I had not accepted his offer. In the back of my mind, I heard his deep, dark voice: *If you require proof of my good intentions, I will give it, Jena.* "I don't need funds, Cezar. Some travelers came by and offered to do it for food. I'm glad it was a good job; I haven't had the opportunity to go up and check it yet."

Once in the workroom, Paula seated herself at Gabriel's desk in the corner, while Cezar and I took opposite sides of the table.

"What is it you want to see?" I asked him, reaching for the current folder of receipts and payments. My hands were shaking. I thought of Tadeusz and his pallid crew up on our fields, walking in our world, setting their elegant hands to straightening withes and tying up fencing twine on our very own land, a stone's throw from where I and my sisters were sleeping. I thought of them prowling around our sheepfolds. What if someone had seen them?

"Are you sure you're quite well, Jena?" Cezar was regarding me closely. "You look very pale."

"I'm fine. There's no need for this, Cezar. The ledgers are up-to-date and everything balances. There's absolutely no reason for you to check on me. Especially now you've taken away the funds. There will be nothing for me to record until you give control of them back to me."

He smiled indulgently, as if I were a precocious infant. Then, as quickly, he was serious again. "I have something to tell you, Jena," he said. "It concerns the priest's visits to this house. I imagine you can guess what it is."

He had my full attention now. "What have you done?" I asked him, and heard the frost in my own voice. I could not look at Paula.

"I took action, as I advised you I would. I had a word with Father Sandu's superior. Were you aware that these lessons were never officially approved by the priory? That your father made a private arrangement with this priest to tutor young Paula? Even you must have been aware of how unconventional such behavior was."

"What do you mean, *behavior*?" Paula was on her feet, shaking with rage. "Father Sandu tutors the sons of many families in the district, you know that. How dare you imply there's something illicit about this? All he does is treat me the way he'd treat a boy student."

Cezar gave a patronizing smile. His eyes were cold. "Exactly," he said.

Arrogant fool.

"Tell us!" I was holding on to my temper by a thread, and willing the frog to keep his thoughts to himself. "What did you do?" In my mind I saw the closed shutters of Father Sandu's little house.

"I have not done as you seem to believe. I did not request that the priest cease his visits to Piscul Dracului. All I did was let his superior know what was going on."

"You must have realized that would have the same result," I said.

Now the little smile was turned on me. "Well, yes, in fact, the good Father will not be coming here any longer." Cezar's tone was rich with self-satisfaction. "A decision was made to recall him to the priory near Sibiu. It happens sometimes: a priest working alone—in a remote corner of the country, out of touch with his brethren—can lose his way a little. I believe they're sending a replacement to the district as a matter of urgency."

Paula got up and, clutching her book to her chest, walked out of the room in total silence. Her face was sheet-white, her jaw clenched tight. If she planned to shed tears, it would not be in our cousin's presence.

"How dare you!" My rage burst out of me. "You don't even realize what you've done, do you? This isn't just about Paula, Cezar. Father Sandu's been here far longer than we have. He's married people and baptized their babies and buried their dead in this community for years and years. People trust him. They rely on him. You've done this without even thinking about what it will mean for the valley!"

"The valley is better off without folk who disregard rules and conventions set up for their own protection. Besides, it was not I who relieved this priest of his position."

"Of course it was! Cezar, your father was deeply respected here. Folk looked up to him as a leader of the community. That's what the master of Vârful cu Negură is supposed to be. You're walking in Uncle Nicolae's shoes now. You must go and visit this Church authority straightaway and ask him to bring Father Sandu back. And speak to Judge Rinaldo while you're about it. Your father would never have dreamed of robbing our community of its beloved priest."

"I've upset you." For a moment, I heard genuine contrition in his voice.

"Promise me you'll make them reverse this, Cezar. Show what you're made of—do what's right." And, when he scowled at me, I added, "At least promise me you'll think about it."

The scowl changed to an expression I could not read. "There might be room for some negotiation," he said. I heard, in the back of my mind, a different voice saying, *Nothing comes without a price.* "You seem tired, Jena."

"I didn't sleep very well. Now, what is it you need to see in these accounts?"

We spent some time going through the latest ledger, which balanced perfectly and was entirely up-to-date. I kept waiting for Cezar to find fault, but he simply perused the figures in silence, asking an occasional question. Once or twice his hand brushed mine on the table and I withdrew my fingers. Once or twice he gave me a particular kind of look that made me wish Paula had not departed so abruptly.

Just as we were nearing the last entries in the ledger, Cezar seized my hand in his, turned bright red, and began, "Jena—"

Uh-oh.

"I've been meaning to ask you something," I said hastily, jumping to my feet. "Have you been opening my letters to Father, Cezar? How would Gabriel know to shield Father from what was in them otherwise?"

Cezar dropped my hand like a hot coal.

Nice work, Jena.

"Of course not! What do you take me for?" The flush faded. He put up a good show of looking bitterly offended.

A man who wants what he can't have.

I drew a deep breath. "I thought I knew you," I said. "There was a time when you used to listen to me. But the boy who was once my friend seems to be disappearing fast. In his place there's an autocratic bully, deaf to any opinion but his own. I know that's impolite, but it would be worse to lie to you. All you want is control. You shouldn't seek to rule over what isn't yours, Cezar."

There was a silence. Cezar's mouth was clamped into a tight line. He closed the ledger and passed it to me, and I replaced it on its shelf. He held the door open; I went through. As we made our way down the narrow stairs, Cezar said quietly, "It must run in the family."

"What?" I was desperate to be back with the others and for him to go away.

"You said all I want is control. That sounds more like you, Jena. A woman who seeks to have her hands on the reins day and night has a lonely future ahead of her."

Wretch. Mongrel.

"You misunderstood me," I said, pausing on the step below him. I was surprised at how hurt I felt—I had thought nothing he could say would touch me. "Being in control is good if one is running a business or a household. It's seeking to extend that control where it's neither needed nor wanted that offends me."

"Are you saying I offend you, Jena?"

Finally he gets the message.

"I don't like your hate and your anger. It's time to let all that go—to relinquish the past. I don't like what you're doing at Piscul Dracului. Taking over. Trying to show we can't cope. You should at least allow us the chance to prove ourselves." I went on down the steps.

"Ah," came his voice behind me, "but you've had that chance. It's not been so very long since your father left, but in that time I've seen your funds squandered, your elder sister failing utterly to support you, Paula spouting dangerous nonsense, and Iulia making a spectacle of herself like a cheap flirt—"

Hit him, go on.

"Don't say that!" I was within a whisker of carrying out Gogu's suggestion. "You were ogling her just as much as your wretched friends! Iulia's only thirteen, and she's a good girl—"

"Maybe so," Cezar said weightily. "But without proper guidance, how long will she remain so? Jena, I value your sense of duty. I admire your attempts to look after your home and family in this difficult time. But—unpalatable as it may be to you—the fact is that the best person to look after business, farm, and household is a man. In Uncle Teodor's absence, that man should be your closest kin: myself. The sooner you acknowledge this simple truth, the sooner the rose will return to your cheeks and the furrow disappear from your brow."

My fingers rose automatically to my forehead. What furrow? I'd been so busy, I couldn't remember when I'd last looked in a mirror.

Is that all?

"Are you quite finished, Cezar?"

"Don't be angry, Jena, I—"

"Are you finished?"

"For now. I simply ask you to think about this. You judge me too harshly."

"All things considered," I said, "I think I've shown remarkable self-restraint. You can forget about my making little trips to your door through the snow to grovel for money. You can forget about sending men over to help on the farm. As you can see, I'm perfectly capable of making my own arrangements. And I'll find someone else to take my letters to Constanţa."

He did not reply. Both of us knew there was nobody else. Few people had the means to travel such difficult ways in wintertime. Our position was so isolated that I'd have no opportunity to seek out other merchants or traders before the spring. When Father was home, much of the business was conducted through his agents in the towns, using Dorin as a go-between. But Dorin had been asked to stay away. If I wanted to send letters to Father, Cezar was my only means of delivery. That meant I could not write the truth—not all of it.

"I'd advise you not to come here for a while," I said, struggling to keep my voice under control. "You've made me quite angry and you've upset Paula. Please take your friends and go home."

Go, go, go, odious man.

"I think—" said Cezar, but I never heard what he thought. We opened the kitchen door on an uproar. In the center of the room stood small, wizened Petru, and by the hearth a younger man of similar build: his grandson, Ivan. Petru was telling some kind of tale, stumbling over his words as Daniel and Răzvan and my sisters bombarded him with questions. Florica, pale as bread dough, was muttering and crossing herself. Tati alarmed me most of all, for there were hectic red spots on her cheeks and she was clutching her tea glass so tightly I expected it to shatter at any moment.

"What—" I began, but Cezar's bigger voice boomed over mine.

"Sit down, all of you, and speak one at a time. Tatiana, what has happened here?"

Tati turned her big violet eyes on him, but did not speak.

"Iulia?" I queried. "What is it?"

"Petru has a terrible story," Iulia said, her lip quivering.

"A killing." Petru's voice was as grim as his seamed and creviced face. "Ivona, daughter of Marius the miller. Only fifteen years old. Her mother went in at dawn, and there was the girl, sprawled across the quilt like a rag doll, white as snow: a bloodless corpse."

"What are you saying?" I whispered, not prepared to acknowledge, even to myself, that I already knew the answer.

"She had puncture wounds on her neck," said Florica heavily. "A bite."

"You know what that means." Petru tightened his lips.

And although nobody actually said it aloud, our blanched faces and shocked eyes spoke the words for us, into the silence of a shared terror. Without a shred of doubt, this was the work of the Night People.

Chapter Seven

Cezar took charge immediately. He would head straight down to the village to meet with Judge Rinaldo. The able-bodied men of the district must arm themselves however they could in readiness for going out into the forest at dusk to hunt down the evildoer. They would bring him to justice or they would kill him. Even as Cezar spoke, Petru and Ivan, Răzvan and Daniel were donning cloaks and gathering their belongings to leave.

Tati had fled upstairs. After a little, my other sisters followed, leaving me to deal with the situation.

"Jena," Cezar said gravely, "I will be advising all households to install appropriate defensive measures—not just on their dwellings, but on barns and outhouses as well. I want Florica to do the same: garlic, iron nails, amulets—whatever you can manage."

"Marius's place was well protected," Petru said, pulling his

sheepskin hat down over his ears. "That didn't stop the creature from coming in."

Tadeusz's words rang in my head: *I am not bound by man's fences
or fettered by his puny charms of protection.* Cezar's eyes were full of
dark purpose. Disgust, guilt, and fear churned inside my belly.

"I don't want any of you girls going outside," Cezar said.
"Nor you, Florica, unless you absolutely must. You'll need to
tend to the work of the farm, I know, at least until we can spare
Petru. But keep it to what is essential, and be always on your
guard. Come back inside and bolt your doors and windows
well before dusk." He was looking at me closely. "It's all right,
Jena," he said in a different tone. "We'll catch this beast—
I give you my promise." He took my hand. "I think, after all, one
of us should remain here with you. Răzvan, will you stay at
Piscul Dracului in my absence? Make sure the young ladies are
not frightened. You should keep your crossbow at hand at all
times."

Răzvan gave a curt nod. He looked annoyed. It was plain
that the task of guarding a household of women was less to his
liking than a manly mission of vengeance.

"Remember my warnings. Keep the doors locked," said
Cezar. "Be watchful, all of you. This is a dark time." And he
was gone.

"I have a confession to make," I said to my sisters a little later as
we sat in our bedchamber, shocked and quiet. "I don't want to
tell you, but I think I have to. This is probably all my fault."

They sat in total silence as I recounted my conversation with

Tadeusz. I did not include quite everything he had said, but by the end of my account they were staring at me, incredulous.

"Jena!" exclaimed Paula. "You're supposed to be the sensible one! What on earth possessed you to listen to him? Have you forgotten everything you know about the Night People?"

"He said that was old wives' tales," I told her miserably. "That we didn't really know what they were like. And that could be true. It sounds as if someone walked right past the charms of ward at the miller's house. So much for all those stories about garlic and silver crosses."

"That's if it was one of them who did it," said Tati. She was shivering even though she had her thick woolen shawl wrapped around her, and her face was pinched and pale.

"Of course it was, Tati," said Iulia. "You heard what Petru said. You just don't want to believe it because of Sorrow. You don't want to admit that he could have been the one responsible."

Tati was on her feet, eyes wild. "He wasn't! Sorrow would never do something wicked like that—he couldn't!"

"We can't know that," put in Paula calmly. "We can't really know much about the Other Kingdom, even though we've been visiting Dancing Glade for so long. It's full of tricks and traps, masks and mirrors. Tati, I know you won't like this, but Sorrow could be anything at all. The face he shows you may be only the one he wants you to see."

Relieved to have my younger sisters' support on the issue of Sorrow, I risked a new suggestion. "There is one way to see the truth about the Other Kingdom," I said. "We could go across at Dark of the Moon and look in Drăguţa's mirror, as Tadeusz told me. We could see the future. And if we could do that, we could change it—take action to prevent the bad things from happening."

There was a silence.

"Jena," said Paula, "I've spent a lot of time with the sooth-sayers and wizards of the Other Kingdom. We've talked about tools for divining the future. We've talked about portals and the way that time and space work between their kingdom and ours. Nobody ever said a thing about a magic mirror."

"Maybe they only tell you what they want you to know." My voice was a little sharp. I felt as if I were walking on a knife edge. A girl had died horribly. The men would be out there tonight with their crossbows and cudgels, their pitchforks and scythes, hunting the Night People down. Yet something still drew me toward Dark of the Moon. It was not so much Ta-deusz's beguiling voice, though I knew that was part of it. Even after this—even after innocent blood had been spilled— I felt its pull. But far more powerful was the thought that Drăguţa's mirror might provide the answers we so badly needed. So easily, I could know whether Father would come home again; I could know whether Tati would get over her foolish in-fatuation and be safe. And if I went there, I could confront Tadeusz with what he had done. I could tell him that this vile act of bloodletting was not what I had wanted; that the price for mending a few fences should not be the life of an innocent young woman. I could make it clear that I had never asked for such offerings and that there were to be no more of them.

"You wouldn't actually go, would you, Jena?" Iulia was looking at me with a mixture of alarm and admiration. "After what's just happened?"

"I don't know," I said. In my pocket Gogu was still, as if frozen. I could feel his horror. *No, Jena. No.* "Maybe I won't have to think about it. Maybe Cezar and the other men will catch the killer. Maybe Ileana will banish the Night People from her realm, and this will be all over."

"It might not be your fault, Jena," Paula said. "It's possible that the girl's father did something to make the Night People angry, like setting fires in the forest or felling an oak. You can't know."

"I do know." I took Gogu out and held him between my hands for comfort. "I can feel it. I can feel things turning dark. It started when the Night People came. It got worse when Tati encouraged Sorrow. Now I'm responsible for someone's death. I have to put it right somehow."

"I told you, this is not Sorrow's doing, Jena." Tati was huddled on the bed now, hugging the shawl around her. "He's the kindest of men, gentle and good."

"To you, maybe," I said.

A small voice spoke. "Tati wouldn't fall in love with a murderer."

Stela's words hung in silence for a little, then Iulia cleared her throat. "You'd be surprised," she said. "Love makes people do some odd things. I mean, Jena loves Gogu best in the world, doesn't she? A frog. That's just about the weirdest thing you could imagine."

Gogu twitched as she spoke his name. Then, abruptly, a

sort of cloud fell over his thoughts, as if he were deliberately hiding them from me. "That's not the same kind of love," I said. "Anyway, Tati hardly even knows Sorrow."

Tati said nothing.

"Love at first sight," put in Paula. "If it happens in stories, why shouldn't it happen in real life?"

"It's a mistake to let your head get full of stories about true love," I said. "It just means you'll be disappointed. There are no handsome heroes in the real world—only boring young men like Răzvan and Daniel. That's probably the best any of us can hope for."

"I can't stop thinking about it, Gogu," I said later in the day, as I threw out grain for the chickens under a leaden sky. "I owe it to that girl, Ivona, to cross over and speak to Tadeusz again, to tell him to stop. What if Cezar's hunt actually kills one of the Night People, and then Tadeusz seeks vengeance for that, and so on, until the whole valley is awash with blood? I can't wait until next Full Moon. It's too long. Think how much damage they could do."

Brave. Brave, but foolish. You can't go.

"The Night People must leave this forest—they have to go home. I don't know why they came here in the first place. If they left and took Sorrow with them, that would remove the danger and solve the problem of Tati, as well."

No response from Gogu. On the far side of the courtyard, Răzvan was shoveling away snow, clearing paths to the barn and outhouses. In Cezar's absence he had surprised me by offering his help with whatever needed doing. It was clear he would rather have work to keep him occupied than stand about with crossbow in hand, trying to look fierce.

"What else am I supposed to do?" I asked the frog. "Stop looking at me like that!"

I could see by Gogu's expression that he thought I'd over-reached myself this time, and it wasn't helping. I set him down to explore the woodpile by the hen coop.

Don't go at all. Full Moon, Dark of the Moon, keep well away.

"You think Tati's going to agree to that? Sorrow's all she can think about. In her eyes he's incapable of an ill thought, let alone an evil deed." At that moment an idea came into my head. In one way it was ridiculous, given what had happened. In another it made perfect sense. "Unless," I mused, thinking aloud, "she met someone else, someone nice and suitable—the kind of young man she could like and Aunt Bogdana would approve of. If I could get her interested in a real man, maybe she would realize how hopeless her attachment to Sorrow is. It might break whatever spell he's put on her. I don't suppose we could give a grand party. It's too soon after Uncle Nicolae's death, and the whole valley's going to be consumed by the hunt for the Night People. Besides, our money's gone; we can hardly feed guests on *mămăligă*. But . . ."

I sat down on a stone wall, wrapping my arms around myself. Gogu had begun to forage in some old decaying wood. I averted my gaze. If he planned on eating beetles, I didn't particularly want to watch. "It's not just Tati," I said. "Iulia's been behaving strangely, too. Cezar accused her of flirting, and I think he did have some cause for it. She's too young for that. I hate to admit it, but Aunt Bogdana has a point about manners and deportment. We all need opportunities to meet suitable young men. Like it or not, if we don't want Cezar in complete control of Piscul Dracului and making all our decisions for us, we need to take this first step. We have to accept that Father may not be coming back." I shivered. "Gogu, I can't imagine Cezar as master of Piscul Dracului. He doesn't love the place as we do. It would be just . . . wrong. Almost anyone would be better than him. Perhaps Aunt Bogdana's friends have sons we could like, given time. Young men who would look after the castle and the forest. Men with good judgment and kind hearts."

Gogu was pursuing a small scuttling creature. His thoughts were held tight.

"All right, then," I grumbled. "If you don't want to talk, don't. Leave me to sort out my problems all by myself. We need an heir for Piscul Dracului. One of us has to marry. If Tati won't do it, I think I'll have to. I'd always planned to do other things with my life—have adventures, go on voyages, become a merchant in my own right. And if I did marry, I'd hoped it would be for love. I used to dream about how I'd meet an exotic stranger in a foreign port and know instantly that he was the one. Of course, anyone wanting to marry one of us would need Father's permission. But—" I choked on the words. If Father should die, Cezar would instantly gain control of everything. It was unthinkable. A man with such anger in his eyes should not be allowed to decide the fates of others. "Gogu," I said, "I need to go and visit Aunt Bogdana. Will you stop crunching those things? It sounds disgusting."

He hunkered down in the woodpile, abruptly silent and

near-invisible. I reminded myself that not long ago I had almost lost him.

"I'm sorry," I said. "The thing is, I'm so close to you I forget sometimes that we're separate people. I just say what I think, and don't realize I've hurt you until the words are out of my mouth. Gogu?"

I peered down between the logs. All I could see were his eyes—wide, unwinking, desperately serious.

"Gogu, I'm sorry. Come out, will you? I really need your advice."

He made me wait long enough to realize how badly I had wounded him. Then he hopped onto the seat beside me, holding something in his mouth. He dropped it into my lap.

"What's this?" A gift, clearly. He'd never made such a gesture before. It was a little seedpod, mousy brown and shaped like a heart. "Thank you! How sweet!"

He cringed. Maybe my tone had been a little patronizing.

"Gogu, I value your gift," I said, taking off my glove to stroke his head with my finger. "On the first day of spring, I'll cook you the finest pondweed pancake you ever tasted, and too bad if people say I'm behaving like a child. Unless there's something else you'd like in return."

I caught something bright and strange in his thoughts, gone so quickly I could not begin to interpret it. After a little, I sensed a more hesitant approach.

You could . . .

"I could what, Gogu?"

You could . . . *Nothing.*

"You're in a very strange mood today. I wonder whether that trip across the Deadwash on your own has scrambled up your head a little. Are you going to tell me how you did it?"

Silence.

"That's a no, I take it." Now I was hurt. We had always shared our secrets, the two of us. Ours had been a friendship of perfect trust.

Jena?

"Mmm?"

A party. You will marry a man you meet at a party?

"I don't even know if we can do it yet, Gogu. It depends on what Aunt Bogdana thinks is right. This will be the first time I've spoken to her since the *pomană*, and I have no idea how she'll react. If she's still terribly upset, I may not even get as far as suggesting this. Anyway, it wouldn't be a party, more like a polite gathering—though I'm hoping we can have music and good food. As for the marrying part, the idea of going about that as if it were a business transaction makes me feel sick. But I'll do it if I must." I slipped the seedpod into my pocket. A number of hurdles lay before me: the fact that Cezar had said his mother wanted no visitors; the possibility that my request might offend her deeply; the need to ask my cousin for funds; the snow lying heavy on the paths around Piscul Dracului, making travel by cart difficult; the Night People. Everything suggested that my idea was foolish and impractical. But with Father in such fragile health, I did not want to wait for springtime. "In the morning I'll go up and see Aunt Bogdana. If she says yes, I'll tell the girls we're not going to the Other Kingdom again until the

Night People have left the valley. So you see, Gogu, I am being sensible. I'm following your good advice."

I'm sorry, Jena.

"Sorry? What do you have to be sorry for?"

I'm sorry I cannot protect you.

Unease was plain in the frog's hunched posture and the forlorn tone of his voice—the voice only I could hear. Abruptly, I was on the verge of tears. "Don't be silly," I told him, sniffing. "Why would I expect that? It's ridiculous. Friendship and good advice, that's all I need from you."

Put me on your shoulder now. I want to go inside.

"Jena! How lovely to see you!" It seemed that Aunt Bogdana was no longer too distressed to receive visitors. Her severe black dress accentuated her pallor and she was looking thinner, but her smile welcomed me as Daniela showed me into the sewing room. "Daniela, we'll have some coffee, please. Come and sit down, Jena. I'm sorry I have not been out and about. It seems such an effort without Nicolae. Everywhere I go, I feel his absence."

"I'm so sorry, Aunt Bogdana. I can't imagine how it feels. If there's anything we can do . . ." I seated myself on a little chair with an embroidered cushion. From the shelf nearby, Costi's painted eyes watched me.

"And now there's this terrible news of the miller's daughter. . . . It's as if a curse has fallen over the valley, a kind of darkness. It makes me wonder what we have done to deserve such ill fortune. And Father Sandu is gone. That was a blow.

It is at times such as these that a community sorely needs its priest."

I refrained from mentioning her son's role in Father Sandu's departure. "Cezar seems to be doing his best to hunt down the offender," I said. "They didn't succeed last night, but I think he will keep going until they do. He's very determined."

Aunt Bogdana sighed. "To be quite honest with you, Jena, I'm not at all sure that is the way Nicolae would have gone about it. A blessing on the settlement and on the margins of the forest, the erection of a crucifix, those things he would have done. But this . . ." She shuddered. "It's answering blood with blood. I fear for Cezar. I fear for all those men. One does not meddle lightly with the forces of the forest." She cleared her throat; her eyes were on Costi's picture. "Cezar, of all men, should know that. Ah, here's Daniela with the coffee. Allow me to pour for you, Jena. How are your sisters?"

"They're well, thank you. Upset by what's happened, of course. Aunt Bogdana, there's something I need to ask you. You must tell me if you think it's inappropriate."

"Go on, Jena."

I stumbled through my proposition, hoping I would not reduce my aunt to tears or make her angry by trespassing on her grief. Aunt Bogdana regarded me over her coffee cup, not interrupting. She did not seem upset, only intrigued. "And so," I said eventually, "I did wonder if we might have a small gathering, perhaps just a few carefully chosen guests. I know it's not the best time, but actually it might lift people's spirits. In fact, I thought the folk of the valley might see it as a good thing to do. A gesture to show we are not afraid, that we are prepared to light lamps against the darkness. You wouldn't need to do anything, Aunt, just advise me on how to go about it and suggest whom we might invite. I realize we should perhaps wait until spring, but—"

Aunt Bogdana lifted a hand, and I halted in midsentence. She sipped her coffee, her eyes thoughtful. Waiting, I gulped mine down. Daniela hastened to refill my cup. Gogu had escaped my pocket and was on my knee. He made a sudden leap, landing on the arm of Aunt Bogdana's chair.

"Oh, I'm sorry—" I began.

"Not at all," Aunt said absently. "Now, Jena, this is a matter of balancing what is right for you and your sisters with community expectations. It happens that an old friend of mine, a lady with extremely good connections, is staying near Braşov over the winter and is likely to have a significant number of houseguests. I think it is possible we might do something, as long as it is kept sedate. The season being what it is, we cannot expect folk to travel far. And with this new threat, it will be necessary to offer guests a night's accommodation at Piscul Draculi—nobody will be wanting to be outside after dusk. You'll need to clear out your storeroom. It's the only place where you can entertain so many guests."

"So many?" I had imagined we might put people in the formal dining room.

"Jena," declared Aunt Bogdana, evidently warming to the challenge, "there's no point in doing this if you don't do it properly. While you cannot expect to find suitors in one evening, if folk see you at your best, they'll talk. Word will get about, even in winter, believe me. By springtime there will be invitations flooding in for you."

She had astonished me. I realized I had been expecting a flat refusal. "You think the guests will come?" I asked her. "Even with the Night People in our forest?"

"We can only try, Jena. As long as movement in and out is by daylight, I think we can achieve something. You'll all need new gowns. My seamstress should be able to do the job, with a little assistance. When did you plan to do this?"

"I thought maybe at next Full Moon." I imagined explaining this to Tati. "If that allows sufficient time to organize everything. I'll work hard, Aunt Bogdana."

"This is quite a change of heart for you, Jena." My aunt's eyes were shrewd. "If anyone had asked me last summer whether I would ever persuade you to show interest in such activities, I'd have said I thought it an impossibility until you grew up a little. What has prompted this?" She had crumbled a dainty biscuit at the edge of her plate; Gogu was investigating.

I gave her as much of the truth as I could. "Uncle Nicolae's death; my father's illness. We do need to look ahead. And . . . I do believe in what I said before, about giving the appearance of being strong and brave. I'm as much afraid of the Night People as anyone is. But I think this would be good for the village, especially if we get folk involved. I would need quite a bit of help getting things ready." I wondered how I might approach the delicate question of payment.

"No dancing, of course," Aunt Bogdana said. "That's a shame, really. Nicolae did so love to dance, and I know he

wouldn't mind, yet it would be inappropriate so soon after. . . .
But I think we could invite the village band, just for some quiet
tunes in the background. The men could do with a few extra
coppers to tide them over the winter. And we'll ask the women
to come up and help Florica with the supper. That way we do
everyone a favor, and if they're all together they will feel safer
after dark."

"Aunt," I ventured, "I'm not sure whether Cezar will think
this a good idea. He has all our funds at present. He's approving
our expenses one by one."

Her brows shot up. "Really? He can hardly raise any objections to this, as long as it has my approval. Don't worry about
the cost, Jena. Nicolae would have been happy to do this for
you. Think of it as his farewell gift." Abruptly, her brisk manner turned to tears, and I got up to put my arm around her shoulders. "You're a good girl, Jena," my aunt said. "Perhaps a little
unusual, like poor dear Teodor, but your heart is in the right
place. I'm all right, my dear. This will give me something with
which to occupy myself. We can start the guest list now.
Daniela, make a note of this, will you? Judge Rinaldo, of course,
and his son Lucian . . ."

I had never seen Tati so angry. When I told her we weren't
going across at next Full Moon, at first she thought I was joking. Then, when she saw I meant it, she shouted at me. I had
closed the bedchamber door; I'd warned the others to stay
away. Tati paced up and down, using all the arguments she
could think of, one by one. We couldn't have a party now, she

insisted, it was too soon since Uncle Nicolae's death. I told her that both Aunt Bogdana and Cezar had agreed to it, as long as we kept it sedate. Then she said, "But we always go. The others will be upset."

"I've already told them, and they've accepted this. It makes perfect sense after what happened to Ivona. It's logical for us to stay away until we know the valley is safe again." I struggled to sound calm and controlled. I would not let her know the compulsion I felt to cross over at Dark of the Moon, to confront Tadeusz and make him understand that I did not want his help—not at such a cost. "And we don't always go. What about the times when one of us was ill or away from home? We've certainly missed a few over the years. Ileana and the others are unlikely to be upset if we don't make an appearance. It's not their way to trouble themselves about such things."

"What about Sorrow? He'll be upset. He'll think I'm staying away because I believe he did it—that he's capable of killing someone in cold blood. I must go, Jena. I must explain it to him!"

"He mightn't even be there anymore," I told her. "Ileana's probably sent the Night People away by now. Their crimes must put her own people in danger. You weren't there when Cezar and the others stormed out of Piscul Dracului with their pitchforks and crossbows."

"Sorrow won't go," Tati declared. Her pale cheeks were flushed a hectic red; she looked as if she had a fever. "Not even if Ileana banishes them. He won't leave me."

"This is stupid! You've only seen him a couple of times, Tati! You know what it means for a human woman to ally herself with someone from the Other Kingdom. You'd go and you'd never be able to come back. You'd get older and he wouldn't. One day you'd be an old woman, all wrinkles and toothless gums, and he'd still be a lovely young man. You'd never see any of us again. Is that really what you want?"

"It might not be like that." Her voice was very quiet. She bowed her head; her ebony hair hung down like silken curtains, shielding her face. "Stories don't tell the whole truth."

"It might be worse. If he's one of the Night People, you might not last beyond a single bite."

"Don't say that, Jena!"

"I'm sorry. But it's true. I'm not asking much. Only that you miss one Full Moon visit."

"That's not really all you're asking, Jena." Tati turned her big eyes on me; their expression was cool now. "Anyway, you aren't asking, are you? You're telling. I can't go through the portal if you won't help open it. What you really want is that I never see Sorrow again. You think the moment I get up and dance with some fellow Aunt Bogdana's dredged up for me, I'll forget all about him. Well, I won't. And I won't go to your stupid party. You don't understand."

She was right. Whatever Tati was feeling, it was something new to me, something I couldn't comprehend: powerful, mysterious, and frightening. I began to wonder whether I had this all wrong—whether I had meddled in something I could not hope to control.

"Tell me, then." I sat down beside her on the bed. "It might help if I did understand."

"You're just trying to be nice to wheedle me into agreeing."

"No, I'm not. I'm finding it hard to believe this has happened so quickly and made you change so much. I feel as if you've gone away from me—that I can't rely on you anymore."

"You know how you felt last time, when you lost Gogu? When you really thought he'd been trampled to death, but you wouldn't say so?"

I nodded, surprised that she had noticed: she had seemed entirely wrapped up in her own woes.

"Multiply that by a thousand, and you know how I feel when I think about never seeing Sorrow again. It's the most awful feeling in the world—like having part of your heart torn away."

"A thousand? Isn't that rather extreme?" I thought the way I'd felt that night was about as wretched as I could possibly get. Gogu had been my constant companion—an unusual one, true, but no less loved for that—for more than nine years. She barely knew Sorrow.

"Well, after all, Gogu's a frog. Sorrow is a man."

It was just as well I'd left Gogu with Paula while I spoke to Tati. I was certain he'd have been offended by this, even though it was half true. "That's the point, isn't it? Sorrow *isn't* a man. I want you to answer a question, Tati."

"What?"

"Have you asked him straight out if he's one of the Night People?"

"We've talked about it, of course. He couldn't tell me."

"Couldn't? What do you mean?"

"It's something he can't talk about. I don't know why. It seems to be somehow forbidden. He wants to, but it's not allowed. He seems so alone, Jena."

"They're all like that. Tadeusz said, 'We all walk alone.' Maybe Sorrow's mother was a human woman." I shivered. "A victim. Only instead of dying, like that girl, she changed into one of *them*."

"He's not at all like the other Night People, Jena. He's so sweet and thoughtful."

"Just a ploy to win your affections." Sweet and thoughtful would work with Tati. For me, Tadeusz had held out the heady prospect of perception beyond my wildest imaginings. He had flattered me, too, and I was forced to admit that I had liked that. His words of admiration had stirred something in me—they'd made me realize I would have liked to be a beauty. Tadeusz had known how to tempt me, and Sorrow knew how to work his wiles on my sister.

"Tati," I said, "what do you and Sorrow talk about? Do you actually have anything in common?"

Tati stared into space, smiling. "We talk about everything. And nothing."

"Everything. And you still can't tell me what he is. How about his teeth? You've had a good chance to see those up close. Are they like yours and mine?"

Tati hesitated.

"Well?"

"Not exactly." She spoke with some reluctance. "They are a little odd. He's very self-conscious about it. But they're not *fangs*."

"Nor are Tadeusz's teeth," I said. "And *he* makes no secret of what he is."

"Jena, I'm not just playing at this, you know, and neither is Sorrow. Do what you like. Have your party. Let Aunt Bogdana trot out her eligible young men. Bar me from Full Moon dancing. I'll find Sorrow anyway, somehow. Or he'll find me. Whatever you do, we'll be together. You can't stop us."

"Ileana can," I said, chilled by my sister's certainty. "If she banishes the Night People, you'll have no way of finding him."

"I will find him," Tati said. "Wherever he goes, however far away she sends him, we'll find each other."

It was then that I noticed what she was wearing around her neck: a very fine cord, black in color—just a thread, really— and on it, a tiny amulet that caught the light. I was certain I had never seen it before.

"What's that?" I asked her, intrigued. Tati's hand shot up to cover it. "Show me, Tati."

Slowly she drew her fingers away, revealing the little charm, dark against her creamy skin—a piece of glass shaped like a teardrop, and red as blood.

"Did he give you this?" I hardly needed to ask. Such an item had Sorrow written all over it.

"We exchanged."

"You exchanged? What did you give him?"

"My silver chain," Tati said in a whisper.

"Mother's chain? You gave it away?" It had been a gift from our father to his sweetheart on the day she agreed to marry him. It had never left Mother's neck, until death took her from us. I suppose my horror sounded in my voice. Tati flinched away from me, but her eyes were steady.

"I'm the eldest," my sister said. "It was mine to give."

Chapter Eight

My idea grew sudden wings and drew the whole community along in its wake. Aunt Bogdana worked behind the scenes. Subtly, she made it evident that I was in charge, under her guiding hand, and that the purpose of the evening was to give heart to the valley in time of trouble. She bullied Cezar into releasing sufficient funds for an excellent supper: the band was hired and helpers recruited for the occasion. As my aunt had anticipated, the folk were all too willing to assist in return for a payment in coppers, fuel, or leftover food—provided that they were not expected to cross open ground between dusk and dawn.

Meanwhile, alongside the cleaning of chambers to accommodate our houseguests, the planning of a menu, and the dispatch of invitations, the grim work of hunting down the Night People went on. Cezar had assembled a ferocious-looking band of helpers for his nightly sorties. Many of them were men from beyond our area. Petru had come back to tend to the farm, muttering one morning over breakfast that he'd had enough of hunting. We did not speak about the fences.

There had been no further word from Father; nothing even from Gabriel. I sat in the workroom with Gogu, staring at Father's empty chair, wondering whether the whole idea for a Full Moon party had been a ghastly mistake. Was it conceived only to keep myself from the peril of *wanting*? Even one wrong thought might bring Tadeusz to me at Dark of the Moon: a wondrous temptation with a hideous price. That had been the most disturbing part of his invitation—the idea that simply wishing something to be, even for one unguarded moment, might make it happen. My instincts told me it was all wrong, yet I could not keep his voice out of my head.

I had a new concern as well. Cezar had moved himself into Piscul Dracului. He had ordered Florica to prepare Father's bedchamber for him and to accommodate Răzvan and Daniel, as well. It was far easier, he declared, to coordinate his hunting parties from here—and besides, he was worried about us. We needed men in the castle: strong protectors. Aunt Bogdana had a houseful of loyal servants. He thought she could do well enough without him.

"There's no privacy, Gogu," I said, crossing my arms on Father's desk and laying down my head. "Everywhere I turn, there's one of them in the way. And it's making extra work for Florica, on top of the party. I want to write to Father again, but I can't tell him a bunch of lies. And I can't tell Father that Cezar's gradually easing himself into his place, that the valley is full of fear, that I no longer have control of his business interests, and that Tati's fallen in love with a . . . whatever he is. I could hardly have done a worse job of looking after things."

You've left something off your list of disasters. You listened to that person in the black boots. You let him flatter you. You want to see him again, I know it.

I lifted my head to glare at the frog. "All right," I growled, "go on, make me feel even worse. I almost fell for an invitation to do something really stupid. And probably someone died because of that. Just because I don't say it out loud doesn't mean I don't think of it every day, Gogu. If I could make time go backward, I'd erase that night completely."

Gogu did not respond. Maybe he realized I was having to work hard not to think about Dark of the Moon, now only days away.

"We'll have to clear out the storeroom," I told him. "That means Salem bin Afazi's shipment must go out to the barn until after Full Moon. We must move everything as soon as there's a fine patch in the weather. I wonder if Aunt Bogdana has some tapestries she would lend me to cover the worst cracks in the storeroom walls? It's going to be cold in there."

You're worried. But not about tapestries.

"No. I'm worried about myself. How weak I've been. What I might get wrong in the future. How much depends on me."

Isn't your grand party supposed to make everything right?

I stared at him, sudden tears welling in my eyes. His silent voice had sounded almost bitter. "You could be a bit more supportive, Gogu," I said.

Don't mind me. I'm only a frog. Wallow in self-pity all you like.

"What's this *I'm only a frog*? You're my best friend in all the world, you know that."

Go and try on your finery. Prepare your grand chamber.

Sighing, I got up. Gogu had been acting very strangely of late. I could not tell whether he thought the party a good idea or not. Something had certainly stirred him up. Perhaps the talk of marriages had made him uneasy about his own future.

"If I could avoid this cold-blooded search for suitors," I told him, "believe me, I would. And I'd never marry anyone who didn't like frogs. You've got a home with me forever. I swear it, Gogu. Stop looking so mournful."

He did not reply. Increasingly, he had taken to going suddenly silent, as if he drew down a little shutter over his mind. It worried me.

Go and try on your finery. Finery was a whole issue on its own. Aunt Bogdana had insisted on new gowns for everyone. We had not told her that each of us already possessed a dancing dress, for fear of arousing suspicion. So we'd agreed to use the services of her household seamstress and allowed our aunt to select fabrics from her own substantial store. Our first fitting had not gone well.

"There's no need to be critical about our getting dressed up, Gogu," I told him now as we descended the stairs from the workroom. "Aunt Bogdana is making us wear what's suitable." It was a pity that none of us liked our gowns, but we could hardly quibble when Cezar was paying for everything. Stela's was to be a lacy white creation with a red sash. My youngest sister had declared it to be "a baby dress." Paula's was pink, which made her look sallow. Iulia's natural beauty would be dimmed by Aunt's choice of a soft gray—the cut extremely demure, with a high neckline and long, narrow sleeves. Iulia called it drab, and I had to agree.

It was clear that our aunt intended for Tati and me to be the sisters who shone at this particular event. Tati's gown was pale blue with silver thread. It had a high waistline and a long, trailing skirt. With every fitting the seamstress, frowning, took the bodice in further. Tati had little appetite these days—at mealtimes she would move her food around her platter, eyes distant. She did not conceal her lack of enthusiasm for the gown, the party, and everything to do with it.

Aunt Bogdana had decided to put me in dark crimson. The fabric was sumptuous and the cut flattering, though it put more of me on show than I felt comfortable with. It was a suitable choice for attracting men, but it was wrong for me. I knew Gogu didn't like it; perhaps that was the reason for his sharp comment. There was no such red in the natural hues of the forest, not even in the most brilliant autumn foliage. I favored russet-brown, shadowy blue, a thousand shades of green. Never mind. It was only for one night. I'd need to make sure we were allowed to do the finishing touches ourselves so I'd have time to sew in a Gogu-pocket. I had a feeling I would need my wise advisor by my side more than ever this Full Moon.

I made my way down to the storeroom, planning how best we might move the many crates, bundles, and rolls of carpet that we had so painstakingly put away there. As I rounded a corner in the passageway, I halted abruptly. The big double doors were propped open. A crew of men was busy lifting

Salem bin Afazi's precious cargo from the shelves and carrying it out into the courtyard.

"What are you doing?" I challenged them, striding forward. "Who gave you permission to move those?"

The men glanced at me but kept on working. I followed them out into the courtyard, where fine snow was falling. If the fabrics were allowed to get wet, they would lose most of their commercial value. We had been so careful.

A long cart was standing just beyond the entry, a team of patient horses harnessed before it. The burly figure of Cezar could be seen giving sharp directions as still more men loaded each item onto the conveyance. I saw that the goods were being layered with oiled cloth for protection; Cezar was a merchant and appreciated the value of such a consignment. That did not alter the fact that he was taking it away and had not consulted me. Why had I spent so long sitting upstairs, stewing over my problems?

"Cezar, what is this?" My tone was sharp. "The things only need to go as far as the barn. Why the cart? Why wasn't I told about this?"

My cousin went a little red and hastened to draw me aside. "Jena, please refrain from speaking to me in that tone in front of my workers," he said. "Save your shrill comments, if you must make them, for a private situation."

Shrill. That's offensive.

"This is my father's house, Cezar, and that is my father's shipment. I'll say whatever I want. What do you think you're doing?"

"Your manner offends me."

"All I want is a truthful answer."

"I thought you'd be pleased. You've been looking so pale and tired. This entertainment you've set your heart on for Full Moon is creating too much work for you, especially at such a frightening time."

"Answer my question," I said, through gritted teeth. They were bringing out the breakable items now—the little scent bottles, the porcelain cups in their padded boxes. Everything was going onto the cart.

"I only want to help you. You do need this chamber cleared for your party, don't you? The goods will be stored at Vârful cu Negură. I have plenty of dry space for them there. That will make it far easier for me to sell them when the weather improves. I will deal with the entire venture from this point on. I can get good prices for you, Jena."

He was behaving as if Father were already dead; he was acting like some kind of patriarch. I wasn't going to put up with it. "I'm not at all sure I trust you to get the best price," I said, "or to pass the full profit back to us if you do. Father trusted me to look after these things. It's a very special cargo. I know he'd prefer the goods not be sold until he comes home."

"I'm a merchant, Jena." His lips had tightened; it was clear I had offended him. "Do me the courtesy of recognizing that I know what I'm doing. You can accept my help with this matter. It must be to your advantage, and mine, if you learn cooperation. Not that I don't enjoy a good spat with you once in a while, but you are a young woman now. Concentrate on your party. I hear from Mother that you are proving quite able at organizing it. I look forward to seeing you in your finery."

He makes me sick.

"This is very high-handed, Cezar. I was left with the responsibility for Father's business, and I expect at the very least that you will consult me before making any major decisions. I think the hunt for the Night People must have addled your brain a little. Maybe you should concentrate on that, and leave Father's business affairs to me." Before I reached the end of this speech, I was wishing I hadn't started. Cezar had narrowed his eyes—his irritation had turned to something far more alarming.

"Since you seem to have taken it upon yourself to point out deficiencies in my behavior," he said, lowering his voice as the workers began to fasten ropes over the neatly packed contents of the cart, "let me return the favor, Cousin. There's a small matter of some fencing you had mended, which you advised me was done by folk traveling through the area. I spoke to Petru about it the day after you told me, and congratulated him on finding such efficient workers. He knew nothing about it. As far as he was concerned, the job was still waiting to be done. It all happened rather quickly, Jena. It seems the repair was carried out overnight, so to speak. Someone was here at Piscul Dracului—someone you didn't want to tell me about."

I prayed that my expression would not give anything away. I was unprepared for this, and could think of no satisfactory answer. Petru had not quizzed me about who had done the job. I had taken that to indicate it was a question the old man thought better not asked, and had offered him no explanation. "Petru was busy when the workers were here," I said, knowing I must say something. "Then you all rushed off after the Night People. I didn't get the chance to tell him."

"*Rushed off.* Are you implying that my pursuit of these bloodsucking fiends was in some way too precipitate?"

"No, Cezar." I was shaking; I stuffed my hands into my pockets, not wanting him to see how nervous he was making me. "They did something terrible. I know you believe it's the right thing to hunt them down. Many people would agree with you."

"But you do not?" His tone was incredulous.

"I wouldn't attempt to pass judgment on such an issue. I understand the desire for vengeance—I imagine that Ivona's family is feeling that right now. But folk say it's dangerous to meddle with the powers of the wildwood. That it's wiser simply to set up wards and take preventive measures. If Father Sandu had been here—"

"Oh, it's that again, is it? Your resentment at my action regarding the wayward priest clouds your judgment once more. This is petty, Jena."

"I'm not a child, Cezar, as you yourself seem keen to point out whenever you get the opportunity. I think taking violent action may only make things worse. That's all I'm trying to say to you." I could not tell him what I really believed: that the miller's daughter had died as payment for the mending of my fences, and that in the accounting of the Night People, the ledger was now balanced. That made a hideous kind of sense. "If we waited and all worked together to protect the settlement, in time this menace would pass us by. The Night People would move on. That's what they do."

He looked at me. Seeing another question in his eyes, I made a desperate attempt to fend it off. "I'm worried about you," I told him, putting a hand on his arm. "You're not safe out there after dark." That was not a lie, either; none of them was safe. Though my cousin was a bully, I had no wish to see him fall victim to Night People or anything else that might be out in the forest by night. That this was a minor worry against so many more weighty problems, I did not say.

Cezar's hand came up over mine. I remembered, vividly, the touch of Tadeusz's chilly fingers and the feeling that had aroused in me. I could not help shivering.

"I'm sorry I upset you, Jena." My cousin's voice had changed. I liked this softer tone even less than his hectoring one. "Believe me, it gives me no pleasure at all to have to reprimand you. Your distress troubles me. As for the Night People, have no fear for me. I'm an expert hunter. We'll track this villain down, believe me. If fortune favors us, we'll have him before Full Moon."

It was a strange time at Piscul Dracului. On the one hand, preparations for our party were in full swing. A stream of women came up the hill each day to help Florica with cleaning and cooking, to lend a special jug or a strip of embroidered linen to cover a bare shelf. The kitchen was full of chatter. Down in the village, the band could be heard seizing any spare moment for a little practice. Against this, every dusk saw Cezar's group of grim-faced hunters setting out up the track toward the forest in their woolen cloaks, their fur-lined hats and heavy boots—some armed with such weapons as a crossbow or knife, others shouldering the implements of farm or forge; it was known that the folk of the Other Kingdom feared iron. The hunters would return at dawn, frozen, exhausted, and thus far, empty-handed. I feared to see them come back triumphant, for my heart told me that more spilling of blood might well plunge the whole valley into chaos and darkness. Perhaps that was what the Night People had wanted all along: to set their terrible mark on Ileana's court and on our peaceful community.

Cezar and his friends snatched sleep in the mornings. It was the only time we did not have their large presences dominating our house and stifling natural conversation. The party and the hunt did not seem like things that could exist comfortably in the same world, yet both were designed to keep the valley safe. I hoped our celebration would be seen by Tadeusz and his dark henchmen for what it was: a gesture of defiance, of independence. A message that I would not listen to them, and that I despised what they had done.

Tati had become eerily quiet. Her appetite had vanished; she found all kinds of excuses not to eat, and I was deeply concerned. She had never been a big girl, and I saw how her clothes hung on her now, as if they had been made for someone far healthier. She made no further attempts to argue with me about going across to the Other Kingdom. Instead, she wandered about the narrow hallways and crooked staircases of Piscul Dracului like a pale ghost. When she managed to evade the watchful eyes of Cezar and his friends, she disappeared for long, solitary walks in the forest. She would come home trembling with cold, with boots and hemline soaking wet and eyes full of a desperate emotion that was somewhere between grief and fury. I took to looking out for her return so I could smuggle her in without Cezar noticing.

Two days short of Dark of the Moon, Aunt Bogdana visited Piscul Dracului with her seamstress, and we gathered in the formal dining room after breakfast for another fitting. Iulia stood on the table in her stockings while the seamstress pinned up the hem of the decorous dove-gray creation. My sister was scowling. She plucked at the high-cut neckline, experimenting to see whether it could be rendered just a little more revealing.

"Iulia, I can see you don't care for this," Aunt said, not un-kindly. "Believe me, it's not the young men you need to impress, it's their mothers, and you won't do that if you're falling out of your bodice, dear. Leave that alone, it's the appropriate cut for you at thirteen. We might add a bow at the back: that will look girlish while showing off your pretty figure. I wonder if we can have just a little dancing. . . . It seems rather silly to refrain on Nicolae's account, when he enjoyed it so much him-self. . . ."

"We'll do whatever you think proper, Aunt Bogdana," I said.

The seamstress straightened up; she had finished adjusting Iulia's hem.

"Very well, Iulia, you're done," said Aunt Bogdana. "Step down. Carefully—mind those pins. Stela! You're next!"

I heard a commotion, voices, footsteps, from the hallway outside. One of the voices was Cezar's. "A celebration!" he was saying, his words loud and uneven, as if he was too excited to control it. "Florica, we'll have hot ţuică and some food. We won't stay here long—this news needs to go straight down to Judge Rinaldo. Who'd have thought it, eh? To feel the wretch's skinny neck in my own hands!"

"Jena," Aunt Bogdana said quietly as she helped Stela up onto the table, "go out and ask my son what has happened."

Heart thumping, I did as she asked. None of my sisters offered to go with me. In the kitchen, Cezar, his two friends, and several other men were shedding their outdoor clothing, their layers of wool steaming in the warmth from the big stove, while Florica busied herself with platters and cups, obeying Cezar's demand that she serve them. I halted in the doorway. Cezar turned from hanging his cloak on a peg and met my eye. His face was flushed with what seemed to be triumph. He strode across and seized both my hands in his.

"Congratulate me, Jena! We made a capture last night!"

I thought of Tadeusz, so cool and controlled; I thought of somber-faced Sorrow, holding Tati's cloak for her. My voice would not oblige me by framing an intelligent question.

"Sit down, Jena. I can see I've shocked you. I should have broken the news more gently. Florica, some water for Mistress Jena, please."

"What's happened?" I croaked. "You caught one of the Night People? Is that what you're saying?"

"Not one of *them*," said Daniel. "Another one of the forest folk, an accomplice. He was hanging about in the woods, up to no good. Cezar thought he might lead us to the Night People. Give us useful information."

"He would have done." It was clear that Cezar wanted to

tell this story himself. "If the wretch hadn't decided to fight us, we could have locked him up and got what we wanted out of him."

Every part of me had turned cold. "*An accomplice.* What kind of accomplice?"

"A dwarf. No doubt where *he* was from. I offered the fellow freedom in return for information, but he wouldn't have any of it. Fought like a little demon. Bit Daniel on the hand; nearly took my eye out with his boot. Didn't have a chance, of course."

Anatolie. I could not ask, *What color was his beard? Did he have diamond studs in his teeth? Was he an old friend of mine?* "You mean you took him prisoner?" I asked, thinking that any dwarf could escape from human custody, given time. What had he been doing out in our world by night at such a time of risk?

Cezar's features were suddenly grave. "No, Jena. These folk are not so easily taken. We used various methods to try to make the little devil talk, but he had nothing to say about Night People or about ways in and out of their realm. In the end, he perished for his silence. There was no alternative. We could not let him go free. These vermin must be cleared from our forest. Those who cover for the perpetrators of crimes are, in their way, just as guilty as the criminals."

They'd killed him. Just like that, he'd lost his life for something he'd had no responsibility for. The dwarves were peaceable folk; they could have played no part in Ivona's death. *Various methods . . .* Surely Cezar didn't mean torture?

"It doesn't sound like cause for congratulation," I found myself saying. My voice wobbled. "You caught, hurt, and killed someone without knowing if he had any responsibility for the murder. And you didn't get any information. You spilled more blood, and for nothing."

There was a sudden silence. All the men were staring at me. By the stove Florica stood utterly still, the kettle in her hands.

"Jena," Cezar said in a dangerous, quiet voice, "I think it's best if you leave us now. We men are weary; it's been a long night's struggle. You need a little time to digest this news. Distress is making you irrational."

"A *long night's struggle*? A pack of—what—ten or eleven men against one dwarf?" I was on my feet, so angry that I let the words spill out without caution. "Forgive me if I cannot agree that this is some kind of victory."

"Leave the room, Jena." Now Cezar spoke sharply; it was a command. "I will not have words of that kind spoken here in the valley, not while I am master of Vârful cu Negură. Please curb your tongue. Florica, where's that ţuică?"

One of the hardest things I had to do was break this news to my sisters in Aunt Bogdana's presence, not knowing how each of them might respond. I was quivering with rage and humiliation after Cezar's reprimand, and full of horror over what he had done. All I wanted to do was run away somewhere by myself with Gogu and cry like a child. But the voices of my cousin and his friends were loud and excited as they went over their exploits; it could only get worse as the ţuică flowed. I needed to be first with this news, to render it gently. I did try.

"Cezar *killed* a *dwarf*?" Iulia found her voice first.

Stela, halfway through taking off her party dress, was staring round-eyed, her chin beginning to wobble.

"Aunt Bogdana," said Paula, her own voice less than steady, "I might take Stela upstairs."

"Of course, dear—your gown doesn't have much work left to do. This is odd news. I did not think Cezar . . . It's quite disturbing." A loud gust of laughter reached us from the kitchen.

I was watching Tati. She stood by the wall, white and staring, as the sounds of hilarity filtered through the door. Then she turned and left the room without a word.

"I don't think Tatiana's very well, Jena," said my aunt quietly. "She's grown so thin, and she often seems . . . not quite all there. I wonder if you should consult an herbalist? I can recommend someone, if you wish."

"Thank you, Aunt. I'll consider that." I realized she was speaking to me as if I were head of the household, as if I were the one in charge. Listening to Cezar's voice, remembering what he had just said to me—wounding words, the words of a tyrant—I knew that if I had ever been in charge of anything at Piscul Dracului, I was no longer.

The next morning, the landholders of the valley awoke as usual and went out to check their stock. On every farm, on every smallholding, an animal was found slaughtered. There was no consistency in what was chosen, only in the method of killing. On one farm it was a sheep, on another a pig. One family found a beloved dog lying limp across the doorstep. Some had been luckier, finding only a chicken gone, while some had lost their cow, the standby of every household. The valley's cows were not simply valued for the milk they provided over spring and summer, or for the calves they bore. Over the warmer months they all went out to graze the mountain pastures together, gathered up by a herdsman in the morning at each gateway, and returned in the evening to be milked again. Each animal knew its own gate and waited there for admittance; each knew its own human family. That morning, eight cows lay in their blood, their throats slit. Eight families had lost an essential part of their livelihood as well as an honored friend.

The news reached us early—Ivan came up to tell us, his face pale. He had been fortunate to lose only one of his ducks. He went out with Petru to check our own stock. Most were housed over the winter in outbuildings near the castle, but we did have a flock of hardy ewes in the sheepfold near the forest's margin. There was nothing untoward in the barn or the byre or the outbuildings—the animals looked healthy and demanded their breakfast. While the men went off to the upper pasture, I fed the chickens and Iulia tended to the pigs, and Paula and Stela made themselves useful in the kitchen, helping Florica with a batch of bread. Cezar and his friends were still asleep after another long night's hunting; they would be hungry when they awoke. Tati had not made an appearance.

Ivan and Petru were gone awhile. The upper pasture was covered in snow; for most of the winter, the sheep were dependent on hay carried up to their shelter. I stayed outside the barn, chopping firewood with unnecessary violence. Images of blood and death passed before my eyes. I did not know any longer whether I believed that filling Piscul Dracului with colored lights and music and laughter could have any effect at all on the Night People. Something was happening that seemed far too powerful for that small gesture of defiance to hold any weight. And, though I was filled with dread at the prospect, I wondered whether I should after all take a different path to try to stop it. Tonight was Dark of the Moon. If I crossed over to the Other Kingdom, could I hope to change the way things were? If I looked in Drăguţa's mirror, would I be given the secrets of the future, so I could make it come out differently? But maybe I was fooling myself, pretending that my motive was selfless when, underneath, it was dark temptation that drew me.

Jena.

Gogu had been sitting on a tree stump, wincing every time my ax split a log. I stopped chopping. "What is it, Gogu?" I took him in my hand; he was trembling. It came to me suddenly that it could have been him, that I could have woken to find him stretched out dead beside me on the pillow, slaughtered as callously as those other animals had been.

Tell me what you are thinking.

"I can't. It will make you angry."

Tell me. I am your friend.

"I'm afraid. All I really want to do is be a complete coward and hide from all this. We can stop visiting the Other Kingdom so we don't give away any secrets. We can hold our party and pretend that we're not afraid of the Night People. But I don't believe those things are enough to put this right. Ileana's folk wouldn't slaughter people's stock. She said it herself—*That is not our way*—when she spoke to me about punishing Cezar. Her folk respect creatures; they don't perform arbitrary killings. This is the work of the Night People. But it's not vengeance for the dwarf—he wasn't one of their kind. It's Tadeusz, playing games. It's sheer mischief, malicious teasing, designed to stir up unrest. I'm sure it's my fault. If I hadn't let him bewitch me . . ." My head was full of that beguiling voice. Its soft darkness still drew me, despite all common sense.

What are you planning?

"Nothing." But I was lying, and I thought he knew it.

When Petru and Ivan returned to the castle, their faces grave, I expected to be told of a loss. But they had counted the flock three times over, and all our sheep were still alive and well. It seemed that Piscul Dracului had escaped the slaughter. Maybe, Petru said, other farms had also been spared—some were too far away to have made a report yet.

Before day's end, Judge Rinaldo called a meeting down in the village. Cezar went, and so did Petru. The news they brought back sent a chill through me. Of all the households in the entire valley, ours was the only one that had not lost an animal to this scourge. Piscul Dracului had been singled out for special treatment. It was not to do with castles and cottages— one treatment for the wealthy, one for the common folk—for Cezar's farm at Vârful cu Negură had lost a breeding ewe.

Cezar was beside himself with fury. Questions had been asked in public as to why our house—situated so close to the edge of the wildwood—should be different from any other. One very old man had muttered something about Piscul Dracului being a place of mystery, a home of hidden perils and secret doors. Petru had told him he was an addle-pated old fool, but the damage was done. Once one tale came out, other folk had more to add. Someone suggested that the reason the place had stood empty for so long was that it concealed a gateway of some kind—that within its walls was a portal where worlds met.

Our cousin assembled us in the kitchen—all five sisters, with Florica and Petru. Răzvan and Daniel were looking uncomfortable by the door, as if stationed there to keep us from escaping. Perhaps Cezar had forgotten that this was our own house.

"I'm very unhappy," he said. "Deeply disturbed by what has happened, and by what folk are saying. If I believed for a moment that any one of you was hiding something, that information existed which could help me apprehend these murderers and that you were holding it back, I would—" He stopped, then turned on Florica. "You've been here for years, since the days of the old owner. What's all this talk of secret passageways and hidden entrances? Don't try to tell me you don't know."

His tone was intimidating: Florica paled and shrank away from him. Petru put his hand on her shoulder.

"Cezar," I said, "you can't interrogate Florica as if she were a criminal."

His brows creased into a ferocious scowl. "I'll do whatever is required to drive this menace from our forest, Jena. Personal bonds and old loyalties must be set aside when people's lives are at stake. You didn't see that fellow we caught. These folk are evil, through and through. And I will not be the target of vicious tongues in the community. I will not allow accusations of this kind to taint my reputation. If there's any truth in them,

I want it out in the open, right now. In your father's absence, I speak as head of the family. Perhaps you girls lack a full understanding of the danger we are facing. But you must know what these rumors could do. Let folk associate such tales with the five of you, and your chances of making advantageous matches will be reduced to nothing. Nobody wants a wife with the taint of the wildwood about her."

Paula made as if to speak—I silenced her with a look. Any comment she might make was likely to inflame the situation still further. In my pocket, Gogu was vibrating with anger.

"Cezar," I said, "since you are so keen on propriety, may I suggest that we discuss this in private, just you and me, with one of my sisters as chaperone? I will not have Florica and Petru bullied."

Cezar's face was calm, the anger suppressed now, but I could see the dangerous look in his eyes. "My intention was to address you all together," he said. "But I've changed my mind. I'll see you one at a time, starting with Stela. Alone. And we'll do it now, before you can concoct a set of matching stories."

"Are you accusing my sisters of lying?" We all looked at Tati in surprise. These days she rarely contributed anything to general conversation. She had certainly got Cezar's attention. He looked at her and his eyes narrowed. It was, perhaps, the first time he had noticed how pale and thin she was—how much she had changed.

"I cannot answer that until I hear what they have to say," he said.

"You're not talking to Stela without one of us there," I told him. "She's only five. And this is still Father's house. You are not head of anything, Cezar, not while he's still alive and no farther away than Constanţa." I drew a breath, fighting for calm. "It's after Stela's bedtime. It's completely inappropriate to subject her to this so late. You can talk to her tomorrow with me present—or, better still, with Aunt Bogdana there as well. Let us see how prepared you are to bully and intimidate us in your own mother's presence—"

He lifted his arm; his hand was poised to strike me. As one, my sisters drew in their breath in a shocked gasp. Then, surprising all of us, Daniel took two long strides across the kitchen and interposed his large body between my cousin and me. Cezar lowered his arm and I stepped back. Nobody had uttered a word.

"Tati," I said, "will you take Stela up to bed, please? Florica, Petru: you are excused for the night. It's been a long day, and you need your rest. Paula, Iulia: please clear away these platters and glasses before you go upstairs. Florica will want everything tidy for the morning."

Cezar had turned his back; his shoulders were tight.

"Thank you," I said to Daniel. He had retreated to the doorway, his eyes wary. I imagined that not even a strong young man would gladly cross Cezar. "I don't know if the hunting party is going out again tonight, but I would ask you and Răzvan to give me a little time to speak to my cousin in private. You can wait outside the door."

They obeyed. My sisters cleared the table rapidly, bearing cups and platters away for washing and drying in the scullery. While they were close at hand but out of earshot, I took the opportunity to speak, addressing myself to Cezar's back.

"You would have hit me." I could hear how cold my voice sounded, not at all the best thing to placate him. I couldn't help it. "Any man who attempts that loses my respect immediately, Cezar. My father would never have raised a hand against a woman. Nor, I'm certain, would Uncle Nicolae. What is it that makes you hate so?"

"I don't hate you, Jena." His tone was constrained. He did not turn. "Quite the contrary. But you try me hard sometimes. I know you want to protect your sisters and your servants—that is admirable, as a general sentiment. But if one of them is concealing something . . . if one of them is in league with these destructive powers . . . I cannot believe that's true, but I have to investigate the rumors. If the worst comes to pass, and someone in my own household has assisted these demonic folk, I must use what information they can give me to root out the evil—to destroy it once and for all."

I was so angry I could hardly speak. "If you're not careful," I said, "your hatred will eat you up, Cezar. I don't understand it. It has changed you so much that I hardly recognize you anymore. I know how terrible Costi's death was for you. But it was so long ago. You have your own estate to look after, your community to watch over, your life to lead. It is frightening to have the Night People in our forest. It is terrible that Ivona died, and troubling that folk have lost livestock. But you're a leader— you should be setting an example, not charging forward with the scent of blood in your nostrils and blind hatred in your heart. No matter how cruel the blow of losing your brother, it should never have made you lose your sense of what is right."

He did not answer for a long time, just turned to stare at

me. It was as if I were the one who had almost struck a blow. Eventually he said, "You can't understand. You can't know what it's like to be offered something and for it to seem as if you've been given it, and then to find out it's all a sham—that what you believed was a wonderful gift is worthless, cold, a dead promise. To pay an impossible price and get dross disguised as treasure; that is the cruelest thing. A leader, me? Hardly. Folk follow me because I'm the best they've got. That's not saying much in a place like this. Yes, I'm angry. I want the truth—and when I have it, I'll use it to destroy those who tricked me, those who played the most evil joke in the world on me. I will tear them apart, limb from limb, and then I will destroy their forest so that they can never return to haunt me. I will drive them even out of my dreams."

"*Evil joke?*" I asked, my voice diminished to a thread. "What joke? What are you talking about?"

"Forget it, Jena," said Cezar. "I don't want to discuss this further tonight. In the morning I'll hear what you have to say, each of you in turn. I'll know if anyone's lying. I won't have the community intimidated by the forces of the forest, and I won't have my household cursed and polluted by association with Drăguţa the witch and her henchmen. Night People or not, she's the one who is behind all this. She did it. She drowned Costi. She's never let me forget that, not for one instant. People think life goes on after these things, that folk recover and get over it, that everything doesn't change. That's wrong, Jena. It never goes away. It won't go away until I make it go. It won't leave me until I crush it completely."

Iulia and Paula had finished putting away the dishes; now

they hovered in the doorway, waiting for me. Thank heaven for my sisters. I could forgive their small failings instantly, as long as they were there when I needed them. I put my hand around Gogu, inside my pocket. He was tensed up into a little ball, deeply distressed. "I don't think I understand," I told my cousin. "I've always believed we should try to put bad things behind us—not to forget them, but to learn from them and make the best use of that learning in our lives. If you can't do that, you shouldn't blame Drǎguţa or the folk of the forest. It's your life—the only one who can live it is you. Now I'm going to bed, Cezar. If you ever try to hit me again, I will tell my father. And I'll tell Aunt Bogdana, as well. Once I might possibly come to forgive. Twice will ensure you never regain my good opinion."

In the quiet of our bedchamber, Stela was tucked under her quilt, almost asleep. There was no sign of Tati.

"Stela?" I crouched down by my little sister's bed. "Where did Tati go?"

"I don't know."

"Jena." Paula turned solemn eyes on me. "Her outdoor cloak's gone."

My stomach dropped; I felt sick. I thought of Tati's wan, desperate appearance over these last days; her odd trips out into the forest; the way she seemed to drift along on the edges, as if she were not really part of our family anymore. I had told her about Tadeusz. I had told her about Dark of the Moon. "I think I'd better go and see if she's all right," I said as calmly as I could while my heart raced with terror. "I'll just settle Gogu down first."

I poured water into his bowl. My hands shook so much that the stream spilled over the rim.

"Jena," said Iulia, "where do you think she's gone? Why are you looking like that?"

"Like what?" I fished Gogu out of my pocket and set him by the water dish.

No, Jena! No.

"You look terrified," Iulia said.

"I don't want her to get in Cezar's way. You saw what kind of mood he's in. I'll just slip out and bring her back."

Jena, don't go. Don't do this.

"It's Dark of the Moon," Paula said. "You don't think she might be planning to—?" She was not quite prepared to put my worst suspicion into words.

"Of course not," I lied. "She doesn't even know where to go; none of us do." *Call to me and I will take you there.* "I'd better go now. Keep an eye on Gogu for me, will you?"

Take me with you. Jena! Don't go without me!

I made for the door before the frog could leap onto my shoulder. I knew that if I picked him up again, I would find it impossible to leave him behind. "I shouldn't be long," I said, snatching my cloak from the peg where it hung. "Just go to sleep. I'll see you in the morning."

I imagined I could feel the horrified eyes of my sisters on my back as I went out. I heard a little thud as Gogu leaped from the table and made to follow me. I shut the door before he could reach it. If Tati was doing what I suspected, my only choice was to follow her, but I would not risk the safety of my little wise friend as well as my own.

I wanted to run, to find her as quickly as I could before it was too late. But I went cautiously, sidling from one corner to another, constantly watchful. If I drew Cezar's attention, I would have to find an excuse for creeping about at night in my outdoor cloak, and then retreat to the bedchamber without my sister. There was no map to follow, no logic to choosing where I might look. An instinct I had not known I possessed drew me down one staircase and up another, past Father's workroom, along a creaking gallery, then down the back way to the chamber that had once been our storeroom and was now swept bare and clean, waiting for the night of Full Moon.

The castle was dark. I had grabbed a candle before I went downstairs, but its feeble flickering did little to illuminate the cavernous spaces and shadowy corners of Piscul Dracului. I walked the length of the big chamber, the pillars rising into darkness on either side, the floor faintly gleaming as my small light passed over it. I went up a set of stone steps at the far end. From here it was possible to enter a musicians' gallery set above the main chamber, or to climb still further to an open terrace looking out over dense forest. With the moon hidden, there would be nothing to see tonight. "Tati," I whispered, "where are you? Don't be gone already—please, please. . . ."

The door to the terrace was ajar, its chain unfastened and dangling. So much for Cezar's precautions. I crept through and ascended another flight of steps to emerge on the stone terrace. The night was pitch-black and cold enough to freeze the breath the moment it left the body. I hugged my cloak around my shoulders, lifting the candle in a feeble attempt to light the darkness. "Tati? Are you here?"

There was a sudden movement by the parapet wall. She was standing close to the barrier, her face a pale oval in the fitful light, her eyes big and wild. The blue cloak shrouded her figure completely; her feet were in soft slippers. My sister was not alone. Beside her stood a tall, black-caped figure. It was not Sorrow. It was not Tadeusz. Those ruby lips, that snow-white skin, that elegant bearing, belonged to the woman of the Night People: the haughty Anastasia.

"Tati," I gulped, "come inside. You can't go. It's too dangerous." My voice sounded tiny—a child's, ineffectual and meaningless.

Anastasia smiled, showing her unusual teeth. The effect was deeply troubling. "Take my arm, Tatiana," she said, and her voice was as musical and as haunting as her brother's, if brother he was. "I will lead you across. Sorrow is waiting for you just beyond the margin. Your sister is wrong. It's perfectly safe. You're women now—you are entitled to this."

"No!" I cried out. "Tati, don't!" I could see the longing in my sister's eyes; Sorrow's name had brought it sharply to life. As for me, I felt the urge to move forward, to obey the coaxing voice and follow wherever Anastasia bid me. I yearned to go. I needed knowledge. What she had said about being entitled warmed me. In her world, there were no men like Cezar to dismiss my aspirations and scorn my quest for independence.

"Come with us, Jenica," Anastasia purred. "My brother waits to show you the mirror. It's just on the other side. Come, take my hand."

I hesitated, remembering the small, wise voice of Gogu

raised in desperate protest. *No, Jena!* When had he ever been wrong?

"You waver," the red-lipped woman said dismissively. "You are too cautious, like an old woman. Come, Tatiana." And, as I watched, Tati slipped her arm through Anastasia's. They moved away, beyond the small circle of light my candle cast on the cold stones. The portal could be anywhere. They might simply vanish; my sister might never come back. I imagined her pale and lifeless like Ivona, with the livid mark of a bite on her neck. I drew one long, uneven breath and launched myself after them.

Chapter Nine

The candle went out, and I was blind. I stumbled along the terrace, hoping I would catch them before they escaped my reach. Surely this was too far—there should be a wall. . . . Groping before me in the darkness, I touched something chill as winter: a thin-fingered, long-nailed hand. I clutched it, reminding myself to breathe. A moment later we were falling, falling, so far down that I knew our landing would be in a tumble of crushed flesh and broken bones. I screamed, but my voice drifted into nothing; instead, the cold air was full of the cries of strange birds, an eldritch music of night. I squeezed my eyes tightly shut, waiting for the ground to slam into my body.

I landed gently, my feet on a soft surface, my eyes still closed. From the distance came a sound of faint music. I opened my eyes.

We were by Tăul Ielelor, on the path to Dancing Glade. There was the avenue of tall trees that led up to the sward; there was the little sandy shore where our boats would glide in to let us out. The lake was frozen over. Tonight its surface did not glimmer, but lay sullen and dark beneath the willows. Up in the trees, lanterns still hung, but their forms were changed: in place of beetle, bird, and butterfly were twisted forms of things not quite right—a cockroach with elongated teeth; a child with grimacing features and stunted limbs; a death's-head; a worm-infested apple. The light they cast was dim and odd, rendering the landscape a greenish purple. Anastasia's pale face was skull-like and my sister's a terrified mask. I swallowed and released Anastasia's chill hand, struggling for words. I could not berate Tati for her weakness. I had felt the same urge to come here. It was in my blood now as I walked after my sister and her guide up the pathway toward Ileana's glade.

I willed myself to be silent. I would not ask, *Where is Tadeusz? Where is Drǎguţa's mirror?* It seemed far wiser not to give the Night People the impression that I cared greatly for anything they might have to offer. I hoped Ileana would be here as usual and that I might petition her again, since it seemed the whole valley had now fallen under a malevolent shadow. I would simply ask her to send the Night People away. And if the queen of the forest laughed at a human girl for seeking influence in such grand matters, so be it.

I tried to grasp my sister's arm so she would stay by my side, for I could see in her eyes that she would not listen to words of caution tonight, but Anastasia hurried her on. I would need to remain on my guard constantly to be certain I could bring Tati home safely. Home. I did not even know how we would get there. Anastasia did not seem like the kind of being who would snap her fingers and transport us back as soon as we grew tired. There were no boats on the lakeshore tonight. Never mind that: there would be folk I knew at Dancing Glade, folk who would help me if I needed them.

"Where's Sorrow?" Tati asked. "You said he was just on the other side. He's not here." Her voice rose. "You lied to me! Where is he?"

Anastasia was walking briskly, her booted heels sinking deep into the damp soil. "Patience, patience, Tatiana. He will be here. He waits for you. He longs for you. I will take you to him." And she drew Tati on, so fast that I had to break into a run to keep up. The trees seemed to reach out long fingers as we passed beneath, sharp and greedy; they clawed at my cloak and tangled in Tati's long hair. She brushed them away, shuddering. "Keep up!" snapped Anastasia, her voice no longer beautiful. "You are too slow!"

On the edge of Ileana's glade, we halted. The sward was full of dancing figures, as at Full Moon, but there was nothing familiar about it. I could not see tall Grigori, or big, blocky Sten, or diminutive Ildephonsus. I could not see the elegant form of the forest queen or the golden hair of her consort. Instead, a company of beings writhed and cavorted on the grass; Night People were among them, but there were also many that seemed part creature, part man or woman—a person with the head of a boar, a lady whose skin was all scales—and, here and there, stunted beings whose bodies were squashed up on themselves, hobbling in a grotesque mockery of a formal dance. Most disturbing of all, I saw human folk among the motley throng—

men and women whose faces were not those of happy revelers but who bore trapped expressions, grimacing or fearful or plain mad. I saw a girl of around Paula's age—pale-faced, solemn, delicately built—her dark hair tied back in a bow of black silk, her gown a small replica of Anastasia's. She stood under the trees by the sward's edge, watching gravely. Two tall women of the Night People flanked this slight figure; I could not escape the impression that they were acting as guards. The girl looked vaguely familiar. There was something deeply unsettling about the sight of her in this unlikely place; her frail innocence surely did not belong here. I saw that she was looking at a group of folk playing some kind of game with long barbed poles. They were throwing high, competing to reach a trussed-up bundle that hung on ropes from a willow bough. The bundle was wriggling, struggling—there was something alive inside it. A stick found its mark; a cry of pain came from the target.

Anastasia was already drawing Tati away. "Over here," she commanded, making her way around the edge of the sward. I followed, my eyes drawn to a circle of Night People who were not dancing, merely standing and watching a figure that capered in the center. It was a man, a human being of middle years, dressed in the ragged remnants of a shepherd's garb—long felt cape, conical hat—performing a crude kind of dance that jerked and contorted his body, as if a mad puppeteer were moving him against his will. I saw the agony in his eyes. He stared wildly at me, and his lips moved in a silent entreaty: *Help me!* Then Anastasia grabbed my arm and moved me on.

"Wait," I protested. "That man—what are they doing to him? And what was that hung from the tree?"

Anastasia's red lips curved in a smile entirely without mirth. "That man, and a woman of your kind, wandered a little too far," she said. "Why would you protest? We have spared their lives: like many other foolish folk, they have become part of our revels."

"But it looked as if that man couldn't stop—as if he was forced to dance on and on, just so they could mock him." I glanced back over my shoulder, but a frenzy of dancing creatures had moved between me and that sad, capering figure.

"Do not judge us, Jenica. Your own cousin tore one of Ileana's folk apart, limb from limb. And for no good purpose, as it came about. Dwarves are ridiculously loyal."

I made myself ask. "Can you tell me which one it was? Was it Anatolie?"

She laughed. The sound of it rang in my ears, derisive and harsh. "What would I care? They all look the same to me."

"Where's Sorrow?" Tati had stopped walking, and there was a new look of determination on her face. "I'm not going a step farther until I see him." She reached back and grasped my hand. "Nor is Jena."

"That's right," I said, fixing Anastasia with an attempt at a glare. "If you can't make good on your promises, we're going straight back home."

She laughed again, and this time the folk who were dancing close beside us halted and fell silent. Suddenly we had an audience—an audience in which not a single figure was familiar. Where were our friends from Ileana's glade?

"Home?" It was Tadeusz's voice. I whirled, letting go of Tati, and there he was, right behind us. "That could prove difficult, Jenica. You will not cross the Dark Between without one of us as your guide. Don't look like that—we mean you no harm. A little insight, some entertainment, then we will take you safely back again. You have surprised me." He moved forward, his hand coming up to touch my hair. "I had believed you lacked the courage for this."

"I'm not here because I want to be," I said through chattering teeth. "I'm here to make sure my sister comes home safely. And to tell you—" I halted. To come right out with a request—no, a demand—that they leave the valley alone, in front of such an audience, did not seem particularly wise. "There's something I need to explain to you," I told him. "I would prefer to do so in private."

Tadeusz gave a knowing smile; it reminded me of the way Cezar sometimes looked.

"I didn't mean—" I blurted out, mortified.

"Oh, but I think you did." The voice was at its velvety best, insinuating itself into the deepest recesses of my mind. "Without wanting, you could not pass over. You and your sister both." The dark eyes flicked to Tati and back again. "There will be time enough for private dalliance later. The night is long. Don't you want to look into Drăguţa's magic mirror? When you have done so, we will have a hundred new things to talk about, Jena."

"I don't care about the mirror." Out of the corner of my eye, I could see Anastasia getting restless, impatient. She was examining her long, polished nails and glancing about her. "I'll say what I need to say now. You've brought evil on the valley, you and your people. You offered me something and I didn't accept the offer, but you took payment anyway—payment in an innocent girl's blood. You started this. You can't say just wanting something means I've agreed to some kind of bargain; that isn't fair. The people of the valley were already hungry: it's winter, and times are hard. Killing their animals isn't only cruel, it's unjust. Not everyone is like Cezar. Most people understand the need to share. They understand that humankind and the folk of the wildwood have to live side by side, with proper respect for their differences. Ileana's folk know that. It seems you don't."

"You promised that I could see Sorrow." Tati's voice was uneven. "If he's here, I want to see him now. Show me that he's safe and well."

"Of course, Tatiana." Tadeusz's voice had become kindly, warm; he sounded utterly trustworthy. "I will take you to him. He's a shy boy, as you know. He won't come out while so many folk are enjoying themselves. This way."

"Wait!" It seemed my night was to be a long sequence of running, clutching, trying to keep up. "Don't go without me—"

"This way," said Anastasia, and I found that she was leading me down a pathway into the woods, and my sister and Tadeusz were nowhere in sight. I tried to pull back, to follow Tati, but my feet were obeying some force beyond me, dragging me along behind my pale-faced guide. I was engulfed by malevolence, in the grip of a fell charm. I tried to call to my sister, but my voice seemed to die in my throat—all I could manage was a strangled gasp. We moved on into the darkness. Behind us, the eerie lights of the glade faded.

"What is this place?" I managed. "Where are Ileana and Marin? Why is it so different?" A terrible fear awoke within me. Perhaps the Night People had changed the Other Kingdom forever. Perhaps Ileana's rule was over, and our friends were all gone.

"You think that within the Other Kingdom there is only one realm?" Anastasia raised her brows at me, as if she found me unbelievably stupid. "Dark of the Moon is our time; we come to celebrate in our own way. It is Ileana's choice to shun our festivities. That's of no matter. My brother's world is stronger than hers. In time, all this will be ours."

My heart went cold. Fear seized me, but not quite enough to stifle common sense. "I thought you were from the east," I whispered. "I thought you were only visiting. And what about Drăguţa?"

"Drăguţa?" She tossed her ebony hair. "A mere mountain witch? She's no more than a puny local herbalist who reaches beyond her abilities. Why else has she failed to make an appearance in all the days since we came to the forest of Piscul Dracului? The crone dares not set foot in the open now the Night People have put their mark on this place."

While my feet carried me along after her, I was thinking hard. "If Drăguţa has so little power," I said, "why did your brother hold out her mirror to tempt me here? It must be a tawdry thing of little value. Why did Tadeusz tell me I would find truth in it? Was everything he said to me a lie?"

"I know one thing," the scarlet-lipped woman said with a twisted smile. "My brother was never interested in *you*, plain little thing that you are, with your unkempt bush of hair and your flat chest and your flood of stupid questions. It's your sister he has his eye on. She's a choice morsel, all pearly flesh and quivering uncertainty. There's no need to look like that, Jenica. We're not so precipitate. He wishes Sorrow to see them together, that is all. He wishes to play a little."

Humiliation, confusion, and terror warred within me. I stayed silent, though inside I was screaming.

"You want to ask questions, don't you? Look in the mirror, then. You may protest that you are here simply to bring your sister back, but I know the real reason. You are thirsty for knowledge. You must have it whatever the cost—because knowledge allows control, and you do love to be in control, don't you, Jenica? And you like flattery, poor, silly girl. My brother knew how to manipulate you; it was the easiest thing in the world."

For a moment I knew what hate felt like. I knew how Cezar felt in those moments when his face went cold and his eyes dark. Then I saw that we had reached a still pool fringed by ferns, a pool that was perfectly round, with a shimmering to its surface that reminded me of Tăul Ielelor on the night of Full Moon. Without a doubt, this was Drăguţa's magic mirror. The forest around us was hushed. No night bird called, no small creature rustled a path through the grasses.

The moment she releases this spell, I told myself, *I have to run. Run back, grab Tati, go to the lake, and get across any way we can.* Even as I thought this, I knew how impossible it would be. I wished with all my heart that I had not left Gogu behind. He would have thought of some way out, I was sure of it. What my stupidity had gotten us into, his sound common sense would have extricated us from. *Run. Run.* I stood paralyzed, waiting for her to release my feet. I looked anywhere but at that circle of bright water, for it seemed to me that once I let my eyes fall on it, I would be trapped: caught by the vision, a victim of my own hunger for knowledge. I looked up into the elder tree that grew by the pond, and in its drooping branches I caught a glimpse of something small and bright—something that reflected the gleam from the water and shone it into my eyes. I blinked, disbelieving, then reached up a hand and lifted it down. It was a tiny crown made from wire and fabric, beads and braid. *I want to be Queen of the Fairies.*

Anastasia gave a hiss. The spell was abruptly undone, my feet freed from what had rooted them to the ground, my throat released from the tight grip that had held my voice to a whisper. I took a step back, ready to flee. The crown slipped through my fingers, and as I reached to catch it, I looked into the water of Drǎguţa's mirror.

I saw a pair of children, pale-skinned and dark-eyed, each as somber-faced as the other. He was perhaps eight years old, she a mere babe. Brother and sister, no doubt, and I was sure I knew them. That sad-looking boy was Sorrow, and the other the fragile girl I had seen not long ago with her minders. The water showed them in the forest, wandering, probably lost—the boy was holding his sister in his arms, trying to make a way through ever thicker undergrowth as the light faded. They came to a clearing as dusk fell, and there, under the trees, was Tadeusz in his black boots and swirling cloak. *Do not be afraid,* he said, and then the vision faded.

Before I could begin to think about what that meant, a new

image appeared in the mirror. I saw myself, dancing with a young man clad in rags. He was tall and lanky, his dark hair hanging wild and unkempt over eyes as green as beech leaves. He was looking at the girl in his arms as if she were his whole world, and the Jena of the vision was gazing back with her heart in her eyes. It made me feel hot and cold and confused— I longed for the vision to be real, and for love at first sight to be a true thing after all. His face was everything I liked: the mouth quirky and sweet, the features strong and well defined, the eyes deep and thoughtful. He seemed in some way familiar, though I was certain I had never seen him before. As I gazed, the man in the mirror turned to look out at the world of Dark of the Moon, and the tenderness in his eyes made my heart turn over. *Be sensible, Jena,* I warned myself. *You are in the Other Kingdom; nothing is as it seems.*

Then, before my eyes, he changed. As I stared, horrified, the pleasant, clever features became a distorted mask. The eyes went from green to red, the skin puckered and blistered and broke out in festering sores. He lifted a hand, and the fingers were tipped with nails so long, they had grown into yellow curls. He opened his mouth, and what came out was a terrible howl, the cry of a savage thing from the darkest places of the forest. The other Jena was gone from the mirror, but my younger sisters were there, all three of them. I stood frozen with terror as the monstrous figure turned on them: slashing, tearing, rending, as he made them run, pursuing them through the wild-wood without mercy. I heard Stela screaming in pain. I heard my own voice, a little, pathetic thing, whimpering, *No, no!*

Trust that one, someone said, *and you will deliver up your heart to be split and skewered and roasted over a fire.* The vision dissipated on the water's surface. All that remained was a leaf or two floating there and a drift of weed below.

I dashed the tears from my face and fought to get my breathing under control. I was free to go; it seemed these cryptic and horrifying glimpses were all Drăguța's mirror had to show me. Anastasia had fallen strangely silent. She was a tall woman and her grip had been strong. I wondered if I had any chance of outrunning her. I turned and saw that her eyes were on the little crown in my hands, the trifle of bits and pieces that, at five years old, I had thought the most wondrous thing in the world. It was fraying and crumbling and falling apart.

"Throw that away," Anastasia said, staring at the crown and clutching at her throat as if something hurt her. "It's an evil charm, one of *hers*. A human girl cannot hold such a talisman— it will kill you, Jenica. Cast it aside."

"Hers? You mean Drăguța's? A mere mountain witch?" I edged away from her. If, startling as it seemed, this childhood creation gave me some kind of advantage here where the Night People held sway, I would not hesitate to use it.

"Give it up, Jenica!" Anastasia lunged toward me. As her fingers reached for the little crown, there was a whirl of white between us and we both flinched back. A moment later an owl landed on the bending branch of the elder tree, its plumage snowy, its eyes an odd, cloudy blue-green. Anastasia's hands moved in a complicated gesture before her, like a ritual charm. It reminded me of the sign the folk of the valley used to ward off evil spirits.

Run, said my inner voice, and I obeyed, the little crown still clutched tight in my hand. "Tati!" I shouted, careless of who could hear me or what they might decide to do. It seemed to me I had been given a second chance and that I must use it quickly. "Tati, where are you?"

I ran back up the path to the sward, my heart pounding, my breath coming hard. In my head I was five years old again and the oak tree I had been told to reach moved farther and farther away the faster I drove myself. I could hear Costi's footsteps behind me, closer and closer, but this time it was Anastasia chasing me, and after a while her steps grew fainter, though I still heard her calling me: *"Jenica! Stop!"*

I reached the turning where I had lost Tadeusz and my sister, and paused, not knowing which way they had gone. I might take a wrong turn and keep blundering through the woods until I was lost forever—as lost as those children in the vision had been. Human children: an ordinary boy and girl who had been captured by the wildwood and now could never be set free again.

The owl flew over my head, making me duck. I ran after it, trying to keep the bird in sight as I brushed past thorny bushes and crept under tangling briars. Surely this was not the way I had come? Where was this creature leading me, into the heart of the wood? "Wait," I panted, but the bird flew on, uttering an eerie hoot as it winged its way down a steep, overgrown hill. At the bottom of the slope, I glimpsed the strangely glowing waters of the Deadwash, brighter now than before. I forced a way through the prickly undergrowth—my cloak tearing on thorns, twigs catching at my hair. Behind me, at a distance, I could hear sounds of pursuit: a howling arose, like that of hunting hounds. And close by me, along the bank, someone else was making a crashing descent. Anastasia—had she caught up with me? I glanced through the bushes and caught a flash of a white, terrified face and a stream of dark hair. Tati—and with her someone in dark clothing, a man leading her along at breakneck speed. He still had her. Tadeusz would get there before me, he would stop me. . . .

The owl cried out again. I saw it alight on a branch down the hill, where the forest opened up to the lakeshore. I was running so fast that I could not stop. I stumbled between sharp-leaved holly bushes and out onto the open ground, the little crown still clutched in my hand.

"Jena! Quick!" my sister was saying, and when I looked up, I saw that the person with her was not haughty, black-booted Tadeusz, but the slighter form of the young man in the black coat: the man about whom, it seemed, I had been quite wrong.

"Are you all right?" I asked Tati, sure that I could hear the sound of running footsteps and of barking not far behind us.

"I'm fine. I ran away and hid, and Sorrow found me." In her chalk-pale face, my sister's eyes were shining bright. "But he says we have to go."

"You should not have come here." Sorrow's voice was muted; he, too, was glancing over his shoulder. "You put yourselves in peril. If I aid you, I break a vow and endanger the innocent. You must go quickly."

His sister, I thought. He must be bound to obey the Night People, or she would be hurt. That was cruel.

"I only wanted to see you," Tati said in a whisper.

"I know that, dear heart, and the sight of you fills me with joy. But you must go now, quickly, before they reach the shore. Do not come here at Dark of the Moon. Promise me you won't come again."

"I promise." She stood on tiptoe to kiss him. Sorrow enfolded her in his arms, and I had to look away, for he held her with such tender passion that it made my cheeks burn. I felt like an intruder. I remembered Tadeusz's insinuating talk about *wanting*. And I remembered the young man with green eyes who had looked at me in just the way Sorrow looked at Tati—as if I were the sun, moon, and stars, all wrapped into one. For a moment I had believed that might be real for me, too, until Drăguţa's mirror had shown how cruelly deceptive such daydreams could be. I gazed over the lake and saw the owl fly out to land in a birch that grew on the first of many small islands there. The Deadwash was hard frozen. With sinking heart, I knew what we must do.

"Farewell," Sorrow said, and his voice was the saddest thing I had ever heard.

"When will I see you?" Tati asked him as I drew her away, down toward the frozen lake. "I can't bear this!"

"Wouldn't Drăguţa help you?" I looked back at Sorrow as I stepped out onto the ice. "Couldn't you approach her?"

"Go!" whispered Sorrow. "Go before they see you." And he vanished under the trees.

The white owl led us all the way across Tăul Ielelor. The ice was slick—by the time we reached the other side we were bruised, exhausted, and freezing. Tati was crying. I was oddly dry-eyed, my heart still pounding with fear and exertion, my mind busily trying to make sense of all that had happened. I had not looked back once. The sounds I had heard behind us suggested that pursuit had come only as far as the lakeshore. Something had helped us, something that was not simply a friendly bird from the Other Kingdom.

I looked at the owl now; it was perched on a tree stump, coolly preening its feathers like any ordinary creature. "Thank you," I said, inclining my head in a gesture of respect. "I don't know why you helped us, but I honor you for it. I don't suppose the usual portal's going to open—not tonight. Can you show us how to get home?"

With a screech, the bird unfolded its wings and flew off. Within moments it was gone. The only light was the faint gleam from the lake's surface. On this moonless night, the path we usually took up to the castle and the long winding stair would be impossible.

"It's all right, Jena," Tati said, surprising me, for I had thought her beyond rational speech. "We can simply walk home through the forest."

"How could that work? We'd probably go around and around in circles and never get home. We might be like that . . ." My voice trailed away. If she had not seen that pathetic puppet on the sward, capering before his tormentors, I would not tell her about him. As for the pale child in her black gown, it seemed that she and her brother were not so different from us.

"I don't think so, Jena. It's the Bright Between that separates the two worlds, and we're already across." She shivered, drawing her cloak more tightly around her. "I think if we're careful which way we go, we can get home from here."

"What are you saying? If that was true, the whole thing with our portal would be . . . It wouldn't be a magical charm at all—it would be meaningless, Tati. What about the shadow hands on the stone at Full Moon? If it's not magic, it should work anytime we try it, and anyone should be able to do it."

"I don't know. But I think we should start walking. I'm cold. We need to follow the edge of the lake until we find a path; at least the water is a little brighter than the forest."

"Tati?" I asked her as we picked our way along the lake-shore.

"What?"

"Are you going to tell me what happened?"

"I told you. That tall one, Tadeusz, tried to take me off somewhere, and I just bolted into the forest, not even thinking where I was going. A moment later, there was Sorrow. I could hear Tadeusz laughing. It was almost as if he knew what was going to happen. As if it was all part of some mad game. He frightened me, Jena."

"Here, there's a way up beside this stream, between the rocks, I remember it. . . ." It led to the secret hollow where Gogu and I had enjoyed many picnics. That meant the place where we had slipped and staggered to shore was the scene of Costi's drowning—the sandy beach where my cousins and I had once placed our precious treasures and started a game whose rules none of us understood. I felt the slight weight of the little crown, which I had slipped into the pocket of my cloak. *I want to be Queen of the Fairies. . . .* I was missing something. I was on the verge of solving a puzzle, but the pieces would not quite fit.

"Wait a minute," I said, and I took the crown out and set it on a flat stone by the stream. "I don't think I'm ready to take it back yet," I whispered.

"What?"

"Nothing. Come on, then. We should go as quietly as we can; Cezar and his hunting party might be out again. I'll tell you my story when we're safely home, with the door locked behind us."

She was right about the portal—at least, right in her guess that we could walk back to Piscul Dracului without the need to pass between worlds once more. We had still more cuts and bruises by the time we came up the track past the barn toward the main entrance to the castle. Our boots were sodden from tramping through the snow and the hems of our skirts coated with forest debris. My ears ached; my nose streamed; I'd never felt so cold in my life. Within the castle, lights still burned. Despite the need to conserve fuel, Florica would not have the place in total darkness on a winter night. One lamp shone over the big iron-hinged doorway.

"It's going to be locked," Tati said. "Everything will be locked, except the door up on the terrace."

If we'd been birds or bats, we could have reached that entry. As it was, I could think of only one solution. "We'll have to take shelter in the barn," I said. "We can slip indoors when Petru comes out in the morning. With luck, he won't see us."

"What if he does?"

"I know whom I'd rather answer to, out of Petru or Cezar," I said grimly. "Come on! At least there's warm straw in there, if you don't mind sharing it with a cow."

If we had reached home just a little earlier, if we'd walked just a little faster, this makeshift plan might have worked. If I hadn't stopped—from some instinct I hardly understood—to leave the crown behind, Cezar wouldn't have seen us. As it was, we were only halfway over to the barn when we heard voices. A moment later he and his two friends came around a corner of the house and stopped dead, staring at us. Răzvan was carrying a lighted torch. Daniel had a crossbow in his hands, with a bolt already in place. Cezar was in front, the ferocious expression on his dark features changing as he saw us to shocked incredulity. He was speechless.

My mind went completely blank.

"Cezar!" exclaimed Tati. "We—we were just . . . We thought we heard something out here. . . ."

My cousin's eyes went from the two of us—shivering and pathetic in our muddy clothes—to the doorway of the house. At that moment, the bolts were slid aside and the door opened to reveal Petru in his nightshirt, with his sheepskin jacket over it. He had an iron poker clutched in one gnarled hand. The knot in my tongue undid itself. I ran across to him.

"Nothing to worry about, Petru. It turned out that it was only Cezar coming back," I babbled, praying that the old man would understand we needed help. "I'm sorry we woke you up. We can all go back inside now. I really am sorry to have caused such a fuss."

Petru didn't say a thing, he just looked at me, then backed into the house. He muttered something about Florica and hot drinks and vanished in the direction of the kitchen. Cezar seized my arm and marched me indoors. I could feel the vibration of anger in his touch, and as soon as we were in the hallway, I wrenched my arm away.

"What have I told you, over and over?" he shouted. "You girls must never go out after dusk, especially on your own! I can't believe you were so foolish as to venture outside at night. It could have been anything out there! And why in God's name didn't you wait for Petru? You must leave these things to me, Jena. I thought you'd grasped that basic fact."

He grabbed me by the arm again and pulled me along after him in the direction of the kitchen. The others had gone ahead without a word.

Florica was boiling a kettle, bleary-eyed, a big coat of Petru's partly covering her night attire. Her silent husband was setting cups on the table. Tati stood shivering convulsively by the stove, her face drained of color. Daniel and Răzvan were standing about, looking awkward.

Cezar was still holding on to me. I made a decision: before he began to pick holes in our account of ourselves, I must take preemptive action. "I need to sit down," I said, finding it all too easy to buckle at the knees and put my other hand on my cousin's arm for support. I had judged him correctly—he put his arm around me and guided me to a chair. I looked up at him. His eyes were full of suspicion. "I'm really sorry, Cezar," I said, hating myself, but unable to think of any other way out of this. "We've been stupid, I can see that now. I promise never to do such a thing again."

Maybe I had overdone it. He narrowed his eyes at me. Florica set a pot of fruit tea on the table, and beside it a flask of warm ţuică, with a little dish of pepper and one of sugar. Neither she nor Petru had said a thing.

"Jena," said Cezar, "I must ask you some questions. I don't wish to seem distrustful, but in light of these wild tales that have been raised about the house, I'm duty bound to investigate anything in the least suspicious. How was it that you were able to hear something out in the yard when your bedchamber looks over the other side of the castle? Whatever it was you heard, it was not our hunting party. Only the three of us went out tonight, and it was no farther than the innermost fence, to check that the stock were undisturbed. We went as quietly as we always do, the better to apprehend an evildoer should we chance on one. If you roused Petru, how was it that the two of you were already in the yard in your outdoor clothing while he was only just opening the door? This doesn't add up. I don't like it. Petru, what have you to say for yourself?"

Petru was seized by a sudden fit of coughing. It was so severe, he had to excuse himself and leave the room.

"I'd best go and help him, Mistress Jenica," muttered Florica. "He's bad when it takes him like this." And she, too, was gone. Tati began to pour the tea, as if this were one of Aunt Bogdana's polite gatherings. Through a haze of weariness I thought that at times, the human world could be every bit as strange as the Other Kingdom.

"Anyway," Cezar said, "it's the middle of the night—you

must have been fast asleep. Surely only a commotion would wake you. If there'd been any disturbance I would have heard it myself."

"Jena's been sleeping very poorly," said Tati, sliding a cup across to Cezar. "We're all upset by what's been happening. She didn't want to worry you." It was a bold-faced lie and utterly surprising in view of my sister's wanly dispirited demeanor of late. Her eyes were still bright, and not just with tears. Perhaps that kiss had given her strength.

"Mmm," grunted Cezar, sitting down beside me, so close his thigh was against mine. I edged away, trying not to be too obvious about it. "I'm sorry, Jena. All the same—"

I yawned; it owed nothing to artifice. "Could we talk about this in the morning?" I asked him in as sweet a tone as I could muster.

"Drink your tea," Cezar said. "Get warm. You're shivering—here." He took off his thick cloak and put it around my shoulders. It was, in fact, wonderfully warm.

"Thank you," I said in a small voice. "I'm truly sorry." And in a way I was; sorry that Tati had taken it into her head to cross a forbidden margin, and sorry that we had not been able to reach home undetected; sorry that such sad things existed as those I had witnessed at Dark of the Moon.

"All right, Jena; don't distress yourself." Cezar patted my hand. "I can wait for an accounting. But when it comes, I want the truth."

Gogu was on my pillow, sitting so still he might have been dead. When I got into bed, he edged away from me.

"I'm sorry," I whispered. "I should have taken you with me."

Crouched between my pillow and Tati's, the frog turned reproachful eyes on me. The shutters were closed over his thoughts, but I needed no words to know what he was feeling.

"We *are* back safely, Tati and I. We didn't meet some terrible fate," I told him.

He blinked. There was a whole world of meaning in it.

"Gogu? Will you forgive me? I can't go to sleep if you're angry. I truly am sorry."

A torrent of furious distress came from him. *You lied to me. I'll just slip out and bring her back, you said. And you'd promised never to go away from me again. How can I look after you if you leave me behind?*

I struggled for an answer that would not insult him.

Beside me, Tati had slipped under the quilt, pulling it up almost over her head. "Go to sleep, Jena," she mumbled. "It's almost morning."

"Gogu," I whispered, "I did slip out and bring her back. It was just a bit farther than I expected. And I'm upset by what I saw—things I wouldn't want anyone to see, not even you. Things so bad I can't even talk about them. But you're right. I needed you. I knew that as soon as I got there."

You think me worthless. You think because I am a frog, I cannot stand by you.

His anger hurt me terribly. I had never seen him like this, not in all the years we had been together. Tears sprang to my eyes. "That's rubbish, Gogu, and you know it," I sniffed. "You're my dearest friend, my inseparable companion, and my wise advisor. You've got as much heart as any knight on horseback."

You say that.

"I mean it. I didn't take you tonight because I was worried I might lose you. That's the truth. If that happened, I couldn't bear it."

"Couldn't this wait until the morning?" Tati's voice was an exhausted whisper.

I laid my head on the pillow and closed my eyes, but I couldn't stop crying. Long after Tati had fallen asleep, I felt Gogu's small damp form jump onto the linen beside my face, and his tongue came out to lick my tears away.

After our Dark of the Moon journey, the idea of our party—which I had hoped might be the solution to several problems—became faintly ridiculous. We were bound to it, nonetheless. The invitations had gone out and acceptances had begun to come in—more than Aunt Bogdana had expected, for she had wondered whether the rumors that were sweeping the valley about us and our home would keep folk away. It seemed that curiosity outweighed fear.

The castle was being given a top-to-toe cleanup by women from the local area. I heard whispered stories about Night People, and about Drăguţa the witch, as our helpers scrubbed and dusted and polished—and I tried to ignore them. I had a story of my own, and I had not yet told it to Tati.

If I was right about what that vision meant—the two children lost in the forest—I owed it to her to tell her the truth about Sorrow. His parting words had seemed to confirm what I believed: that he was in some kind of servitude to the Night

People, with his sister's safety the price of obedience. I wondered why he had not told Tati himself.

I held back from giving my sister the news. Once she heard that Sorrow was, in fact, a human boy who had strayed into the Other Kingdom and been kept there for years, growing into a man far away from his own people, how would she ever be persuaded to give him up? The cruel thing about it was that even if he was a mortal man, he was still beyond her reach as sweetheart, lover, or husband. It seemed that he and his sister had been living in the Other Kingdom since they were children. One could not stay so long in Drǎguţa's realm without partaking of food and drink. Tadeusz had lured them and kept them; kept them too long. They would never be able to live in our world again. They might both be halfway toward becoming Night People by now, or worse. And if Sorrow could not stay here, the solution Tati might seize on would be for her to go there. I knew her kind heart. As soon as I told her his story, that was what she would want. Even if it meant a future in that shadowy, cruel realm we had glimpsed at Dark of the Moon, I thought she would do it for him.

I could hold back from divulging the story, of course. I did not plan to tell her of my other vision in Drǎguţa's mirror: that of a young man with green eyes whom I had thought for a wonderful moment I could love, until the image revealed the monster beneath. I had no idea what that meant. Perhaps it was a warning not to trust too easily. I had not passed on Anastasia's crushing words to me, nor the news that it had been my sister whom Tadeusz had wanted all along. Indeed, Tati and I had hardly spoken of our experience since we came home, despite our younger sisters' volleys of questions.

Paula was our most reliable source of information on just about anything to do with the Other Kingdom. I seized my opportunity to quiz her while we were doing the final hemming on our party gowns. The two of us had taken our work up to a little tower room where the light was good. Our only companion was Gogu, crouched down in a roll of green silk thread, sulking. He still hadn't entirely forgiven me and, in a way, I could see his point.

"Paula, I want to ask you something."

"Mmm?"

"When people go to the Other Kingdom and stay there, they can't ever come back, can they? Not if they've been eating the food."

She nodded. "Everybody knows that."

"But folk do come back sometimes. I've heard stories of people vanishing and being gone for hundreds of years, and then suddenly appearing in the woods again. They're out of their wits, usually. So it must be possible."

"Time works differently there," said Paula, pushing her spectacles higher on her nose and peering closely at her sewing. "It can be quicker or slower than our time, whatever they want it to be. You might be gone for years and years in our time, but you'd only have been in the Other Kingdom a day or less. You might not have touched the food. That's why people go mad. Imagine coming back and finding everyone you knew had been dead for a hundred years. Why do you want to know that, Jena? I wish you'd tell us what happened that night."

I shuddered. "It was horrible. Dark and cruel. I don't want any of you even thinking about such things. Be glad you didn't see it."

Paula gave me a funny look. "How did you get there?" she asked me.

I ignored the question. "Paula, what if someone from the Other Kingdom wanted to stay in our world? Is the rule the same?"

"I don't know, Jena. Anyway, I suspect the rules can be broken if Drăguţa decides that's the right thing. I've wondered whether the only reason anyone can cross over is her deciding to let it happen."

I looked at her. "Really? Tati said that, too: that the way we open the portal doesn't mean anything special; that it's only because Drăguţa approves that we can go to the Other Kingdom at all. At Dark of the Moon, once we'd gotten back across the Deadwash, we just walked home."

"Is this about Sorrow?" Paula was astute as ever.

"I can't say. I have to talk to Tati first. There's something I need to tell her."

Cezar had been asking questions of his own. It was clear to me that he did not believe our explanation for being out at night. But since we maintained our story about strange noises, and Petru managed to back us up without quite telling lies, my cousin made no progress in his search for answers. Cezar was edgy; his ill temper manifested itself without warning, and nobody was safe from his sharp tongue. I gathered from Ivan that more and more of the valley men were trying to get out of the hunting party. It had been many days since Ivona's death. With nothing useful discovered, and not so much as a sniff of a Night Person detected, folk were starting to say they'd rather be safe in bed behind a locked door at night and spend their energies by day looking after their stock and keeping their families fed and warm. Someone had suggested, behind my cousin's back, that continuing the hunt could only offend the folk of the wild-wood further—that Cezar risked bringing down another act of violence on the community. A group of the local men made a formal request that the master of Vârful cu Negură erect a new crucifix on the slopes above the mill, and Cezar agreed to pay for it. But he was angry, and we crept around the house as if on eggshells, trying to keep out of his way.

With seven days to go until Full Moon and the party, Aunt Bogdana paid us a visit to check on the supper arrangements. While she was closeted with Florica and her helpers, deep in discussion of pies and puddings, I took Tati up to the tower room. I bolted the door and told her my theory about what I had seen of Sorrow in Drăguţa's mirror.

"So I owe you an apology, if I'm right about what it means," I said at the end of my account. "It seems as if Sorrow isn't one of the Night People—he isn't even from the Other Kingdom. Or wasn't. But he's trapped there now, he and his little sister. I didn't like seeing her there, Tati. It looked as if they were making her watch: as if she'd been shown so many bad things that she hardly understood what they were anymore."

"But why didn't he *say*?" It was clear she believed my theory.

Her eyes were wide with horror. "Why didn't he tell me? This is terrible, Jena! We have to help them. I must go there at Full Moon. I must talk to Ileana—"

"No," I said, before she could work herself up any further. "You're not going—not this time. We have our own party, remember? We all have to appear at that. Cezar's suspicious enough already without any of us going missing. Besides, I don't know how we could help. From what Sorrow said when we were leaving, he's obliged to do the Night People's bidding in order to stop worse harm from coming to his sister. And the Night People are powerful. Ileana didn't even put in an appearance at their revels. You must have felt it, Tati—the way they twist and turn things, and meddle with your thoughts. Against that kind of strength, we're like little feathers drifting on a stream, carried along wherever it decides to take us."

"You said yourself"—Tati was fixing me with her eyes—"that Sorrow should ask Drǎguţa for help. She's supposed to be the real power of the wildwood. Couldn't she change things, if we explained how important it is?"

"You make it sound easy. I don't even know where she is. I don't think anyone does. Anyway, if she really is so powerful, why has she let the Night People keep Sorrow and his sister prisoner so long? Even if they can never come back to their old lives, at least in Ileana's world they wouldn't be . . . well, slaves, or whatever they are."

Tati's voice was a whisper. "Are you saying you don't believe in Drǎguţa? Are you saying you don't believe there's a power in the wildwood that's strong enough to defeat evil, Jena?"

I felt as if I were suddenly teetering on a precipice.

Of course we believe. Every morning, when I wake up on your pillow, I see that certainty in your eyes, Jena.

"Of course there is, Tati. We have to believe it." I thought of the little crown that I had decided, for a reason I did not understand, to leave behind in the forest. "And if it's safe for us to go across at next Full Moon—the one after the party—I suppose we can ask Ileana what to do."

The day of the party came, and Piscul Dracului began to fill with guests. Every chamber that was even slightly suitable had been dusted and mopped, bed linen had been borrowed and quilts aired. Space had been cleared in our stables for many horses. Our activities had provided work for almost everyone in the settlement, and I imagined it was costing Cezar a pretty penny. Folk came early—wanting to be safely within our walls before dusk fell—then retired to their chambers to rest before the party began.

I felt sick with nerves. I wished I had never had such a mad idea. How could I make polite conversation with suitable young men and their mothers when I was all churned up with worry about the Night People and Sorrow and what Cezar might do if he found out the truth? He'd been questioning Florica and Petru further, I knew it: I could see the signs of strain on their faces as they went steadily about their work.

At the appointed time, I ran upstairs from the kitchen, where I had been helping with some last-minute baking. I found Tati sitting on our bed, still in her working dress, and

Iulia with her shawl on over the gray creation and a forbidding look on her face. Paula had a pair of heavy irons heating on our little stove. She was pressing Stela's frock with each in turn.

"You'd better start getting ready," I told Tati. "Aunt Bogdana wants us to help her formally greet the guests as they come down." I got into the crimson gown, wishing Aunt had not told the seamstress to make it quite so tight in the bodice or so low in the neck. In this dress, I certainly didn't look flat-chested. "Iulia, would you mind doing my hair?"

When the time came, I went downstairs alone. Tati muttered that she would come later. I thought she would put in an appearance, if only for the sake of avoiding Cezar's attention, but it was clear that she intended to play as small a part in the festivities as she could get away with. Since Iulia was refusing to come down early in the gray gown and Paula was occupied with helping Stela get dressed, it fell to me to stand beside Cezar and my aunt to greet the first arrivals. In the crimson gown I felt as though everyone was staring at me. Iulia had pinned my hair up high, exposing my neck and upper chest, and Cezar's eyes had gone straight to me the moment I appeared in the party chamber. I would have felt very much alone in the crowd if I had not had Gogu nestled safely in my pocket. After Dark of the Moon, I hadn't dared suggest he stay upstairs.

The weather was bitterly cold. Outside, men from Vârful cu Negură were leading horses away to the shelter of the stables and setting chocks under the wheels of carts. The kitchen was full of women from the neighborhood, putting finishing touches to pastries and sweetmeats under Florica's supervision. In the grand room with the pillars, where a fire on the broad hearth was smoking more than was quite desirable, the air was chilly. The village band sat in the little gallery, blowing on their fingers.

"It will warm up when everyone's down," Aunt Bogdana whispered in my ear. "Now, be especially sweet to that lady in the purple, Jena—her son stands to inherit a very grand estate near Sibiu, and the uncle's a *voivode*. Ah, Elsvieta, how delightful to see you! Paul, how are you? And this is your son? Vlad, is it? Allow me to introduce my niece. . . ."

One by one, my sisters came downstairs to join the increasing crowd. Paula—uncomfortable in her pink—had a forced smile on her face as she greeted Aunt Bogdana's friends. Stela, who did in fact look charming in her lacy dress, glanced desperately around for anyone her own age. No Ildephonsus here; no friends for dances and daisy chains. If these folk had younger sons and daughters, they had left them behind, in the care of servants. At least Stela could plead weariness and go to bed early.

Next down was Iulia. There was a ripple of disapproval as she came along the line, and I heard a whistle, *sotto voce*, from one of the young men. Now the shawl was gone, I saw that the neckline of the gray gown had been drastically altered and a generous expanse of winter-pale flesh was on view. The kind of bodice our aunt had deemed acceptable on me was decidedly immodest on Iulia, with her far more womanly figure. For a thirteen-year-old, the gown was shockingly inappropriate. As if to have the last laugh on Aunt Bogdana, Iulia had sewn a tiny frill of fine lawn across the plunging décolletage, a wisp of transparent fabric that only served to emphasize what was on show. Her shoulders were back; she held her head high. Cezar was staring, and so was every other young man present. Aunt Bogdana's cheeks went scarlet.

"Good evening, Aunt," said my sister. "Good evening, Cezar." Her smile was sweet, her eyes sparkling. I saw that she felt like a woman—she felt beautiful.

Cezar's eyes raked over her. He did not smile. "Go back upstairs and fetch a shawl," he said. "Cover yourself up before your guests."

Iulia went white. It was as if he had hit her. She turned without a word and fled. Perhaps Cezar thought this had been a prank; I recognized it as simply a misguided attempt to be more grown-up. Paula excused herself and made for the stairs.

"Jenica," said Aunt Bogdana loudly, pretending that nothing had happened, "this is Raffaello, son of my acquaintance Maria Cataneo and her husband, Andrei."

Raffaello was tall and pimply. He bowed over my hand and introduced his friend Anghel, who was short and had a weak chin. Gogu stuck his head out of the pocket for a better look, and I squashed him back in. The music began—something not too lively, out of respect for the family's recent loss. I wished Uncle Nicolae were here tonight, with his twinkling eyes and bluff humor.

"They say your elder sister is a rare beauty," said Raffaello. Evidently this was his idea of starting a conversation.

"Yes, they do," I said. "She'll be down soon, I expect."

There was a little silence. Anghel cleared his throat.

"You enjoy hunting?" Raffaello asked, his eyes scanning the crowd.

"Not much," I said. "And since my uncle's recent death, even less."

"Mmm-hm," he responded, proving that he was not listening. *A fool. An idiot. Strike him off the list.*

"I'm so sorry," said weasel-faced Anghel, who was paying marginally more attention. "A terrible tragedy—"

Before I could say a thing, Cezar was beside me. "Mother seems to think that dancing is in order," he said. The look in his eyes made the two young men step backward. "Jena, will you honor me with the first?"

"I suppose that would be appropriate, Cezar." This was going to be the longest night of my life. "You upset Iulia."

"Your sister requires discipline. Lacking your father's presence, and in view of the evident inability of Tatiana and yourself to provide strong guidance, the job falls to me. Iulia must learn not to make a spectacle of herself."

I thought of poor Iulia's stricken face and the fact that even in the unseemly gown, she had looked remarkably pretty. "Discipline," I echoed, with my heart full of resentment—not least because, in part, he was right. "Maybe so. But discipline should be administered kindly, don't you think? Girls of Iulia's age are so easily hurt."

"I've no interest in talking about your sisters tonight, Jena," Cezar said, drawing me closer as the dance began. "Let us enjoy the evening. Mother tells me you're all novices at dancing. Do you know any of the steps to this one?"

I looked into his eyes and shook my head.

"Never mind," he said. "I'm expert at leading."

Do we have to put up with this?

"You haven't brought that wretched frog, I hope?"

"I always bring him, Cezar. Don't worry, I'll keep him in my pocket, out of sight."

But not out of earshot. Why are you dancing with him?

Grimly I danced, trying to ignore Gogu. As Cezar and I moved about the room—and as I discovered how hard it is to dance badly when the skill of doing it well comes naturally—my sisters returned to the party: Iulia, red-eyed, with an embroidered silk shawl artfully draped across her cleavage, and Paula by her side. And Tati. I faltered, stepping hard on Cezar's foot. Tati, not in the blue and silver of Aunt Bogdana's choice, but ethereal in the pale butterfly gown, the gown that had been made to wear for Sorrow. It revealed a startling change in her appearance: she had lost more weight than I had realized. Her back was all bones, her arms fragile, her waist tiny. The pallor of her garb drew the eye to the strange pendant around her slender neck, a crimson drop of blood on the white skin. Her hair was newly washed—it hung, dark and lustrous, across her shoulders. There was not a trace of color in her face, save for the vivid violet-blue of her eyes.

"Tati's looking very unwell," observed Cezar, leading me through a complicated maneuver that turned me away from her.

"Mmm," I murmured, thinking I had better do as Aunt Bogdana had suggested and consult the herbalist. Under the bright lights of the party chamber, Tati looked not so much ethereal as wasted. It frightened me.

"A brighter color would have been more appropriate," he went on. "She looks quite washed-out. And it's important that she present herself at her best."

"Oh?" I would not help him through this particular conversation.

"Well," Cezar said, putting his hand on my waist as we made our way down the line, "isn't that what tonight is all about? Beginning the search for possible partners?"

"More or less," I said. "It's not something I particularly relish, Cezar. But I'm happy that your mother has enjoyed helping. And I suppose I should thank you for paying for everything. I don't imagine you actually wanted to."

He grunted some kind of response, and his hold on me tightened, brushing me up against him. In the formal line of the dance, I could not wriggle away. "You hope that Tatiana will attract the interest of these young men? You think any of them eligible?" He ran his eyes over those closest at hand; his expression was one of disdain.

"Aunt Bogdana chose them. They're all eligible. If Tati doesn't snare one, maybe I can." I attempted an insouciant laugh, without a great deal of success.

"You far outshine your sister tonight, Jena."

I stared at him, full of suspicion. His expression alarmed me. It was deadly serious.

"Besides," said Cezar, "for you, there is no need to go through this exercise—this fishing for suitable husbands."

"Really?" I remembered a conversation with Aunt Bogdana. "Because I'm the one destined to stay at home and tend to Father in his old age, you mean?"

"Don't tease, Jena," Cezar said. "You know what I mean."

I hate him. The frog was trembling with fury.

A horrible possibility suddenly occurred to me. I recalled

that awkward conversation with my cousin in the workroom, the one in which he had seemed on the point of some declaration. I thought of certain other things he had said recently, certain other gestures he had made. Surely I must be wrong. I was the sensible sister, not the beautiful one. Besides, even Cezar must see it was ludicrous. The two of us did nothing but argue.

The music came to an end. Across the room, I spotted Tati sitting quietly beside Aunt Bogdana and a group of older women. She looked like a grieving young widow. Shockingly, she looked as if she belonged there.

"You must dance with each of my sisters," I told Cezar. With Gogu in my pocket vibrating with ill will and my cousin's conversation troubling me more than I wanted to admit, I decided I would avoid Cezar for the rest of the evening. "And make sure you're nice to Iulia," I added. "Remember, she's only thirteen."

Cezar smiled at me. Then the pimply Raffaello asked me for the next dance, and my cousin let me go. I could feel the imprint of his hand on my waist, like a brand of ownership. Perhaps that *had* been what he meant: he and I. The look in his eyes had frightened me. It had been a look of utter certainty.

I danced with Raffaello, whom Gogu had already dismissed as an idiot. I danced with Anghel.

I can't see from in here. Put me on your shoulder.

Anghel glanced down: the wriggling form of the frog was clearly visible under the close-fitting skirt of the red gown.

"My pet frog," I muttered. "He would insist on coming."

Pet. The tone was accusatory.

"A frog?" Anghel struggled for words. "Or did you say a dog?"

"Er, no—although it's not unlike one of those little dogs, the kind ladies carry about . . . ," I babbled, hating myself.

"Yes, my mother has one," Anghel said, holding me at arm's length lest he come in contact with Gogu, even through a layer of fabric. "Hideous little thing. It sheds everywhere. One can't wear black."

"What a trial for you," I murmured, calculating how soon I could politely excuse myself.

Looks like a stoat. Gogu's head was out of the pocket. *Sounds even sillier than the first one. You can do better.*

I danced with Vlad, whose uncle was a *voivode.* Vlad was better-looking than the others—tall and broad-shouldered, with thick dark hair. His manners were exemplary. We chatted about the weather and the music. We talked about his home near Braşov and his horse and his hunting dogs. He complimented me on my hair and on the party, which Aunt Bogdana had told him I organized all by myself, and on the red gown. He asked me for a second dance and I accepted. He fetched a little platter of pastries, which we sat down to share. Gogu had retreated to the depths of the pocket. Quite against logic, the sense I was getting from him now was: *No. No. No.*

"I have to ask," said Vlad, smiling to reveal perfectly even white teeth, "whether it's true you have a pet frog. Someone told me you carry it around everywhere."

"Well, yes," I said cautiously. "His name's Gogu. I rescued him a few years ago."

I waited for the nice young man to shrink away, to make

an embarrassed comment, or to fall silent. Instead, he leaned forward.

"May I see?"

I was charmed. I got Gogu out and held him on my palm, where he embarrassed me by cowering in abject terror. "He's usually quite friendly," I said. "I don't know what's come over him."

Vlad reached out to touch, and such was the shock emanating from Gogu's small body that I drew my hand away.

"Oh, yes, I find them fascinating," Vlad enthused. "I have a big collection myself, you know. It's a special study of mine."

"Really?" I began to wonder whether it was possible that there might be a man who was not only eligible, but genuinely suitable—someone I could actually come to like. From over by the hearth, Cezar was staring at us with an expression dark as a thundercloud.

"Yes, I have one of every species to be found in the Carpathian region, and a number of more exotic ones as well. But nothing quite like your little fellow. I can't tell exactly what he is. You realize how very unusual it is for him to be active in winter. A scientific curiosity of the first order."

"Yes, well, I think Gogu's one of a kind," I said.

"I can see that we have a great deal in common, Jenica," said Vlad. "I'll ask Mother if she can arrange a return visit in the spring—I could show you my laboratory. I've devised a wonderful new method for preserving my specimens. They keep more or less indefinitely, you know. I start with a few drops of ether on a cloth, and then—"

"Excuse me." I felt sick. In my hands, Gogu was trembling like a leaf. "I think I hear Aunt Bogdana calling me."

I fled to the safe company of my aunt and her friends. Tati was no longer with them. I scanned the crowded room, wondering whether she had gone back upstairs already.

"Tatiana is such a lovely dancer," observed my aunt's friend Elsvieta. "And what an exquisite gown . . ."

"If it's possible to obtain something similar," said another woman, "I think your son will be flooded with orders after tonight, Bogdana."

"You're a nice little dancer, too, Jenica," Elsvieta went on, smiling at me. "I could see my son was enjoying himself. Vlad is rather too fond of his own company and his experiments. I hope you may come to visit us in the spring. A little riding, perhaps, and some music. It would be so good for him."

"I'm sure Jena would welcome that," said Aunt Bogdana, alarming me. "If her father approves, of course. We hope very much that Teodor will be home by springtime. Jena, who is that young man dancing with your sister?"

I looked across the room and froze. Maybe there was no black coat tonight, but I knew instantly who it was, and my heart filled with terror. Tati was in a trance, moving in his arms like a graceful bird. Sorrow wore a mask—black, of course—which didn't do much to disguise his snow-pale skin and burning dark eyes. He had made some concessions to the nature of the gathering. His hair was tied back at the nape of the neck, and he wore a white shirt under a traditional waistcoat: black, embroidered with red flowers. Black trousers and boots completed the outfit. Around his neck was our mother's silver chain. He held Tati reverently, as if she were the one thing he valued in the world. Their eyes remained locked as they went through the steps of the dance—there might as well have been nobody else here.

"He dances well," commented Elsvieta. "But he does look rather . . . *intense*. Who is he, Jena?"

I thought frantically. "Er—I think he came up with Judge Rinaldo's son, Lucian," I mumbled. "I'm not sure what his name is."

"The mask is too much of an affectation," said another woman. "But he's quite striking, isn't he, with that very dark hair and the pale complexion? Your sister certainly seems to think so."

I looked around wildly for Cezar and saw him near the passageway to the kitchen, talking to Iulia. He looked distracted and she looked miserable. I muttered an excuse and dived into the crowd. What was Sorrow thinking? Did the man have a death wish? And how could Tati have encouraged him? They'd planned this—the butterfly dress proved that. I had to get rid of him now, immediately. If Cezar realized where Sorrow had come from, our sedate party would descend into violent, bloody tragedy.

They had left the hall before I reached the spot where I had seen them—close to the steps up to the terrace from which Tati and I had made our terrifying passage to the Other Kingdom at Dark of the Moon. The door stood slightly open. Through the gap, the freezing air of the winter night seeped into the crowded chamber.

I went halfway up the steps before I called. "Tati?" I glanced back over my shoulder. Beyond the half-open door, the music played on—nobody had followed me. I went higher. "Tati, where are you?"

At one end of the parapet, a long black coat lay neatly folded on the wall. At the other end stood my sister and her lover. Tati's arms were wound around Sorrow's neck, her body pressed close to his, as if she would melt into him. His hands were enlaced in my sister's long hair as he strained her slight form against him, white on black. Their eyes were closed; their lips clung; they were lost in each other. It was beautiful and powerful. It was impossible. I cleared my throat, and they opened their eyes and turned to look at me.

"If Cezar sees you, he'll kill you," I said bluntly, picking up the black coat. "You must leave now, right away. How could you risk yourself like this? Tati, come inside."

Sorrow took the coat. He did not put it on.

"Jena, just a moment longer," pleaded Tati.

"Now!" I hissed. "Do you want to see him run through with a pitchfork? Sorrow, go, please! Just go!" As I spoke, I heard someone coming through the door at the foot of the steps, and a voice.

"Jena?" It was Cezar.

Sorrow slung the coat over his shoulder. He reached out, and Tati threw her arms around him, burying her face against his chest. He stroked her hair, murmuring something.

"Jena, are you up there?" Cezar sounded anxious rather than suspicious.

"I'm just coming down!" I called in what I hoped was a

casual tone. I jerked my head violently toward the other end of the terrace as Sorrow disengaged himself from my sister once more. Anastasia had used some kind of portal to reach the Other Kingdom from here—I hoped he could do the same. "Go!" I mouthed. "Now!"

"It's freezing cold out here, Jena, and you don't even have a shawl. You'll catch your death!" I could hear my cousin's heavy tread as he climbed the steps.

Tati was standing frozen, her eyes on her lover as he swung up onto the parapet. "Goodbye," she whispered.

"Goodbye," Sorrow said, and, slipping his arms into the black coat, he stepped off the wall and into space. I sucked in my breath, then let it out as Cezar appeared at the top of the steps.

"Come inside, girls," he said. "Get warm by the fire. Jena? Are you all right?"

Tati walked past him, unseeing, and vanished down the stairs. I wanted to go to the parapet: to look over, to see whether Sorrow lay among the trees far below like a broken doll.

"I'm sorry to have worried you, Cezar," I said shakily. "I needed some fresh air."

"Maybe we can find a quiet corner, just the two of us, eh?" He put his arm around me. Under the circumstances, I let him. Anything to distract him from the oddity of the situation. "Come, my dear, let's go in."

As we made our way down, it came to me that a sudden descent from a castle wall might present no difficulties at all for Sorrow. He had been in the Other Kingdom a long time. Perhaps he had indeed changed: become less like a human and more like one of *them*. Maybe he'd gone through a portal; when Anastasia had taken us across, it had felt like falling. But maybe he could spread out his black coat and fly like a bat. I shivered. That had been too close, by far.

"It's all right, Jena," said Cezar. "I'm here."

Chapter Ten

My heart, still thumping from Sorrow's narrow escape, slowed with relief when Cezar left me to go off and find the quiet corner he had mentioned. I kept myself very busy: first chatting to Aunt Bogdana, then dancing with Răzvan and Daniel and some other young men, whose names I instantly forgot. Gogu's comments were predictable:

Too tall, you'd get a sore neck just talking to him.

This one smells.

Lavender silk. What more need I say?

I imagined a different face on my partner: a tangle of dark hair, a sweet mouth, wary green eyes. Beside the man in Drăguţa's mirror, tonight's collection of suitors seemed entirely without character. Then, in my imagination, I heard my sisters' screams as the green-eyed man turned to something monstrous, and I knew how foolish it was to let myself think of him. Dark of the Moon had opened up a realm of peril—dream about it too much and I might be drawn into forgetting my sense of right and wrong. *This world,* I told myself sternly. *These suitors, this life. If you want your family to be safe, if you want to protect Piscul Dracului, this is the way.*

I kept watch over my sisters, something that was second nature from our visits to Dancing Glade. I spotted Tati and Stela retreating upstairs together—Stela stifling a yawn, Tati drifting along at her side. Iulia was talking to Răzvan. Whatever he was saying to her, it had coaxed a smile to her face.

The supply of pastries began to run short, and people still seemed to be hungry. I headed for the kitchen to check with Florica. As I entered the passageway, my cousin stepped out of the shadows and grabbed me by the arm, making me gasp in fright. There was nobody else around.

"Don't do that!" I snapped as my heartbeat slowly returned to its normal pace.

"Are you trying to avoid me, Jena?" Cezar asked, not letting go. "I need to talk to you alone. I said so when we came inside, but you're always somewhere else. Come and share some țuică. Rest for a little." When I opened my mouth to tell him that Aunt Bogdana had asked me to come straight back, he added, "I have something to say to you. You must know what it is. Jena, this needs to be in private."

I glanced around frantically. The sound of laughter and clinking platters filtered up from the party. From the other end, behind the closed kitchen doors, came the sound of scrubbing: Florica and her assistants, starting to clean up. In the middle, Cezar and I stood in our own little patch of awkward silence.

"If you've got something to say, better just go ahead," I told him.

He had held on to my arm all this time. Now he grabbed the other arm as well. I had my back to the wall, and his face was unpleasantly close to mine. I could smell *ţuică* on his breath. I gritted my teeth.

Get on with it, wretch.

"You know what it is. You know how much I want you, Jena. You look wonderful in that red gown. I can't keep my eyes off you. Jena, you will marry me, won't you?" The words came out in a rush. Before I could draw breath—let alone start to say I wouldn't marry him if he were the last man in all Transylvania—Cezar bent forward and kissed me.

I had often dreamed of my first proper kiss, though the dreams had not contained a particular man, just a vague idea of one. The kiss itself, I knew all about. It would be tender and sweet and exciting all at once. It would make my knees go weak, and at the same time it would make me feel safe, and loved, and beautiful.

The touch of Cezar's mouth on mine destroyed every trace of that dream. His kiss was not about love or tenderness. It was a kiss of possession, and it bruised my lips and wounded my heart. When he was done, I wrenched my arms from his grip and stood there shaking, using all the strength I had to stop myself from hitting him.

Tell him.

I drew a deep breath. There were words bursting to get out of me—furious, hurtful words. Though I was shaking with humiliation, I kept them back. Cezar held power in our household. If Father died, that power would become absolute. My refusal would offend my cousin, there was no avoiding that. But I must do it as tactfully as I could. He had the capacity to cause terrible damage to all the people I loved.

"Thank you for your proposal," I said in a tight voice. "Cezar, this just wouldn't work, you and I. We're too different. We don't think alike. We don't enjoy the same things. We'd argue all the time, and be desperately unhappy—"

"Jena, Jena, Jena," he muttered, moving in close again. He pressed his body up against mine and put his lips against my ear. "You don't mean that. Haven't we been friends since we were small children? All lovers quarrel, that's the way things are. Besides, this solves the problem of your father's estate. I'm family already. I'm sure this is what Uncle Teodor would want. Come on, Jena, you're just teasing me. . . ."

His hand went down the front of the red gown, and my rage finally got the better of me. In the pocket, squashed between Cezar and me, Gogu was quivering with fury. "Stop it!" I shouted, and hit Cezar across the cheek, hard. "Don't you dare touch me like that! What do you think I am, some girl who lets every drunken oaf pinch and fondle her in dark corners? I'm not going to marry you, Cezar, and if I have anything to do with it, nor are any of my sisters. Don't ever put your hands on me again. I'm saving that privilege for my future husband. And there's one thing plain as a pikestaff: that won't be *you!*" I turned on my heel and marched off to the kitchen, and I didn't look back.

After the guests had retired for the night, I retreated to our bedchamber, exhausted and distressed. My mind hardly had room to hold the double shock of Sorrow's foolhardy appearance in our midst and Cezar's crude behavior.

I took off the red gown, knowing that I would never wear it again, and slipped into my night robe. I put Gogu on the side table. Stela was asleep. Tati lay in bed with her eyes open. The others were sitting on Iulia's bed, conversing in whispers. Nobody looked happy. On some level, perhaps, our party had been a success, but the possibility of finding suitors we genuinely liked seemed farther away than ever. I remembered Tati saying once that the Other Kingdom might spoil us for life in our own world, because nothing could ever match up to it. Tonight I was beginning to wonder whether that was true.

"Jena!" exclaimed Paula as I turned and she caught sight of my face. "You look terrible! It wasn't as bad as that, was it?"

I cleared my throat. "Cezar just proposed to me," I said. "I turned him down." I had not planned to tell them just yet—the hurt of his abusive kiss was still raw. The words had spilled out despite myself.

There was a stunned silence. Even Tati stared at me, getting up on her elbow to do so.

"True," I said. "He kissed me, and groped me, and it was disgusting. I tried to be nice about refusing, but I lost my temper. I've made him angry. Even angrier than he was before." I poured water into Gogu's bowl. There was comfort in the small daily routine.

"I bet he thinks you're a challenge," said Paula.

"Yes, like wild boar to be hunted," I said. "If I married him, he wouldn't be satisfied until he'd crushed the last spark of spirit in me. I can't think how he ever believed I'd say yes." But, I thought, perhaps underneath the man who seemed hungry for power and dominance—the one who feared the Other Kingdom so much he felt bound to destroy it—a little boy still existed: the solemn child who had idolized his big brother, and had felt responsible for an even smaller cousin since the day tragedy struck the three of them. Perhaps he had always believed that one day he and I would be together. If so, it was sad. I would never marry him—his touch disgusted me, and his anger frightened me.

I snuffed out the last candle and got into bed beside Tati. I could not even begin to talk to her. Curiously, as the image of my sister and her lover wrapped in each other's arms came to my mind, what I felt most strongly seemed to be envy. To love like that, to be so lost in it that you forgot everything else in the world, must be a wonderful feeling—powerful and joyous. I wished the green-eyed man in the mirror could be what he had seemed at first. I wanted him to be real, and to love me, and not to be a monster from the Other Kingdom. Why did things have to keep twisting around and going dark when all I was trying to do was keep my family safe and live my life the way Father would expect? Tears began to trickle down my cheeks.

A little later, Gogu hopped across and settled damply on the pillow.

"Jena?"

I had not expected Tati to say anything. "Mmm?"

"Thank you."

"For what?"

"You saved Sorrow tonight. If you hadn't warned us, Cezar would have seen him. Caught him. I didn't think you would do that."

"You can't have thought I'd stand by and let Cezar run him through with whatever was handy."

"No, of course not," Tati said in a murmur. "But you still want the problem to be gone, don't you? You're still hoping Ileana will send them away and that I'll never see him again. You were angry with us."

"Of course I was angry," I said. "He must never come here again, Tati. Did you plan this? How?"

"I see him sometimes in the woods." Her whisper was barely audible. "I told him about the party. I didn't think he would come, Jena, truly."

"He shouldn't have. It's not just Cezar he has to fear, or the other men of the valley. Coming here to see you might get him in trouble with Tadeusz as well." I thought of the terrible things I had seen at Dark of the Moon—the imaginative ways the Night People had devised for tormenting those human folk unlucky enough to become their slaves. I remembered Anastasia telling me that Tadeusz wanted Sorrow to see him with Tati. That would be a very particular kind of torture. "Sorrow must love you very much," I said, "to take such a risk for you. Please don't do this again, and please don't go out into the forest looking for him. Promise me."

"All right. As long as we go across at next Full Moon."

"I think," I said grimly, "that's going to depend on Cezar. Good night, Tati. Sweet dreams, Gogu." I did not tell my sister how much Sorrow's leap from the wall had troubled me; how it seemed to me that if he could do that, he was no longer so different from the folk who had captured him as a child. I wondered what they ate in the realm of the Night People, he and his poor sister. I fell asleep with dark images in my mind. My dreams were a chaotic jumble of angry voices and violent hands.

Cezar didn't say a word about what had happened. In fact, he seemed to be on his best behavior with all of us. Still, I was suspicious. It wasn't like Cezar to forgive and forget.

The conduct of the business had been taken right out of my hands. Cezar claimed Father's desk and told me, politely enough, that for the rest of winter there would be no figures for me to reconcile since his own people at Vârful cu Negură would deal with everything. In short, there was nothing for me to do, and no reason for me to be in the workroom. He didn't actually say this last part, perhaps knowing the explosion it would generate, but he made the message clear.

I protested, but not for long. To tell the truth, after the night of our party, I could hardly bear to talk to my cousin. I was finding it hard to sleep. When I did, my dreams were tangled and distressing. I'd be dancing with a young man: not Cezar, or the odious Vlad of the frog experiments, or any of the folk from Ileana's glade, but a man with green eyes and unkempt dark hair, who held me firmly but gently and smiled his funny smile as he looked at me. I'd feel radiant with happiness, full of a contentment I had never known before, not even on the most thrilling of all our nights of Full Moon dancing. Then the man would bend his head to say something—perhaps *Trust me, Jena*—

and his face would change to the grotesquely ugly thing I had seen in Drăguţa's mirror. Around me, the bright chamber would fade away. The light would become livid, green and purple, and sounds of screaming would fill my ears. My partner's sweet smile would become a grimace—all long, sharp teeth and pale, flicking tongue. I would wake up covered in cold sweat, my heart racing in terror. Sometimes I shouted and woke my sisters. Sometimes my dream was different: in this one, I was chasing Tati through the forest as someone led her away. Whether it was Sorrow or Tadeusz I could not see. I ran and ran, and the harder I tried the farther ahead they moved, until they reached a cliff top looking out over a great ravine filled with mist. *Jump,* said the man, and as I tried to reach her, my sister leaped out to be swallowed up by the vapor.

I kept these dreams to myself, but the memory of them was with me even in waking hours. To keep the nightmares at bay, I tried to make plans. I must get a letter to Father somehow, without Cezar knowing. A truthful letter, perhaps addressed to Gabriel, in which I set out what I could about our problems and let them know how badly we needed help. Who would take it? The snow still lay in heavy drifts, piled up against walls, blanketing roofs, burdening trees. Winters were long in the Carpathians. A possible solution presented itself—but I did not write the letter, not yet. Cezar had a habit of reading anything left lying around.

The days passed. The young men helped Petru with the farm chores, which was a good thing. They also accompanied us girls anywhere we went outside the castle, which was not so good. Cezar had tightened his watchfulness, and it became near-impossible for any of us to slip away for a solitary walk. I spent a lot of time in the tower room, a favorite haunt for me and Gogu. Piscul Dracului was full of nooks and crannies. I liked the notion that however long we lived here, there would always be new ones to discover. This particular tower had seven arched windows with views out over snowy wood-land, and the ceiling was blue, with stars on it. A long time ago I had brought an old fur rug up here and a pile of threadbare cushions.

I was lying on my back on the rug, looking up at the painted stars and doing my best not to think of our problems. Gogu was perched on my midriff, unusually still.

"We're not going to talk about anything bad today, Gogu," I told him. "We're going to discuss only things we like. You start."

It was your idea. You start.

"Paddling in the stream in springtime," I said. "Making pan-cakes. The smell of a wood fire. The sound of a waterfall."

Gogu made no response.

"Come on," I said, a little disheartened. "You must be able to think of one good thing."

Sleeping on our pillow, side by side.

"Mmm-hm." His choice surprised me. "If I go a long way back, my memory's full of good things. We used to fill up the day with adventures. Skating in winter—not on the Dead-wash, of course—and swimming in summer, though we weren't actually supposed to, not when we were playing with Costi and Cezar. Aunt Bogdana had the idea that it wasn't appropriate for boys and girls to strip off their clothes and swim together, even though we were only little."

She thought you'd catch cold.

"How could you know that? I bet you weren't even born then."

No response.

"Actually," I told him, "you're probably right. Aunt Bogdana adored Costi. I suppose I was lucky she let him out to play at all."

Green.

"What?"

Nice things. Green is nice. Your green gown with the deep pocket.

I smiled and stroked his back with my finger. "Gogu," I asked him, "do you think I've been unfair to Cezar? He was all right as a little boy. But he's grown up so obnoxious and so sure of himself and . . . well, I am actually quite scared of him. He's so much bigger and stronger than any of us, and people don't stand up to him when they should."

A pause, then: *I thought we were only talking about things we like. Your brown hair, so soft—lovely to hide in.*

"Hmm," I murmured, surprised again. I wasn't sure how I felt about this description, which would have been apt for a favorite bit of undergrowth. "Father coming home. That'll be the best thing of all. Father coming home fit and well—and *soon.*"

True love.

I lifted my head off the musty cushion and stared at him. "True love is looking less and less likely, if it's my future you're talking about," I said. "Or do you mean Tati and Sorrow? That's not a good thing—it's a disaster waiting to happen. We weren't meant to be talking about that."

True love is the best thing. It's the thing that makes troubles go away.

"Even for frogs?" I couldn't help asking.

Gogu's eyes closed to slits, and he went silent on me.

"Gogu, I was joking," I said, sitting up and, in the process, dislodging him onto the fur rug. "I know you're not an ordinary frog. It's just that . . ."

He hopped off the rug and concealed himself somewhere on the elaborate mosaic floor, which was patterned with tiny dragons. In the muted blues and greens and grays of the tiling, I could see nothing of him.

"Gogu," I said, "come out, please. There's enough trouble right now without you and me getting cross with each other. If I upset you, I'm sorry."

Not a twitch.

"Gogu," I said, kneeling on the tiles and waiting for him to move so I could pounce, "if you would tell me what you are and where you come from, it might make things between us far easier. You've never said. You've never given me even the tiniest clue. We're supposed to trust each other better than anyone, aren't we? Surely it would be easy enough just to *say*. I always tell *you* the truth." I realized that this was no longer accurate: I had not told him much at all about my visit to Tadeusz's dark revels. I had not told him about the young man in the mirror, or about what Anastasia had said to me. He'd been too upset and too angry with me to hear it. As for what he really was, I had long ago given up trying to guess. To me he was simply Gogu, and perfect just as he was. It was a shame he was increasingly unhappy with that. "If you don't like it when I treat you as a frog," I went on, "maybe you should be honest with me and tell me exactly what you are."

He made no appearance. His mind remained shut tight against me. Gogu was expert at camouflage. It took a hammering at the door to startle him into moving; I picked him up, my heart thumping, and went to open it. Paula was standing outside, her expression anxious.

"I'm sorry to disturb you," she said. "I know you probably came up here to be by yourself. But Florica's crying. I know Cezar's been asking her questions. She's really upset, Jena. I heard her say something about leaving Piscul Dracului. I think you'd better come."

In the kitchen, Florica was shaping rolls on the table while Stela made little dogs and gnomes and trees out of the scraps. Our housekeeper's distress was obvious. Her eyes were red and swollen and she would not look up at me, even when I spoke to her by name. As she lifted a roll from the table to the tray, I could see her hands shaking. Iulia, who was feeding wood into the stove, gave me a meaningful look as I came in. They were all expecting me to put things right. It was alarming that my family still had such faith in my ability to solve problems—thus far, I had been a woeful failure.

"Florica," I said, coming over to sit at the table, "what's wrong?"

"Nothing, Mistress Jenica." The formality of this address told me that something was badly amiss.

"Come on, Florica, tell me. You've been crying. It *is* something."

Florica muttered a few words about not getting us into trouble and not making things any worse. A moment later she sat down abruptly, her shoulders shaking.

"He said . . ."

"What, Florica?"

"Master Cezar's been asking questions around the valley—trying to find out about things so he can go ahead with these plans of his. Someone mentioned Full Moon to him, Jena—told him that was a time when barriers were open. He's taken it into his head that you and Mistress Tati know something you're not telling him."

"Why would this upset you so much, Florica?" I had taken over the task of forming the dough into rolls while Iulia had started brewing tea. Stela put a small arm around Florica's shoulders.

"He said if we didn't tell him everything we knew, he'd see that we lost our places here. He said we were too old to work. I've been here since I was fifteen, Mistress Jena. Petru's been in the valley even longer. We've given good service all our lives. Piscul Dracului is our home. And Ivan has enough mouths to feed already—we can't expect him to take us in as well. Master Cezar wouldn't really send us away, would he?"

"Father's still the head of this household," I told her firmly. "You know he'd never send you or Petru away. You belong here. Florica, if you've told Cezar something, you'd better let us know what it was."

"He asked about Full Moon: whether you went out at

night, whether there had been folk hanging about in the woods, odd folk. I said no, that Full Moon was a night when you girls kept to your bedchamber, and that there was never a peep out of you, although you always seemed tired the next morning. I shouldn't have told him that. I could see the look on his face. He's going to use it against you—against all of us. Such men have no understanding of the old things."

"Florica?" asked Paula in a whisper. "You know, don't you?"

"Hush," I said quickly, seeing the look on our housekeeper's face, a look of sheer terror. "We won't speak of that. Florica, what's done is done: don't feel guilty about it. If there's anyone who should feel guilty it's Cezar, for browbeating you like that. Tell Petru that if Cezar tries to make you leave, it'll be over my dead body."

"You're only a young thing, Jena. How can you do it? If your father never comes back—"

"He will come back." I had seen Stela's face. "He's just not sending letters, because of the winter. In springtime everything will be back to normal. And I will stop Cezar from doing what he threatened. He can't send you away. It's not right."

I went straight to find Cezar, knowing that the longer I delayed the confrontation, the harder it was going to be. He was in Father's workroom, but he did not seem to be doing anything in particular. He was simply sitting at the desk, brooding. I could not look at him without remembering that kiss—and before I had even begun to speak, I was afraid.

"Jena," Cezar said coolly. "To what do I owe the pleasure?"

Pleasure? Not for us. Gogu was sitting on my shoulder. Not wanting to draw undue attention to him, I left him there.

"I need to ask you about something, Cezar."

"Sit down, Jena. What is it?" There was a little smile on his face, as if he had a secret.

"I've just spoken to Florica. She and Petru say you threatened to turn them out of Piscul Dracului if they didn't answer your questions—questions about me and my sisters. Is that true?"

Cezar leaned back in his chair, arms folded, eyes on my face. "You need younger staff here," he said mildly. "No wonder you got into such difficulty this winter. I know girls are soft-hearted and become attached to their old servants, but really, Jena, those two are long past being useful to you. They should be retired, like worn-out horses put to pasture. Don't look like that; it's a perfectly practical suggestion. They've a grandson in the settlement, haven't they? Let their own provide for them."

"If it *is* only a suggestion, not an order, that's all right," I said. "Florica and Petru are part of our family. They're not going anywhere—not while I'm in charge here."

He looked at me as if waiting for me to realize that I was speaking nonsense.

"Do I need to tell you again that my father has not died, and that he asked me and Tati to oversee things at Piscul Dracului until he came back?" I tried to keep my voice calm. "You don't seem to have recognized that yet, Cezar. Nobody asked you to take over the funds. Nobody asked you to move in here. Nobody asked you to ban me from having anything to do with the business. And nobody asked you to browbeat Florica and Petru. If you have questions about Full Moon, I'm the one you need to speak to. Leave the others alone."

"Jena, what is your interpretation of your father's failure to send a single letter during all this time away?"

I felt cold. "He's unwell, I know that. He did get worse, as Gabriel told us. That doesn't mean he won't get better, Cezar. Once the weather improves, I'm sure a letter will come advising us of that."

"You'd be wiser to prepare yourself and your sisters for the worst," Cezar said. "That would include moderating your behavior, Jena. I'm not just referring to your outspokenness, your desire to hold all the strings, your wayward choice of that wretched creature"—he eyed Gogu—"as a constant companion. I mean much more than that. I was deeply shocked to see you and Tatiana out in the courtyard that night, looking as if you'd just come in from running about in the forest. I was still more alarmed when the questions I asked, both here and in the valley, elicited the information that one can somehow cross over to the realm of the fairy folk and back again on the night of Full Moon. Florica tells me that's a night you girls always spend on your own, in your bedchamber, behind locked doors. So quiet, she said, that you might almost not be there at all."

I said nothing. I had my hands tightly clasped together behind my back. I was glad Cezar could not feel how fast my heart was beating. "May I remind you that our party was held at Full Moon," I said, "and that we were all here at home?"

"Ah, the party." Cezar was suddenly solemn. "That marked

a low point in our friendship, Jena. I'm still hoping you will change your mind about a certain issue."

"I can't—"

He lifted his hand, silencing me. "You know, it would make life so much easier for all of us if you would," he said. "It's what is meant to be, Jena: you and I—I know it. But that can wait. I'm interested in this Other Kingdom that folk mention, and the talk of portals. Should such an opening be available, that would simplify the process of destroying the Night People and all those that consort with them. One could prepare thoroughly—reduce the risks considerably. There's been plenty of talk about Piscul Dracului and the likelihood that entries to the other realm may lie within the castle. It seems that as soon as one old fellow starts talking, a dozen others remember tales of their own. It came to me that if you girls generally spent the night of Full Moon locked inside your bedchamber and came out exhausted in the morning, it could very possibly be deduced that one such portal was located within that very chamber."

Uh-oh.

I stood frozen. I had not expected him to deduce anything of the sort—it was a big leap of the imagination for a man like him. "What are you suggesting?" It wasn't at all difficult to sound shocked. "That my sisters and I are crossing over to another world and coming back again every Full Moon? That's ridiculous."

"So I might once have thought, Jena. I would once have believed you girls incapable of such folly: especially you, who saw what these folk could do on the day we lost Costi in the Deadwash. But there's your night escapade. And Mother mentioned the appearance of a strange young man on the evening of the party—a young man she's certain was not on the invitation list. Apparently you told her he was a friend of Lucian's. Lucian tells me that is not so. This stranger was dancing with Tatiana. Who was he, Jena?"

Think fast.

"You mean the man dressed in the black waistcoat? I have no idea. I did think I saw him come in with Judge Rinaldo and Lucian. I must have been wrong."

"Really? Then I'd better ask Tatiana. Maybe she will be more forthcoming."

My heart sank. Tati was in no fit state to stand up to Cezar's bullying. "She's not well," I said. "If you like, I will ask her for you."

"I have a far better plan, Jena. You should be happy with it; it obviates the need for me to question any more members of the family. My hunting parties are becoming a waste of time. It seems it's all too easy for Night People and other denizens of this fairy kingdom to slip away to their own realm, apparently using these portals or gateways that folk speak of. I don't want to believe this of you and your sisters, Jena. If the people of the valley learned you knew of such an opening and had concealed it, in the light of the murderous activities of those who live beyond, the reputation of our family would be destroyed for all time. But if it's true, we can make use of it, without letting the community know the secret."

"There is no portal." I tried to keep still so he would not see me shaking. "All that happens here at Full Moon is a private night for girls, when we dress up and share our secrets. You should be pleased that we lock ourselves in, if you believe it to be the most dangerous night of the month."

Cezar narrowed his eyes at me. "It may not be," he said, and I did not like the edge in his voice. "I also heard another tale, a tale in which Dark of the Moon was mentioned. Ah, I see that means something to you, Jena. That, too, is a night on which mysterious ways may be open and uncanny creatures come out into our world to terrify and attack our kind. Wasn't it Dark of the Moon when I found you and your sister wandering about in the snow?"

"I didn't notice," I said. "You've had an explanation for that night, Cezar. You cannot set yourself up as some kind of guardian to us. You're only a couple of years older than Tati. This is ridiculous. We've done nothing wrong."

He remained silent.

Ask him. Ask him what this plan is. It sounds bad.

"Are you going to tell me what you intend? Since this is our house, I'd appreciate the courtesy of knowing what it is you plan to do here."

"Oh, Jena." He looked genuinely regretful; it made me remember the boy he had been. "I would far prefer us to be friends, you know. More than friends. I meant everything I said to you, the night of the party. Every word."

"So did I, Cezar."

"You've often told me I am too angry—that I haven't learned to put the past behind me. Oh, yes, I've been listening: don't look so surprised. But I can't do it. Not without this—not without pursuing those who ruined my life all those years ago. Their promises are false, their words are foul lies. When they are all gone, then I will have no more reason for anger." He had gone unaccountably nervous, twisting his hands together on the desk, avoiding my eye. "Jena, I need your friendship. I need your love. If you help me, I can do this. I can make my life worthwhile again. Don't you see, I must have vengeance for Costi, and for what was done to me that day. You could help me do that. And when it's over, you could stay by my side and support me, as you did long ago by the Deadwash. . . ."

Gogu had tensed up alarmingly as this speech unfolded. I put up a hand to stop him from doing something silly. I was struggling for a way to answer Cezar. "On the night of the party," I managed, "you didn't say anything about love."

Cezar looked up; his eyes met mine. "I didn't think I needed to, Jena," he said quietly.

This was bad. It made it much harder to say what I must. "I don't understand any of this talk about making your life worthwhile," I said. "Isn't it worthwhile already? You have your mother, you have Vârful cu Negură. In time you can become a man like your father was: a stalwart of the community, someone folk look up to. You're a merchant, you can make a success of that. As a man you can travel, see things, make your mark in the world. I know you've had losses, terrible ones. But you shouldn't need to crush and destroy the folk of the forest, or to take control of Piscul Dracului and of our family, in order to compensate for that. You've got a good life now. Or could have, if you would simply get on with living it."

He was waiting for something more.

"I can't love you, Cezar. Not in the way you mean. And I don't believe you love me. If you did, you would have taken the time to understand what was important to me. I couldn't ever love a man who tried to get his own way by frightening people."

There was a silence. Even the frog had no contribution to make. Then Cezar got up and opened the door. "You may as well leave, Jena. You've made your attitude perfectly clear," he said. His tone chilled me.

The plan.

"You mentioned a plan, Cezar. Am I allowed to hear what it is?"

"It will become plain to you in due course."

"Cezar, tell me. Please." I had to force the word out.

"Let us simply say that should you girls make use of any secret passageways or hidden doors at next Full Moon, you won't be doing so alone. Between now and that time I will be establishing improved security at Piscul Dracului. I know you've been breaking the rules I set down to preserve your safety, Jena. Tati, in particular, has shown an alarming tendency to go off for walks on her own. I overheard something in the village recently, something that wasn't intended for my ears. Folk have noticed the change in your sister's appearance. They've been putting it together with what happened to the miller's daughter, and some of them have leapt to a conclusion that deeply disturbs me. I don't know how much you understand about the Night People."

Now I was really frightened. "Not much," I whispered.

"They feed, and folk die. Ivona was victim to that. But sometimes they feed and folk remain alive, but changed. If this is distressing to you, Jena, I can only say it is something you need to know, in view of the foolish risks you girls have been taking. I heard someone suggest that Tatiana might have been singled out in this way. The fellow said it explained why Piscul Dracului's stock had been spared the knife, and would also account for the dramatic change in Tati's appearance. People saw her at the party, they could hardly not notice it. Folk muttered that she was sure to be visited again, and you know what that means."

I could hardly speak. "I don't, Cezar. Tell me."

"After a certain number of bites, the victim becomes one of the Night People, Jena. Once the process begins, folk see such an individual not as a victim, but as a threat to the community. There's no reversing this. She would become an outcast, hunted, her own bite the stuff of desperate fear. I assume there is no substance in this rumor." He was deadly serious, his eyes sternly fixed on me.

"Of course not!" I felt cold all through. Deep inside me, there was a terrible suspicion that, just possibly, what he suggested could be true. I didn't want to give it credence, but part of me couldn't help it. Sorrow had been in Tadeusz's realm for years and years. Before she met him, Tati had been healthy and happy. Folk didn't actually waste away for love, did they? So perhaps this was something else. That someone in the village had thought of this possibility was terrifying. I pictured the hunting party—expressions dark, weapons glinting—crashing through the forest, and Tati fleeing before them. I'd still never had a proper look at Sorrow's teeth.

"We must put an end to such talk," Cezar said. "Tati has been astonishingly stupid to allow any grounds for it. And she's the eldest. It is no wonder your younger sisters are growing up so wayward. There will be guards here as of tomorrow. I expect you girls to keep to the house and courtyard."

I stared at him, my feet rooted to the spot. "You can't do that," I whispered, unable to believe that even he would be so heavy-handed. "You don't mean guards to protect us, do you? You mean jailers—folk to keep us in."

"You could cooperate, Jena." That soft voice again, the one that frightened me most. "Tell me the truth and we can go about this quite differently. Just give a little. I don't want us to be enemies."

Ask about Full Moon.

"You said something about not being alone at Full Moon. I told you, all we will be doing is having a little fun among sisters. Nothing untoward. What are you planning to do, set a woman to spy on us in our own bedchamber?"

"Not a woman, not if there is the least possibility of a trip to this Other Kingdom, with its attendant perils."

Just say it, scum. The frog was a tight bundle of nerves; I was no better.

"I think you'll have to spell it out for me, Cezar. You can't mean that you yourself are planning to spend the night in our private quarters, not if you care about the family reputation. If such an episode ever became public knowledge, your own good name would be destroyed along with ours."

"Of course I would not consider such a thing." I could see the terror in his eyes at the very thought of exposure to the Other Kingdom; it made me wonder how he had managed his nightly hunting parties—and whether he had, in fact, ever believed they would bear fruit. "I'll find a man in need of a few coppers to keep body and soul together," he said. "Someone prepared to take a risk. He'll be locked in with you overnight, and be bound to find out the secret and follow you wherever this portal leads. Once I know the truth about it, I can prepare properly for an all-out assault. Don't look like that, Jena. Didn't you swear to me there was no portal? If you were telling the truth, there's nothing to worry about, my dear."

I'll dear him. How dare he? Wretch! Coward!

"You would put a *man* in our *bedroom*." My tone was flat with disbelief. "Overnight. Clearly it's only your own reputation you're worried about, not those of your marriageable cousins. Cezar, this is ludicrous. I'm going up to see Aunt Bogdana first thing in the morning. She will never allow such a breach of propriety."

"My mother is not home. She's gone to visit her friend near Braşov."

I was immediately suspicious. "She never mentioned that to me."

"It was a sudden decision. Don't trouble yourself, Jena. I will provide a woman from my household as chaperone, someone discreet. We'll make sure this doesn't get out."

"Then I'm going down to the village to see Judge Rinaldo.

You've exceeded your authority too far, Cezar. This talk of guards . . . It's not something you can do."

"You will explain to the judge about your nighttime escapades, then? The uninvited guest at your party? He knows already of your difficulties in managing your father's funds and in running your farm with only old Petru to help. He knows this household was singled out to be spared the marauding attentions of the Night People. Very probably he's heard the theory about the cause of Tati's illness, as well. I think you'd find it hard to make a convincing case against my providing a force of men to protect you and your sisters, Jena."

"I'll try, despite that. I'm not letting you do this." There was a feeling like a cold stone in my stomach, a dread of what was to come.

"You weren't listening, Jena. I told you, none of you girls is to go beyond the house and courtyard. Most certainly not down to the village. Not until this is resolved to my satisfaction."

Prisoners in our own home. Not so long ago, the fool was talking about love.

"And what if this spy of yours discovers nothing at all?"

"Then I will find a new man for next Full Moon—and then another man, and so on—until the truth comes out. You'd do far better to tell me now, Jena. Save yourself all that embarrassment. I could have the woods swept clean of these presences even before spring. It's within my grasp, I feel it." He was no longer seeing me; his eyes were full of blood and vengeance.

"I can't believe you thought I might change my mind," I said, backing away toward the door. "I can't believe you thought I could ever possibly love you. The real monsters aren't folk from the Other Kingdom, Cezar. They're men like you: men who won't stop grasping for power until they've destroyed everything. You think you're going to put an end to the folk of the forest. But if you don't take a step back, you're going to end up destroying your own life."

Cezar looked at me. His dark eyes were bleak. "No, Jena," he said quietly. "I think that's already been done."

Chapter Eleven

There was worse to come before bedtime. Cezar decided to perform a search of our room without warning, so we'd have no time to hide anything suspicious. He made Florica come all the way up the stairs and stand in the doorway lest I accuse him of improper conduct. Such a concern was ridiculous, given what he had threatened for Full Moon.

Before we could go to bed, we had to sit there and watch him rummage through all our things—from shoes to small-clothes to silk shawls, from trinkets and keepsakes to combs and scent pots—frowning and muttering. I was furious, but I sat there in silence and let him make his comments on our worn-out dancing slippers and the elegant gowns he had never seen us wear. I'd been able to give my sisters only a brief warning about his plans. Tati had her back to the room; I knew she was trying not to cry. She had pinned all her hopes on Full Moon.

"We like sewing," Paula told Cezar as he lifted a fold of Iulia's blue silk dancing gown. As a merchant, he would know all too well the quality of the fabric, with its woven-in silver thread. "Aunt Bogdana approves of it as a pastime for young ladies."

Cezar glanced at her sharply—it was evident he thought she was mocking him.

"All girls love to dream, Cezar," Paula added. "All girls like to dress up, even when they have nowhere to go."

He opened the little brass-bound lacquer box in which Paula kept her papers, but it seemed she had already moved them to safer keeping, for all he found was a pot of ink and a few split quills. He went around the chamber checking each window, each alcove, each joint in stones or boards, for secrets that might uncover themselves. All of us carefully avoided looking at the corner where the portal was. He picked up Gogu's bowl and eyed the jug of water. He scrutinized my pillow, which was still slightly damp from last night. "Oh dear, Jena," he said.

Oh dear, yourself.

"You should ask yourself whether that creature is the key to your problems," Cezar went on. "I have grave doubts about it. It's clearly no ordinary frog. Have you considered that it may be of another kind entirely? That it may be . . . influencing you?"

"A frog?" I made my voice scornful. "Give me a little more credit, Cezar. You already know I have a mind of my own." I would apologize to Gogu later.

Cezar kept us up until Stela was dropping with weariness. At last he seemed to be done—his flinty expression told me he was far from satisfied.

"Finished?" I inquired as he stood in the center of the room, hands on hips. All around him was disarray: clothing was spread out everywhere, shoes and other bits and pieces littered the stone floor. Furniture had been dragged out from walls, and even the bedding had been turned upside down.

"For now," he said. "I don't for a moment believe Paula's story of sewing for fun and dressing up for amusement. What would Uncle Teodor think of such reckless squandering of fine fabrics and trimmings, I wonder?"

"In fact," Iulia said, "we never take anything without asking Father if it's all right. He doesn't mind. Sewing's a good wifely skill." She was glowering; Cezar's reprimand at the party would not be soon forgotten.

"A man would be out of his mind to look for a wife among the five of you," Cezar said, his tone chilly. "A washed-out bag of bones; a domineering shrew; a cheap flirt; a know-it-all scholar; and an impressionable child—a man would do best to stay clear of the lot of you."

"We'd be very happy if you'd do just that, Cezar," I said quietly. I was fighting to keep my dignity and not shriek at him like the shrew he'd named me. "We'd love for you to go back to Vârful cu Negură and leave us to our own devices until Father comes home—"

"That's enough, Jena." There was something in his voice that silenced me. At that moment I had no doubt at all that he would go through with his threat. Unless, somehow, he could be stopped. Unless there was someone powerful enough to prevent it.

"Good night, then," I said politely. The others sat on their beds, watching in complete silence. Cezar went out without a word.

One by one, my sisters fell asleep. Outside, snow was drifting down onto the many roofs of Piscul Dracului—I could not see it, but I could sense it in the quality of the silence. The four colored windows were winter-dark. On the little table by my bedside, one candle burned. The castle was still, save for the creaks and groans and shifting murmurs an old house makes as the winter chill touches its bones.

"Gogu?" I whispered.

I'm here, Jena.

"We have to do something before Full Moon. Something to stop Cezar from going through with this." It was a puzzle. We could not use our portal until the night of Full Moon. I had no intention of crossing over at Dark of the Moon again, to visit that realm of shadows and trickery, and Tati had promised Sorrow she would not. That meant we could not seek help or give warnings in the Other Kingdom until the night Cezar put his henchman in our bedchamber: too late. "The simplest thing would be not to go at all," I murmured. "Not to use the portal. At least, that way, Cezar wouldn't find it. But he will eventually, I know it. He's so angry he's forgotten what's wrong and what's right." I shivered, imagining where that anger might take him. If he threatened violence against one of my sisters, I'd have no choice but to give up the secret. Would he stoop so low? What he had said about Tati, about folk in the village suggesting that the Night People had begun to change her, was most terrifying of all. That rumor could be a powerful tool to force our obedience.

Drăguţa.

"What? Oh. You mean because folk say she's the real power in the wildwood? But is she? She's never put in an appearance, Gogu. And I'm starting to doubt the magic mirror story. Why would her mirror be there at Dark of the Moon when she isn't?"

Mirror? What mirror?

I remembered that I had not given him a full account of that night. That was probably just as well. "You think Drăguţa would help us? Grigori did say to me, *If you truly need her, you'll find her.* So maybe she can be found even when it's not Full Moon. I've heard other stories that say she comes out often, like the dwarves, but not always in her own form." I suddenly remembered the white owl. "Gogu, do you really think we should try this?"

Silence. He was shivering the way he did when we crossed the lake. I felt cold, too. There would be guards to get past, Cezar's wrath to face if he found out I had gone into the forest, a trip in the cold to the Deadwash, and then . . . Finding Drăguţa, without knowing where to look, might prove harder than Grigori had indicated. We might wander about in the snow until we were dying of cold, and get nowhere.

"We have to do it, Gogu," I whispered. "You and I. I'm not putting any of my sisters in danger—this is bad enough already."

D-dawn, Gogu conveyed to me. *First thing tomorrow, before the g-guards come.*

I peered at him. In the candlelight he was just a green blob on the pillow. "You can stay home if you don't want to do this, Gogu," I said, realizing that he was as terrified as I was. "I can go by myself." At Dark of the Moon, I'd left him behind. The thought of doing that again, of braving the witch of the wood without my dearest companion by my side, made me feel sick. But it was unfair to drag him along when he was so scared.

You d-don't want me to c-come? You would l-leave me b-behind again? His whole body drooped.

"Of course I want you, stupid! I'm petrified of going alone. I'm just trying to spare you."

Then we will g-go together, Jena.

"You realize I've got no idea how to find her?"

We'll find her.

"I hope so," I said, sitting up to blow out the candle. "And I hope she's prepared to help us. Good night, Gogu. Sweet dreams. Up at dawn, remember."

This pillow is my best place, Jena.

"What?" I squinted at him in the darkness, but his eyes were already closed.

I settled Gogu in my pocket, wrapped in the sheepskin mitten, and tiptoed downstairs with the first lightening of the sky. Florica already had the fire roaring in the kitchen stove and was kneading dough on the well-scoured table. Petru sat by the stove, his hands curled around a steaming cup of last night's soup. Both looked up as I tried to pass the open doorway in my hooded cloak with my winter boots in my hands.

I went in. This was the first test of the day. "Florica, Petru,

I need a favor. I must go out on my own, without Cezar knowing. Please . . ."

Two pairs of dark old eyes regarded me shrewdly. "You'd want to hurry," Florica said. "The boys will be down early today. Daniel and Răzvan. They're leaving."

"Really? Isn't that rather sudden?"

"There was a lot of shouting last night, after you girls were in bed," Petru said. "They didn't like what Master Cezar planned to do. The two of them told him they wouldn't have any of it. Packed up to go home."

"Oh." I would once have been glad to see those two gone, but now their departure felt like bad news. They had willingly performed a hundred and one tasks on the farm. I thought their presence had gone a certain way toward moderating Cezar's behavior.

"What are you planning, Jena?" Florica muttered. "It's not safe out there, you know that—especially for a girl on her own."

"I do have to go, Florica. It's really important. I'll be safe, I promise. The folk of the forest don't harm people who show them respect. You said that yourself. And I'm not alone, I've got Gogu. I'll be safer out there than I am here in the castle, with Cezar in his current mood. All you need to do is keep quiet. Please?"

"Off you go," Petru said. "We never saw you. Or the frog. Here, take this." He put his little knife into my hand, the one he used for a thousand jobs on the farm. It had been next to him on the table, ready to cut the bread Florica would give him for his breakfast. "It's sharp," he warned me. "Keep it in the sheath until you need it. And make sure you bring it back."

Florica sniffed, wiping her floury hands on her apron. "May all the saints watch over you, Jena. Take this, too." She reached into one of many capacious pockets in her apron, fished out a little figure made of garlic cloves, and pressed it into my hand. "Go on, now. The boys will be here any moment; I'm just making them a little something for the road. Jena, you've had no breakfast. Let me—" She was already rummaging on the shelves, finding the crust of yesterday's bread, a wedge of hard cheese, an apple, and wrapping them in a cloth. "Take these. Petru will be in the barn—find him first when you come back, and he'll see you safely into the house."

"Thank you," I said, and moved to hug them, each in turn. "I don't know what we'd do without the two of you. I'll be back before dusk. If anyone asks, you have no idea where I am."

At first I didn't even try to work out where Drăguţa's lair might be, or how to reach it quickly. My main aim was to disappear into the forest, somewhere Cezar could not readily track me. That wasn't easy with the paths all thick with snow. If the imprints of my boots didn't give me away, I thought, Cezar only needed to send the farm dogs after me and they'd find me by smell. So I did what I could to make my scent difficult to follow. I tried to walk along frozen streams, and Gogu and I sustained bruises. I clambered up a steep rock wall, and came close to a fall that would have broken an arm or a leg or worse, if I hadn't grabbed on to a prickly bush just in time. Unfortunately, I had removed my gloves so I could climb better. My palm was full of thorns; at the top of the wall, I sat down to remove the worst of them with the numb fingers of my other hand, and Gogu licked the sore places better.

Poor Jena. Is the hurt gone now?

"Yes," I lied, thrusting the aching hand under my cloak. "We'd better go on. I don't think he'll track us here. Now what? Which way do we go?"

The D-Deadwash.

"Do you want to go back in the pocket? It's freezing out here." In there, I thought, he could shut his eyes and pretend he was somewhere else.

No. I will ride on your shoulder.

"Gogu, are you sure? You sound strange. Sad. You didn't have to come, you know."

I know, Jena.

So we went to the Deadwash: not just as far as the little stream where we'd made pondweed pancakes in autumn, but right down under the dark trees to the shore itself. The water was sheeted with ice; the mist hung close, a shifting gray shroud. There was an odd stillness about the place. Not a bird called in bare-limbed willow or red-berried holly, not a creature rustled in the undergrowth. Above the canopy of interlaced branches, the morning sky was a flat gray. It would snow again by nightfall.

Now what?

"I don't know," I whispered, my heart hammering. "Calling out to her seems wrong. Praying would be blasphemous. Searching for her might take all day and be no help at all. I wonder what it meant, what Grigori said. *If you truly want to find* her, *you'll find her.* . . ." I hugged my cloak around me. "Gogu," I said in a very small voice, "I think what we need to show is . . . well, blind faith. Do you trust me?"

With my life.

"All right, then." I took the frog in my hands, drew a deep, shuddering breath, closed my eyes, and stepped onto the frozen lake. I walked, unseeing, step by step. The ice made moaning, cracking sounds under my boots. The hard freeze of Dark of the Moon was beginning to weaken; the waters of Tăul Ielelor had scented spring. I kept my eyes screwed shut, and with each step I thought about why I needed Drăguța to help me: Father; Cezar; Tati and Sorrow; . . . Piscul Dracului; my sisters' future; the folk of the wildwood . . .

"Drăguța," I whispered, pausing to stand completely still, Gogu cupped between my palms. "Drăguța, can you hear me?"

Get rid of the man.

"What?" I hissed. Drat Gogu, he had completely broken my concentration.

Throw away the little garlic man.

I dug into my pocket, fished out Florica's tiny charm, and threw it as far as I could across the frozen lake. Maybe the folk of the Other Kingdom feared garlic or maybe, as Tadeusz had said, that was a myth. Better safe than sorry. I shut my eyes again. "Drăguța," I said, "I love the forest. I love the Other Kingdom. I love my family, and I love Piscul Dracului. Please help me to save them." My heart was drumming hard, and so was Gogu's. Hadn't my cousin Costi been drowned right here where I stood? I tried not to think about the probability that if the ice broke and I fell through, I would freeze so fast I wouldn't have time to drown.

We waited. I felt the cold seep under my cloak and my warm gown and my woolen stockings and into the core of my bones. My nose was numb, my ears ached. I thought I could feel ice forming on my eyelashes. Gogu was shivering in great, convulsive spasms. I refused to believe she wasn't coming. Allow that thought in and she probably wouldn't. Faith was required, and faith was what I planned to demonstrate, for as long as it took.

It's hard to stand still with your eyes shut for a long time: eventually you start to lose your balance and feel faint and dizzy. I kept it up a good while, listening to the silence of the forest and willing Drǎguṭa to put in an appearance before I was frozen through. But it wasn't the witch of the woods who finally made me open my eyes, it was Gogu. He started so violently that I almost dropped him on the ice. As I bent to grab him, I found myself looking into the face of someone very small, who had been standing quietly in front of me, right by my feet.

That's her.

"What?"

That's her. Cupped in my hands, Gogu buried his head against my palm, trembling.

I took another look. White shawl, more holes than fabric. White hair, long and wild. Cloudy green eyes, like ripe gooseberries. Wrinkled face, beaky nose, fine parchment skin. A little staff of willow wood, with a polished stone like a robin's egg set at the tip. Little silver boots with pointed toes, glittering against the ice where she stood. In the hand that did not hold the staff, she had a delicate silver chain, and at the end of it sat a white fox in a jeweled harness. The woman herself stood not much higher than my knees.

"You stink of garlic!" she said sharply, eyes fixed on mine. "Can't stand the stuff, myself. What have you brought me?"

"Ah . . . are you Drăguţa?" I could not believe this tiny, frail-looking creature was the feared and fabled witch of the wood.

"What do *you* think?"

I couldn't afford to waste even one question. If she was Drăguţa, she might decide to vanish at any moment. I had to get this right.

"I think you are, and I offer you my respectful greetings," I said, giving her a curtsy. She sniffed, but stayed. The fox was pawing at the ice, wanting to dig.

"I have some good bread and some tasty cheese," I said, cursing myself for not thinking of bringing gifts. "And a red, rosy apple. You are welcome to those." Putting Gogu on my shoulder, I undid Florica's cloth from my belt and knelt down to offer it.

"Hm," the tiny woman said, prodding at it with her staff. "Anything else?"

I thought frantically. "My gold earrings? A nice silk hand-kerchief?"

"Are you afraid of me, Jenica?" the witch asked suddenly.

And suddenly I was, for she stretched her mouth in a smile, revealing two rows of little pointed teeth. She was looking straight at Gogu, who was trying to hide under my hair. Drăguţa put out a long, pale tongue and licked her lips.

"You *do* have something I want," she purred. "Something juicy. Something tasty. Something green as grass."

"You can't have Gogu!" I gasped, horrified. "Anything else, but not him!"

"Oh, Jena, you disappoint me. All this way in the cold, and such a heartfelt plea, and you give it all up for a mere morsel like that? Perhaps you don't quite understand. Give me the frog, and I'll tell you everything you need to know. The solutions to all your problems. It's easy. Just pass him over. It'll save me from having to decide what's for supper." She grinned.

Gogu went suddenly still. I thought his heart had stopped beating from sheer fright. "Gogu!" I hissed. "Don't give up on me now, I need you!" He moved just a little and I drew a breath for courage. "I won't do it," I said, staring the witch straight in the eyes. "I can't give up my dearest friend. We're a team, Gogu and I. We do everything together. Do take the bread and cheese, they're Florica's best. And the apple's from our own orchard at Piscul Dracului. They'll make a much nicer supper. Trust me."

Drăguţa stared at me a moment, then threw her little head back and burst into peals of laughter. Her laugh was so loud it made the trees all around the Deadwash shiver. The white fox laid back its ears. "Florica, eh? She'll be an old woman now, just like me. I remember her when she was a mere slip of a thing, with the young men all dancing after her. Ah, well. Me, I was old even then. Drăguţa's always been old." She gathered up the bundle and stuffed it into one of the silver bags the fox wore behind its miniature blanket saddle. "Tell me your story, then, and be quick about it."

I told her everything, starting with Father's illness, going on with the catalog of Cezar's misdeeds, and throwing in Tati and Sorrow and the prospect of young men being locked in our bedchamber every Full Moon until we gave up our secret. "And I've tried and tried to keep control of things, but it keeps on getting worse," I finished miserably. "Now I think Tati may be in danger soon, from folk who think . . . who think she's changing into something else." It was hard to get the words out, for to give voice to this most terrifying of possibilities seemed to make it real. "She's so pale and distant, and so thin. . . . It could be true that Sorrow—that he—" I couldn't bring myself to say that he might have bitten her—that he might have drawn her into his own darkness. "I'm hoping you can tell me what to do."

She cackled. "Easy, eh? A simple set of instructions. Or a spell, one that turns back time. I doubt if your Tati would welcome that. You've surprised me, Jena. My great-nephew Grigori told me you were a capable girl."

"Not anymore," I said. "These days I seem to be getting everything wrong."

Drăguţa reached out to stroke the fox's muzzle. Then, with an agility astonishing in one apparently so ancient, she leaped onto the creature's back. She gathered what I now saw were reins.

"No—please—" I spluttered. "Please wait! I need your help!"

The witch paused, reaching into a pouch at her belt under the voluminous tattered shawl. "Where is the wretched thing—ah, here!" She tossed something straight at me, and I dodged instinctively. The small item bounced on the ice and went spinning away. I slid to retrieve it, keeping Gogu safe in place with one hand. It was a tiny bottle of greenish fluid, tightly corked. "It gives long sleep," Drăguţa said. "Two drops, no more. Almost tasteless in wine, completely so in ţuică. You'll have no problem with your nocturnal visitors."

"Thank you," I managed, desperate to keep her near until all my questions were answered. "Drăguţa—Madam—can anything be done for Sorrow and that little girl, his sister? It seems so terrible that they are trapped in that dark place, and perhaps doomed to become Night People themselves. I would like to help them. But Sorrow and Tati, that's impossible—"

Drăguţa regarded me gravely. "Your sister is a grown woman, Jena," she said. "Let her live her own life."

"But—"

"Would you challenge me?"

There was something in her voice that stopped further words. Small she might be, but I heard her and trembled. "N-no. I just don't want to lose my sister."

"What will be, will be. I have one piece of advice for you, Jena. Listen well, because it's all you'll be getting."

"I'm listening."

"Trust your instincts," Drăguţa said. "And remember, nothing comes without a price." She kicked her little silver boots against the fox's sides. The creature took off at a brisk trot over the frozen plane of the Deadwash. Within a count of five, the two of them had vanished into the mist.

"Wait—!" My shoulders slumped. She was gone, and all I

had was a finger-sized bottle of some dubious potion and a piece of advice I knew well enough already. "Curse it!" I said, stamping my foot in frustration. The ice let out an ominous snapping sound.

C-can we g-go back to shore now?

It seemed Drăguţa had decided not to drown us. We reached the shore of Tăul Ielelor safely, minus our provisions. It was time for the long walk home. I felt desperately tired and utterly despondent. I sat down on a log and found that I didn't have the energy to get up again.

"She did try to help, Gogu," I muttered. "But I feel so disappointed, I could cry. What about Sorrow and Tati? And a sleeping potion is all very well, but once he finds out about it, Cezar will use other ways to make me do what he wants. And what's the point of saying nothing comes without a price? I'd be stupid if I hadn't learned that. Everyone says it."

D-don't be sad. I'm here.

"So you are," I said, taking Gogu in my hands and holding him against my cheek. "How dare she threaten to have you for her supper? You're my truest friend in all the world." I turned my head and kissed him on his damp green nose.

Everything went white. I found myself flying through the air, the sound of a shattering explosion assaulting my ears. I landed with a bone-jarring thump, flat on my back in a scratchy juniper bush. Gogu had been torn from my hands by the blast and was nowhere to be seen. I sat up cautiously as the bright light faded and the lakeshore came back to its gray-green, shadowy self.

"Gogu?" My voice was thin and shaky. My heart was pounding and my ears were ringing. Distantly, I thought I could hear the sound of an old woman's derisive laughter. "Gogu, where are you?"

No response. A terrible, cold feeling began to creep through me. This was Drăguța's doing. She'd never meant to help me without payment. She'd given me the potion and she'd smiled, and the price she'd wanted was the one she'd asked for in the first place: my precious companion. "Gogu!" I shouted. "Gogu, if you're there, come out right now!" I crawled around in the undergrowth, clawing wildly at ferns and creepers. "Gogu, be here somewhere—please, oh please. . . ."

I was bending to look under a clump of grass when I saw him: a lanky, sprawled figure lying on the shore at some distance from me, as if thrown there. He was pale-skinned, long-limbed, his dark hair straggling down into his eyes. The rags he wore didn't cover him very well: a considerable amount of naked flesh was on show. He lay limp, perhaps unconscious. Maybe dead. A wanderer, a vagrant. Drunk, probably—perhaps mad. I was alone out here in the forest. I should run straight home and not look behind me. On the other hand, he might be hurt, and it was freezing. Father had taught us to be compassionate. I couldn't just leave him.

I crept nearer, my hand gripping the hilt of Petru's little sharp knife. The young man lay utterly silent. I came still closer, crouching down an arm's length from him. Not dead: breathing. His face was bony and well formed, a familiar face with a thin-lipped mouth and a strong jaw. No, I told myself.

No, please. He opened his eyes. Behind the strands of dark hair, they were green as grass. My heart lurched in horror. This was Drăguţa's joke, her cruel joke. This was the lovely young man who had haunted my dreams since Dark of the Moon. Behind that appealing face was the evil creature I had seen in the magic mirror, pursuing and hurting my sisters. And . . .

My skin prickled, my heart felt a sudden deathly chill. Perhaps I had known who it was from the first, although my mind shrank from it. Who else would be there beside Tăul Ielelor in the middle of winter? There had been nobody—just me and my frog.

"Gogu?" I whispered, backing away with the knife in my hand. "Is it you?" My heart was breaking.

The young man looked at me, not saying a thing. That was cruelest of all: if he had managed even a word or two, some expression of regret, it might have eased the pain just a little. He sat up, wrapping his long arms around his bony knees. Suddenly he was racked with convulsive shivering.

"Here," I said, taking off my cloak and putting it around his shoulders. "It *is* you, isn't it? It has to be. Can you get up? Can you walk?"

I knew I should flee: I should run as fast as I could, away from the Deadwash and out of the wildwood, back home to my sisters. He was a monster. I had seen it with my own eyes. But deep inside me, something wanted to help him—something that could not disregard his beseeching gaze. This was like being ripped apart. I hated Drăguţa as I had never hated anyone in my life. If this was the price for a few drops of sleeping potion, it was too high.

"Gogu?" I ventured again, my voice shaking. If only he would say something—anything—while he was still in this form. How long, I wondered, until that kind, sweet face turned to the mask of hideous decay? How long before this semblance of a human became the thing underneath, an evil being from the world of Dark of the Moon? How long before it turned its rending claws and vicious teeth on me as I fled through the forest? It was a long way home to Piscul Dracului. But how could I turn my back on him? It was cold, and we were in the middle of the forest. And it was Gogu, whom I had promised never to leave behind.

"Have you got somewhere to go?" I asked, hating the way those green eyes were looking at me, full of love and reproach. "Can you get up and walk?" Despite myself, I held out a hand to help him to his feet. He tried. After a moment, his legs buckled under him and he collapsed in a heap, trembling violently.

"Who were you before?" I asked him. Fear tugged at my feet; sorrow and pity held me still. He wasn't Gogu anymore. Surely he could answer the question now, the one he'd never been able to respond to before. "Before you became a frog, were you a man or something else? Tell me, go on. Who were you?"

The young man stared at me without a word. His expression was so sad, it made me want to throw my arms around him and reassure him that everything would be all right. But the words that had come to me at Drăguţa's mirror were still in my head: *Trust that one, and you will deliver up your heart to be split and skewered and roasted over a fire.* It felt as if that were happening right now.

"If you won't tell me, how can I possibly understand

anything?" I burst out. "I don't want to walk away, but I can't stay here." Saying this, I could not look at him. "It's going to take me a long time to walk home. I don't think I can fetch help. There's only Cezar, and—" I thought of trying to explain this to my cousin; of what would likely be the violent and bloody result: this young man pursued and butchered by a mob of scythe-wielding hunters—or, worse still, turning into his true self and inflicting deadly damage on the men of the valley before he was captured and killed. "I wish you would say something," I whispered. "It seems terrible to leave you like this. Please tell me who you are."

Nothing; not a word.

"Then I'm going," I said, fixing my mind on the vision in Drăguţa's mirror, the bad part of it. "I have no choice." I took a step away, but something was holding me back. I turned, looking down, and saw that he was clutching a fold of my gown, his long fingers gripping the woolen fabric, desperate to delay the moment when I would walk away. I made myself meet his eyes; tears welled in mine. He looked forlorn, bereft. His expression was just like the frog's, those times when I had somehow offended Gogu and he had retreated to the bushes. *He's from the Other Kingdom*, I told myself sternly. *You've seen what he turns into. Don't let him charm you: he can't be allowed near Iulia and Paula and Stela.*

I reached down and opened his fingers, undoing his grasp as if he were a small child clinging to something forbidden. His fingertips brushed the back of my hand, and I felt his touch all through my body, flooding me with tenderness and longing. I remembered Tadeusz's chill fingers against my skin, his soft voice and tempting words, and the sensations they had aroused in me. I knew that they had been nothing—nothing at all compared with what I felt now. This was deep and strong and compelling, and I needed all my strength to fight it. It was all wrong. It was something I could not have. Yet, cruelly, it felt more right than anything in the world.

"Goodbye, Gogu," I whispered, then turned my back and fled.

Chapter Twelve

I arrived home freezing, exhausted, and utterly miserable. Petru
smuggled me inside. All around the place there were men with
clubs or crossbows or knives, some whom I recognized from
Vârful cu Negură and some who were strangers. I spotted
Cezar giving them stern instructions. All I could think of was
the horrible thing Drăguţa had done to me—the cruel trick that
had turned my world upside down.

My sisters bundled me out of my damp clothes and into
warm, dry ones. Stela brought a stone hot water bottle for my
feet. Iulia fetched a jug of tea from the kitchen, with a little
dish of bread and pickled eggs, but I could not eat.

"Let's go through this again, Jena," Paula said carefully, as if
humoring a hysterical child. By this stage I'd stammered out the
story, more or less, including a brief account of the young man I
had seen in Drăguţa's mirror and what he had become. I had not
given them details of the scene in which the monstrous figure
had pursued and hurt them; there was no need for them to share

my nightmares. I had shown them Drăguţa's sleeping potion. I couldn't expect them to understand how I was feeling. If anyone said, *Oh well, it was only a frog*, I'd scream. "You did actually kiss Gogu? That was what made him change?"

"I don't want to talk about it."

"Maybe Gogu was just an ordinary boy once," suggested Stela solemnly. "Until Drăguţa enchanted him."

"There's nothing ordinary about him. He belongs in the world of the Night People. He looks good on the outside and he's all bad on the inside. I saw it."

"And you believe it." Paula sounded doubtful.

"I heard Drăguţa laughing after she'd done it. Paula, there's no point in talking about this. He's gone. I was wrong about him all those years—stupidly wrong. Instead of a friend and companion, I was carrying about some"—I shuddered—"some thing that belonged in the dark, out of sight. How could I have made such a mistake?"

"Or perhaps she changed him," suggested Iulia. "It's hard to believe that Gogu was an evil creature, Jena. Maybe she took him and left you this other thing in his place. To teach you a lesson."

"So it was true, then." Paula was looking thoughtful. "About you being able to hear Gogu's thoughts, I mean. When she transformed him into a frog, Drăguţa probably gave him that voice to make up for not being able to talk. Otherwise he'd have gone crazy."

Tati had been silent so far. Now she gave the others a particular kind of look, and the three of them retreated to sit on Paula's bed.

"Jena," said Tati. "Jena, look at me."

She hadn't sounded so sensible for quite a while. I looked at her, and she reached out her fingers to wipe the tears from my cheeks. Her hand was all skin and bone. "Surely this can't be the first time you ever gave Gogu a kiss," she said.

"It's not. I don't think that's what made him change. Drăguţa just wanted a dramatic moment to do it, and that's the one she chose. Maybe I deserve punishing, Tati. I've messed up everything, and now he's gone, and I don't have any answers, and Cezar's down there, putting armed guards all around the castle." The tears flowed faster. "Sorry," I hiccuped. "I just can't believe I've lost him. It's even crueler than it seems. . . ." No, I would not tell her that the young man with green eyes had appeared nightly in my dreams. That I had considered him far nicer than any of the young men at the party. That I had imagined dancing with him, and had wished he could be real. That meant nothing: every single time, the dream had ended with his changing to reveal the monster beneath.

"Jena," said Tati softly, "we can go across at Full Moon. Drăguţa's potion will put Cezar's man to sleep. You can ask Ileana about this, and I can ask about Sorrow. Maybe it can still be set right, all of it. I'm going to ask her whether she will let Sorrow and his sister live in her realm, away from the Night People. You've done something really brave, getting the potion for us. Don't cry, Jena, please."

"Do you think Gogu will remember the way home?" asked Stela, whose mind was dwelling on the fact that, unaccount-ably, I had left my friend on his own out in the forest. If she had missed the point about exactly what he was, I was glad of it. "I hope he doesn't freeze to death, like birds that fall out of the trees in winter."

"Shh!" hissed Tati. "Don't upset Jena. She did give him her cloak."

"If this was one of those old tales," said Iulia, "he'd turn up on the doorstep here, and Jena would have to grovel to get him back."

"Hush, Iulia!" Tati's arm tightened around my shoulders. "Don't make this any worse. Until you lose someone you love, you can't understand what Jena's feeling."

"You know," Paula said, "it would really be more sensible not to go, this Full Moon—even if there are questions you want to ask. If we never opened the portal again, Cezar couldn't find it."

Tati and I both looked at her.

"We can't not go," Stela said, all big eyes and drooping mouth.

"You're saying we should never go to the Other Kingdom again?" Iulia had understood what lay behind Paula's words, and her voice was hushed. "Not *ever*?"

"That's common sense," said Paula. "I don't like it any more than you do. Where else am I going to be able to talk about the things I love—history, philosophy, and ideas—now that Father Sandu's gone? But it's probably the right thing to do."

There was a silence. As it drew out, I imagined the sounds that might once have filled such an awkward pause and never would again: Gogu's wry comments, which only I could detect; his little splashing noises in the bath bowl; the soft thump as he landed on the pillow, ready for good-nights and sleep.

"We do need to go once more, if we can," I said as tears began to roll down my cheeks again. "I think we have to let Father know what's happening here. The only way I'm going to get a letter past Cezar is to ask for help in the Other Kingdom." I would take Grigori up on his offer. I thought he was strong enough to look after himself from here to Constanṭa and back. "What will happen after that, I don't know. Paula may be right. Maybe it is the end."

As we lay in bed later, Tati reached out under the quilt and took my hand in her own. Hers was cold as a wraith's. "Jena?" she whispered. "I'm sorry you're so sad."

My cheek was against the pillow, on the spot where Gogu always slept. The linen had been almost dry; I was wetting it anew with tears. I said nothing. It troubled me that when we had spoken of ending our visits to the Other Kingdom, Tati had raised no objections. I wondered what she saw in her own future. From where I lay, I could see her hair spread across her pillow like a dark shawl, the pale expanse of her neck exposed. I shut my eyes. If there was evidence there, a mark on her pearly skin, I was not ready to see it—not brave enough to accept what it might mean. The truth was, at Dark of the Moon, Sorrow had seemed to be a good person, as kind and thoughtful as Tati had always said he was. I did not want him to be one of *them*.

"Jena?"

"Mmm?"

"If Ileana won't help about Sorrow, I don't know what I'll do. I can't go on without him. I just can't."

It seemed an enormous effort to answer. All I wanted to do

was curl up into a ball with my misery. I hated Cezar. I hated fate for making Father ill and for not sending anyone to help us. I hated Drăguţa most of all, for twisting my dearest friend into a thing to be feared and loathed. I hated myself for still loving him.

"We just might have to go on, Tati," I said. "There might be no choice." I thought of a future in which Cezar was master of both Vârful cu Negură and Piscul Dracului. That future seemed to be almost upon us. Without Gogu, I wasn't sure whether I would be strong enough to protect my sisters— strong enough to act as Father would wish.

"There's always a choice, Jena." Tati closed her eyes. "Even giving up is a kind of choice."

As Full Moon approached, Cezar's mood deteriorated. He could often be heard yelling at the guards, who had evidently been chosen for both their intimidating size and their reluctance to engage in conversation. I wondered that he had anything to chide them about, since they seemed utterly obedient to his rule. They slept out in the barn.

Petru, displeased with the new arrangements, grew still more taciturn. Florica was distracted and fearful. The five of us applied ourselves to helping her in the kitchen and around the castle and to keeping out of Cezar's way. He was furious, and Petru had his own theory as to the cause. "Can't find a taker for this job he's thought up," he muttered as I passed him in the hallway. "Nobody wants to venture into the other realm. All too frightened of the Night People. A reward's no good to you if you're dead."

Iulia had become unusually quiet and often had red eyes. We were all uneasy at the presence of armed minders in our house, but this seemed something more.

"It's Răzvan," Paula told me when Iulia had burst into tears over a trivial matter and rushed out of the room for the tenth time in a week. "She's upset that he left so suddenly."

"Răzvan?" I stared at her. "She liked him that much?" I had noticed the boys' admiring glances at Iulia, and thought them inappropriate. My sister looked like a woman, but she was only in her fourteenth year—surely too young for such attentions. I had seen, later, how kind Daniel and Răzvan were to my younger sisters. All the same, this was a surprise.

"He has a sister Iulia's age, and his father keeps a stable full of fine riding horses," Paula informed me. "He half invited her to visit in the summer; she was really excited about it. Now that's all changed. The boys left without saying goodbye, and Cezar's not letting us go anywhere, let alone all the way to Răzvan's father's estate—it's on the other side of Braşov."

"Why didn't Iulia tell me?"

Paula regarded me a little owlishly. "You've been wrapped up in your own misery, Jena," she said. "With you brooding over Gogu, and Tati counting the minutes until Full Moon, Iulia's got nobody to confide in except me. And Stela's got nobody to be a mother to her except me. She's frightened. She can't understand why all these men are suddenly hanging around. It would actually be quite nice if you went back to taking a bit more notice of the rest of us."

Her words were a slap in the face. Was this really true? In my misery over Gogu and my concern to keep Piscul Dracului and the Other Kingdom safe, had I forgotten that my sisters, too, were unhappy? "I'm sorry," I said, tears welling in my eyes. "It's just that I miss him so much."

"All the same," Paula said, "you could make a bit of an effort."

"What do you want me to do?"

"Talk to Iulia. Make some time for Stela. Tati doesn't tell her stories and play with her the way she used to, and Stela thinks that's somehow her fault. I wish Tati would be herself again. She doesn't just look thin, she looks really ill. I wish Full Moon was over."

When I saw Iulia, I told her I thought Father might consider her old enough, next year, to go on a visit by herself, provided Aunt Bogdana approved all the arrangements. The expression on her face was reward enough: her eyes lit up. My little sisters were growing up faster than I had expected. It seemed that the prospect of a summer of riding in the company of an admiring young man was now more enticing to Iulia than the magic of Full Moon dancing. Was it possible to grow out of the Other Kingdom?

I took over the job of teaching Stela her letters—a task that Tati had abandoned when thoughts of Sorrow began to crowd other matters from her mind—and was rewarded by my small sister's smiles. I made myself available for bedtime stories. There was not much I could do for Tati herself. I could not force her to eat, and the rumors that were going about the valley made me reluctant to send for a doctor. I watched her fade a little each day, and prayed that Full Moon would bring solutions.

Up in our chamber, Gogu's jug and bowl stood empty on

the side table. Eventually I would put them away, but not yet; it seemed so final. Although I knew that beneath the semblance of the green-eyed man there was something dark and terrible, part of me still longed to go out into the forest and search for him, to see whether he was safe and well, to ask him . . . what? Why it was that Drăguţa had made him into a frog and put him in my path so I could save him and befriend him and love him and then have him torn away from me and revealed to be a monster? What she had done seemed not only pointless, but unreasonably cruel. I struggled to make sense of it.

On the eve of Full Moon I took ink, quill, and parchment up to the little tower with the starry ceiling and sat on the rug to write a letter. This was one place Cezar's watchdogs had not discovered. I recalled Gogu sitting on my midriff here and astonishing me by talking about true love. Telling me he liked my soft brown hair and my green gown. Saying he liked sleeping on my pillow so we were side by side. "I love you, too, Gogu," I whispered into the silence of the tower room, where the rays of the setting sun came low through the seven windows, touching the painted stars to a rosy shine. "At least, I loved you when you were a frog, before I knew the truth. But . . ." It was unthinkable that I could still feel that tenderness, still remember the good things as if they were not tainted by the horror of his true nature. He had watched me undressing, had traveled everywhere in my pocket, warmed by my body. He had snuggled against my breast and cuddled up to my neck under the fall of my hair. He'd been dearer to me than anyone in the world.

"I wouldn't mind you being a man, once I got used to the

idea," I muttered. "I could have liked that man, he seemed kind and funny and nice. Why couldn't he be the real Gogu?" I imagined my friend hopping across the dragon tiles to conceal himself in their green-blue pattern. I remembered his silent voice: *You left me b-b-behind.*

No more tears, I ordered myself. I'd had enough days of weeping myself into a sodden mess. There was a letter to be written and it must be done just right. Without Gogu to advise me, I must try to think of what he would suggest and do the rest myself.

Dear Gabriel, I wrote, *I have addressed this to you, hoping you will read it first, then share it with Father. I have already sent several letters, but we have received only one from you, telling us he was too unwell to have the news of our uncle's tragic death. I am sending this by a different messenger. Gabriel, if Father is dying, I need to know. My sisters and I would want to be at his bedside to say goodbye. If he is improving, then he should be told that we are having some difficulties at Piscul Dracului. . . .*

I kept it brief. Nothing about Sorrow or our Full Moon activities, of course. I told him what Cezar was doing: from the one-sided decision to take over our finances to the establishment of a force of guards to curtail our freedom. Telling that last part without revealing what we knew of the portal was tricky, but I managed it. I told him Cezar planned to start cutting down the forest as soon as spring came, and that I believed he had sent Aunt Bogdana away so she could not hold him back. I told him there were dangerous rumors in the valley, rumors about Piscul Dracului and about us.

If Father cannot come home, Gabriel, I ask that we be provided with some other assistance. I am afraid of Cezar and his interference, and I want him kept away from Piscul Dracului. I do not know where to turn. Please discuss this with Father. Do not send a reply with Cezar's usual messengers, the ones employed for the business, as I believe letters may have been intercepted. My own messenger is prepared to wait for your response. You must honor his wish to remain unidentified. You can trust him. I and my sisters send you our respects and our heartfelt thanks for your loyalty to Father. Please give him our love and fondest wishes for a good recovery and a speedy return home. Jena.

I folded the parchment and slipped it into my pocket. Then I lay on the rug, staring up at the ceiling as the sunset moved through gold and pink and purple and gray, and birds called to one another in the dark forest outside, winging to their roosts. I made myself breathe slowly; I willed myself to be calm. It wasn't easy. As far as we knew, Cezar had found nobody willing to undertake his mission. But I knew he would make it happen somehow, even if he had to do it himself. An elderly servant called Marta had come down from Vârful cu Negură earlier in the day, her job to act as our chaperone. We had made up a pallet for her in our bedchamber. It all seemed quite unreal.

I hoped the letter would reach Father before Cezar did anything worse. Tonight, at Dancing Glade, I would ask Grigori to take it to Constanţa for me, and both Tati and I would seek an audience with the queen of the forest. If Ileana had no further answers for us, I thought this might be the very last time we would visit the Other Kingdom. To risk exposing the folk of that realm to Cezar without good reason was something we could not do, not if we loved them and valued the wonderful opportunity they had given us month by month and year by year since we'd first found the portal. Tonight we might be saying our last farewell to Grigori and Sten, to Ildephonsus, to Ileana and Marin and all our friends from the Other Kingdom. I knew I must drink my fill of the colored lights, the exquisite music, the glittering raiment and delicious smells, and store it all up in my memory. The rest of my life might be a long time. When I was an old woman, I wanted to be able to remember every last jewel, every last gauzy wing, every last thrilling moment.

"Jena?" A tap at the door.

"Mmm?"

"Come downstairs! Quick!"

My heart plummeted. *What now?* I got up and opened the door.

No fewer than three sisters were clustered outside, their expressions mingling excitement and anxiety.

"There's a man here," Iulia babbled, "for the quest. Cezar's absolutely beaming! I think he thought he'd have to do it himself—"

"So you need to get the potion ready—" put in Paula.

"Quick, quick!" urged Stela, grabbing my arm and pulling me toward the steps.

We reached our chamber. Marta was down in the kitchen with Florica right now, waiting to find out if there would be any call for her services.

"Make sure none of your party clothing is in sight," I told my sisters. "We want both Marta and this man asleep before we show any signs of getting ready. Where's that *ţuică?*"

We had a silver tray ready, with a pretty Venetian flask and a set of matching glasses, though none of us actually drank plum brandy. Tonight, Tati and I would make the gesture of taking a small glass each, just so our victims would not be too suspicious.

"Put the marked glasses on this side," I said. "Good. Now the potion . . ." I retrieved Drǎguţa's tiny bottle from its hiding place under my mattress, uncorked it, and let two drops fall into each of the two glasses that had an unobtrusive ink dot on their stems. "There. We just pour the ţuicǎ on top, and—if the witch was telling the truth—this man won't detect a thing, and nor will Marta. Then we wait. I hope it works quickly. I can't believe Cezar is making us let a stranger into our bed-chamber."

We sat through supper. There were so many guards now that Florica couldn't feed them all in the kitchen, so she had to send provisions out to the barn. Cezar failed utterly to conceal his excitement. The look in his eyes sickened me.

There was no conversation. Florica brought dishes in and out; Cezar smiled his little superior smile; I divided the mǎmǎligǎ and shared out the boiled mutton and pickled cabbage. My sisters ate what they were given without a word. Apart from Tati, that is: she cut up her meat into tiny pieces and prodded her mǎmǎligǎ with a spoon. I didn't see her eat so much as a crumb.

After that, things grew more and more unreal. A man was waiting outside in the hallway, cap in hands, feet shuffling awkwardly. He looked rather pale. Our cousin introduced us by name, as if this were a polite tea party.

"Now, Ioan," said Cezar expansively, "you understand what is required of you tonight?"

"Yes, my lord. Find the entry; go in; come out; make sure I don't attract notice. Bring back information. I'm sure the young ladies will assist me."

Cezar raised his brows. "Well, good luck to you. I'll be waiting at dawn to let you out."

"What do you mean, let him out?" I asked, alarmed. "We'll be doing that. The bolt's on the inside."

"I have made suitable provision," Cezar said. "There's to be no trickery, no funny business, understand?"

"I understand that it excites you to shame your own kins-folk in front of strangers," I said, seething.

"You've brought it on yourselves." Cezar's tone was dismissive. "Go on, then. Take Ioan here up to the bedchamber and get on with things. Where's that frog, by the way? I haven't seen it at all lately. I must say I very much prefer taking supper without the wretched creature dripping all over the table and slurping its soup."

"I let him go," I said through gritted teeth. "This way, Ioan."

There was indeed a new lock, on the outside. One of the men must have installed it while we were at supper. When all of us were in the bedchamber, including Marta, who had toiled up the stairs after us, Cezar closed the door and we heard him slide the bolt across. The inside bolt had not been removed. I fastened that as well. Then we all stood about, awkward and silent: we sisters, our chaperone, and the unfortunate man.

"Would you care for a drink?" Tati asked politely.

Ioan muttered something and took the glass she offered.

"Marta?" Iulia favored our chaperone with her most charm-ing smile. "I'm sure you'd enjoy a small glass?"

"Thank you, Mistress Iulia." Marta was clearly embarrassed by the whole situation. She accepted her glass and retreated to sit on the very edge of her pallet, ill at ease.

All of us tried hard not to stare at either of them. We were deeply suspicious of the contents of Drăguţa's potion. Tati poured drinks for herself and for me; we perched on the end of our bed, sipping.

"Chilly weather, isn't it?" observed Paula brightly.

"Brilliant observation, considering it's winter," snapped Iulia, on edge with nerves.

"That's rude, Iulia," hissed Stela.

There was a sigh from Marta's corner. When we turned to look, she was collapsing onto her pillow, eyes shut. Iulia re-trieved the glass before it could fall from her limp fingers, and Paula tucked the blankets over her. Ioan swayed, staggered, then lay down on the floor, snoring faintly. After a moment, I picked up my pillow and put it under his head. It wasn't really his fault that he'd been so desperate for a few coppers that he'd been willing to risk the reputations of five wellborn young ladies.

"So far, so good," I said shakily. "We just have to hope it will last until we get back. Drăguţa's unreliable—she might try anything. Get changed quickly."

Tati put on the gossamer dress. White silk on white skin: she looked like a sacrificial victim. The crimson teardrop around her neck, on its black cord, was her only note of color.

She seemed all bones and hollows, a shadow of herself. Look-ing at her, I felt a chill deep inside me.

"Jena." Iulia's voice broke into my reverie. "Are you plan-ning to get dressed, or come in your working boots and apron?"

Quickly, I put on my green gown and pulled my hair back in a ribbon.

"Come on!" Tati was already crouched at the portal. "Hurry up!"

It felt very strange indeed. I could hardly believe this might be the last time we would gather here, a semicircle of pale faces by candlelight, a pattern of shadows on the wall, conjuring the magical, long-ago day when we had first discovered our won-drous secret.

Tati looked at me; I looked back. Her eyes were full of anx-iety, but there was a brightness there all the same: the gleam of love and of hope. She had not quite lost that, not while Sorrow might be no farther away than a single doorway and a walk through the forest. I shivered. It seemed to me there was noth-ing ahead for them but heartbreak and loss.

The portal opened.

"It's the last time." Stela's chin was quivering. "The really, really last time."

"Maybe not," said Paula briskly. "Anything's possible, Stela. Come on, take my hand." They vanished down the spiral ahead of us, and we followed. I was the last out; I looked back over my shoulder as I went. Both Marta and Ioan lay where they had fallen, motionless.

We reached the bottom of the steps and headed along the Gallery of Beasts. The gargoyles were hanging down from their vantage points, staring at us with their big, vacant eyes. None made a move to join us. Tati had gone ahead, but there was no call to the boats. As we approached the shore, I heard her urgent undertone. "*Jena!*"

Someone was there before us. A young man stood by the water's edge, and my heart stopped as I saw him. Pale skin, dark, tangled hair, steadfast green eyes . . . I could move neither forward nor back—my feet refused to budge. What was he doing here? This was Full Moon, Ileana's night: the night of lights and music, of friendship and good things. It was our chance to make things right again, if the queen of the forest would help us. If anyone did not belong here, it was him—the creature from the mirror, fair mask over foul reality. And yet I longed to go over to him, to touch him, to ask him if he was all right.

"Jena," whispered Paula, "who is it? What do we do?"

"It's him: Gogu," I said grimly. I walked on, ignoring my sisters' gasps of shock and murmurings of curiosity. "You mustn't go anywhere near him—it's dangerous. Don't speak to him. And don't let him in your boat, if he tries to get a lift."

We advanced to the shore. "*Ooo-oo!*" called Tati, glancing nervously at the young man. "*Ooo-oo!*"

Not so long ago I had wished Ileana would banish the Night People for good, and Sorrow with them. I had hoped fervently that my sister would never see her black-coated sweetheart again: it had seemed to me that even if he truly loved her, he could bring her only grief. Now, as I watched the little boats come one by one through the cracking ice of the Deadwash, part of me was willing Sorrow to be there, just to keep the spark of hope in Tati's eyes alive. One, two, three boats came. The first was poled by a dwarf—not Anatolie, but one of his many cousins or brothers—and a cold hand clutched at my heart. Paula, Iulia, and Stela were swept away across the water. The boatmen glanced at Gogu as they came in to shore, and their faces showed nothing but mild curiosity. None seemed afraid.

"He has to be here," Tati muttered. "He must be, he must be. . . ." She had her arms wrapped around herself: the ice might be melting and the winter starting to lose its grip, but this shore was no place for fine silk gowns. She looked at Gogu again. "Aren't you going to say *anything* to him?" she whispered.

"What is there to say? He's a monster—a thing from the darkness." I peered over the water, wondering whether I could see a light through the curtains of mist. I willed myself not to meet the gaze that I knew was fixed on me from a little way along the shore. He'd made no attempt to go with any of the others, though the ferrymen had looked amenable enough. With luck, we could leave him behind us.

"They're coming!" Tati exclaimed, peering across the ice-strewn water into the vaporous cloud. A moment later her shoulders slumped, for the two craft that emerged were poled by the massive troll, Sten, and tall, dark-locked Grigori. Sorrow had not come.

Tati went with Sten. I could see her questioning him as they crossed the lake. I went with Grigori. As our boat moved away from the shore, I caught Gogu's eye. His face was white, his mouth twisted in what looked like self-mockery. *Don't think about him,* I ordered myself. *You have a mission to perform tonight, so do it*. But I thought about him all the way across the Bright Between. He wouldn't go out of my mind.

I asked Grigori whether he would take the letter. "I'm desperate. There's nobody else I can trust."

"I'll take it, Jena. This Gabriel—can *he* be trusted?"

"He may look at you twice, but I know he has Father's best interests at heart. He's not the kind of man to make a fuss about things. All the same, be careful. I've made too many mistakes this winter and hurt too many people. I don't want to put you at risk, Grigori."

He smiled widely. "So my great-aunt finally turned the frog back into his old form," he said.

I was taken aback. "You know about that? Does everyone know?"

Grigori nodded. "Drăguţa made no secret of what she had done. All of us knew when the spell was cast, and when it was broken."

"You knew what Gogu really was, all the time?" I was shocked. "Why didn't anyone tell us? And what do you mean, his old form? What was he before, man or monster?"

"There's a right time for such answers to be made known, Jena, and it's not up to me to determine it. Drăguţa's rules bind us all. We were forbidden to tell."

"There was no right time for what she did to us," I said. "To Gogu and me. It was unforgivable."

"My great-aunt enjoys setting tests and playing tricks. There's a reason for every one of them. It pays to listen carefully to her words."

"Tell me about Anatolie." I forced the words out, wanting the truth before we reached Dancing Glade.

Grigori bowed his head. "We lost him," he said simply. "Some cruelties are beyond the endurance of the most stalwart. We will remember his laughter, his heroic strength, his nimble feet. No need to speak, Jena. I understand that this wounds you as it does every being in the Other Kingdom. Here we are," he added as the little boat grazed the far shore. He laid the pole in the craft and stepped out, extending a hand to help me. "There is a right time, Jena. You simply need to be open to it. Anatolie would want you to be happy."

Chapter Thirteen

I knew I would not have the heart to dance, even though this could be our last visit to the Other Kingdom. The confirmation of Anatolie's death weighed heavily on me. I could not escape the feeling that I could somehow have stopped Cezar if I had been just a little stronger, just a little braver. I was on edge, waiting until Ileana was ready to hold her audience so I could tell her what I needed to. Tati was in a worse state than I was. There was no sign at all of Sorrow, or of the other Night People. My sister was circling the sward, speaking to one person after another. As she came past me, I heard her asking where he was, where they were, and everyone giving the same answer: *Ask Ileana.* But Ileana and Marin had not yet appeared. I wondered how I would get Tati home if she refused to come.

The young man who was Gogu had managed, somehow, to get across the Deadwash. He was not dancing, either. As I refused one invitation after another, I stole glances at him and

wondered why he had come here. If Tadeusz and the pale Anastasia had not put in an appearance, along with their somber
retinue, why was this one creature from Dark of the Moon
among us? And why did none of the patrons of Ileana's glade
seem afraid of him? When I tried to warn people, they simply
laughed.

My younger sisters had not been able to resist the lure of
the music; even Paula was out on the sward, dancing. My feet
were itching to be out there in the midst of it. The lilt of the
bone flute, the throb of the drum, the thrum of the harp, stirred
my blood. My mind showed me, cruelly, the dream in which I
circled and swayed in the arms of the green-eyed man and felt a
happiness akin to nothing else in the world. I couldn't do it. I
was too full of sadness and guilt and fear.

Sten loomed by my side, huge and craggy. "One dance," he
said. "Come on."

"I can't. I'm waiting for Ileana."

"The queen's audience won't be until later."

"I'm worried about Tati. I need to keep an eye on her."

"Come on, Jena," the troll said. "I want to see you smile."

"I shouldn't—"

"Yes, you should. Come on! Iulia and Grigori are waving
us over."

"I—"

The troll seized my arm in a friendly grip. In a trice we
were out in the double circle of merrymakers, facing Grigori
and Iulia for a dance called Haymaking. The band struck up the
tune, and I had no choice but to join in. It was a dance in which

the circles moved in opposite directions, so everyone changed partners after sixteen measures. In the Other Kingdom this was an interesting experience, since some dancers were only as tall as one's knees, some had a tendency to use their wings to accentuate their moves, and some were so big that a girl my size had to crane her neck to make conversation. For a little, I half forgot my troubles in the constant effort to keep up and remain on my feet. The pace was frenetic.

I danced with Grigori and with the dwarf ferryman. I danced with the tiny Ildephonsus and with a mountain goblin who complimented me on my light feet. Then everyone moved on again, and the man standing opposite me was Gogu.

A chill ran through me. I whispered, "I can't—" but there was no extricating myself from the circle of folk moving in intricate pattern to the quick beat. With a crooked smile, the green-eyed man took my hand in his and led me around in a figure-of-eight. His touch alarmed me: it felt every bit as tender, as thrilling, as it had the day he'd first become a man again and I'd had to leave him. It seemed to hold out the promise of a joy beyond measuring. He made no attempt to converse with me, simply looked. In his eyes I could see confusion and reproach and a forlorn sadness that made me want to draw him out of the circle, to sit down and sort things out sensibly once and for all, to get to the truth. . . . But I could not find any words.

The circle moved on, and he was gone.

A forest man in a garment of salamander skins took my hand and led me into the next maneuver. At the far side of the sward, I spotted Gogu again, moving out of the crowd to stand alone under the trees. Somewhere in the throng there was a person without a partner.

When Haymaking drew to a close there was a fanfare, and the throng parted to allow Ileana her grand entry. She wore a cloak of peacock feathers and, under it, a gown that sparkled with silver. I wished she would go straight to her willow-wood throne, ready to receive folk with requests or praise or complaints. Instead, she went from one dance to the next, her tall headdress bobbing like a bright banner above the sea of revelers. I sat on the sidelines, watching Gogu, with a mass of conflicting feelings chasing one another around my heart. I had such a longing to get up and dance with him again that I had tears in my eyes.

"Trying to fill a lake with your tears?" A little voice spoke up right beside me, making me start. I looked down. There was Drăguţa, in a long cloak of tattered green and a hat of leaves, under which her white hair shone like moonbeams. Around her neck she wore an ornament of tiny bones threaded on a cord.

"I got it wrong, didn't I?" I said, wiping my nose. "I messed it up."

The witch grinned. In the undergrowth not far away, a pure white snake raised its head to stare at me: I had no doubt that it was her creature in another form, for its eyes were just the same. "Mess and mend," Drăguţa said. "Lose and find. Change and change again. The solution was right at your fingertips, and you never saw it, Jena. Now it's moving farther away every day. Best wake up soon, or it'll be beyond your reach."

"What solution? What do you mean?"

"Sometimes you have to let go. Sometimes you should hold on with all the strength you've got. And you have a lot of strength, Jena—too much for your own good, sometimes." She clicked her fingers; the snake wriggled toward her, hissing. She stooped and it flowed up her arm to settle around her shoulders like an exotic garment. Then she marched off into the forest without another word, and the shadows swallowed the two of them.

At that moment a horn sounded from down by Ileana's little pavilion. At last it was time for the royal audience. As I made my way across the sward, I found that I had a companion. The green-eyed man was walking beside me, a discreet distance away, not saying a word.

"What do you want?" I snapped, fighting an urge to move closer.

He remained silent; the look he gave me was gravely assessing. We advanced side by side. Although he kept a decorous arm's length away, my whole body felt his presence as if we were touching—as if we were walking arm in arm, like sweethearts. My face was hot; I knew I was blushing. I kept my eyes straight ahead. I had to keep my sisters safe. I could not afford to weaken.

Ileana was seated on her throne, the long train of her gown arranged artistically around her feet. Marin stood beside her, the lanterns turning his hair to brilliant gold. He needed no crown to show his royal status. Standing on tiptoe and craning my neck over a mass of shoulders, I caught a glimpse of Tati in her gossamer gown, white arms stretched out in supplication.

". . . and nobody will tell me where he is," she was saying. "I must know! I have to find him!"

"Ah, true love," said Ileana with a little knowing smile, and a ripple of laughter went around the gathered crowd. I tried to get through to the front, but the throng was too tightly packed, and I stumbled. Almost before I could draw breath, Gogu's hand was there at my elbow, steadying me. A moment later he was alongside me, clearing a way for us to go through. Folk took one look at him and simply moved aside.

"Thanks," I muttered ungraciously. We halted at the front, he behind me.

"Please help us, Your Majesty." Tati's voice was trembling. "Tell me where Sorrow went, so I can look for him. He's all alone. He needs me."

"Child," Ileana said, "do you recognize the gravity of what you intend to do? Do you know what a human woman must sacrifice to wed one of our kind? You are young. You will have suitors aplenty in your own world. Give this up. Sorrow is gone. If he did not keep faith with you, why should you do any more for him?"

Tati clenched her fists. "You're lying," she told the queen. A ripple of shock ran around the circle. "I know Sorrow wouldn't turn his back on me. If he's not here, there must be another explanation. Anyway, we think maybe he's not one of your kind. Jena saw a vision: it looked as if he and his sister were human children captured by the Night People. That means he's the same kind as me. You can't forbid us to be together—"

"May I speak?" I interrupted. I had seen the look in Ileana's eyes. I knew I must stop Tati before she angered the queen beyond helping us. I had never witnessed one of Ileana's rages, but the folk of the Other Kingdom spoke of them with awe. Her screams had been known to crack ice and make birds fall from the trees. "Your Majesty, perhaps you know that my sister and I crossed over at Dark of the Moon last month. It was not a very wise thing to do, but Tatiana was concerned about Sorrow's safety."

"And you had your own reasons, no doubt, Jenica." Ileana's pale blue eyes bored into me, seeking out my most carefully guarded thoughts.

"I wanted information," I said cautiously. "I'd been invited to look in Drǎguţa's magic mirror." I heard a gasp from the assembled folk; this meant something to them. "I thought if I could see the future I might be able to change things, Your Majesty. That was foolish—I know that now."

"What did you see in this mirror? Enlighten us, Jenica." Ileana's tone was quite chilly.

"What Tatiana told you. Sorrow and a little girl as children, and the leader of the Night People offering them shelter when they were lost. I saw that same girl at the Dark of the Moon gathering. It alarmed me that such a young person should be exposed to the evil things I saw there. It is hard to believe that world exists alongside yours, Your Majesty. Until we crossed over, we had no idea of it."

"And what else did this magic mirror show you?"

"I . . ."

"Come on. You went there—you let temptation rule you. Tell the truth!" Suddenly she was on her feet: tall, fell, and terrible. The glade seemed to darken.

"I saw this young man, the one who is standing behind me. As I watched, this mask of—of ordinariness—slipped off, and there was a terrible creature underneath. A creature that belonged *there*, in Tadeusz's dark world. He . . . I saw him do some cruel things, Your Majesty. Things that turned my blood cold." I could not look at Gogu.

"You are telling us that the creature you have carried close to you all these years—the little frog who enjoyed our midnight frolics and journeyed among us held safely on your shoulder—is a monster beneath the surface?"

Misery shrank my voice to a whisper. Without looking, I could sense Gogu's utter stillness. We had not been so close all those years for nothing. "That's the way it seems. When Drǎguţa turned him back into a man, that's the man he was. I think it was all some kind of cruel joke." I pulled myself together. "But I'm not here to ask about that, Your Majesty. Tati and I are deeply concerned about Sorrow and his sister. I understand that even if they are human folk, they have been in the Other Kingdom too long now to come back to our world. I saw Sorrow jump off a high parapet at Piscul Dracului. No human man could do that and survive. I understand that perhaps, after so many years, they have become something very like the Night People. But, Your Majesty, if you could find a place for them in your own realm, safe from those who hold them in thrall, that would be much better than leaving them where they are. That little girl is almost a woman: I don't like to think what might become of her. . . ."

"Ah," said Ileana. "You are able to see somewhat more broadly than I gave you credit for, Jenica. Good. You realize, of course, that nothing comes without a cost."

"So folk keep telling me."

"You may have to give up something precious, Jena. Something very dear to your heart."

I was five years old again, and offering my crown. *I want to be Queen of the Fairies.*

"Can it be done, Your Majesty?" Tati breathed. "Can you bring them here?"

"Sorrow's gone," said Ileana flatly. "You weren't listening, Tatiana."

"Nor were you!" Tati's voice was rising. "I told you, he loves me! He'll come back for me—I know he will!"

"Love, hope, trust," Marin said lightly. "These are strong in you, Tatiana: so strong, your belief in them seems almost foolish. Are they so important?"

Tati squared her frail shoulders and lifted her chin. "They're everything," she said, and her voice rang out around Dancing Glade like a clear bell. "That's what life is all about— love and loyalty, truth and trust. I'm not giving that up. And I'm not giving Sorrow up. Tell me where he is. Tell me what I have to do to find him."

Behind me, Gogu shifted. I glanced up. He had a funny look in his eyes, and his fingers were by my shoulder, close to the place where he was once accustomed to sit under the shelter of my hair. I edged away, alarmed by how badly I wanted him to touch me. His hand fell back to his side, and his face went blank.

"Well spoken, Tatiana," Ileana said, a little smile curving her lips. "You have passed the first part of your test. The second requires that you maintain hope for somewhat longer, for Sorrow is indeed gone—gone far away. As it happens, we have made an arrangement with the Night People. We were very displeased that they did not keep their bloody activities outside this valley. We have watched over your small community since time before time. We do not indulge in senseless acts of violence; wanton bloodletting sickens us, whether it be of human folk or creatures. In Tadeusz's world it is different. His exists alongside mine—indeed, within the Other Kingdom are many worlds. At Full Moon dancing, you sisters have seen but the merest sliver of our realm. You were young when we first admitted you here, young and vulnerable. We showed you what was appropriate. When you chose to visit Tadeusz's world, you entered a far different place. In your world and in ours, darkness and light exist side by side."

She turned and beckoned, and one of her attendants—a tall woman clad in dry beech leaves, with wisps of fern tangled into her hair—came forward, with a pale-faced girl by her side. The girl was all in black. She looked much as she had when last I saw her—dazed, unseeing—but there was more color in her face now, as if a long frost was starting to thaw.

"We bargained for Silence here," Ileana said. "I share your concerns, Jenica. She is with us until her brother can achieve the quest we have set him. Much rides on it. Sorrow has three prizes to win, should he fulfill his task in time."

Tati stood silent, waiting for more. I could see her trembling.

"He has until midnight at next Full Moon to execute it and

return. Fail, and he must leave our forest forever. If he prevails and returns in time, he will win his sister's release to my realm and my rule. The Night People will move away from our valley. And we will give Sorrow permission to bring you across, Tatiana, and to dwell with you among us as man and wife."

"Oh . . . oh, thank you," said Tati, clasping her thin hands together. "Thank you . . ."

My heart was hammering. I had wanted Tati to get her answers, but not this. This just could not be. "My lady," I blurted out. "Your Majesty . . . this is not right. Don't you realize what it would mean, if my sister wed Sorrow? She'd have to leave our world forever. Our father is very sick, perhaps dying. This could be the final blow for him—" I saw Tati's eyes fill with tears. Ileana's regal features became glacial, but I didn't seem to be able to stop myself. "You can't allow this! There has to be another way!"

"Of course, Sorrow may not succeed in the quest," Ileana said crisply. I wilted under her stare. "We made it difficult, in recognition of the value of the reward. If he never returns, or does so without fulfilling our requirements, you can keep your sister. For you are right: Sorrow and Silence have been here too long to go back to the human world. Each has developed qualities that would lead to great trouble if they tried to return. Neither could last long."

What could I say? That I would rather my sister not marry the man she loved, even if it meant she would be unhappy all her life? When I looked at it that way, it did not seem to matter what Sorrow was or what he might have become. How could I wish his quest to fail, if that meant he and the fragile-looking Silence must return to the dark world of the Night People? But if he succeeded, Tati would say goodbye to her family and home forever. We might never see her again. Torn two ways, I held my silence.

"What is the nature of this quest, Your Majesty?" Tati's voice was trembling.

It was Marin who answered. "He must journey within both your world and ours. Five items are to be brought back. A jewel from the ceremonial headdress of the Caliph of Tunis. A tail feather from the sacred phoenix of Murom-Riazan. A cup of water from the healing well of Ain Jalut, filled to the very brim, but not overflowing."

"A tooth from the loathsome bog-beast of Zaradok," added Ileana. "And a lock of hair from the head of a truthful man."

"In one turning of the moon?" The incredulous voice was that of Paula, whose knowledge of geography was extensive. "You can't be serious! There's no way a person could travel so far in so little time."

"You've set Sorrow up to fail," said Tati in a whisper. "You never meant him to—"

"Enough!" Ileana's voice was imperious. "Perhaps you do not comprehend how rarely such an opportunity is offered—how privileged the two of you are, to be granted our approval for your union. If Sorrow's will to succeed is strong enough, he will complete the quest. If not, he does not deserve our favor. Step back, Tatiana. Your audience is over. Jenica, you spoke out of turn. Leave us now."

I cleared my throat. "I have something else to say," I croaked, trembling with nerves.

"Be brief." The forest queen had risen to her feet. She towered over me, eyes baleful. "You have offended me."

"I—it is possible I and my sisters may not return here after tonight," I said. "Our cousin . . . He has a plan to get the secret of the portal from us. He intends to come through and use violence against you. We need to protect you: we owe you that, and much more. I think this may be our last visit. Even so, I can't be sure we will be able to stop him—but we'll do our best."

Around Dancing Glade there was total silence.

"So . . . I want to say thank you. We have been so happy here, so honored. I know few human folk are granted the privilege of crossing over as we were, and the joy of meeting so many wonderful friends—" Across the circle, Ildephonsus broke into noisy sobs and flung his short arms around Stela's neck. Sten was wiping his eyes on a crumpled gray rag. "There is no way we can thank you enough." I was struggling now, my own tears welling.

"Of course," Ileana observed, "there *is* a way to thank us. Should Sorrow achieve his quest, you can agree to let your sister come across to us—to become one of us. That would balance the ledger perfectly. Or don't you set such a high value on your lovely Tatiana?"

"You know I do," I said, blinded by tears. "I understand what you said, that everything has a price. But that's too much to ask. Tati's my sister. I love her. It's too final."

"Death is final," the forest queen said. "The felling of trees is final. What we ask of you is simply the recognition of change, Jena. Yours is a world of constant change. You must learn to change, too. You spend a great deal of time worrying about others: trying to put their lives right, trying to shape your world as you believe it should be. You must learn to trust your instincts, or you are doomed to spend your life blinded by duty while beside you a wondrous tree sprouts and springs up and buds and blooms, and your heart takes no comfort from it, for you cannot raise your eyes to see it."

Gogu made a sudden movement, as if in anger.

Ileana regarded him gravely. "I'm growing weary of this audience," she said. "Young man, have you something to say?"

He stepped forward, bowed courteously, then lifted his hands and indicated his mouth and throat. Then he spread his arms wide, palms up, as if asking a question.

"You've lost something?" Ileana queried. A new warmth had entered her tone.

The young man nodded, pointing to his throat again.

"Ah," said Ileana. "Drăguța's been up to her tricks again. Not content with tormenting the young lady, she's decided to play games with you as well, frog boy. You want your voice back?"

So that was it: not that he would not speak, but that he could not. A spell of silence. I had been less than fair to him.

Ileana sighed. "The witch of the wood is overfond of such charms," she said, snapping her fingers. One of her attendants came forward with a wand of plain willow, with a small star at the end—the kind of thing I would have loved as a child when I was playing at fairies. "You've been a model of control over the years, young man—so much of one that even your best friend failed to see what you really were. Kneel down!"

He obeyed. The cloak he wore, my cloak, brushed the ground before Ileana's throne. Anticipating magic, the crowd hushed again. The forest queen stretched out her arms, and the sweep of her vivid peacock garment caught the lights of Dancing Glade. "Speak again, young man," she said quietly. "You have been silent long enough." She touched Gogu gently on his bowed head with the tip of her wand.

There was no sudden flash of light, no explosion, no flying through the air. The young man said, "Thank you," and got to his feet. He turned toward me, his eyes blazing. "Jena," he said, "don't you know me?"

I stared at him. In my head, the mask of sweetness peeled back and I saw the monstrous reality beneath it. *Don't trust, don't trust, don't trust*, a little voice repeated inside me. *Don't put your sisters at risk.*

"Jena, I'm Costi. Your cousin. You must recognize me."

"What—!" That was Paula.

"But Costi's dead." That was Stela.

"I'm not listening to this," I said shakily. How dare he! How dare he come up with something so outrageous and offensive? "You can't be Costi—he drowned. Cezar saw it with his own eyes. You're just saying that to . . . You're just—" I could not look at him: I could not bear the look on his face, wounded, disbelieving.

"I'm not dead! I'm here. I am Costi—can't you see? I've been with you all along, since the day you found me in the forest. Waiting—waiting until she lifted the spell, and I could be my self again, and tell you."

"A spell of silence," Iulia breathed. "Like Sorrow—a ban on talking about who he was and what had happened to him. But Jena's right. Cezar saw what happened. So did she. They saw Costi dragged under the water. He couldn't have survived." Despite her words, there was a note of wonder in her voice, as if she would be all too easily convinced.

"The audience is concluded," Ileana said. "Young man, I wish you well. Strike up the music! The queen wants to dance!"

But for us, there was no more dancing. As the queen and her retinue headed back onto the sward, Tati crumpled to her knees. "Jena . . . ," she whispered, "my head hurts. . . . I don't feel very well. . . ." A moment later she fell to the ground in a dead faint.

"She's hardly eaten a thing since the last time she saw Sor row," Paula said, crouching down to feel for Tati's pulse. "And she's overwrought. We should go home, Jena."

"What's wrong with her?" Stela was crying, half in sympa thy with Tati, half in sadness and exhaustion. Ildephonsus clung to her, his gauzy wings enfolding her in a kind of cape.

"She's fainted, that's all," I told her, not wanting to make things any harder. "Paula's right. We need to go now."

"I have to say goodbye," Stela sniffed. "I'll be quick, I promise."

"We'll meet you down at the boats," said Iulia.

"Wait—" The two of them were already gone.

"Jena," said Paula, "we need to get her down to the lake."

"I'll take her," the young man said. "She's very cold. Is there a spare cloak?"

"No—!" I began, not wanting him to put his hands anywhere near my sister, but he ignored me, picking Tati up as easily as if she were a doll. Paula and I followed him around the margin of Dancing Glade and down the path to the Deadwash. None of us said a word. I was full of mixed-up feelings, uppermost being a sense of betrayal: how dare Drăguţa meddle so cruelly? How dare this *thing* in a man's guise play with my heart and disturb my mind? Of course he couldn't be Costi. I'd have known! I'd have known, even when he was a frog. Wouldn't I?

By the time we reached the boats, a silent crowd was following us: red-eyed Stela, somber-faced Iulia, and all our usual escorts and hangers-on. There wasn't a smile among them.

Grigori took Tati from Gogu and laid her in his boat. She was beginning to stir, putting a hand to her brow and murmuring something. Then Drăguţa's great-nephew extended his hand to me. "You, as well," he said.

Sten took Iulia, and the dwarf was boatman to Stela. Ildephonsus, refusing to accept her departure until the last possible moment, clambered into the small craft to sit by her, sobbing. A hooded soothsayer ferried Paula, who was now carrying a mysterious bundle. On the shore behind us, the young man with the green eyes stood quietly, watching. He did not ask for a lift, and nobody offered one.

"Goodbye!" my sisters called. "Goodbye! Thank you!" But I had no heart for farewells; all I could feel was a numb disbelief.

The folk of the Other Kingdom waved and shouted and sang, and one or two flew over us, blowing kisses and causing the dwarf to curse as he nearly lost his pole. Then the mist came down to cover us. Behind us, the Other Kingdom shrank . . . and faded . . . and vanished.

"All will be well, Jena," Grigori said quietly. But it couldn't be. A terrible sense of wrongness was coming over me: the feeling that I had just thrown away my dearest treasure and that I would never, ever get it back.

I reached out to take Tati's hand. She seemed fragile as a moonflower—destined to bloom for a single lovely night, and then to fade and fall. A whole month until next Full Moon: it was a long time for her to wait. And yet, for me, it was short. Only a month, and my sister might be gone forever. How could I let that happen?

On the far shore, Ildephonsus refused to be detached from Stela. Both were in floods of tears. Paula disembarked, bundle in hand, and bade her boatman a grave farewell. She moved to Stela's side.

"Stela," she said with remarkable composure, "I've been given some books and maps and other things, see? Even if we can't use our portal anymore, there must be other ways we can find. There are clues in here. We just have to work them out. You can help me. I don't believe it's farewell forever."

Stela dashed the tears from her cheeks, took a deep, unsteady breath, and stepped away from her friend. "Goodbye, Ildephonsus," she said, hiccuping. Her expression told me she had suddenly grown up rather more than she wanted to. "We'll come back sometime. Paula knows these things." She kissed him on his long pink snout. Ildephonsus wrung his paws and began a high, eldritch wailing. The dwarf bundled him back in the boat and, with a shout of farewell, bore him away.

Sten lifted Iulia out onto the shore. "Of course," he said, "*we* can come across if we're careful, so it's not really goodbye forever. But we'll sorely miss you at Full Moon. You make lovely partners." He planted a smacking kiss on my sister's cheek. "Don't go marrying a heavy-footed man now, will you?"

"I'll see you soon, Jena," said Grigori. He had brought Tati to land. She was conscious again, though shaky—between us, Iulia and I supported her. "I'll be back with your father's answer as quick as I can."

"Be careful. Cezar's hunting parties are still going out from time to time."

"I will. Farewell, then."

"Farewell, Grigori. Thank you for everything."

"My advice to you," he said with a grin, "is to seek out my great-aunt before you go home. I don't think you've asked her all the questions you might." He stepped back into the boat and dug in the pole. Within a count of three, the vessel had disappeared through the shrouds of mist, and we were alone on the shore. Or not quite alone, for another boat was approaching through the vapor—a flat little craft that bobbed on the surface, the ice shards jingling around it. On it stood a familiar figure: thin arms wielding the pole, green eyes set on the shore ahead, hair tumbling wildly over his brow. His jaw was set tight; he looked every bit as angry and upset as Cezar on one of his worst days. As we watched, he maneuvered his craft to the shore and stepped off it. A raft. A raft made of weathered timbers, bound together with twists of flax and fragments of fraying rope.

"I'm sorry," Iulia said, staring. "We should have offered you a lift in one of our boats."

"As you see," said the young man, "I have my own."

"You—" I managed. "You—" But my tongue would not deliver the words. I'd been foolish before, letting myself be taken in by Tadeusz and his coaxing. I'd been so foolish that I'd nearly let him take Tati while my attention was all on my own concerns. I would not give way to such foolishness now. "That could have been here all the time," I said. "Anyone could have found it and used it. You're lying. You're not Costi. You can't be."

He looked as if I'd just smacked him in the face. The green eyes went bleak. The thin lips were not humorous now, but set in a tight line. "If you can't trust, you can't trust," he said. "Goodbye. I'm going home now." Without another word, he turned on his heel and walked away along the lakeshore.

The five of us stood in silence, watching him, until he vanished into the darkness of the wildwood. He still had my cloak on.

"We need to get Tati home, Jena," said Paula. "It's cold out here."

"You can't just let him go like that," objected Iulia. "He was upset. He was really sad. Jena, he does look quite a lot like Cezar. And even more like that old picture of Uncle Nicolae, the one Aunt Bogdana has hanging in her hallway. Are you sure—?"

"Run after him, Jena." Stela was shivering with cold.

"Run after him? In the forest at night? I don't think so." My feet were on the verge of doing just that. How could I let him walk off with that expression on his face?

"Go on, Jena." Tati's voice was a thread. "We'll wait for you at the top of the steps. He can't have gone far."

I ran. I did not allow myself to think of Night People, or of wolves, or of any other dangers that might be lurking in the darkness. I ran along the shore of Tǎul Ielelor, and as I went I spotted something shining in the undergrowth—a little crown of wire and beads, ribbon and braid. Following my instincts, I grabbed it as I passed. "Gogu!" I shouted. "Wait for me!" But there was no response, save the hooting of an owl and the patter of a small creature in the bushes.

At the spot where the track branched away from the water I halted, my chest heaving in the chill air. I would not attempt the walk through the woods, the long way home to Piscul Dracului. The others were waiting; without me, they could not open the portal. How had he managed to vanish so quickly? Perhaps he had slipped away to Tadeusz's world—perhaps, if I tried too hard to follow, I, too, would find myself in that dark realm. "Gogu?" I said, my voice shrunk to a little, fearful thing in the immensity of the shadowy forest.

"Gone," someone said from down below. "Gone for good. Foolish girl. Why didn't you *listen*?"

I looked down. She was there, green cloak wound around her small body, broad hat partly concealing the gooseberry eyes and the wrinkled, canny old features. Not far away, the white snake twined in a bush, its forked tongue flickering.

"Gone where?" I asked her, my mind searching for the right questions, not to waste the opportunity as I had before.

"Home. Vârful cu Negură. Where else?"

"You're talking as if he *is* Costi. But he can't be. Costi drowned. Cezar and I saw it. One moment he was swimming, the next he was gone."

"Think, Jena. You're on the raft. You've just given up your treasure and received a gift of great power in return. You're frightened. The raft floats out on the water, far out, beyond a safe margin. What then? Tell me the story. Think hard."

"How do you know all this?"

"I was there." The witch smiled; the moonlight glanced off her little pointed teeth. *Nothing comes without a price.*

She was right: I really had been stupid. I looked down at the crown in my hands. "A gift of great power," I said softly. "What are you saying? I couldn't be queen of the fairies. That was a child's wish."

"You won the nearest thing I could grant you, little brave adventurer that you were: free entry into the Other Kingdom for you and your sisters, for as long as you needed it. Each of you got what she most desired from it: for Paula it was scholarly company, for Stela little friends to love. Iulia's wishes were simple—to dress up and dance, to enter a world more remarkable and vibrant than your own could ever be. Tati waited a long time for her reward. She is still waiting, but what she most longs for will come soon enough, if Sorrow can win it for her."

I could hardly breathe. "And what about me?"

"The satisfaction of pleasing those you loved. The escape; the freedom; the Otherness. And more, if you learned to recognize it. You had to grow and change, Jena. So did your cousins. I did not act from sheer mischief that day by the lake. For the good of Piscul Dracului, for the wildwood, for the valley, I made a choice. Three choices. Three wishes."

"I was on the raft." I grasped for old memories. "It floated out too far. Costi swam after it to save me. He was scared. Nobody swims in the Deadwash, not if they value their life. But he did. He got his hands on the raft; he got me more than halfway back. Then . . ." *Then he got into difficulties, and I had to rescue you, Jena. I went back in for Costi, but he had disappeared under the water. Hands pulled him down—the witch's hands.* I could still hear Cezar telling the story, coaching me, word for word, so I would get it right when we had to tell our parents. It wasn't my story—it was his.

"Go on, Jena."

"I was scared. I had my hands over my eyes. I didn't see anything until I got back to the shore. I know the raft tipped up and I nearly fell in. I opened my eyes when I landed, and it was Cezar pushing the raft, not Costi."

"And after that? Did you look out across the water? Did you see Costi?"

"No," I whispered, a terrible feeling creeping over me, the cold knowledge that I had misjudged my best friend in all the world. "I ran off into the bushes and hid. I put my little blanket over my head. When I came out, there was only Cezar. Costi was gone. And Cezar told me what had happened."

"And you believed him."

"I was only five." It seemed a poor excuse. "Besides, why would you turn Costi into a frog? You said he had to grow and change. How could that help?"

"He got his wish, as you did yours. He gave up what was most precious to him: his badge of family. He was an arrogant boy—impetuous and exuberant—but he did have duty at heart, and love for his parents and his home. There was a lot of good in him, enough to make his future important. I could not allow that arrogance to go unchecked. He wanted to be King of the Lake, and he got his wish. Isn't a frog the master of the water, free to go wherever he wishes, lord of all he surveys—as long as he keeps a lookout for large fish?"

"But he wasn't," I said. "When I found him later, he was weak and sick and frightened. He didn't know how to be a frog, not properly."

"Part of his learning, and of yours," said Drăguţa, her beady eyes fixed on me from the shadow of her broad-brimmed hat. "He learned patience and humility; you learned compassion. You both learned love. At least, that was the intention. Don't look at me like that, young lady. I have your best interests at heart."

I found this very hard to believe. "Then why the magic mirror? Why show me Costi's face and make it into something hideous that gave me nightmares? Why show him attacking my sisters? I thought the mirror showed the future. I thought it offered warnings. All it's done is make me hurt him terribly. He'll never forgive me for this."

"He will find it difficult to forgive, yes," Drăguţa said. "I saw the anger in his eyes—the sorrow and shock—when I gave him back what he had given up to me, all those years ago. Costi has a difficult time ahead of him. It is unfortunate that he cannot have his heart's dearest by his side, but this is the path you have chosen, and you must follow it as best you can."

"You saw him just now? Gave him back his family ring?"

She nodded. "And I have sent Cezar back his own treasure," she said. "A surprise—he'll get it tomorrow. Now that Costi is home, his brother can no longer be King of the Land."

I stared at her, horrified. "What?" I whispered. "You mean . . . Cezar becoming the eldest son, and later on getting control of the estate, and taking ours as well, and . . . You mean that was all part of granting a *wish*? That he actually wished he could take Costi's place?"

"At eight years old, Cezar was not wicked; he was an ordinary little boy who loved his brother dearly. When I asked him what was most precious to him, that was where his eyes fell: on Costi—his hero, his idol. But he did not make his choice in innocence. As he realized what he had been offered, his childhood fell away from him, and he set his feet on a new path. He chose power before love. He could have saved Costi. I offered him that opportunity after he brought you to shore: his brother was still swimming, but was held there by the current, unable to come in. Instead of helping him, Cezar stood and watched his brother go under the waters of Tǎul Ielelor. In that moment, he shaped his future. He has fought that decision over and over as he has grown to be a man. But he could not unmake it. He could not change the fact that when the choice faced him, he took the darker path."

"Oh, God." The strange things Cezar sometimes said began to make a kind of sense: the mutterings about promises that were shams, about gifts that turned to damage those who received them. I understood, at last, his powerful hatred of Drăguţa. "That was . . . unspeakably cruel. Without that, he might have grown up to be a good man."

"The choice was not mine. It was Cezar's. Every choice he has made, these ten years past, has been his own. Now he has run out of choices. He has lost his chance to rule the valley. He has lost his brother's love, and yours. His father is gone. His mother has done her best to love him, but her feelings for this son have always lacked the warmth she turned on Costi, her adored eldest." She turned her head, snapping her fingers to summon the snake to her.

"Please don't go yet," I begged. "The mirror—why that image in the mirror?"

"The monster? Not my doing," Drăguţa said dismissively. "Hers, I imagine: Anastasia's. All it would have taken was for you to have a moment of doubt, a moment when you mistrusted your instincts. That moment of weakness would have allowed her control of the image. Such creatures as she take delight in tormenting folk, Jena. She wanted to send you nightmares—to make you squirm."

"Why?"

"Oh, I imagine she was jealous. She didn't like the way her brother, if brother he can be called, was looking at you. She didn't take kindly to his partiality to you."

"Tadeusz was never interested in me. She told me so. She told me very plainly that I was beneath his notice."

"Exactly. *She* told you. *He* never said anything of the kind, I imagine. And since you are bidding the Other Kingdom farewell tonight, you won't be getting the opportunity to ask him. Perhaps you are not such a plain, unattractive thing as you imagine, Jena. You might consider why, with two eligible young men on one estate and a family of five girls on the next, both men fell in love with the same sister: not lovely Tati or blossoming Iulia, but flat-chested, bushy-haired, opinionated Jena."

"In love? Cezar doesn't know what love is. As for Tadeusz . . ." I faltered. I had allowed the cruel logic of Anastasia's words to overrule what I sensed: that the leader of the Night People was indeed drawn to me. I remembered Tadeusz telling me that his kind were misunderstood; that superstition had painted them darker than they really were. I wondered if there was any truth in that. I'd never get the chance to find out now. "And if Costi felt any love for me when he was a frog," I went on, "it will all be gone after what's happened. How could he love someone who's shown such a lack of trust? If only he'd had his voice as soon as he changed back. He could have told me who he was and what had happened to him, and none of this misunderstanding need have happened—"

The witch cleared her throat, and I fell silent. "You have a short memory," Drăguţa said. "*Trust your instincts,* I seem to recall advising you. But did you listen? It would seem not. He was your dearest friend, and in your heart you knew it. You knew it from the moment you saw him sprawled out on the shore—you knew it as he walked through your dreams and every part of you yearned for his touch. But you wouldn't let yourself trust those feelings, would you? I couldn't give the boy back his voice straightaway, Jena. That would have made things too easy for both of you. Even now, you need more time to learn what love really means."

"Time to do what?" My voice came out tear-choked and harsh. "He just walked away. I don't know how to mend things now."

"I can't help you with that," Drǎguţa said briskly. "Now are we done here? It's not my habit to answer so many questions. I hope you don't have any more; I doubt if I'm up to it."

I swallowed a further plea for help. I had not forgotten who she was, or what she could do.

"It's for you to sort out, Jena," the witch said, her tone not unfriendly. "You are, in fact, highly capable and full of goodwill. You can do it." The white snake slid up her arm to twine around her shoulders. She picked up her staff, which had been lying in the bushes. "Goodbye, Jena," she said. "Hurry back. Your sisters are getting cold."

"Goodbye," I said as she slipped away, vanishing within moments. "Thank you for giving me the truth."

There was a diminishing cackle, high-pitched and scornful, then silence.

At the top of the winding stair my sisters were waiting, white-faced and silent. Paula had the lantern that we had left ready at the foot of the stairs when we came down, and Stela was carrying the bundle. Tati was sitting on the ground with her back against the portal, her eyes shut.

"She says she's not coming," said Iulia, who was crouched by Tati with a hand on her shoulder.

"Tati!" I said sharply, kneeling down and touching my sister's wan cheek. "Tati, wake up! Put your hand on the door— come on!"

"Not going . . . must wait . . . Sorrow . . . ," she muttered.

"Tati," said Paula, "we can't get home unless you help us. We'll all be trapped here in the middle. Come on! Sorrow's going to be away for a whole month." I saw in her face the unspoken thought: *And probably far longer—that's if he ever gets back*. The quest had seemed formidable to me, and I had never even heard of Ain Jalut or Zaradok.

Tati opened her eyes. "I'm not going," she whispered. "I'm waiting for him here."

It sounded like nonsense. But something deep inside me had changed tonight. Now I could understand so well what she was feeling: the longing, the grief, the fragile hope. "Tati," I said, "if you truly love Sorrow and he loves you, you need to do what Ileana asked you to do: to keep faith until he achieves the quest. Let us go home, and we'll help you get through the wait until next Full Moon. Remember what you said: *love and loyalty, truth and trust*? You can trust your family."

"You really believe that?" she asked me in a wisp of a voice. "That love will make it right?"

I longed for the certainty that would let me speak as Tati had to Ileana, pleading Sorrow's case and her own. If only I could believe that love must triumph over all adversity. But my head was full of doubts. "Of course I do," I said, wishing with all my heart that it was not a lie.

"Come on, then," whispered Tati, kneeling and placing her hand on the stones. We set ours beside it so the five of us touched the portal together. It slid open, and we entered our bedchamber. There, both Ioan and Marta lay sleeping, exactly where we had left them. Our last visit to the Other Kingdom was over.

Chapter Fourteen

We heard the bolt slide open soon after dawn, and Cezar's voice. "Where's my man?" he demanded. "What's he got for me?" He was in the doorway.

We had changed back into our day clothes; our dancing finery was neatly packed away. I had unfastened the inner bolt. Stela had slept for a little, but the rest of us had been too nervous to rest.

"Ioan's still asleep," I said as calmly as I could. "So's Marta. It's very early."

"Wake him." Cezar was keyed up, his hands clenched into fists. His tone shocked me. "I need his account now."

"I'm not your servant, Cezar." Something had made me strong this morning. Perhaps it was the knowledge of what he had done, all those years ago. "I'm taking my sisters down to breakfast. I won't be treated as some kind of lackey in my own home."

"Wake him!" He lifted his hand and struck me; my cheek burned. I heard my sisters' horrified gasps behind me.

"You can't do that!" protested Iulia.

"Excuse me." My voice was not calm now, but shaking. I walked past Cezar, palm to my face. The others followed me without a word. As we made our way down the stairs, I could hear him shouting at Ioan, "Wake up, man! What's the matter with you?"

It was a difficult day. Without making any kind of decision, we sisters did not say anything to Florica or Petru, or to Cezar, about Costi's reappearance, though I had told the others after we came home that I had been terribly wrong. It was true: Gogu and Costi were one and the same. I feared to tell Cezar the truth. I did not know how he would respond, with anger and suspicion or with love and relief that the adored brother whose death he bore on his conscience was, after all, alive and well. I did not know what Costi would do, how he would manage his return. Would people know him? Or would they be like me—wary and doubtful, unable to trust? I should have known him better than anyone; he'd been my constant companion since I was six years old.

My face hurt. In the mirror, I could see a livid bruise flowering across my cheek, the imprint of my cousin's angry hand. I was sad, guilty, and afraid.

There was a row. I heard Cezar yelling at Ioan; clearly he was throwing him out of the house. Marta made a hasty departure for home, accompanied by one of the guards. Then Cezar strode into the kitchen, where we were sitting in silence over our breakfast, none of us able to eat much. He confronted me, hands on hips, his broad features flushed red with anger. "You used something, didn't you? Some kind of potion, something to send them to sleep? Don't deny it, Jena, I know your tricks! Answer me! What did you do?"

"Leave her alone!" Tati protested, half rising, her hand on the table for support.

"Master Cezar—" began Florica.

"Enough!" His voice was thunderous. "Jena, tell the truth!"

"I have nothing to say to you," I said, shivering. "Only that if Uncle Nicolae could see you now, he would be bitterly ashamed of you."

"How dare you—"

"Don't even think of hitting me again," I said. "I have nothing to tell you."

"Then we'll see whether your sisters do," Cezar said. "Not now—I have business to attend to across the valley. I'll be home before supper, and I'll be speaking to each of you on your own before you go to bed tonight. If you don't like the sound of that, Jena, you know how to prevent it. You need only tell me the truth."

The day seemed interminable. Tati went back to bed and lay there, very still; I could not tell whether she was awake or asleep. Iulia helped Florica with some washing. Up in our chamber, Stela fretted, unable to settle down to anything. She flounced around the room, kicking at the furniture and disarranging things on shelves. When she started to fiddle with Gogu's jug and bowl, I snapped at her.

"Stop that, Stela!"

Her lower lip trembled.

"Stela?" Paula put aside the book she had been trying to read and went over to her little storage chest. "You remember how you asked me to teach you to play chess? Shall we do it now?"

"Thank you," I said as Stela began to unpack the chessmen from their bag while Paula unfolded the hinged board that was one of her prized possessions.

"That's all right," Paula said. "Jena, what do you think Costi will do? Will he come here?"

"He has to, eventually. He must confront Cezar. I suppose he might need time to prove his identity. Maybe I should have told Cezar what happened. But it sounds so mad: *Your brother's alive—he was a frog all those years.*" I had not told my sisters about Cezar's choice. I had not explained how Drăguţa's gift had turned our cousin's life gradually to the dark.

"I can't believe Cezar hit you," Paula said in a small voice. "Jena, if he insists on talking to us one by one . . ."

"Don't worry," I said with false confidence. "I won't let that happen." But my stomach was heavy with dread, and my bruise throbbed as I remembered the look in Cezar's eyes. It was the look of a man who believes the whole world is against him—of a man who will do anything to change the ill hand he thinks fate has dealt him. And although part of me shrank from seeing Costi again, for the memory of his set face and wounded eyes filled me with guilt, another part of me was wishing, wishing above anything, that he would come.

*   *   *

Being cooped up indoors was driving me crazy. Toward the end of the afternoon, I seized a moment when there were no guards around and slipped out, bucket in hand, to give the chickens their mash. The light was fading and the shadowy courtyard was deserted, save for a solitary figure standing stock-still, right in the center. It was an old woman dressed in black, with a basket over her arm. The basket was empty. I felt a prickling sensation all over my skin. A moment later I heard a horse's hooves approaching along the path that skirted the woods. Cezar was back.

"Go," I muttered, setting down my bucket and hurrying over to the old woman. "Go quickly!"

The crone made no attempt to move away. She had shed the tiny uncanny form that I was accustomed to, but I had known her instantly. She looked just as she had long ago, when three children had ventured to a forbidden place to play at kings and queens. The old woman grinned at me, and her little pointed teeth confirmed her identity.

"Go!" I urged her again. "Cezar's coming!" Images of the hunt were in my mind: those men with their iron implements, their tight jaws, and their eyes half angry, half terrified.

"I know," said Drăguţa calmly.

And it was too late. He was there, riding into the court-yard. He dismounted by my side, glaring at the unexpected vis-itor. "Be off with you!" he said. "If you're expecting handouts, you've come to the wrong place. We've nothing for beggars at Piscul Dracului."

"Not at all, young man," said the crone, gazing up into his

scowling face. "It's my turn to bestow largesse. I have some-thing for you."

Cezar opened his mouth to speak, then shut it again as Costi stepped out from the shadows by the hen coop to walk across to us. His dark curls had been cropped short and he was freshly shaven. He wore a plain white shirt, a waistcoat em-broidered with ivy twists, and dark green trousers with riding boots. He looked just as wonderful as he had in my dreams. The green eyes were cool and the mobile mouth unsmiling as he came up to me. Over his arm was my cloak.

"I think this is yours," he said politely, holding the garment out to me.

Cezar froze, staring at him. I took the cloak but said nothing—for the moment, I had no words. I had known that Costi would come back, but not like this, not suddenly, with-out any warning, and with the witch of the wood beside him.

"Jena," said Cezar in a strangled whisper, "who are these people? What are they doing here?" His eyes went from Costi to Drăguţa and back again; he looked as if he were caught in a terrifying dream.

"I'm your brother, Cezar," Costi said. His voice was un-steady; I saw in his face that he was half expecting the same rebuff I had given him last night, and dreading it. There was anger there, certainly, but it was not as strong as the love and the desperate hope in his eyes. "Maybe you've forgotten me. It's a long time since that day by Tăul Ielelor when we gave up our most treasured possessions."

I found my voice. "It's true," I said. "He didn't die. He was bewitched into another form until he came back to himself not long ago. Drǎguţa didn't drown him, she saved him. She made him into a frog. He's been here all these years, Cezar. He was Gogu."

"The frog," Cezar said blankly. "No. No, it can't be. It's nonsense. Are you saying . . . Are you telling me—? I don't believe you. You're not my brother, you can't be. Costi died. I saw it." He was looking at the witch now, and I saw him open his mouth again to call out, to summon the guards and have her seized.

"No—" I began, but Drǎguţa gave the tiniest shake of her head. I fell silent. In her eyes I saw that the guards would not hear my cousin shout, that nobody would come until her business here was done. It was as if Piscul Dracului and all the woods around it were frozen while the four of us played the game to its conclusion in the quiet courtyard.

"This is your doing, Jena!" Cezar blustered. "You encouraged this—this *thing*—right onto our doorstep! You harbored that wretched slimy creature, you lied and cheated and used every trick you could think of to stop me from finding out the truth about your escapades. You've probably been crossing over into the dark realm whenever it suited you, as if that didn't set a curse on the whole valley. No wonder evil made its way into our midst. No wonder—"

"Cezar." Costi's voice had gone ominously quiet. "How did Jena get that bruise? Did you strike her?"

"A misunderstanding," Cezar muttered. "Anyway, that's none of your business. You can't just walk in here and tell me you're Costi—it's ridiculous. Who would believe you? You can't prove a thing. You don't have a scrap of evidence."

"There's this," Costi said, and he drew out a chain he had around his neck. On it hung the silver ring of Vârful cu Negură, the ring given only to each generation's eldest son.

"You could have found that in the forest—"

"Cezar," said Costi simply, "you are my brother. You did wrong that day, long ago. But we were all very young, perhaps too young to understand what our choices would mean. It has been a long time of learning. We can mend things now; we can work together to set this right. That is what Father would wish, for he always put the good of the valley first. There's plenty of work here for both of us. I will gladly share the responsibilities of estate and business and community with you, if you agree to let our cousins and the folk of the wildwood lead their lives without interference. Cezar, it's never too late to take a different path. Come, take my hand, and let's start afresh. Will you?"

There was a moment's charged silence, in which I held my breath, watching Costi's face. It made my chest ache to see the longing there. Until now, I had not really understood how lonely and terrible those years as a frog must have been. Soft pillows and loving words do not make up for the cruel punishment of being trapped, helpless, in a body that does not allow you to live your life as your true self. I marveled at Costi's capacity to forgive. I willed Cezar to put out a hand, to stumble through an apology—to begin to be the man his brother believed he could be. But he stood there rooted to the spot, and there was a darkness on his face.

"Think well on this," Drăguţa said. Cezar started; he seemed to have forgotten she was there. "Today I return your gift, for the game is almost finished. This is a second chance, Cezar—the opportunity to choose again. As your brother says, you were young, though not so young as Jena, who made her choice more wisely than you. Each of you gave up a precious treasure. That, you chose out of love. But when the meaning of the game became clearer to you, you sacrificed love for power. You were caught up in a terrible snare, a net in which you wrapped yourself more tightly as the years passed. Now your brother offers you the chance to untangle it; to step free and move on. He has learned his lesson. Have you learned yours?"

It seemed to me that as the witch of the wood spoke these words, a shadow grew around her. Now she was not a bent old woman, but a towering sorceress—her face pale as ice and her eyes full of a terrible judgment. A wind blew across the court-yard, scattering dead leaves before it.

"Vârful cu Negură is mine," Cezar said, and I saw Costi flinch as if he'd been struck. "It's mine. I've worked for it and suffered for it. You'll never prove your identity: nobody will believe such an incredible story. And don't expect Jena to back you up—she's in enough trouble already, with her foolish es-capades. She knows what will happen if she doesn't obey me. Try telling your lies to Judge Rinaldo, and see how far they get you." His words were defiant, but he was shivering. "And you," he added, not quite looking at Drăguţa, "get off my land, before I call the guards. Try this again and my men will hunt you down, and every last one of your foul demons with you."

"Oh, I'll be gone soon enough," the witch said. "A little of your company goes a long way. Costi, you'd best tell your brother how you spent your day."

"I've been with Judge Rinaldo and the village elders," Costi said quietly. "Doing a lot of talking; a lot of explaining. Maybe you've forgotten that the judge and our father were educated together; they knew each other as very young men. Apparently I look a lot like Father did back then. He and the elders have accepted my identity, though not without considerable surprise at the tale I had to tell. They asked many questions."

Cezar was ashen. "You told them?" he whispered. I saw acceptance of the truth in his face at last, and with it a terrible realization of the dark thing he had set on himself. "You told them what I did?"

Costi regarded him levelly. "That my life was your price for a chance to be the eldest son?" he said. "No, Cezar. I would not shame my own brother thus. Besides, I did not want to damage your chance of a better future. I told them the tale of a boy become a frog—of enchantment and promises and the power of the Other Kingdom. They thought it strange and wondrous. For a little, it will be the talk of the valley. In time it will be forgotten that I was ever anything but a man. The story will become folklore, another strange tale of witches and goblins to tell around the fire at night. Now I think it's time the two of us went home and discussed this further, for there must be changes. The first will be the removal of these guards you have set all about our cousins' house. There's no need for them. Piscul Dracului is safe from the Night People."

Cezar stared at Costi, at me, at Drăguţa. "How can you know that?" he asked.

"There's much to speak of; this is not the time or place," said Costi. "I will say one thing to you before we leave here. If you ever hurt Jena again, I'll strangle you with my bare hands. That's a solemn vow, Brother."

He made this startling speech without once looking me in the eye. I did not know what I was feeling; my head and heart were full of confusion. He had seemed so cool to me, and now . . .

"I'm not accepting this," Cezar said, glaring at him. "What about all the work I've done: looking after the business, watching over the girls, organizing the hunt for the Night People? You can't just walk in and take it all!"

"*Watching over the girls?*" The last of the warmth had gone from Costi's voice. "Have you forgotten that I've been here all the time? I saw you set guards on them and threaten them. I watched you crush Paula's aspirations and rob the valley of its good priest. I saw you humiliate Iulia. I saw you put your clumsy paws on Jena and expect her to like it. Being a frog didn't relieve me of my intelligence or my powers of observation."

"You piece of pond scum!" hissed Cezar. "You think you can march in here and help yourself to everything! You don't deserve to be master of Vârful cu Negură: you haven't done a scrap of work to earn it—you don't know the first thing about running the business! All you know about is . . ."

"Being a frog?" Costi raised his brows. "Believe me, if there had been any choice in the matter, I would have stayed in human form. In fact, I don't think I'll have as much difficulty picking up the reins as you believe. What Jena learned about the business, I learned, too. Her shoulder made an ideal vantage point for reading all those ledgers."

I was watching Cezar's face—pale as parchment and distorted with outrage. Before my horrified gaze, something snapped. He strode forward to seize his brother by the throat. I screamed. Costi struggled, long limbs thrashing. His face turned crimson as he fought for air. His eyes bulged. Cezar was backing him toward the high stone wall by the hen coop. Drăguţa stood quietly, watching the two of them.

"It's her fault, that witch's, she tricked me!" Cezar babbled. "It was supposed to be mine, all of it, the estate and Jena, too, that was what it meant, King of the Land, but it was a hollow promise! Even with you gone, I could never be more than second best! It's wrong! Wrong!" With each repetition he shook Costi as if he would smash his head against the stone.

Nobody was coming out: my screams had not brought a single guard. "Stop it!" I yelled. "Let him go!" I grabbed Cezar's arm in a desperate effort to intervene. The game was not supposed to end with me watching one brother kill the other, right before my eyes—it could not be so. "Stop it, Cezar!"

Cezar knocked me away and I fell, painfully, onto the stones of the courtyard. In the moment's respite allowed him, Costi performed a sharp upward jab with his knee. Cezar sucked in air—his grip slackened. Quick as a flash, Costi wriggled out of his brother's hold and retreated, both hands up in front of him, palms out. "Enough," he wheezed. "You don't want to do this."

"The game is finished." Drăguţa's voice was solemn. Her gooseberry-green eyes moved over each of us in turn: me struggling to my feet, Costi gasping for breath, and Cezar just standing there with a look on his face that made me want to cry. He had made his choice, it seemed, and it was a waste—a waste of what could have been a good life.

"My work is done here," the witch said. Basket over her arm, she turned and trudged away across the yard as if she were indeed just another wanderer who had passed by, hoping for a crust of bread or a few coppers. None of us said a thing.

When she was gone, Costi cleared his throat and looked his brother in the eye. "We're going home now," he said, and his voice was as bleak as winter. "I'm sorry you are not prepared to accept me. I never forgot that we were brothers, even as I watched you bully the girls and mismanage Father's affairs. After this, I don't want you anywhere near our cousins, Cezar. We'll discuss what few options are still available to you. Come—I'm certain Jena is longing to see the last of us."

I opened my mouth to speak, to say something—anything— for the look Costi turned on me was tight and hurt and made me want to curl up and cry. But I didn't say a word, for someone was coming on horseback, and the moment was over. Into the courtyard rode the gray-bearded figure of Judge Rinaldo, and after him a familiar figure seated sideways on her fine mare, her face pale and tense. It was Aunt Bogdana. She slid down from her horse, her gaze on Costi. As she came across to him, first walking, then running, I saw a wondrous sequence of expressions cross her face: utter trepidation, reawakening love, transcendent joy. She threw herself into his arms, hugging him like the child he had been when she lost him, and Costi held her with tears streaming down his cheeks. My own face was wet; I scrubbed a hand across it.

"Jena," Judge Rinaldo said, "my apologies for coming without warning. Your aunt passed by on her way home, and I felt obliged to explain to her what had occurred. I offered to escort her straight here, since I knew that Costin was coming up to see his brother. This will silence doubting tongues. Nobody can dispute that a mother knows her son."

I murmured something polite, hardly hearing him. Cezar was watching his mother sobbing in Costi's embrace. Over Aunt Bogdana's shoulder, Costi's eyes looked into his brother's. What I saw in them was as much sorrow and regret as judgment. I did not think Cezar recognized that. He saw only confirmation of what he knew already: that he would never be more than second best. His mouth tightened. Turning on his heel, he strode off across the courtyard and away down the track toward the forest. He seemed hardly aware of what he was doing. It was almost night; the shadows swallowed him quickly.

"I hope this matter will not create confusion and discord at Vârful cu Negură," said the judge. "The valley sorely needs a time of peace, and it needs its leaders."

"I know I'll have to work hard to gain the community's trust," Costi said. "I'll try my best to do things the way my father did—with wisdom and compassion." He patted his mother on the back. Aunt Bogdana was laughing and crying at the same time. I doubted that she had noticed Cezar was gone. "I hoped that my brother . . . I did hope—" Costi seemed to gather himself together. "We've all suffered some blows this winter. It cuts deep to lose the trust of those who were once dearest to the heart. I think that is a wound that can never heal."

I felt the poisoned arrow of his words right in my heart: it hurt more than I could have imagined possible. He sounded so sad, and so unforgiving. I stood silent, shivering.

"Judge," Costi went on, and now his tone was that of a leader, "I thank you for your help and your belief in me, and for bringing Mother here so promptly. Jena, I'll take most of the guards up to Vârful cu Negură with me. I'm sure you can't wait to have your house to yourself again."

There were plenty of things I could have said, but all I did was mutter, "I'll find Petru for you," and head back indoors as folk began, at last, to spill out of the castle to see what was going on. I did not know what I was feeling, only that my heart was being torn in all directions at once. Furious tears welled in my eyes. Those words about trust had been cruel. It sounded as if he'd decided he wouldn't even try to forgive me. Perhaps we would live our lives a stone's throw from each other, never exchanging so much as a friendly greeting.

I sent a bemused Petru to sort out guards and horses. As briefly as I could, I told my sisters and Florica what had happened. I could see that they were bursting with questions, but instead of asking them, the girls tiptoed around me, eyeing me warily as I helped set the table for supper, crashing plates and jangling cutlery. Whatever story my face told them, it didn't have a happy ending.

Chapter Fifteen

A strange quiet settled over Piscul Dracului. Cezar was gone. He had not waited to talk further to Costi or to bid Aunt Bog-dana farewell, but had left the valley that very night. Nobody knew where he had gone. The guards had departed, leaving our household at seven once more: we sisters, Florica, and Petru. The earliest traces of spring were touching the forest, cautious yet, for the winters were long in our mountains: a clump of tiny wildflowers, a bird bearing a beakful of dry grasses for its nest. Insects on a pond; the hens starting to lay again.

From Ivan, who traveled to and fro, we heard news of Costi in those first weeks after his return. He was working hard to establish himself as master of Vârful cu Negură, and to take the reins of Uncle Nicolae's business affairs. Aunt Bogdana was torn between joy and sadness. She had found one son, only to lose the other. She did not invite us to visit, and we did not walk up to her house. All the same, we could not be unaware of Costi's presence so close to Piscul Dracului. Small reminders kept coming. One day not long after Cezar's departure, two men rode into our courtyard bearing our strongboxes: one for the family expenses, one for the business. A third man brought a stack of ledgers, which he obligingly carried up to the work-room for me. Everything Cezar had taken was being scrupulously returned.

The business coffer was entirely in order, containing both ample funds and full receipts for Salem bin Afazi's goods. The household box had more silver in it than it had when Cezar took it, but not enough to embarrass me. I judged that Costi had calculated an amount that would see us comfortably through the next three months or so, well past the time we hoped Father would be home. The gesture was generous and sensitive. It was just what I would have expected from Gogu—and from Costi—and it made me feel both relieved and ashamed.

"You can't go on blaming yourself forever," Iulia told me bluntly one morning as we were feeding the chickens. "So you didn't trust him straightaway. I can understand why he was upset, but you did have a very good reason for it."

"Evidently Costi doesn't think so," I said, throwing out a handful of grain. "He remembers when he was Gogu, and the way the two of us trusted each other more than anything. We were so close, and now that seems to be gone, gone as if it never was."

Iulia glanced at me sidelong. "Didn't you say he threatened to kill Cezar if he hurt you again? He loves you, Jena. It's obvious to the rest of us. All you need to do is go up there and say you're sorry."

"I can't." The very idea of it made my stomach tie itself in knots. If he spoke to me again the way he had that day in the courtyard, it would be more than I could bear.

"So you plan to be enemies for the rest of your lives?" Iulia asked me. "That could be awkward, with him living next door."

"I don't plan anything," I said. "I'm too worried about Tati even to think about Costi." Not true, of course; I thought about him all the time—and if I could have rewritten the past, I would have.

As for Tati, we were all worried about her. She had barely spoken a word since Full Moon, and she was eating scarcely enough to keep a bird alive. Her cheeks were hollow and her eyes looked too big for her face. I thought she was living the quest with Sorrow, that she was attuned in some way to his journey and his struggle, every part of her fixed on bringing him safely back, his mission complete. As the moon had gone from full to gibbous to dark, she had retreated gradually into a shadowy world of her own. It seemed to me she was letting go, slipping away to a place where we would not be able to reach her.

I heard from Ivan that there was talk in the valley about which sister had kissed the frog back into a man and what the likely outcome might be. He said nothing about a portal or nocturnal journeys, and neither did folk in the village, although we did attract some curious looks. Whatever version of events Costi had told Judge Rinaldo, it seemed that the full truth had not come out, and I was glad of it.

At Dark of the Moon I dreamed not of a young man who

turned into a monster, but of Tadeusz, with his cynical smile and wandering fingers. He was saying to me, *You missed your opportunity, Jena. Now what? Marriage to some worthy young landholder, and a baby in your belly every spring? You can do better than that. I'm not far away. Just wish for me, and I'll be there.* I woke in a cold sweat.

Tati's side of the bed was empty, and the door ajar. Heart in my mouth, I threw on my cloak and ran through the darkened house, straight up the steps at the end of the party room and out onto the terrace.

She stood there in her night robe, looking out over the dark forest. Alone: no cloaked figure by her side. I breathed again.

"Tati, what are you doing? It's freezing out here. Come back inside."

She said nothing. I went up to her, taking off my cloak to put it around her shoulders. I felt a deep shivering in her. Her eyes were blank.

"Come on, Tati. Step by step, that's it. Come with me."

Back in the bedchamber, I put the quilt around her and sent Iulia, who had awakened at our return, down to the kitchen for dried berries so we could make fruit tea. I set the small kettle on our stove. After a while, Tati's trembling subsided. She said in a whisper, "I had a terrible dream, Jena. I think Sorrow's hurt. I don't think he's coming back."

"Tell me. Remember, dreams aren't always true."

"He was fighting some kind of monster, like a wild boar, only much bigger, and he . . . he fell, and the thing gored him with its tusk. . . . He was bleeding, Jena. He was just lying there in the mud. He looked so pale, as if he was already dead. . . .

And I couldn't do anything. I couldn't touch him, I couldn't even say goodbye. . . ."

"Shh . . . shh . . . Don't think about it anymore. It doesn't mean anything, Tati, just that you're worried about him."

"He's not coming back," my sister said flatly, staring into space.

After that she stopped eating altogether. Already she was skin and bone, her appetite whittled away to a nibble of fruit here, a morsel of bread there. Now she refused to touch any-thing. I could hardly get her to swallow a sip of water. Logic got me nowhere. I told her again that what she had seen was only a dream, not reality, that with half the month still to go, Sorrow had a good chance of getting back in one piece with all the required items. I had scant grounds for such confidence, after what Paula had said about the quest. But I knew the im-portance of hope. If there was a decision somewhere in what I was saying, I did not acknowledge it even to myself.

As Full Moon drew closer, Tati became too weak to get out of bed. I sent for a doctor. We had one in the valley, an old man who had once traveled with great armies on the march, and whose skills ran more to bone setting and stitching up knife wounds than to tending young ladies fading away for no appar-ent reason. He applied leeches; the treatment effected no visible change. He suggested bleeding the patient, but I said no, for it seemed to me she was too frail to endure it. My heart was chill. When I had made my confident assurances to Father that I could look after things in his absence, I never dreamed that I would be watching Tati dying before my eyes. It seemed we might lose her even before we knew whether Sorrow had achieved his quest. I spent a lot of time praying, and even more time thinking.

Florica had heard about the rumors in the village. She did not actually ask us whether our sister may have been bewitched by forces from the Other Kingdom, but she climbed the steep stairs to our bedchamber and festooned the place with plaits of garlic, enough to keep out anything that might conspire to snatch Tati away from us. She put a hand to Tati's brow and looked closely at her neck—something I had not been brave enough to do myself—and then she went back downstairs. Her expression troubled me: it combined grief and acceptance.

"What will you do when Full Moon comes?" Paula asked me as we sat by Tati's bedside one evening, listening to the labored sound of her breathing.

"What will I do?"

"It's not an unreasonable question. You usually do make the decisions, Jena. Do you think Sorrow will come? If he does, how can she go across? She's barely conscious. She won't be able to walk."

"I know that."

"So what if he does come, and there's some way he can take her? Will you let her go?"

I gazed down at Tati. "It's not my choice," I said, realizing that I had learned that much from all this. "It's Tati's and Sorrow's. I don't know what we'll do." I knew whose advice I wanted. I knew whose support I needed. But I wouldn't go to Vârful cu Negură. I couldn't ask him. There was too much

between us: too much love, too much hurt, too much misunderstanding. We'd made a gap too wide to bridge.

"Is Tati going to die?"

I had not heard Stela come in. She stood at the foot of the
bed, her eyes on our sister's fragile form—the tight-stretched
skin, the shadowed lids.

"I hope not." I wasn't prepared to lie to her.

"Doesn't she believe in true love anymore?" Stela asked.

The moon grew from new to half to almost full again, and the
first lambs were born. Men came up from the village to help
Petru, willing and able now I could pay them a fair wage. Tati
was sinking steadily. I knew she could not last many days more
unless we could get her to eat something—a little soup, a sliver
of cheese. But she refused everything.

Not knowing what else to do, we told stories of true love
in an effort to coax hope back to Tati's heart. It was often hard
to tell whether she could hear them, for she lay mostly limp and
unresponsive. Late one afternoon, when Stela was down in the
kitchen, Paula told a striking tale she had heard among the
scholars of the Other Kingdom. The sun had almost set beyond
the green window; the light in our chamber was mellow. *Green
as grass*, I thought, *green as pondweed, green as home*. Maybe I was the
one who needed to believe in true love.

Paula's was a dark tale, in which a father desired his daughter. She fled to conceal herself in the kitchens of a great house,
ash smeared on her face, her body hidden by a coat of many
small skins—rabbit, fox, stoat, mole, badger. She fell in love

with the young master of the house, and drew his attention with a series of gifts.

"So she dropped her gold ring in the bowl of broth, and gave it to the kitchen maid to place before the young lord at table. And this time, he demanded to know who had served the soup, and where he might find her. . . ."

When Paula reached the end of the story, Tati's eyes were open. It was the first time in days she had shown any awareness of her surroundings. I took her hand and felt her fingers squeeze mine weakly. They were deathly cold. It came to me that if I said the wrong thing, she would shut her eyes again and sink away beyond reach. Paula's story had sown a seed in my imagination.

"Iulia," I ventured, "you remember when Costi first changed back into a man, and you said if it were a story I'd have to grovel to get him back? Was that what you meant—ash and rags and mysterious gifts?"

"I suppose it *might* work," Iulia said doubtfully. "Are you saying you're actually prepared to try now?"

I took a deep breath. "I might be," I said. "If I can work out the best way to do it. Costi's not the sort to respond to a gold ring. And you know I'm not the groveling type. But there must be a way to show him that—that—"

"That you love him?" Tati whispered.

I felt my cheeks flush red. "Well, yes," I admitted. "I'm terrified of going to see him. Why hasn't he invited us to Vârful cu Negură? If he's forgiven me, why hasn't he come to see me?"

"He loves you, Jena." Tati was too weak to lift her head, but she turned her eyes to meet mine. "You must know that in your heart."

"He needs to know he can trust you," Iulia said. "That if something bad happens in the future, you won't let go again."

"I've already broken two promises," I said. "I told him I'd never leave him behind, and then I did. First to find Tati, then all by himself in the forest, with no voice. If I promise again, why should he believe me?"

Paula was thinking, her chin in her hand. "He shouldn't be so hard on you," she said. "When you wouldn't accept that he was Costi, you were just being careful. That was reasonable enough, considering all the things that had happened. Surely he hasn't forgotten that you protected him and loved him and put him first for nine whole years. That can't be wiped out in a single day."

"But it was," I said.

"Remind him." Tati's voice was like a leaf stirred in the wind. "Remind him how things were."

"And show him they haven't really changed," said Iulia.

"Do it while you've got the courage," Paula added. "Go tomorrow. One of you has to take the first step."

"It's too soon. I'm not ready." My heart was pounding; it was as if I'd been asked to fight a dragon single-handed. I got up and fetched a glass of water.

"Jena," said Tati, "I want you to talk . . . Costi. To be . . . happy. I want you . . . go . . . before Full Moon. . . ."

"That's not very long," I protested. "Only five days. And I haven't worked out how to do it yet." But a plan was forming in my mind, for Paula's story had reminded me that Costi loved games.

"Go . . . soon."

The look in Tati's eyes frightened me. It was a farewell, and it seemed to me it did not mean she believed Full Moon would see her safe and happy, either in our world or the Other Kingdom.

"Tati, stay with us," I said. "Wait for Sorrow. It would break his heart if he came for you and . . ." I could not put this into words.

"You think he's all right?" Her voice was a plea. "You really believe he'll come back?"

"I do believe it, Tati. I've seen how he looks at you, how he touches you. You're his whole world. The quest is difficult, yes. All the same, I think Ileana wants him to succeed. Don't lose hope. Sorrow will come for you—I know it."

"So you *do* believe . . . true love?" she whispered.

I took a deep breath. "I think I have to," I said, blinking back tears. "Without it, we're all going nowhere."

"Then talk to Costi. . . . Go tomorrow. . . ." Her eyes closed.

I tried. In the morning I put on my outdoor boots and went down to breakfast, fully intending to make my way to Vârful cu Negură as soon as I'd eaten. What I would say to Costi was not yet clear in my head. My whole body was strung tight; my nerves were jangling.

"Your cup's rattling, Jena," said Florica, looking at me closely. "Are you quite well?"

"I'm fine." I tried for a casual tone. "I thought I might go up to Vârful cu Negură today and visit Costi, since the weather's improved so much."

"Your aunt would like to see you, I'm sure," Florica said, "but Master Costin's not there, Jena. The word is he's gone off down the valley for a couple of nights."

"*A couple of nights*," I echoed, the tension draining from my body to be replaced by bitter disappointment. It had taken all my courage to decide to go and face him. "When is he expected back, Florica?"

Florica's eyes sharpened. "Before Full Moon, I expect," she said. "Why not go up and ask your aunt Bogdana?"

"No, I . . . It's Costi I need to talk to. Florica, could Petru arrange for someone at Vârful cu Negură to let us know as soon as Costi comes home? Right away?"

"I expect so, Jena. So you won't be going up today?"

I shook my head. "I'll go when he's back home. I just hope it's soon."

It suddenly seemed urgent to speak to him before Full Moon, to be able to prove to Tati that happy endings were possible in real life, as in tales. If I sorted out my own problem, I thought, the solution to my sister's might fall into place, too. There was no great logic to this. After all, I was the one who had refused to recognize true love when it was no farther away than my own pocket. I knew I needed his help. *Hurry up, Costi, I* urged him silently. *Come home. I need you.*

The sun set beyond the colored windows four more times, and inside our chamber the stories went on. Not all were joyful tales; we needed to acknowledge that love was not just kisses, smiles, and fulfillment, but also sacrifice, compromise, and hard work. Tati hung on. My promise to mend things with Costi had awakened a fragile hope in her. She swallowed water obediently, but would not eat. She submitted to sponge baths and let Stela brush and plait her hair. All the same, I saw what a shadow she had become. When the sun rose on the eve of Full Moon and there was still no word of Costi's return, despair began to creep into my heart.

Tati awoke restless and confused. She kept asking me whether I had talked to Costi yet and what he had said. She would not be calmed. When Iulia tried to begin another story, Tati whispered that she didn't want to hear any more and closed her eyes. Iulia retreated to her bed with shaking shoulders. When I went over to her, I heard her whispering to herself, "First Mother, then Father, now Tati; I can't bear it." I tried to comfort her, murmuring that Father was not dead yet and neither was Tati, that things could change, that she must be brave. It wasn't much help; the two of us ended up in tears together.

At breakfast, Petru told me that Costi was expected home sometime today. "Stopped for the night down at Judge Rinaldo's house. The word is he's riding on up to Vârful cu Negură this morning."

This morning. There might be time, if I was quick.

"Jena," said Paula quietly, "just get your bag and go. I know you have your things ready. Go now. We'll look after Tati."

"Going up to see Master Costi today?" queried Florica, eyes knowing. "I'll pack you some provisions. It doesn't do to get hungry out in the woods."

"I'm not sure if I should go." Instinct pulled me powerfully in the direction of Vârful cu Negură, but common sense made it hard to leave home. How could I possibly go, with my sister so ill and the night of Full Moon almost upon us? If she slipped away from us while I was gone, I could never forgive myself.

"Yes, you should," said Stela. "That's what Tati wants."

"Florica," I said, "could you pack up exactly what I used to take when Gogu and I went out in summer?"

"It's hardly the weather for outdoor cooking," muttered Florica, but she was already gathering a little bag of flour, an egg, some butter, and a twist of salt. She wrapped them neatly in a cloth. "Here you are, then. Go carefully. Put a couple of cloves of garlic in your pocket, Jena. It may be daylight, but that doesn't mean there's nothing lurking out there. And keep away from the Deadwash."

Upstairs, I told Tati where I was going and why. She showed a flicker of interest; I had to hope it would be enough to get her through the day. Then I put on my green gown and packed Florica's provisions in my knapsack, on top of various other items I had ready: a bowl, a spoon, my little frying pan, a flint.

"Wait," said Paula as I began to fasten the strap around the bag. My younger sisters were standing there in a row, each of them holding something.

"We thought," said Iulia, "that as this is a bit like a quest, you'd need magical objects to take with you."

"This was the closest we could get," Paula added. She held out a small box. I opened it to reveal a quill, a tiny pot of ink, and three miniature squares of parchment. "We've each chosen something special; imagine you're taking us all with you to help."

Stela gave me a green ribbon, and Iulia her rabbit-skin hat. On the verge of tears, I stumbled over words of thanks as I put on the hat and packed the other gifts in the bag.

"It's all right," Paula said, grinning. "We know you appreciate us, even if you've been too busy to say it much recently."

Tati was too weak to find me a token, but Iulia brought out her sewing scissors and snipped a few hairs from the head of each sister, me included. These she twisted into a little ring. She tucked the knotted ends in and put it on my finger. "Sisters and friends," she said. "We know you're doing this for Tati as well as yourself. We're all willing you to succeed."

It was a long walk up to Vârful cu Negură. I did have a plan, but exactly how to act on it was far from clear. I needed to see Costi without the rest of his household knowing. I must get as close to the house as possible, then hope an opportunity would present itself.

Where would he go after a long ride? Would he take his own horse to the stables, or get a groom to do it? If he went off to bathe and rest, I would have to change the plan. There was a secluded spot I thought I might use, down by the orchard; it was close to the stables, but not close enough to be spotted by the grooms and other folk who worked there. I just had to get there before Costi came home.

As I walked briskly through the forest, I had the sense that I was being watched. I'd catch a flash of movement behind a holly bush or a gleam of bright eyes amid the thick needles of a pine, following my progress. It made me feel better. Drăguţa's plans were big ones; she had been shaping our lives since we were little children. It was easy to believe my small quest today was linked to Tati's ordeal and Sorrow's; that the folk of the Other Kingdom were watching me and Costi as closely as they were my sister and the young man in the black coat. Something would be decided today, one way or another.

The day was half gone before I reached the outskirts of Vârful cu Negură. My stomach was churning again; in my imagination, Costi looked at me with bitterness and turned his back. *Trust your instincts,* I reminded myself. *And trust your sisters. Without them, you wouldn't have made it this far.*

At the far end of the leafless orchard there was an old stone bench crusted with moss. I unpacked my knapsack, gazing between the bare branches at the stable building and, beyond it, the house itself. It was an expansive place, the walls of mellow stone, the roof red-tiled. In springtime the birches that grew close to the house would wrap it in a silvery, whispering cloak. Smoke rose from the chimneys; Aunt Bogdana was home, but I could not see her until I had spoken to Costi. If he and I could not sort out our differences, I did not think I would be coming here again. It would be too painful. Even now, I felt sick at the thought of seeing him.

I was glad of the rabbit-skin hat. Spring had barely begun, and I did not know how long I might have to wait in the cold. I took out Stela's ribbon; on it, I threaded the seedpod in the shape of a heart, which had lain in my storage chest since the day Gogu gave me his token of love and I dismissed it with a patronizing comment. I tied it around my neck.

I began to gather fallen wood for a fire. Stacking it methodically, I spotted something small and bright lodged in a crack of a splintery old branch. I fished it out, and a smile came to my lips. I was certain now that someone from the Other Kingdom was helping my quest along. I placed the tiny item carefully with my other things and returned to the fire, with knife and flint in hand.

I was well practiced at building campfires, for Gogu and I had spent many long summer days out in the woods. Once the stack of wood was burning well, I opened Florica's bundle and began to mix my ingredients in the little bowl. One essential item I had gathered on the way through the forest: a handful of fresh pondweed.

The sun moved overhead behind the clouds. The day passed, and I grew colder and more nervous. I stamped up and down, and clapped my hands together to keep warm. Nobody seemed to be about; the smoke from my little fire had not attracted attention. Perhaps the folk of the house thought someone was burning rubbish. I began to wonder whether Costi had decided not to come home today after all. Then I thought maybe he had already been in the house when I arrived, and that I would have to knock on the front door and think of something to say. The light changed. I judged it to be mid-afternoon, and I still had to walk all the way home. I must be there before dusk: it was the night of Full Moon. Whatever happened, Tati needed me.

Come on, Costi. Perhaps if I put the pan on the fire and started cooking, it would somehow make him appear. I set it over the embers, dropped in a pat of butter, and listened to it sizzling.

When it was hot enough, I poured in the contents of the bowl and watched until bubbles began to rise through the miniature pancake. As I flipped it, I heard the sound of approaching horses. My little bit of magic had worked—he was home.

They rode up to the stables: Costi and two well-dressed men whom I did not know. They dismounted. A groom came out to lead all three horses inside. *Stay*, I willed my cousin. I slipped the pancake onto the platter I had brought and decorated it with a garnish of pondweed.

They stood there, talking awhile. I stood watching, a bundle of tension, with my little gift in my hands. Games were all very well, but sometimes the effort of playing them was almost too much. Then the three of them headed off toward the house. Short of calling out to him, there was nothing I could do about it. Now what? Walk in and accost him, in front of his guests? I could imagine his face, embarrassed and awkward; I could see the look of disdain in his eyes.

The groom came back out of the stables with bucket in hand, heading for the well. I seized what was perhaps my last chance.

"Excuse me."

He started, then bobbed his head. "Mistress Jena! Shall I tell the mistress you're here?"

I dredged my memory for his name. "No, Geza, I don't want her knowing—not yet. I need your help. You may think it's a little odd, but I have a job for you."

"Of course, Mistress Jena. But I must water the horses first."

The pancake was still warm when he got back. There was

a certain curiosity in his eyes, perhaps sparked by the story of the girl and the frog that everyone in the valley had been discussing over the last few weeks.

"Take this to Master Costin," I said. "Make sure he gets it. I know he has guests, but you must disturb him, even if he's busy. Don't tell him who this is from. If he gives you a message, bring it straight back. If he doesn't, come back anyway."

"Yes, Mistress Jena." He held the platter with the utmost care.

"Thank you, Geza. I know it seems a little strange."

I waited, pacing up and down, too keyed up to be still for long. It was getting late. I imagined Sorrow, a cup of water balanced in one hand, a little bundle on his back, running, running, eyes burning with determination in his chalk-white face. I saw Tati as she had stood in Dancing Glade, frail as a birch in winter, her words an iron-strong declaration of faith. I thought of Costi eyeing my gift with a sad smile and turning his back. *Trust,* I told myself. *This is Gogu, remember: your best beloved.*

It seemed forever, but at last Geza appeared again, hands shoved under his arms to keep warm. The light was fading already; sparks from my fire spiraled upward, like tiny wild dancers.

"Did you give it to him?" I grabbed his shoulders, then made myself let go. "What did he say? Why did you take so long?"

"He has two merchants from Braşov with him, Mistress Jena. I couldn't go straight in—"

"I said to disturb him!" I snapped, then relented at the look on his face. "I'm sorry. It's just that I have to be home tonight, and it's getting late." I knew I should be setting off right now, if I was to be certain of reaching Piscul Dracului before dark. "Any message?"

"No, Mistress Jena."

"Nothing at all?" My heart plummeted.

"Well, he did eat it all up, even the green part. I think he liked it." Geza sounded astonished.

I breathed again. Hope was not lost, after all. "Thank you," I said. "Will you take this to him now?" I gave him the item I had found earlier. It was the discarded carapace of a beetle, iridescent green and shaped like a heart. "Please be as quick as you can. Here, take this quill and parchment, too." Maybe those were a heavy hint, but I had to speed things up somehow.

I waited again. My heart seemed to sound out Sorrow's footsteps as he made his desperate way back toward Dancing Glade. I thought of my sister, so weak she could barely lift her head from the pillow. *Stay with us, Tati,* I willed her. *Keep faith with him.* And I wondered whether I should forget my own dreams and run home now so I could be by her side, but my feet did not want to carry me away from the quiet orchard and the plume of smoke from my little fire.

"Come on, Costi," I muttered, wiping out the frying pan and starting to put things away in my pack, "meet me halfway, can't you?"

This time Geza was much quicker, and he brought me a note, scrawled on the tiny square of parchment I had sent. It read: *Don't good things generally come in threes?*

I felt a big smile spread across my face. Costi was prepared to play. Geza had brought back Paula's quill. Dipping it in the ink pot, I wrote: *If you want the third one, you'll have to come and find me.*

"Right away," I urged Geza. "Please take this to him right away. How did he look?"

"Terrified, Mistress Jena."

"Terrified is good," I said. "That's just how I feel. Hurry, please."

I sat on the old seat, shivering with anticipation. With every rustle and creak from the forest, with every drone of passing insect or peep of home-winging bird, I glanced across the orchard toward the house. I tried to guess what Costi would say first and how I might answer.

He didn't take long. I suppose my using his groom as my messenger made guessing where I was easy. He was carrying a lantern, something I had assumed I would not need, for I had not expected to wait here for so long, nor to be walking home after dusk. We didn't have much time. But I couldn't think of that. Here was Costi, coming across the orchard toward me, the firelight dancing over his face. His expression was terribly serious. He had cut his hair again—it curled around his ears and exposed the back of his neck, a spot my fingers might find rather nice to stroke. He wore plain, good clothes: a white shirt, trousers in a muted green, serviceable boots, a warm cloak. He looked as nervous as a miscreant about to face judgment. I had absolutely no idea what he would say.

Some three paces away from me, he halted and extended his hand toward me. "Would you c-care to d-dance, Jena?" he asked, summoning a ghost of a smile.

"I'd be glad to," I said in a woefully unsteady voice, and put my hand in his. His touch warmed my whole body. I was longing to throw my arms around him and hold him close, but the magic of this moment was like a single, lovely strand of cobweb, fragile and delicate. One wrong move and it would snap beyond mending.

"Can you hear the music?" Costi murmured as he put his hand on my waist. I put mine on his shoulder, and we began a slow, circling measure that took us to this side and that between the trees.

"Mmm," I said, moving in a little closer, and I could hear it: out in the forest birds were singing, and a stream was flowing, and the wind was whispering secrets. His heart and mine added a rhythm all their own. We turned and turned, and with every turning we breathed a little more quickly and held on a little more tightly, and when we came back to the place where we'd started, we stopped dancing and stood with our arms around each other, holding on as if we would never let go, not if the sky fell and the whole world came to an end. And even though there were still things to say, and decisions to make, and apologies to get through, I could feel a delicious happiness spreading through me, starting in my heart and moving outward.

"Costi?"

"Mmm?"

"I'm sorry I hurt you. More sorry than I can say. I can't believe I didn't know you instantly."

"I'm sorry I was so cruel that day. After what happened with Cezar, I hardly knew what I was saying. I was trying so hard to sound assured and capable, and underneath I was a quivering mess. I should have tried to talk to you—to understand why you'd been so afraid of me. When you turned your back on me, when you accused me of lying, I felt . . . I felt shattered. As if part of me had been torn away. That day, I suppose I let that all spill out."

"It's all right, Costi. As long as we forgive each other now, we can put all that behind us."

"Are you sure you forgive me, Jena?" His tone was quite wobbly. I was not the only one for whom this game had been difficult.

"Completely," I said.

"Then can I have my third gift now?"

I took a step back. "Shut your eyes," I told him.

He obeyed. But when I put my palms against his cheeks and stood on tiptoe, his eyes snapped open again. "Wait! Jena—"

"You don't want a kiss?"

"It's just that . . . What if—?"

The same idea had occurred to me. "I don't think you'll turn back into a frog," I said. "That wasn't the first time I'd ever kissed you, after all. I think we had to wait until Drăguţa decided we'd learned our lessons. It sounded to me as if she wanted you to be a man from now on."

Costi shut his eyes again. "I'm willing to risk it if you are," he said with a lopsided smile.

So I kissed him, and he kissed me back. There was no explosion. There was no blinding light. Costi's arms came around me again, strong and warm, and I pressed against him, stroking the back of his neck. The touch of his lips made me feel safe and loved, and at the same time it made every part of me tremble with excitement. The memory of Cezar's uncouth effort was instantly wiped away. This was my first proper kiss, and it was everything I had always dreamed it would be. When, after a long time, we paused to draw breath, Costi showed no signs of becoming a frog.

"Costi," I said breathlessly, "I hate to say this, but—"

"But it's Full Moon and you have to get home?"

"Tati's terribly ill. We're scared she may not even survive until Sorrow gets here—if he does. I should start for home now. You took ages to get here."

"I'll walk you to Piscul Dracului, Jena. We'll go in a minute. I have something to do first. . . ." I felt his hand lift my hair away from my neck, and then his lips brushed the place where he had so often sat in frog form, below my left ear. "I've been wanting to do that for years," he whispered. "It's just as nice as I expected. You can't imagine what thoughts your little frog had, Jena. Far more than he ever dared share with you."

"I'll look forward to hearing them," I said. "We have to go, Costi. The light's fading."

Costi went over to the stables, where Geza was hovering with a grin on his face. He gave the groom some kind of instruction, then we set off down the hill through the forest.

"Is it true there was a spell of silence on you all the time you were a frog?" I asked Costi. Questions were bursting out of me, now that we were together again. "A ban on telling me who you really were?"

"Drăguţa never actually told me so; I never even saw her. The closest I came was that time you left me at Dancing Glade. A fox carried me across the ice on its back. I guessed it was hers. Somehow I always knew about the silence spell. I knew I had to wait."

"It was a long time. A terribly long time."

"I'm just sad Father never knew I was still here."

"He knows, Costi. He's here somewhere, watching. He was a lovely man, so kind and good. Like you."

"You think that, Jena? Really? I haven't b-been much of a friend to you, this last month. It was a big change—it took a lot of getting used to. And there was Cezar . . . I've gone over and over what happened, wondering how I could have handled it better. And . . . I wasn't sure you'd feel the same about me, now that I wasn't Gogu anymore. I was afraid to ask you. I couldn't b-bear it if you said no."

"Costi, I don't remember you stammering like this when you were a boy."

"I don't think I did. It's just when I'm scared. Back then, I wasn't afraid of anything."

"You're scared now? Why?"

"Because this is new and good and so p-precious I'm afraid it's just a dream. I had a lot of d-dreams when I was a frog, and I hated waking up."

I stopped walking, took both his hands in mine, and looked him in the eye. It was dark in the forest, but not so dark I could not see that here was my childhood playmate, my beloved companion of nine years, and the man of my dreams—

miraculously rolled into one. Suddenly this wasn't difficult at all. "I love you, Costi," I said. "That's the truest truth I ever said. Forever and always. There's no need to be afraid anymore."

"I love you, Jena. I always did. When you couldn't trust me, you broke my heart."

Tears spilled from my eyes. He leaned forward and kissed them away.

"Me too," I said. "But it looks as if broken hearts can mend. It's quite remarkable. A phenomenon, Paula would say."

"I suppose," said Costi, "it is no more remarkable than boys turning into frogs, and frogs into men. Oh, Jena . . . When we're married—that's if you'll have me—I want to keep on coming out here, and sitting by a campfire, and doing all the things we love doing."

"Was that a proposal?" I asked, smiling through my tears.

"I can do better with practice," Costi said, a little abashed. "Shall I try again tomorrow?"

"If you want. I plan to say yes. It's best if I tell you that now, so you won't get anxious and go off to hide in the leaves. I hope Aunt Bogdana will approve."

"Mother will be delighted. She's been nagging me ever since we got home to go down and mend things with you; she could see how miserable I was. But I couldn't make myself do it. You were braver than I was."

"I was petrified," I said, slipping my arm around his waist. "But it was worth the effort. You played my game very well."

"You know," said Costi, "I did think I smelled pancakes the

moment I got off my horse. But I dismissed it as wishful thinking." He was suddenly serious. "Jena, what's going to happen
tonight? Sorrow and Tati, I mean?"

"I don't know." As we walked on I explained how weak
and dispirited Tati was, and what she had dreamed about Sorrow's journey. Then we fell silent, thinking about what might
happen if Sorrow didn't come back. If Tati was prevented from
being with her sweetheart, she might actually allow herself to
die of a broken heart. It hardly seemed worth considering such
practical questions as how we could get her across. Now that I
had taken back my little crown and given up my free entry to
the Other Kingdom, I did not think the old way would work
anymore. Drăguţa had granted Costi, Cezar, and me our wishes
for a purpose, and that purpose was achieved now. Still, there
must be some way for Sorrow to win his reward if he completed the quest. Let him reach us first, and perhaps the issue of
a portal would take care of itself.

"You're shivering," Costi said, wrapping his arm around
me. "Not far to go now."

Then we froze. Someone was coming up the path through
the forest. A small light bobbed into view, accompanied by
scrabbling, hurried footsteps and the gasping breaths of someone who has run a long way in the cold. Costi moved me behind him. A moment later we could see a cloaked figure, face
white and pinched, with lantern in hand.

"Paula!" I exclaimed. "What is it? What's happened? Is
Tati—?" I could not say it.

My sister was bent double, trying to catch her breath. She
had set the lantern down.

"Take it slowly, Paula," said Costi. "We're here, and we'll help, whatever it is. Deep breaths if you can."

"Sorrow—" she gasped. "Someone saw Sorrow in the woods. Now the men from the village are out after him—scythes and pitchforks—come now, quickly!"

Chapter Sixteen

"Where are they?" I asked as terror filled my heart.

"I saw them . . . I hid while they went past. They were saying . . . they were saying"—Paula hugged her arms around herself—"horrible things, Jena. . . . I heard what they'll do to him if they catch him—"

"Which direction, Paula?" Costi had put a reassuring hand on her arm.

"Over toward the Deadwash, northeast of Piscul Dracului. Jena . . . Costi, I . . ."

"What, Paula?"

"I know where Sorrow is," she whispered. "I saw him on the way here. I know where he's hiding."

"Tell us while we're walking," I said. "Are you all right? Can you manage to take us there right away?"

As we headed down the steep track under a stand of old oaks, Paula told us what had happened. Ivan had come to the

door near dusk to fetch Petru. The villagers had assembled farther down the hill and were heading up past Piscul Dracului to
the northeast, where a farmer bringing his pigs out of the forest
had spotted the pale young man in the black coat. Petru had refused to go—he was too old, he said. Iulia and Paula had been
in the kitchen and had overheard.

"And Sorrow? How did you find him?"

"He called out to me." Paula was doing her best to keep up
with us; in the lantern light her face was wan and exhausted.
We could not run. The moon had not yet risen, and to try for
haste in the growing darkness would be to risk broken limbs.
"He's in a little cave not far from here. He asked me for help."

"Why didn't he wait near the castle? Tati's much too weak
to come out into the forest."

"He went down to Piscul Dracului to try to find Tati, and
Petru saw him. So Sorrow ran. He'd heard those others crashing about in the woods."

"What about the quest?" I asked. "Has he—?"

"He had the things with him. But he won't go back to
the Other Kingdom without Tati. He's hurt his leg and he
seemed . . . desperate. As if he might do something foolish.
We have to help them, Jena."

I looked at Costi, and he returned my look with a question
in his eyes. I didn't want Tati to go. I loved her. If I helped this
to happen, I'd probably never see her again. Father would be
distraught. And how would we explain Tati's disappearance to
Aunt Bogdana, and to Florica and Petru, and to all the folk of
the valley? Besides, I still didn't really know what Sorrow was,

or what he might do. But this argument hardly seemed to matter anymore.

"Of course we'll help them," I said as we followed Paula down a little branching track to the east. Scared as I was for Sorrow and for Tati, a deep joy still warmed me. I had Costi by my side and my world was back to rights again. How could I deny my sister the same chance of happiness? If I really loved her, I was going to have to let her go. In my heart, I recognized that I had been making this decision, gradually, ever since our visit to Tadeusz's realm at Dark of the Moon. On that night, I had begun to see that Sorrow wanted only good for those he loved: for his sister, and for mine. "How much farther, Paula?"

"I'm here." A white-faced figure stepped out of the bushes, making me gasp with fright. His eyes were wild. He had a bundle slung over one shoulder, and in his right hand he balanced a dark metal cup, so full of water the surface seemed to curve upward. There were scratches on his pale skin, and here and there the fabric of the black coat was rent, as if by great thorns or the claws of savage animals. "We must go quickly."

"Where?" I asked, my voice dropping to a whisper. Distantly, I thought I could hear the hysterical barking of dogs and the voices of men driven on by fear and anger. "I think our portal is closed now. Anyway, I can't get you into the house past Florica and Petru."

"There is another way," Sorrow said. "Bring Tatiana to me at a certain place in the forest, and I can take her across. But we must hurry—I'm afraid I cannot run much farther." He moved forward and I saw that he was limping. "My leg is damaged. I have traveled a long way thus injured—I am paying the cost now." He struggled to keep the cup level, and I remembered Marin's words: *filled to the very brim, but not overflowing.* This was cruel.

"Tati's very weak," I said. "She's been seriously ill."

Sorrow went still whiter. The cup shook. I regretted telling him.

"She won't be able to walk; she shouldn't even be moved," I went on. "Where should we meet you?"

"I will show you."

We went back the way we had come, then along the valley toward Piscul Dracului. I began to wonder, as Sorrow put one flagging foot before the other, whether midnight would come and go before we got as far as our own courtyard. Then there was a rustling in the bushes. A little voice hissed, *"Dark! Quick!"*

"Cover up the lanterns," whispered Paula, and we did. A moment later we heard the voices of the hunting party not far up the hill. As they came into view between the trees, the light of their flaring torches glinted on well-honed scythe and deadly pitchfork, on crossbow and cudgel and long serrated knife. One man was armed with a sharpened stake. A dog barked, and someone shouted.

"Fox, away!" said the same odd little voice that had warned us. There was a sudden pattering in the undergrowth, making steady progress straight toward the huntsmen. An owl hooted. A flock of high-voiced, creaking things passed over, making Costi duck.

"It looks as if we've got help," I murmured. "We'll have to keep going in the dark."

"I will walk first," Sorrow said. "I need no lamp."

So we followed him, and I thought his ability to find his way in the dark was yet another indication that over the years in the Other Kingdom, he had steadily become more fey and less human. Farther up the hill there was a clamor of hounds and an outcry of excited voices, and the hunt took off in a different direction, following what I was sure was Drăguţa on her little white creature. It was a night of surprises, a night of magic. My mind shied away from what might happen to the witch if they caught her.

The moon rose; a cold light began to filter through the woods.

"Here," Sorrow said suddenly, halting by a round pond under a rock wall latticed with juniper. It was a place that Gogu and I had visited often, a good spot for gathering watercress. Beyond that, I had never thought it particularly special. "This is the crossing. Be quick! My strength is waning. Will you bring her, Jena?" He sank to the ground, the cup still balanced in his hand, not a single drop allowed to trickle down its curiously patterned exterior.

"I'll do my best," I said, wondering how Tati could possibly manage such a journey in the cold. Costi and I were both looking at Sorrow, who was plainly at the last point of weariness. It seemed to me that before we had any chance of reaching home, he would be sprawled on the ground in an exhausted stupor—the cup would be spilled, the quest lost. Besides, he must stay alert or the hunters would surely find him.

"I'll stay here," Paula said, squatting down beside him. "Be as quick as you can, please. It's not the warmest of nights." She was shivering; I knew it was not only from cold.

"We'll run," I said, taking Costi's hand. And we did. "I must be mad," I gasped.

"It'll be all right, Jena," panted Costi. I took heart, for there was no trace of a stammer in his voice.

We ran along the track and down the hill to Piscul Dracului. We sprinted across the courtyard and into the castle. As we passed the kitchen doorway, Iulia stepped out and hastily closed the door behind her, blocking anyone inside from seeing us.

"Hurry up!" she urged. "Tati's really sick. Is he coming?"

We ran upstairs toward the bedchamber, Costi with lantern in hand. "You'll be shocked," I warned him. "Tati's much weaker than at last Full Moon. She shouldn't even get out of bed, let alone go into the forest at night."

Costi nodded, sober-faced, and then we were there. I knocked, and Stela opened the door.

"Oh, Jena, you're here! I can't even hear her breathing anymore." The words ended in a sob.

"Sorrow's back," I said, coming to kneel by the bed. "He's out there with Paula, waiting. Tati? Tati, can you hear me?"

Stela crouched on the other side with tears streaming down her cheeks. "We can't wake her up," she said.

Faith. Trust. Love. I put my ear to my older sister's parched lips and thought I could feel, faintly, the whisper of her breath. "Tati, Sorrow is here," I said. "And I have Costi with me. We're going to wrap you up and take you outside. Sorrow has completed the quest—he's got all the things Ileana asked for.

He just needs you to come out, and you can cross over together, if that's what you want. Come on, Tati, please."

She did not stir. Like an enchanted princess in some dark tale, she lay immobile against her pillow. The red glass teardrop glinted on her neck like blood on snow. Just the smallest stir of breath revealed that she had not already slipped away: the tiny, slow rise of her chest under the fine linen of her night robe. Doubt seized me. If I insisted on taking her out in the cold, it would more likely be the death of her than a happy ending. How could I live with that? But if I left her here, we would surely lose her anyway.

"Fetch her warmest cloak," I told the weeping Stela. "We're going to do this. Costi, help me lift her. . . . That's it. . . ."

We wrapped her up as well as we could. "Stela, it's best if you stay here until Costi and I get back. I'm sorry. Say goodbye now. Iulia will come upstairs soon. Please don't cry. Maybe it's not forever. Maybe nothing's forever."

It was cruel to give her so little time. Tati lay in her own world, cold as ice within her night robe and shawl and cloak. I doubted she could hear her little sister's farewell. Costi carried her downstairs and past the kitchen door. Iulia heard us; she came out and touched a hand to Tati's brow.

"I can't believe this," she whispered. "It's like a bad dream. Petru and Florica are just sitting in there, staring into space."

I made a decision. "We should tell them," I said. "They've known Tati since she was little—they should be allowed to say goodbye."

"I think they've worked it out already," Iulia said.

So we called them out, the two of them with their seamed,

strong faces and their work-worn hands. I told them, in as few words as I could, that Tati was going to the Other Kingdom, that she wanted this, and that it was the only thing that could save her life. They didn't ask a single question. Florica kissed Tati on the brow. Petru touched her on the cheek, muttering something that might have been a prayer or a charm.

"What's going to happen, Jena?" asked Iulia, tears beginning to stream down her cheeks. "Do you really think she'll be all right?"

"We must believe that," I told her. "Now say goodbye. Maybe she can hear you. Then you'd best go up to Stela. I'll be home again soon."

It was no longer possible to run. Costi carried Tati in his arms and I held the lantern.

"She's as light as a child," Costi murmured. "What's wrong with her, Jena?"

"I think she's dying for love," I said. "If I'm right, and broken hearts can mend, we may still have time to save her. Hurry, if you can." I pictured Sorrow with his injured leg, trying somehow to carry both Tati and the brimming cup of water away to the Other Kingdom. "You have to have faith," I muttered. "Faith in true love."

"I do," Costi said. "I always did."

"Always?"

"Well, maybe my faith was shaken for a little. But it survived. Can you hear that sound, Jena?"

"Yes." I shuddered. "They're not very far off, are they? Drăguţa must be leading them in circles."

We reached the round pond. Sorrow was sitting on the

ground, the cup still in his hand, and Paula was holding his arm, helping to support it. When he saw my sister limp and white in Costi's arms with her hair spilling down to the ground, he sprang up. But even then he held the vessel balanced, not allowing the least drop to fall.

"Tatiana! No—please, no!" Sorrow sounded very young, utterly distraught, and entirely human.

"She's breathing," I told him as Costi came closer. Sorrow reached out a trembling hand to touch Tati's dark hair. His eyes were full of terror. "But only just. If you think taking her to the Other Kingdom will save her life, then you must take her now."

"Who has done this to her?" Sorrow's customary cool air was completely gone. His voice swung between fury and anguish.

"Lack of food and creeping despair," I said. "I think if anyone can mend this, it's probably you. She started to lose her faith in true love."

"But . . . ," began Sorrow, incredulously. Then we heard the hounds again, much closer, and the shouts of men: "Down there! Heading for the pond!"

Costi knelt and laid Tati on the ground with her head on Paula's knee. "Jena," he murmured, "I'll try to keep them off. But it won't be for long." With that, he strode away toward the torches that could now be seen again, flaring under the trees not far up the hill. My heart was in my mouth as I watched him go, then turned to the others.

"Wake up, Tati!" I gave her cheek a gentle slap. "Tati, please!"

Costi could be heard giving what sounded like a series of calm instructions. The men had gone quiet; the dogs still gave voice, perhaps scenting us within range of a short bolt through the bushes and a quick snap of the jaws. I rose to my feet, craning to see whether they were any closer.

"Sorrow!" Paula's voice was sharp with alarm. "The quest! What are you doing?"

Sorrow had put one arm around Tati's shoulders, lifting her to a sitting position. Her head lolled against his shoulder. Now he raised the cup—the brimming cup that was a requirement of Ileana's quest—and set it to her lips. "Drink, heart's dearest," he whispered. "Drink and be well again."

In the space between one breath and the next, Tati opened her mouth and drank, and it was too late to say a word. I did not know if what filled the cup came from our own world or the other. She drank, and the vessel was no longer full. Her frailty had stricken Sorrow with such terror that he had sacrificed the quest. He would let her go rather than see her die in his arms. This was the embodiment of true love in all its wonder and sadness. How could I ever have thought his intentions evil?

Tati opened her eyes and looked at Sorrow. His face was filled with love and longing and fear. She lifted a hand to touch his cheek. A flush of color crept back over her lovely, wasted features. "My love," she murmured. "You're here." Then she put up her arms and embraced him, and he almost dropped the cup.

"Give that to me," said Paula briskly. "It's all right, it's only for a moment." Taking the cup, she knelt down by the pond and scooped up water in her hand, dribbling it in until the vessel was once more full to the brim. I stared at her. "Do you have a better suggestion?" she queried, brows raised.

Sorrow helped Tati to her feet. She was unsteady, but could stand with support. *A cup of water from the healing well of Ain Jalut.*

"Tati." I could hardly speak for the lump in my throat. "You'll have to make a choice. There's a hunting party just up the hill. Costi may be the new master of Vârful cu Negură, but he can't keep them at bay forever."

"Will you come with me, Tatiana?" Sorrow's voice was so hesitant and sweet—so full of care, of love—that it made my heart turn over.

"I love you," Tati whispered, resting her brow against Sorrow's shoulder. "I will come."

"Paula," I said, clearing my throat, "give Sorrow the cup."

But it was Tati who took it, between hands grown so delicate they seemed transparent as white moths in the moonlight. She held the cup perfectly steady. Sorrow adjusted the bag on his back, then lifted her in his arms.

"Goodbye, Paula," Tati murmured, her head cradled against Sorrow's shoulder. "Tell Father I love him, and I'm sorry if I've made him sad. Say farewell to Iulia, and Stela, and to Florica and Petru, and . . . Oh, Jena, I'll miss you so much."

"Be happy, Tati," I told her through my tears. "I hope and pray that we'll meet again someday."

Tati said nothing more. Her eyes were on the pale face of her beloved. Her expression told me she had been moving down this pathway since the very first time she set eyes on him. I saw that in him she had found her sun and moon, her stars and her dreams.

Sorrow moved toward the rock wall. I could see no cave, no crevice, no crack wide enough for anyone to pass through. Behind us, where the torches burned in the forest, a new commotion broke out. "There! No, there! What in God's name was that?"

"Jena," said Sorrow gravely, "I thank you from the bottom of my heart. Silence and I have seen little of love and kindness in our lives. I did not know what happiness was until I met Tatiana. I did not understand the nature of true friendship until I encountered her family. We owe you everything." He smiled. It was the first time he had ever opened his mouth properly in my presence. As he stepped back and the rocks seemed to swallow him and Tati up in a kind of shadow, I saw that his teeth were indeed irregular: not the pointed fangs of the Night People, but a very crooked set of quite ordinary ones. In an instant, his smile turned him from coolly handsome to charmingly plain.

"Goodbye," I whispered.

"Goodbye," murmured Paula, but they were already gone. A shimmer of darkness remained against the rock, a place where the fabric of our world was interrupted.

"Wait for me!" someone shrieked. We sprang aside as the white fox came pelting down the hill, its rider kicking her little boots against its flanks to urge it on. Drăguţa's long hair streamed out behind her, a silver streak in the moonlight. Her face wore a savage grin—Paula sucked in her breath at the sight of those rows of little pointed teeth. The creature skidded to a halt beside us, and the witch turned her baleful eyes straight on my sister.

"I saw that, young lady!" Drăguţa's voice was sharp as a boning knife.

"It was the only thing I could think of." Paula squared her shoulders, meeting the witch's gaze directly. My sister did not lack courage.

"Showed great presence of mind," said Drăguţa, grinning still more widely. She appeared oblivious to the rapidly approaching men, the barking of dogs. There was a glint of gold threaded through her silver hair. I stared. It looked terribly familiar. Was that a little medallion in the shape of a hunting horn?

"What the queen doesn't know," Drăguţa said, "I won't tell her. Tati's safe—Sorrow, too. Silence will sing again. I'm the one who stirs the pot! Ileana just keeps the fire going." Her voice rose to a sudden shriek. *"Fox, within!"* With a yelp and a cackle, the two of them surged forward to vanish into the rock. There was a shifting and a settling and the stones came back to themselves.

"Interesting," observed Paula shakily.

The hunt approached at full tilt: boots crashing through the undergrowth, hounds slavering and straining on leashes. In the middle of it was Costi, busily talking. "A man in a black coat? That looked more like a fox to me. Or maybe a small wolf."

They reached us and halted, staring suspiciously. It was an odd time for the daughters of Piscul Dracului to be out walking in the forest. I opened my mouth, still unsure which excuse would be the least implausible, but Costi got in first.

"Did you see anything, Jena?" Then, before I could reply, he said to the other men, "I should be getting on; I was just walking the young ladies home from a visit."

"It went past too quickly for us to get a proper look," said Paula. "Then it just vanished. It was as if the earth swallowed it up."

"A fox, no doubt of it." Costi nodded sagely. "Gone to ground. I think you fellows should follow my lead and head for home. You're not likely to flush out the quarry tonight."

There was a chorus of protest.

"But it was right here—"

"Plenty of light, Full Moon and all, we should—"

"Cezar would have—"

Costi cleared his throat, and the noise subsided to angry mutterings. "I've discussed the issue of Night People with Judge Rinaldo and the village elders," he said. "You've played your part bravely, all of you. But spring's coming: we all have work to attend to. In time we'll hold a village council and develop a new strategy together. For now, you need a good night's sleep, or you'll be unfit for anything in the morning. I appreciate your efforts to keep the valley safe. They won't go unrewarded. Come up to Vârful cu Negură tomorrow, and I'll have two silver pieces for each one of you in recognition of your efforts. Just understand that from now on, we'll be approaching the problem differently."

"But—" ventured one man.

"Shh," the others hissed, and he fell silent.

"Thank you, Master Costin."

"We'll be off home, then."

They dipped their heads, shouldered their weapons, and left. No matter that Costi was only twenty years old and, in a manner of speaking, new to the valley. He had stepped into his father's shoes with a natural authority. Folk knew a born leader when they saw one.

In the moonlit forest the three of us stood silent awhile, the weight of what had just happened holding us immobile. I thought of asking the others whether they had noticed that the witch was wearing Cezar's medallion, but decided I wouldn't. Paula put up a hand to dash tears from her cheeks. I started to shiver again and found I couldn't stop. Costi put one arm around me and the other around my sister. He said, "Shall we go home now?"

That was not quite the end of our story. We put it about that Tati had gone on an extended trip to see distant relatives in the east. Later she would conveniently marry in those parts, too far away for easy visits. We told Aunt Bogdana the truth, and she accepted it with lifted brows and little comment. After all that had happened, she was, perhaps, beyond being shocked.

A few weeks after that eventful night, we had the most welcome of surprises. Father rode into the courtyard, much thinner but undoubtedly in good health. Gabriel was by his side, with two baggage ponies bringing up the rear. The letter brought to them by a certain preternaturally tall messenger had been the only one of mine to reach them. Father had received several from Cezar during the winter, assuring him that all was well with us. He was much relieved to find that this was indeed so, and that everything was as it should be at Piscul Dracului. Almost everything.

Father went very quiet when we told him about Tati, and for a little I feared a relapse. But the fact that Costi was alive, and that he and I wished to marry, was a powerful force for healing. We reassured him that Tati would be well and happy, and that she was among good friends.

As for Costi and me, Father's return home gave us a little longer to enjoy getting to know each other as girl and boy, rather than girl and frog, before we needed to organize a wedding and start work on producing the male heir required for Piscul Dracului. More time: more walks in the forest as spring slowly crept back to our valley, more campfires, more adventures. More kisses. We were getting better at those all the time. We talked a lot about the future, a future in which we would work together in the business and travel together to those exotic places I had dreamed of.

Aunt Bogdana invited Iulia up to Vârful cu Negură to help with planning a betrothal party. Răzvan and his sister would be invited. Paula and Stela worked on the papers Paula had brought home from the Other Kingdom. I had told them about the King of the Lake game, and how my taking back my little crown meant our portal would be closed to us from now on. They were trying to find another crossing human folk could use. Paula was sure the secret was hidden somewhere in those documents.

I wished them luck. In my heart I knew that for me and for Costi, the visits to Dancing Glade were over. We had moved on to a new adventure, one that belonged wholly in our own world, and the prospect of it was so joyful and so exciting that I had few regrets. Only Tati: my lovely sister, destined to fade from human memory and become a princess in a fairy tale, captured by a dark suitor from the realm beyond, sacrificing all for love. I hoped they were truly happy, she and Sorrow.

I did not think I would ever see my elder sister again. But Piscul Dracului was a place of unexpected corners, of eccentric ways and sudden surprises. In time, a new generation would play here, would climb the crooked stairways and run along the galleries and make daring forays out into the great mystery that was the wildwood. Perhaps a pair of children would one day stumble upon a secret portal, and open it by accident to find a wondrous world of magic beyond. They might see the glowing lights and hear the beguiling music of Ileana's glade. And if they dared to cross over, perhaps they would dance with Tati's children.

Author's Note

Transylvania is a region rich in mythology and folklore, with a long and tumultuous history. Traveling there, I found that it lived up entirely to its reputation, with visible links to an ancient past as well as uglier remnants of more recent times. Villagers scythe hay in the shadow of crumbling Communist-era factories; horse-drawn carts traverse roads leading to clusters of concrete apartment buildings.

During my time there, I visited such well-known attractions as the walled medieval city of Sighişoara, but also strayed off the beaten track to meet some of the extraordinary people of the Transylvanian villages. From the protective red tassels on the harness of draft horses to the many crucifixes by the wayside, from the delights of *mămăligă* served with cream and fermented cheese to the first toe-curling mouthful of home-brewed plum brandy, I had a rich and unforgettable taste of life on the Transylvanian plateau, surrounded by some of the grandest mountains and wildest forest in the world.

On hearing the name Transylvania, many people think of vampires and werewolves. Bram Stoker has a lot to answer for! His novel *Dracula*, published in 1897, sparked readers' imaginations. It gave rise to an elaborate vampire mythology, which became so popular over the years that many people came to believe it represented the authentic folklore of the region. There is a whole "vampire tourism" industry in Romania, which encourages the (incorrect) belief that the fifteenth-century prince Vlad Țepeș was the original Count Dracula. Vlad inherited the right to use the name Drăculea (son of Dracul) from his father, Vlad III, who was a member of the chivalric Order of the Dragon.

In Romanian, the word *drac* means both dragon and devil, and it is not difficult to see how this led to a devilish reputation for Vlad the son. He did carry out some cruel and barbaric acts during his time as prince of Wallachia, but he also led his people in a strong defense against the Turkish invaders. There is, however, no evidence at all that he was a vampire.

Stoker's novel is a work of imaginative fiction. But his story does owe something to the original myths, legends, and beliefs of Transylvania. In *Wildwood Dancing*, I have tried to go back to earlier sources for my inspiration, and it is for this reason that Tadeusz and his followers are not referred to in the book as vampires, but by the more general name of Night People. I have deliberately made their portrayal ambivalent—are they all bad or partly good?—in order to avoid the Dracula stereotype.

Crucifixes stand all over the rural landscape of Transylvania. They are erected to deflect not only the powers of the devil in this mostly Romanian Orthodox region, but also other entities that may live in the forest—ancient forces that may threaten those who do not respect them.

This is a land where bears and wolves come close to human settlements, a place where snow can lie heavily for up to six months of the year. To survive in such a harsh environment requires a particular understanding of the balance between humankind and wild nature. Certain rituals in which animal masks are worn take place in the more isolated villages at appropriate times of year. These may go back to the practices of the Transylvanians' ancient ancestors, the tribe of the Dacians, among whom there were both shaman-healers and a warrior caste dedicated to the wolf.

As Paula explains in *Wildwood Dancing*, the forest provided a refuge for the people of the plateau through hundreds of years of unrest. This enabled Transylvania to retain some autonomy, and a strong sense of identity, despite the presence of such invaders as the Tartars, the Magyars, and the Turks.

Glossary

Braşov	A merchant town in central Transylvania. Pronounced Brah-*shove*
ciorbă	Traditional Romanian broth. Pronounced *chor*-buh
Constanţa	A trading port on the Black Sea coast. Pronounced Kahn-*stahn*-tsah
mămăligă	A porridge or cake made with cornmeal (polenta), and often cooked with sheep cheese. A staple of the Romanian diet. Pronounced muh-muh-*lee*-guh
Piscul Dracului	Devil's Peak. Pronounced Pis-kul Drah-koo-looy
pomană	A feast for the dead, at which their worldly goods are given away. Attended by friends; relatives; important folk from the village, such as the judge, priest, and teacher; and poor people. A spiritual value is attached to the distribution of the departed one's possessions. Can be held at several significant times after the death: e.g., seven days, seven months, one year, or

seven years afterward. Pronounced
poh-*mah*-nuh

Sibiu	A merchant town in central Transylvania. Pronounced See-*beeyoo*
Țara Românească	A region south of Transylvania, also known as Wallachia. Pronounced *Tsah*-rah Roh-muh-*neeyes*-kuh
Tăul Ielelor	Lake of the *Iele*. *Iele* are female spirits who lure folk to their doom. Pronounced Tah-*ool* *Yeh*-leh-lor
țuică	Plum brandy. Pronounced *tswee*-kuh
Vârful cu Negură	Storm Heights. Pronounced *Vur*-fool koo *Neh*-goo-ruh
voivode	The head of a Transylvanian territory; princeling. Pronounced voh-yeah-*vode*

Pronunciation Guide
to Character Names

Anastasia	Ah-nah-*stah*-see-yah
Anatolie	Ah-nah-*toh*-lyeeah
Bogdana	Bohg-*dah*-nah
Cezar	*Cheh*-zahr
Costi, Costin	*Kohs*-tee, Kohs-*teen*
Drăguţa	Druh-*goo*-tsah
Florica	Flo-*ree*-kah
Gogu	*Goh*-goo
Grigori	Gree-*goh*-ree
Ileana	Eel-leh-*ah*-nah
Iulia	*Yoo*-lee-ah
Jena, Jenica	*Jeh*-nah, Jeh-*nee*-kah (J pronounced like *g* in *mirage*)
Marin	Mah-*reen*
Nicolae	Nee-koh-*lie*-eh (*lie* rhymes with *sky*)
Paula	*Pow*-lah
Petru	*Peh*-troo
Răzvan	Rahz-*vahn*
Salem bin Afazi	*Sah*-lem bin Ah-*fah*-zee
Sandu	*Sahn*-doo
Stela	*Stel*-ah
Tadeusz	Tah-*deh*-oosh (deh-oosh almost one syllable)
Tati, Tatiana	*Tah*-tee, Tah-tee-*ah*-nah
Teodor	Teh-oh-*dor*